Pr   **Cumbria**

Lynsay Sands and the Ar

'Sands writes books that keep readers coming back for m..
clever, steamy, with a deliciously wicked sense of humour
that readers will gobble up'
Katie MacAlister

'Inventive, sexy, and fun'
Angela Knight

'Delightful and full of interesting characters and romance'
Romantic Times

'Vampire lovers will find themselves laughing throughout.
Sands' trademark humour and genuine characters keep her
series fresh and her readers hooked'
Publishers Weekly

Immortal Ever After

LYNSAY SANDS

The right of Lynsay Sands to be identified as the author of this
work has been asserted by her in accordance with the
Copyright, Designs and Patents Act 1988.

First published in Great Britain in 2013 by
Gollancz
An imprint of the Orion Publishing Group
Orion House, 5 Upper St Martin's Lane, London WC2H 9EA
An Hachette UK Company

1 3 5 7 9 10 8 6 4 2

A CIP catalogue record for this book is available
from the British Library

ISBN 978 0 575 10726 7

Printed in Great Britain by Clays Ltd, St Ives plc

The Orion Publishing Group's policy is to use papers that are
natural, renewable and recyclable products and made from wood
grown in sustainable forests. The logging and manufacturing
processes are expected to conform to the environmental
regulations of the country of origin.

www.lynsaysands.net
www.orionbooks.co.uk
www.gollancz.co.uk

One

Valerie's eyes blinked open to darkness. For a moment she was disoriented and wondered what had woken her, but then she became aware of footsteps overhead. She lay still and listened as someone puttered in the kitchen at the top of the stairs, but tensed when the footsteps paused and she heard the slide and click of first one, then another, and finally a third bolt being slid open.

A moment of silence passed before the door swung open. Light immediately raced down the steps and across the basement's concrete floor. By the time it reached her cage, it was weak and dull, but even that bit of light made her blink after the pitch black they were left in most of the day.

She could hear the other women stirring and feel the tension building behind her. Fear was suddenly a living, breathing thing in that dark, dank room. Valerie tried not to let it claim her as well and began counting backward from one hundred to distract herself. A clear head was necessary if she wanted to escape. Fear led to panicky actions and reactions. It led to mistakes, and there was no room for mistakes if she wanted to get herself and the others out of this house of horrors.

Her attention was claimed when the bit of light from above was suddenly blocked by a large figure filling the doorway. It was Igor with a tray in hand, she saw as the light framed his silhouette. That light danced around his body and shifted on the floor as he started down. The heavy thud of his boots on the wooden stairs was loud in the sudden hush. The women were now as still as deer caught in head-lights.

Valerie held her breath and waited as Igor reached the bottom of the steps. He walked past her cage without a glance, heading for the back of the room and the cages there. He always started at the back, distributing a bottle of water and bowl of oatmeal and fruit to each captive until he reached the front. Everyone would get a meal except for the woman who had been chosen for that night's fun. Knowing that, Valerie tried to make out who was getting food and who wasn't, but her cage at the front of the room and the virtual darkness the other women were in made it hard to see anything. She thought Igor had stopped at every cage but couldn't be sure.

When he stopped in front of her cage and Valerie realized that he was now dangling the tray by one handle alongside his leg, empty, she let her breath out on a slow, silent hiss. It was her turn for a "night out" then. Finally. She remained still as he set the tray on the ground and retrieved his keys from his front pants pocket. The tray would remain there until he returned her to her cage. He'd use it to carry away all the bowls he'd just handed out, she knew.

Well, he would if he were to return, but she didn't intend to allow that.

The door of her cage swung open, but Valerie waited for his terse, "Come," before shifting to her hands and knees to crawl out. Her home for the last ten days was four feet high, four feet wide, and the same deep. There wasn't room to stand, or even lie inside it. For ten days she'd either lain curled in a ball on the floor, or sat with her knees tucked to her chest. The only time she got to straighten her legs fully was when she was let out of the cage, like now, and that had only happened once before since she'd been dragged here. Other than that, she'd spent all her time in this cage, eating and even relieving herself there in the bedpan provided. The bedpans were removed once a day when he collected their bowls after feeding, and returned after emptying.

"Up," came the terse order as she paused on her hands and knees on the cold concrete floor. Valerie wasn't surprised when the order was accompanied by Igor grasping her arm and dragging her upward. After so long without being able to straighten her legs, she needed the help and barely restrained a groan of pain as she came upright. She was even grateful for his supporting hand on her arm as he walked her silently up the stairs.

Much to Valerie's relief, the worst of the pain eased by the time she reached the top step, but she continued to lean into his hold, even deliberately stumbling on the last step to give the impression that she wasn't completely steady on her feet. He'd expect that. Normally, the drugs they put in the oatmeal would only now be wearing off and she would be expected to be slow and a little uncoordinated.

She wasn't.

Valerie had stopped eating the oatmeal after her last "night out." She was clearheaded. Her only worry was that she would be weaker than usual after four days without food. But there was nothing she could do about that and would just have to count on her skills, her strength, and the element of surprise to see her through what was coming. She had no intention of dying in her own filth in that damned, stinking cage in the basement.

Valerie continued to lean into Igor's hold and throw in an occasional stumble as he led her across the kitchen. She let her head hang forward as if she was too weary and stoned to hold it up. Doing so allowed her to dart her eyes swiftly around under the cover of her long hair as she searched for a possible weapon, or chance at escape.

There was nothing. The kitchen counters and table were clear of anything useful. There were no knife handles sticking out of a handy knife block, no glasses or cups sitting about that she could shatter and use as a weapon, not even a coffee machine or toaster. It could have been an empty house.

Valerie continued forward, eyes searching as he led her into a hall and up another set of stairs to the top floor of the house. She wasn't surprised when he steered her left at the landing, urging her toward the back of the house. She'd been this way before, but had been drugged at the time. Her recollections of the hallway, the renaissance portrait on the wall, the paneled walls, and the blue carpet were all slightly distorted in her memory.

The hallway ended at a large bedroom. She refused to look at the old-fashioned four-poster bed as they walked past it to the en suite bathroom. The house was probably over a hundred years old, but the bathroom spoke of a renovation at some point. She'd guess it had taken place in the fifties or sixties. It was green; the walls were painted green, the toilet was green, the sink was green, and there was a green tub with small green tiles covering the wall around it.

It was incredibly ugly, Valerie thought as Igor urged her to the side and moved past her to bend over the tub and start a bath running. Valerie knew what came next, but refused to panic. Her gaze slid around the small room, settling on a collection of items on the sink counter: a towel, a washcloth, a bar of soap, shampoo, conditioner, and a clean white robe. All of it was meant for her, set neatly on the sink counter to "prepare her for dinner," as Igor called it.

Valerie had started to look away from the collection when she had second thoughts. Igor was straightening from setting the stopper and turning on the taps. He would turn his attention to her next. With no time to lose, Valerie snatched up the shampoo, popped the lid, and squirted it at Igor's face as he turned toward her. When the man gave a startled cry, fingers reaching for his eyes, she followed up with a roundhouse kick to his abdomen.

Valerie had hoped to send him tumbling backward into the bath, but either he was more steadfast on his feet than most, or she was weaker than she'd expected after four days without food. He did stagger back a step, but that was it, and even as he did, he lashed out with one arm, hitting her in the chest.

The blow was like an explosive charge going off in front of her. Valerie was sent flying through the air, and out of the bathroom. She landed on something with enough impact that it collapsed beneath her weight with a clatter, and then her head was bouncing off the floor. Valerie was left gasping for air with stars exploding behind her closed eyes.

Fighting off the pain radiating through her head and body, she sucked in great drafts of air, relieved when her lungs expanded. For a moment she'd feared the wind had been knocked out of her, which would have left her temporarily helpless, and she didn't have time for that. Igor was even now stumbling out of the bathroom, wiping the shampoo from his red, angry eyes.

Valerie turned onto her stomach, intending to push herself to her feet and start running, but she paused when her hand came down on a shaft of wood. It was the better part of one of the legs from the dressing bench that had sat at the foot of the bed.

So that was what she'd landed on, Valerie thought as she noted that the once rectangular leg had splintered diagonally as the bench had collapsed. It left a rather pointed tip. A stake of sorts, she thought, grasping the item just as Igor's hand clamped onto her shoulder. His fingers dug painfully into skin and muscle as he jerked her over onto her back.

Valerie didn't fight. Instead, she used the momentum to help her stake the oversized bastard in the chest. They both froze then and simply stared at each other, but then Valerie glanced down to his chest to see where she'd got him. It had all happened so quickly, she hadn't had much chance to aim. Luck had been with her, however, because she'd hit him dead on in the heart. If he had a heart, she thought grimly, refusing to feel guilty for what she'd just done.

A raspy breath from Igor drew her eyes back up as he released her. He stumbled back a step, gaping at the makeshift weapon in his chest, and then he suddenly fell back. Igor hit the hardwood floor with a solid thump that didn't cover the sound of his head cracking on the wood.

For a moment, Valerie allowed herself the luxury of simply staying where she was. Her chest was burning where Igor had landed the punch that had sent her flying, her head was pounding like crazy from its meeting with the floor, and the rest of her body—her back especially—was complaining about the abuse it had suffered when she'd landed on the bench. But she'd felled the monster who had subjected them all to such rough treatment and humiliation.

Well, one of the monsters, Valerie acknowledged on a sigh. Igor was not the one in charge. He worked for the bastard who had dragged her off the street and brought her here. And since Igor had been preparing her for dinner, his boss was no doubt expected back soon. She didn't have time to sit about re-gathering her strength or nursing boo-boos.

Grimacing, Valerie forced herself to sit up straight, then grabbed the nearest bedpost and pulled herself to her feet. Her head spun and a shaft of pain shot through her back, but she managed to get upright. As she waited for the spinning to stop, Valerie glanced down and saw that there was a bloodstained piece of wood poking up through the also bloodstained upholstered seat of the broken bench she'd landed on. It seemed Igor wasn't the only one who'd gotten staked.

A quick search revealed that the back right side of her filthy T-shirt was bloodstained. Valerie jerked up the cloth and craned her head to get a better view of the damage. Much to her relief, it looked like it was just a flesh wound. It was bleeding freely, but as far as she could tell, no vital organs had been hit.

Valerie pressed her hand to the wound, trying to slow the loss of blood, and then spared a glance for Igor. He lay prone, seemingly dead. Reassured, she turned her attention to the room itself. There was a phone on the bedside table farthest from the en suite bathroom. Like the décor, the phone was old, but she didn't care so long as it worked.

Pushing away from the post, Valerie moved to the bedside table, a bit alarmed to find she was unsteady on her feet. Ignoring it, she dialed 911.

Her legs were shaking and her head swimming as she waited for her call to be answered. Afraid she'd collapse, Valerie almost sat on the bed, but then changed her mind. She might not be able to get back up.

Fortunately, the table was between the bed and the outer wall, and a window was only a foot away. Pulling the old-fashioned cord taut, she eased to the window and leaned against the sill as her call was answered.

"911."

"I need the police and an ambulance. Immediately," Valerie said, frowning at how weak and shaky her voice sounded.

"What's your emergency and the address?" the dispatcher asked.

"I don't know the address. I've been kidnapped and—"

"Kidnapped?" the dispatcher interrupted.

"Yes. And there are six other women in the base-ment. Or were," she added grimly, glancing toward Igor. "I think he took too much blood and one or possibly even two of them might be dead."

"Took too much blood?" the dispatcher asked, surprise showing in his previously professional voice. "Did you say you've been kidnapped, ma'am? And were these other women kidnapped too?"

"Yes," she answered impatiently. "You'll need more than one ambulance. I'm wounded, Igor's dead, and then there are the other women."

"Igor?" the dispatcher's voice took on an edge of suspicion as he picked out the name Valerie and the other women had given to their caretaker. "Did you say that *Igor* is dead?"

"Yes," she said, closing her eyes with frustration and wishing she'd kept that bit for the emergency workers to learn when they got there. Since she hadn't, she had to explain or risk the dispatcher thinking she was crazy. "Look, Igor's just the name we called him. None of us knew his real name. He was the one who fed us and fetched us from our cages for his boss to bite us. And, yes, I'm pretty sure I killed him. I staked him in the heart."

"Did you say bite? And that you *staked* him in the heart?" There was definite suspicion now. No doubt he now thought she was pulling a prank call or something.

Valerie leaned her cheek wearily against the window. The glass was cold against her skin as she tried to clear her increasingly sluggish thoughts and sort out the best way to ensure her call was taken seriously and help was sent.

She finally said, "I realize some of what I've said

probably sounds crazy and I'm sorry. The man who
kidnapped us is a nutcase. He likes to play vampire
and bite us. But I think he took too much blood from
Janey and Beth. They haven't talked much the last
couple nights and if they aren't dead, they're probably dying. You need to send help, EMTs and the
police, lots of them, and fast. He—" She paused and
stiffened as she became aware of a faraway whirring sound. The automatic garage door opening, she
realized as adrenaline shot through her. It was probably the only modern item in this place and she was
grateful as hell for the warning it was giving her.

"Ma'am?" the dispatcher asked when she went silent.

"He's back. Send help," she hissed.

"Who's back?" the dispatcher asked.

"Who do you think?" she asked harshly. "The
man who kidnapped us. And when he gets up here
and sees that Igor is dead, he'll probably kill me and
maybe even the other women. Send help now."

"Ma'am, just stay calm. I—"

"Have you traced the call yet? Do you know the
address?" she interrupted, and then as the whirring
stopped she added, "It doesn't matter. I'll leave the
phone off the hook. Trace the call and send help."

"Ma'am, I need you to remain calm and stay on
the line. I—"

"Yeah, well, I need an UZI and silver bullets, but
I guess we're both out of luck," she said dryly. "I'm
leaving the phone off the hook and booking it. Trace
the call and send help," she repeated grimly as the
whirring below started again. The garage door closing, obviously, Valerie thought as she set the phone
on the table. He'd parked and would enter the house
and come up here next. She only had moments.

Rather than risk moving back through the house and running into the monster she was trying to escape, Valerie turned to the window, relieved when it slid up easily. She was even more relieved to find there was no screen to have to deal with. Thank God it was an old house and obviously let go. If it had been a new house with those fancy newfangled windows that didn't open all the way and had screens, she'd have had to take a chance and leave the room to find an exit.

Valerie leaned out the window and peered down. She was on the second floor overlooking a large backyard. There was no handy tree or trellis to climb down from, but bushes lined the house below. If nothing else, they'd break her fall.

Grimacing at the thought, she swung one leg over to straddle the ledge, then paused as she heard a door close somewhere in the house. Probably the door from the garage to the house, Valerie realized and threw her other leg over the ledge, only to pause again. There was a window below this one. She didn't know the layout of the house very well and had no idea if he might now be in the room below her. If he was and he saw her drop past the window . . .

Valerie closed her eyes and forced herself to wait and listen to the faint sounds of movement in the house. But the moment she heard the thud of footsteps on the stairs, she pushed herself off the ledge.

Anders stepped out onto the porch and sucked in a breath of fresh air. The house he'd just left didn't smell pretty, but then the situation it presented wasn't pretty either. He hadn't seen many worse.

Spotting Justin Bricker coming back up the drive-way, he started down the porch steps, asking, "Did you handle the police?"

"Done and dusted," Bricker assured him as they both stopped. Glancing curiously to the house, he asked, "Did you find the caller?"

"No," Anders said grimly, his gaze now sliding over the house as well. Their team had been brought here thanks to a 911 call that had suggested there might be something unusual about the situation. One didn't usually wish for silver bullets or stake mortal attackers.

All 911 calls were monitored for anything that might include rogue activity in need of cleaning up. This call had definitely fit that bill, but they'd arrived to find the mortal police already on scene. A quick read of their minds had alerted Anders and the others to the fact that this was no crank call and that inside they would find seven cages in the base-ment: one empty, five holding live women, and one with a dead woman. There were also half a dozen corpses in a back room. All of them, both the living and dead, had bite marks that had completely bewil-dered the mortal officers.

Unable to open the locks on the cages, the officers had done a cursory search of the main and upper floor of the house for the 911 caller, but then had come outside to call for back up, and find something to break open the locks on the cages and release the women. That was when Anders and the others had arrived. While Bricker had seen to erasing the mem-ories of the police officers, the rest of the Enforcers had entered the house.

They'd searched the main and upper floor first,

much more thoroughly than the police had. When that hadn't turned up the 911 caller, the others had gone to the basement to free and tend the caged women while Anders came out to continue the search for the missing woman.

"There's an open window in the master bedroom. She may have escaped," Anders announced now.

"Damn," Bricker grimaced. "If she gets to the authorities and tells them about this she'll undo all the work I just did erasing those cops' memories before sending them away."

"That won't happen. She's wounded," Anders said. He didn't bother mentioning that there were signs of a fight and a hell of a lot of blood in the master bedroom. Or that if even half of that blood was hers, she couldn't have got far on her own.

"Wounded, huh?" Bricker frowned at the house. "She might not have got away at all then. The rogue might have caught and taken her with him. He did return during her call."

"A possibility," Anders acknowledged and thought it would be a shame if it were true. How terrible would it be if this nameless, faceless caller had escaped long enough to alert the authorities, saving the other women, only to be recaptured and taken by the rogue before those authorities arrived to save her?

"I suppose we have to be sure, though," Bricker muttered.

Anders nodded. "Decker and Mortimer are seeing to the women in the basement while we look around and make sure she isn't lying out here somewhere."

"Right." Bricker's gaze slid over the house front again. "Where was the open window?"

Rather than answer, Anders turned and led the way around to the back of the house.

They'd rounded the corner and Anders had just spotted the open second-floor window of the master bedroom when Bricker's phone began to ring. Pausing, he glanced to the younger man as he retrieved his phone and checked the caller I.D. When Bricker then sighed, Anders raised his eyebrow in question. "Problem?"

"It's Lucian." The explanation was accompanied by a grimace.

Anders managed to smother the smile that tried to claim his lips. Lucian was the head of the Immortal Council as well as the Enforcers who hunted down those who ignored or broke council laws. He also had a wife who was a week overdue giving birth to their child . . . which was making the man a little crazy and prone to annoy his Enforcers with phone calls to keep on top of things.

"You'd better take it then," he suggested mildly.

"Yeah." Bricker sighed the word and then muttered, "He probably wants me to pick up something else Leigh is craving. Lord knows he couldn't leave her alone and go get it himself."

Lips twitching, Anders left him to it and continued forward alone. It was late, past midnight, but there was a full moon tonight and his eyes worked nearly as well in the darkness as in light. He headed first for the bushes along the back of the house, eyes scanning for any signs of disturbance or blood on the ground as he went. Anders was standing in the dirt below the window before he saw any indicators of someone having been that way. The bush there was crushed, with broken branches, and loose leaves lying around it. The dirt surrounding it was also disturbed.

Anders followed the trail along the back of the house for ten feet and then paused when he spotted a foot sticking out from under the bushes. His eyes moved past the bare foot to the bottom of a pair of jeans. But he couldn't see the rest of the body, which was well hidden by the bush.

It had to be the female who'd made the 911 call, Anders decided. And from the markings in the dirt, it looked like she'd dragged herself here and tried to hide herself under the bush before passing out . . . or dying, he thought grimly. The noise of his approach hadn't stirred her at all.

Bending, Anders caught her ankle and stepped back, dragging her out from under the foliage. She was a young woman with a filthy face, and equally dirty long, light brown hair. Her clothes were an utter mess, the jeans looking more brown than blue, and her T-shirt was both dirty and bloodstained, leaving only a patch here or there to tell that it had once been white. Her chest was rising and lowering though. She was alive.

Squatting, Anders tugged her T-shirt up in search of wounds, but brought it quickly back down when he saw that her chest was not only woundless, but braless. He sat her up then and immediately spotted the puncture wound on the side of her lower back. It was a good-sized hole, and still bleeding, he noted, but didn't want to tend to it here in the dirt. He had to get her back to the van and the first-aid kit there.

Anders was scooping her up off the ground when he heard Bricker speak behind him.

"Yes, he's found her."

A glance over his shoulder showed Bricker approaching, his phone still pressed to his ear.

"Lucian wants to know if she's alive," Bricker said, pausing behind him.

"She is." Anders straightened with his burden. "Wounded though. Her back. She needs Dani or Rachel to look at her."

Leaving Bricker to relay that information, Anders started away. He'd just reached the front yard when Bricker caught up.

"Lucian says we're to bring her to his house," Bricker announced, falling into step beside him. "He wants to talk to her as soon as she's conscious. He'll have Dani or Rachel come there."

"You'd best go tell Mortimer then," Anders said with a shrug. "I'll wait for you at the van."

"Right." Bricker split away and headed for the front porch, leaving Anders to carry his burden to the van. He managed to get the side door open on his own with a little juggling of the woman, then set her inside and reached for the first-aid kit they always brought along. He had turned her on her side and was cleaning her wound when she regained consciousness and cried out in pain. Anders automatically slipped into her thoughts to soothe her so he could finish his work unhindered. And failed.

Eyes widening with surprise, he peered at the woman more closely, noting that she had a pretty face under all that dirt, and that her hair was a greasy blond rather than the light brown he'd first thought. She also had beautiful green eyes that were staring up at him uncertainly.

"You're safe," he said gruffly.

She continued to stare, eyes searching . . . for what

he didn't know, but apparently she found it because she suddenly relaxed, some of the fear slipping from her expression.

"What's your name?" he asked, trying to slip into her thoughts again. But it was no use. He couldn't get into her head. And that never happened.

"Valerie." The name was a rasp of sound.

"Valerie," Anders repeated softly. It suited her, he thought and said, "You're safe, but wounded. I need to stop the bleeding."

She nodded in understanding.

Anders hesitated, but there was nothing he could do to lessen her pain and it needed to be done, so he set to it and quickly finished cleaning the wound. He wasn't terribly surprised when she passed out halfway through his work. She'd lost a lot of blood and between that and the pain he was unintention-ally causing . . . well, he was just surprised that she'd withstood it as long as she had without screaming in pain.

By the time Bricker rejoined him, Anders was done cleaning and bandaging the wound and simply standing at the door of the van staring at the mortal woman.

"Do you want me to drive?" Bricker asked, peer-ing curiously at the woman in the van.

"Yes." Anders hadn't intended to say that, but wasn't surprised when the word slipped out. It was a good idea. Bricker could drive and he could ride in the back with Valerie. If she woke during the jour-ney, he would be there to keep her calm and prevent her doing herself further injury during the drive.

"Let's move," he ordered, getting into the back and pulling the door closed.

TWO

Valerie woke up feeling like a train wreck victim. Every inch of her seemed to be aching or sore. But when she tried to shift to a more comfortable position she learned her back right side was the worst. Moving had sent a shaft of pain shooting through her that made her suck in a sharp breath. Memory followed on the heels of the pain, crashing into her head like an angry bull. Her eyes immediately shot open. They just as quickly blinked closed when they were assaulted by bright light. After ten days spent mostly in utter darkness, it appeared her eyes were sensitive. But she had to know where she was and what the situation was. Valerie was pretty sure she was no longer lying in the dirt outside the house of horrors, but where was she now? Had help come? Was she in a hospital? Or had her kidnapper spotted her outside on the ground under his bushes and taken her with him? The bright light rather than the pitch black she was used to suggested she was safe, but Valerie had to know for sure.

She forced her eyes open a crack, and then a little more, and more still until she could make out the white ceiling overhead. That was reassuring, she told herself and opened her eyes a little further, her head shifting on what felt like a pillow so that she could take in her surroundings. The first thing she saw was an IV stand to her left with a half-empty bag of clear liquid in it.

She allowed herself to relax a little then, but continued to force her eyes open and peer around. Some of her tension returned when she noted the dark wood furnishings in the room and the pale blue walls. She was lying in a sleigh bed, but there was also a dresser, two bedside tables, and then a chair against the wall on one side of the bed, and two chairs and a small table by a window with baby blue blinds on the other side of the bed. It was all very attractive and soothing . . . and not a hospital.

That realization had her trying to sit up. It was a bit of a struggle. She was weak and so achy and sore everywhere, but she managed the feat and followed it up with removing the IV needle from the back of her left hand.

Valerie gave herself a moment to enjoy the first accomplishment, then shifted her feet to the floor and eased off the edge of the mattress to stand on shaky legs. So far, so good, she told herself when they didn't collapse under her.

"Oh good, you're awake."

That cheerful voice drew her gaze to the door to see a very pregnant brunette entering . . . extremely pregnant. The woman was petite everywhere except for having an almost freakishly huge stomach bulging out in front of her. Valerie didn't know how the woman was carrying that burden around without some kind of sling around it to aid her in bearing the weight.

"I know. I'm huge," the woman said, rubbing her stomach with a self-conscious laugh as she approached the bed.

Realizing she was staring rudely at the protuberance, Valerie forced her eyes to the woman's face. "Where am I?"

The question came out in a cracked, raspy voice and actually hurt her throat. It felt like someone had scoured the lining of her throat with an SOS pad while she was sleeping. Nasty.

"A safe house," the brunette answered as she reached her side. She then leaned past her to pick up a glass of clear fluid from the bedside table. She offered the beverage to Valerie. "It's water. Room temperature by now, I'm sure, but it will wet your whistle."

Valerie hesitated, but then accepted the glass. She didn't know the brunette from Eve, but she'd said this was a safe house, and the woman was pretty non-threatening. It was hard to imagine her being in league with the likes of Igor or his boss and drugging her water, so she risked it and took a tentative sip. When she didn't taste anything amiss, Valerie relaxed and gulped down half the glass in one go. The liquid was silky and soothing in her mouth and throat, and made her realize how parched she'd been.

"Thank you," Valerie murmured as she lowered the glass.

"You're welcome." The brunette smiled widely and held out her hand. "I'm Leigh Argeneau."

"Valerie Moyer," Val responded, placing her free hand in the woman's to shake.

"It's nice to meet you, Valerie," Leigh said with a smile. "How are you feeling?"

"Sore, weak, and like I need a shower," Val answered honestly.

"I'm not surprised you're sore," Leigh said with a nod. "You took a heck of a beating. You have bruises everywhere, and your back wound is probably tender as well. I'm afraid only time is going to help with that," she added apologetically. "But we can do something about a shower. Can you walk on your own, or shall I help you?"

"I can manage," Valerie assured her.

"Then follow me," Leigh said, turning on her heel. She headed for a door on the other side of the bed, adding, "The weakness shouldn't last long. You lost a lot of blood before our doctor could get you sewn up, but she gave you a couple of pints to replace it before switching you to saline in the IV. Hopefully, between that and the fact that you only sustained a flesh wound, you should quickly regain your strength and feel more yourself."

Valerie didn't comment, but suspected Leigh was right. She was already feeling less shaky, and suspected after a shower and some food she'd feel better still. She couldn't wait. But she also had some questions. "This safe house—"

"Is my home," Leigh said as she opened the door and led her into a bathroom decorated in dark shades of blue. Casting a smile over her shoulder, she added, "Well, mine and my husband's, Lucian.

He runs the Enforcement team that responded to your 911 call." She paused and then turned to Valerie to admit, "Well, actually Mortimer is the one in charge of the men, but he answers to Lucian." She shrugged. "Anyway, they found the other women in the basement and then searched and found you in the bushes. They took the other women to the Enforcer house, but brought you here so the doctor could tend you. It's for the best," she added quickly when Valerie frowned at the knowledge that she'd been separated from the other women. "There weren't enough beds at the Enforcer house for all of you and this way you could get more individual attention."

Valerie relaxed and nodded, but asked, "Why not a hospital?"

"Your kidnapper got away and they were afraid you wouldn't be safe in a hospital," Leigh said quietly.

Valerie stiffened at this news. She'd killed Igor, but his boss, the one behind all of the ills that had befallen her, had got away with it. Son of a bitch.

"You're safe here," Leigh said. "Lucian won't let anything happen to you."

Valerie didn't comment. She was more pissed than worried about the escape of Igor's boss. She might have been knocked out and dragged off once, but she wouldn't allow it to happen again. And she resented the fact that the bastard had got away with it. However, there was nothing she could do about that, so she pushed the thoughts away as Leigh said, "I'll leave you alone to take your bath."

"I'd rather shower than bathe," she said with a grimace.

Leigh paused at the door and turned to face Valerie. "I'm sorry, but it's better if you bathe this time. You aren't very steady on your feet and I don't want you to slip in the shower and add to the bruises and bumps you already have. Besides, Dani said you weren't to get your bandages wet and this is the easiest way to ensure that."

"Dani?" Valerie asked.

"Dr. Dani Pimms," Leigh explained. "She's the one who sewed you up and took care of you."

"Oh," Valerie murmured, then sighed and moved to the tub to set the stopper and turn on the taps, muttering, "I suppose a bath will have to do then."

Leigh smiled faintly at her grumbling, and moved over to collect a washcloth and towel from the cupboard beside the sink, saying, "The shampoo, conditioner, and soap are on the side of the tub."

"Thank you," Valerie said, taking the towel and washcloth from her.

"You're welcome. I guess I'll leave you to it then," Leigh said cheerfully, moving to the door. "Don't forget you aren't supposed to get your bandages wet, so you don't want the water too deep. I'll stay in the bedroom in case you run into any problems. Yell if you need me."

Valerie said, "thank you," again as the door closed, then turned to survey the bath. The water was almost halfway up the tub and that was without her in it. She set the towel and washcloth on the closed toilet seat and turned off the water, then straightened and peered down at herself.

Her eyebrows rose as she took in the pretty white cotton nightgown she wore. It wasn't really her style. An overlarge T-shirt was her usual nightwear.

Valerie suspected it was probably Leigh's, put on her after her arrival here.

Whether it was her style or not, she appreciated the loan. Her clothes had been filthy after ten days in them, but jumping out the window and crawling through the dirt under the bushes had made them positively disgusting.

Maybe even more disgusting than her hair presently was, she thought, catching sight of herself in the mirror over the sink. Either Leigh or the doctor had obviously made some attempt to clean her up because her face was clean, as were her arms, but her blond hair was greasy and limp, with clumps of dirt in it, and her scalp was brown between the strands. Cripes, she didn't recall landing after jumping out of the window, but if she were to guess from looking at her head, she'd say she'd landed on it.

Smiling slightly at the ridiculous thought, Valerie turned and quickly stripped off the nightgown, then stepped into the tub. She settled carefully into it, but had to shift her foot under her butt and sit on it to keep her bandage above the water line. With all her aches and pains, it wasn't a comfortable position. It was going to be a fast bath.

As she quickly washed away almost two weeks of sweat and stench, Valerie thought of all the things she hadn't asked Leigh yet. Her host had said the other women had been taken to the Enforcer house, which Valerie assumed was a real safe house. But Leigh hadn't said how they were physically and mentally and that was something Valerie was wondering about now that she knew she was safe.

"How are you doing?" Leigh called through the door.

"Good," Valerie answered.

"You'll probably need help washing your hair," Leigh said. "Let me know when you're ready and I'll help you."

Valerie gave a noncommittal grunt, but she was now considering the problem. She couldn't just lie back and dunk her head in the water. She was supposed to keep her bandage dry.

Her gaze slid to the showerhead a good distance above the tub taps. It was one with a long metal-covered hose attached. It could be used as a normal showerhead, or removed from its holder and hand-held for more interesting angles.

"Perfect," Valerie murmured as she stood up and stepped out of the tub. After quickly drying herself, she wrapped the towel around herself sarong style and then turned back to retrieve the hand-held showerhead. She was standing outside of the tub, bent forward, soaking her head over the tub when she thought she heard her name. Pausing, she glanced toward the door and listened, but wasn't sure if she'd heard anything or not over the rush of water. Then the door suddenly opened and Leigh peered worriedly in.

"Oh, good, you're all right," she said, and then set another white cotton gown on the counter as she explained, "I stepped out for a minute to fetch you a fresh nightgown and called out to be sure you were okay when I got back, but you didn't answer." She hesitated, then stepped into the room, saying, "Let me help with that."

"I can manage," Valerie assured her.

"I'm sure you can, but it will be faster with help and I'm concerned about you pulling your stitches."

Since the stitches in her back were already tugging a bit painfully, Valerie didn't protest further. The moment she lowered her arms, the pulling eased so she supposed it was for the best.

"I meant to ask earlier," she said as Leigh finished dampening her hair and squirted on some shampoo. "How are the other women? Did they all make it out all right?"

Leigh was silent as she finished lathering her hair, then sighed and admitted, "I'm afraid one of the women was dead when the men arrived. Another died during the first night."

"Bethany and Janey," Valerie said, her mouth tightening. If she were walking down the street and ran into any one of the women from that house of horrors, she wouldn't even recognize them. She only knew them as voices in the dark, but those voices had helped keep her sane. They'd all encouraged and given each other hope in that hell. However, Bethany and Janey had grown quieter each day she'd been there. Janey had fallen completely silent the second to last night there, Bethany that last night. Valerie had feared the worst and it seemed her fears had been well founded.

"The others are all right though," Leigh continued encouragingly as she started to rinse out the shampoo. "One or two were pretty weak, but bounced back after a few good meals and a couple nights' sleep."

"A couple nights' sleep?" Valerie asked with a start and instinctively tried to turn her head to look at her, but jerked her head down again when she got a face full of water.

"Sorry. Are you all right? Do you want a towel or something to dry your face?" Leigh asked.

"No, it's all right." Valerie wiped the worst of the water away with her fingers. She then asked, "How long have I been here?"

"I'm sorry, I should have said," Leigh muttered as she rinsed her hair. "This is the third night that you've been here."

"I've been here three nights?" Valerie asked with disbelief. "I don't remember any of it until waking up here today."

"You wouldn't," Leigh assured her. "Dani cleaned the wound and gave you antibiotics the minute she got to you, but it was too late. Infection had already set in. You were feverish until this morning. There. All done," Leigh added and quickly turned off the water. "Hang on, I'll get you a towel for your hair."

Valerie remained bent over the tub and wrung out her hair as Leigh set the showerhead back in its holder and moved away. The woman was back at her side a moment later with a towel in hand.

"Thank you." Valerie took the towel and wrapped it around her head before straightening.

"Better?" Leigh asked as Valerie turned to face her.

"Much," she said and meant it. She already felt a hundred times better. After something to eat and drink, Valerie was sure she'd be almost completely back to normal . . . well, except for some aches and pains and a healing gore wound in her back, she acknowledged wryly to herself. But she was used to aches and pains. Valerie had taken martial arts since she was five and had been in competition since shortly after she started. Bumps and bruises were the norm for her.

"One of the men is going to fetch clothes for you

from your house, but for now I'm afraid you're stuck
with this," Leigh said, picking up the fresh nightgown she'd brought for her.

Valerie peered from the nightgown to Leigh and
asked carefully, "How do they know where my
house is?"

"It was on your driver's license. They found your
wallet the night they raided the house. No purse
though, just a wallet and some keys in the pocket of
a coat in your cage."

"I didn't have a purse," Valerie said, relaxing.
Smiling faintly, she added, "So you didn't need me
to introduce myself earlier?"

"No," Leigh acknowledged. "But introductions
are always a nice way to start a conversation."

For some reason that drew a small laugh from
Valerie. Shaking her head, she took the nightgown
Leigh was holding out. "Thank you."

"You're welcome," Leigh said, and then glanced
toward the bathroom door as a knock sounded from
the other room. "That will be Anders. He's the Enforcer who found you at the house. My husband
assigned him the task of keeping you safe until
they catch the rogue who kidnapped you and the
other women," she explained and then grinned and
added, "He's here to guard your body."

Valerie smiled faintly at her teasing, but asked,
"Enforcer? You keep saying that. You mean police
officer, don't you? Or is he RCMP?"

Leigh hesitated, and then said, "They're neither
police nor Royal Canadian Mounted Police. They're
a special unit that handle unique cases such as
yours." Before Valerie could ask any more questions,
she added, "While you were bathing I went down

and asked him to fetch you some soup. You haven't eaten since you got here and must be starved."

Valerie nodded. Not only had she not eaten in the three days since getting here, she'd refused to eat for four days before that to avoid the drugs they were putting in the oatmeal. She wasn't complaining. It had worked and she was free, but one of the aches and pains she was suffering was definitely gnawing of hunger.

"I'll let him in. Come on out when you're ready," Leigh said, opening the bathroom door. "There's a hairbrush in the drawer to the right of the sink."

Valerie waited until the door closed behind the woman, then let her towel drop and quickly pulled the borrowed nightgown on over her head. She had a lot of questions, but most of them could wait until after she'd eaten. She had no idea what the special unit was that Anders and Leigh's husband worked for, but apparently the 911 dispatcher had sent them in response to her call. Or perhaps the police had responded first and these Enforcers had taken over when it turned out to be a kidnapping. Kidnapping was a federal offense, wasn't it? Or was that only in the States?

It didn't matter. She was free and safe. The other women were free and safe. She was hungry and everything else could wait until she'd eaten.

Valerie moved to the sink and peered at her reflection. Her face was pale but clean. It was her neck though that drew her attention. A large, angry red scab covered the right side of her throat; a second almost healed wound was on the left side.

Mementos from the house of horrors, Valerie thought grimly and wished she had a scarf or something to cover them. She didn't, however, and wishing wouldn't make one appear, so it was best just not to worry about it, she told herself and tugged the towel from her head. Her hair fell around her shoulders wet and tangled and she searched in the drawer for the brush Leigh had mentioned. It was exactly where she'd promised it would be and Valerie quickly dragged it through her hair until all the tangles were gone and her hair lay in quickly drying waves around her face and neck. It wasn't as good as a scarf, but hid the worst of her neck and the wounds with it.

Deciding she was ready, Valerie turned and opened the door to head back into the bedroom, but then paused in the doorway. Leigh was standing at the table by the window, taking bowls and spoons from a tray and setting them out in front of each of the two chairs. But it was the tall man dressed all in black that brought her to a halt. She watched silently as he carried the third chair from the other side of the bed to join the two at the table, noting that he was slim hipped and had a narrow waist, but that in comparison his arms and chest were rather large under his tight T-shirt. He had one of those gorgeous figures that sculptors loved to sculpt and companies hired to model their swimsuits and underwear. She could imagine him sprawled on a beach, skin glistening with suntan lotion, lips spread in a wide smile and those big beautiful eyes dancing with the joy of life.

Valerie didn't know why that thought popped into her head. He was nowhere near smiling right now. In fact, his face was expressionless and kind of grim.

Leigh had talked about an Anders, and Valerie

presumed this was him. She hadn't expected him to still be here, though. She'd expected he'd bring up the soup and leave, but it looked as if he were going to join them.

"There you are," Leigh said cheerfully, and when Valerie glanced her way, she gestured to the seat across from her and said, "Come, sit down while the soup is hot."

Valerie moved to the chair and paused behind it, her attention on the bowl Leigh had set at that place setting. It appeared to hold a beef soup, hearty and thick with potatoes, carrots, turnip, and what appeared to be homemade noodles. It smelled amazing and the gnawing in Valerie's stomach quadrupled in response.

Swallowing the saliva suddenly filling her mouth, she glanced toward the man as he set down the chair he'd fetched, placing it between hers and Leigh's.

"This is Anders," Leigh introduced as she took a glass of milk from the tray and set it beside Valerie's bowl.

Valerie nodded at the man and he nodded back.

Leigh raised an eyebrow at the silent greetings, and then shook her head and said, "Sit down and eat, Valerie. You must be starved."

She didn't need a third invitation. Valerie sat down, glancing around with a start when Anders moved up behind her chair to shift it in for her. It was an old-fashioned, courtly gesture that she didn't recall ever having witnessed outside of old movies. She'd certainly never enjoyed it herself until now . . . and for some reason it left her a little flustered.

"Thank you," she muttered, embarrassed when her voice came out raspy.

When Anders merely grunted in response, Leigh pursed her lips and said dryly, "He's a man of few words."

Valerie smiled crookedly and turned her attention to the bowl of food in front of her. The most delicious aroma was coming from it, and her stomach was growling impatiently and tying itself in knots demanding she feed it. She scooped up a spoonful of the fragrant meal and raised it to her lips for a tentative taste. She could have wept when the flavor burst on her tongue. It was hearty and so flavorful. Definitely homemade. Valerie dug in with enthusiasm.

"Slow down, woman," Leigh said on a laugh a moment later. "I'm pleased you're enjoying my cooking, but you haven't eaten in a while. Your stomach may not be able to handle too much too fast."

Valerie grimaced, but set her spoon down for a moment to allow her food to settle. She drank some milk while she waited, something she hadn't had since she was a kid, but she figured it couldn't hurt. Milk was good for you, right? Unfortunately, things that were good for you often didn't taste good. Valerie didn't care for milk and set it back with a grimace after one sip.

"Valerie?"

"Hmmm?" She glanced to Leigh in question.

"The other women were fed one meal daily. But when Dani examined you, she seemed to think you hadn't eaten for a while."

"I was given oatmeal and fruit once a day like the other women," Valerie said slowly. "But I figured out that the oatmeal was drugged to keep us docile, so I stopped eating. The night I called 911 was the fourth night I didn't eat."

"And they let you simply not eat?" Leigh asked.

"Oh." Valerie smiled grimly. "The other girls warned me that if I didn't eat, Igor would force-feed me, so I hid my daily portion in my jacket, bunched up in a corner of my cage."

"Ah, that explains it," Leigh said with amusement, and then told her, "One of the Enforcers said your coat was soiled. He thought it was vomit. Must have been the oatmeal."

Valerie nodded.

"Igor didn't catch on?" Anders asked.

Valerie glanced at him, startled by his deep sexy voice. She shouldn't have been, because it suited him perfectly, she thought, and then turned her attention to her soup and picked up her spoon again. "He would have had I been there much longer. It was starting to smell."

He nodded, and then said, "Tell us about Igor."

"Anders, let her eat," Leigh said, sounding annoyed. "You can grill her for information later."

"It's okay," Valerie said quickly. She didn't think she had much information that could help them, but if she did and it led to the capture of Igor's boss, she was willing to answer now.

Turning to Anders, she peered at him for a moment. Up close he was even more good-looking. It wasn't just his body that would look good in glossy prints, his face was worth a look or ten. His skin was a lovely mocha, perfect and unblemished, his eyes, large and black with what appeared to be gold flecks in them, though she was sure it was pale brown and a trick of light or something. His lips were nice too, full and soft looking. They were the only thing on the man that looked soft though. He definitely worked out. As she'd noted, his chest was ripped, the muscles rippling under his tight T-shirt. His shoulders were wide, his arms muscular and his stomach flat. She was now curious to see him from behind. She suspected he'd have a nice tush too.

Startled by the path her mind had taken, Valerie cleared her throat and glanced down at her soup as she tried to gather her thoughts. What had they been talking about?

"I'm sure a description of Igor can wait a few minutes while we finish our soup," Leigh said gently.

"Oh right," Valerie said with relief as her memory was nudged. He wanted to know about Igor, she thought and then raised her head and stared at Anders. "Why would you need a description? You should have seen him. He was the dead man on the bedroom floor."

When Anders and Leigh exchanged a silent glance, she sat back slowly in her seat. "He *is* dead, right? I killed him. At least, I think I did. He should have been there on the floor."

When Anders just shook his head, Leigh suggested, "His boss must have taken him."

"Why? It would have slowed him down. He wouldn't bother. Unless he wasn't dead." Valerie frowned at the possibility. She'd never thought that she'd want to hurt anyone, let alone take their life. But after her experiences in the house of horrors, she was coming to think there just might be some people that didn't deserve to live. Was that horrible?

"Perhaps this Igor was dead and was taken because his identity would reveal his boss's identity," Leigh suggested.

"How did you kill him?" Anders asked and for

some reason the question made Leigh glance at him sharply.

"I stake—stabbed him with one of the legs from a broken bench," she answered and then added, "I'm pretty sure I got him in the heart."

"You made the 911 call right afterward?" Anders asked and when she nodded, added, "And his master returned during the call. That couldn't have been more than five minutes later."

Valerie's eyebrows rose at the use of the word *master*, but she nodded again.

Leigh and Anders exchanged another glance and then Leigh said, "Then I'm sure he was dead."

The woman was a rotten liar. It seemed obvious that she wasn't sure at all, but Valerie didn't know how that could be. Unless everything she'd witnessed, and all the suspicions the other women had spoken were true. A vampire? But that was ridiculous. Wasn't it?

"The other women said you arrived ten days before the 911 call," Anders said now, distracting her from pursuing that line of thought . . . which was probably good. She was pretty sure that way lay madness.

Nodding in response to his question, Valerie peered down at her soup, staring at the bits of beef and potato half submerged in the thick broth. "That's my count too. Ten days."

"Where and when did he grab you?" Anders asked.

"Ten o'clock on Wednesday night. I was walking Roxy before bed and . . ." She paused at the thought of her dog. Despite her own situation, she'd worried repeatedly about Roxy while in the house of horrors, but this was the first time she'd given a thought to the German shepherd since waking up here. That realization roused some guilt in her. Had anyone found Roxy or fed her these past two weeks?

"I'd better go look for her," Valerie said, pushing back her chair.

"For who?" Anders asked.

"Roxy," Leigh explained as he stood and stepped in front of Valerie as she got to her feet.

Valerie stared at the wall that was Anders's chest, noting with some distraction that he smelled rather lovely, and that his chest was incredibly wide, his tight T-shirt seeming to highlight the curve of his muscles and—why was it so warm all of a sudden? She wondered as a wave of heat slid over her. Perhaps her fever hadn't completely passed, she worried, unaware that Leigh had stood up too and moved around the table until she touched her arm, saying, "You can't."

Relieved by the distraction, Valerie turned to Leigh, but asked with confusion. "Can't what?"

"Go searching for Roxy. You're in no shape to go anywhere just yet. You need to rest and recover," Leigh said.

Roxy, Valerie remembered. How could she forget Roxy? Frowning, she gave her head a shake and said, "She's been out there for two weeks, Leigh. Anything could have happened to her. She might be at the pound. What if they put her to sleep or something?"

"They won't put her to sleep," Leigh assured her firmly, urging her back into her chair. "She has a license, doesn't she? Maybe even a name tag with your number on it? They'd know she has a home and have probably been looking for you."

"And haven't been able to find me. I should go—"

"You haven't got any clothes, Valerie," Leigh pointed out patiently. "And you're taller than me. None of my clothes would fit you. The best thing you can do right now is sit down and eat and re-build your strength. I'll call around to the animal shelters myself while you eat. Go on," she added firmly when Valerie didn't pick up her spoon right away. She didn't wait for her to start, but turned away, saying, "Anders, make sure she eats while I make the calls."

Three

Anders watched Valerie as Leigh left the room. The woman's expression was full of concern and dissatisfaction. She obviously cared for, and wasn't pleased not to be looking for, her pet. His gaze slid over Valerie, noting that her hair was nearly dry and now fell in soft, golden waves around her face. Her clean face, he noted. Anders hadn't seen Valerie since delivering her to the Enforcer house. The dirt that had covered her then had hidden what he now saw were very fine features.

The woman had incredible eyes: wide, almost emerald green, with long thick lashes surrounding them. She had a pert nose and lips that were lovely: full and puffy like tiny perfect, pale, rose pillows that needed kissing. Beautiful.

"Do I have something on my face?"

Anders's gaze flickered at the question as he realized he'd been caught staring. Shaking his head in answer to her question, he glanced away, but then he shifted his eyes back and gestured to her bowl. "Eat."

Valerie picked up her spoon, but she didn't start eating. Instead, she simply fiddled with the utensil and bit her lip, her gaze shooting to the door again. Thinking about her dog, he guessed.

Sighing, she set down the spoon. "I'm afraid I'm not hungry anymore. I mean, it's very good, but it is a very thick soup, more like stew, really, and I haven't eaten much lately. I should be hungry, ravenous even. I've always been a healthy eater, and . . ." She paused, biting her lip, and then muttered, "Sorry. I'm rambling. I guess I'm worried about Roxy."

Anders began loading Leigh's empty bowl and glass back onto the tray, and simply said, "Drink your milk and finish telling me about the night you were taken."

Valerie nodded, but didn't speak right away. Instead, her expression became thoughtful and Anders suspected she was mentally taking herself back to the night she'd been kidnapped. It worried him. He couldn't read or control her. If putting herself back in that moment upset her to the point of hysterics, he couldn't slip into her mind and soothe her. He was just thinking that it might have been better if he'd waited for Leigh or someone else to be present to ask these questions, when she began to speak. Much to his relief, her voice was perfectly calm.

"It all happened very fast. I'm not even sure what exactly took place. I remember Roxy going suddenly still and barking, and then I felt someone grab me . . ." She paused and Anders watched her closely. Several expressions flickered across her face in quick succession. Fear, anxiety, and anger were among them. Finally she said unhappily, "I think he kicked Roxy. I remember her yelping in pain and then he dragged me up against his chest and . . ."

Valerie hesitated again and he suspected she was trying to decide what she should and shouldn't tell him. No doubt she felt mentioning fangs and being bitten might make him think she was crazy. He wasn't surprised when she suddenly shook her head and muttered, "The next thing I knew I woke up in that cage in the dark. My neck was bleeding and I was weak and disoriented. I couldn't see anything, but I could feel the bars of my cage and hear a woman sobbing. I called out and . . ." She closed her eyes briefly before continuing, "They answered one by one, scared voices in the dark; Cindy, Bethany, Janey, Kathy, Billie, and Laura. One of us for every night of the week." Swallowing, she met his gaze and said, "Leigh told me Bethany and Janey didn't make it."

It was a statement rather than a question, but he nodded anyway, verifying that it was true.

Valerie sagged in her seat, looking more resigned than anything as she said, "Both of them sounded pretty weak and exhausted the night I arrived. They just got worse as the days passed. They'd been there the longest and weren't doing well. I guess that's why they weren't taken up the first week I was there. It was only five days after I was kidnapped that I was taken upstairs myself."

"You ate at first?" he asked, but thought she must have. She'd been there ten days. She wouldn't have had the strength to do what she had if she hadn't eaten the whole time.

Valerie nodded. "The first daily ration of oatmeal and fruit was brought around the night after I got there. At least I'm guessing it was a full day and night after." She shrugged. "Igor took Cindy upstairs after passing out the bowls. I asked the others why he'd taken her and where, but they didn't want to talk about it and just told me to eat or Igor would force-feed me. I was starved, so I ate."

She grimaced. "Things got pretty fuzzy after that. I know he came back and cleaned Cindy's cage while she was gone. But I don't think he collected the bowls until he brought Cindy back. I'm not sure. Like I said, things got fuzzy and all I wanted to do was sleep." She shook her head. "I should have realized it was the oatmeal, that it was drugged, but I just thought the exhaustion and constant sleeping were due to the wound on my neck."

Anders nodded, and then asked, "When did you figure out the food was drugged?"

"After my own first 'night out,'" she answered with a grim smile.

"Night out?" he asked.

"It's what we called it. The night out of our cage. Not a full night, just a couple hours really." She shrugged. "Five nights after I got there, everyone else got a bowl but me, and I was taken upstairs."

She paused again, this time holding her breath, and Anders tensed, afraid that these memories might be too much for her, but after a moment, she let her breath out on a small puff and continued, "I don't usually lose my cool in a crisis. I mean running a veterinary clinic can sometimes be as stressful as a hospital ER. Dogs are hit by cars, or have other accidents or ailments and are rushed in, and we have to be able to jump into action. We can't freak out, or fall apart."

"Of course," he said when she fell silent. It seemed to encourage her.

"By the time Igor came for me it had been twenty-four hours since our last feeding, and the drugs must have been wearing off, but I was still off balance. My vision was affected, or maybe it was my brain," she muttered grimly. "Whatever it was, everything seemed distorted, my hearing was going in and out like a bad radio station, and my emotions were exaggerated and all over the place. But worst of all, my coordination was non-existent and I couldn't seem to remember a damned thing from my martial arts training. It was like all those skills I'd honed and practiced for years had just fled."

She sounded bewildered, and maybe even a little betrayed by that fact, Anders noted. He tried to think of something to say to make her feel better, but before he came up with something, Valerie continued wearily, "By the time Igor got me upstairs, forced me through a bath and into the white silk robe, I was a complete mess. There didn't seem to be a lick of my usual calm, rational self left. I was just this bundle of raw emotion and terror when he dragged me out into the master bedroom. I was sure I was going to be raped. I mean why keep seven women if it wasn't rape, right? There were no men in the basement. So it had to be rape, and that infuriated me because I wouldn't be able to stop it. I didn't seem to have the wherewithal or coordination to fight it."

She was obviously still angry about that, Anders decided, noting the way she was clenching her hands. Her knuckles were white.

"Igor's boss was dressed in a red velour robe and lounging against a mound of pillows on this huge king-sized bed like some pasha or something," she said suddenly with disgust. "I struggled, but . . . damn, Igor was a huge guy. A behemoth. And superstrong too. There was just no escaping at that point."

When she paused again, Anders waited patiently. But this time there was a huge struggle taking place on her face. He didn't have to be able to read her mind to know that she was having an inner battle over what to say next. And it wasn't that she'd been raped. Anders knew she hadn't been. While he couldn't read Valerie, he hadn't had any problem reading the other women who had been prisoners along with her. Each of them had experienced the very same thing on their "night out," so he had no doubt she had too. Aside from that though, Dani had examined Valerie thoroughly. She hadn't been raped. But she had been terrorized and mauled, her throat mangled by what she would call a vampire. She'd hardly think she could tell him that though. None of the women had felt they could. They'd all said he was crazy. That he *thought* he was a vampire. That he had fake teeth or something, or maybe it was a knife, but he'd messed up their neck somehow.

Anders had no doubt Valerie would say the same thing; partially to avoid sounding crazy, and partially because speaking the truth was intolerable. Her mind simply couldn't accept that such things existed. It was too horrible for most mortals to contemplate . . . and that was his big worry. If she couldn't accept that vampires existed, he'd never convince her to be his life mate.

The sound of the door opening made them both glance toward it. Leigh was back.

"She's not at any of the animal shelters," Leigh announced, waddling across the room to reclaim her seat at the table. "So I called Lucian and he said one of the men was at your house collecting some clothes for you and he'd have him check with the neighbors. I'm sure someone recognized and took her in until your return. He'll find her and bring her here."

"Thank you," Valerie said quietly, but worried what she would do if Roxy wasn't with one of the neighbors. What if the blow that had caused Roxy to yelp had killed her?

"The good news is that she can't be dead," Leigh continued. "Otherwise she would have been taken to one of the shelters to be disposed of and they would have told me."

"That's true," Valerie said slowly and felt some of her tension ease. If Roxy was alive, she'd find her. She'd had a chip put in the dog when she was just a pup. If one of the neighbors didn't have her, she'd call and have the chip tracked.

"Now, what did I interrupt?" Leigh asked cheerfully.

"Valerie was telling me what happened," Anders said quietly, then glanced to her and reminded her, "Igor made you bathe and don the white robe?"

"Right," she muttered, memory taking her back to that room again and her terror that she was going to be raped. She hadn't been raped, but what had happened had been almost as bad. As soon as she was close enough, Igor's master had caught one of her flailing hands and pulled her out of Igor's grip and onto the bed.

At first, he'd just held her in place and laughed cruelly at her terrified struggles. But then he'd toyed with her, playing with her like a cat plays with a mouse, letting her think she was getting loose, that she might escape, then catching her and flipping her back onto the bed before him to laugh some more. He'd seemed to enjoy tormenting her, but when her struggles weakened, he'd grown tired of the game. He'd grabbed her by the scruff of the neck, dragged her onto his lap, smiled into her ashen face and opened his mouth, revealing huge, pointy fangs.

Valerie had freaked out. It was like some waking nightmare. In fact, she hadn't been sure it wasn't one. But then he'd ripped into her throat with those fangs and the agony that tore through her had convinced her it was no dream. The sound of his sucking and slurping away her lifeblood had only added to the nightmare quality of the whole experience.

As least that's what she'd *thought* she'd experienced. When she'd woken up in her cage the next day as Igor had come to hand out the bowls of oatmeal, Valerie had convinced herself it was nuts, a ridiculous hallucination brought on by terror, exhaustion, and the situation.

Realizing that they were waiting for her to say something, Valerie blurted out, "After the bath and making me put on the robe, Igor took me to his boss who was a whacked-out freak vampire wannabe who gnawed on and tore up my throat with fake fangs."

Valerie paused briefly, noting an exchange of glances between Leigh and Anders, but not terribly surprised by it. She was just surprised they weren't gasping, "*Fake fangs?*"

Since they weren't, she continued, "I lost a lot of blood the night he kidnapped me, but this was worse. I passed out and when I woke up I was in the cage and Igor was distributing the next night's oatmeal and taking Cindy away again." Her mouth tightened at the memory of Cindy begging through her sobs not to be taken up again. She couldn't bear it. Please just kill her.

Valerie swallowed and pushed those memories away, saying, "I wasn't hungry, and I was too weak to even chew anyway, but I didn't want to be force-fed, so like I said, I upended the bowl in my jacket, and pushed it in the corner. Then I just curled up in a ball and slept until he came again the next night with food. I was feeling better by then, a little stronger, hungry even, but also clearheaded for the first time since the night I was kidnapped. Which is how I realized they were drugging the food," she explained.

It was also when Valerie had decided that, one: the drugs had been playing tricks on her and she hadn't really seen fangs, at least not real ones. And two: that she wasn't going to eat again while held in that cage, that she would skip the meals to avoid the drugs and keep enough of her wits about her to escape the next time she was taken for her "night out."

Clearing her throat, Valerie shrugged. "So I stopped eating. I drank the water, because that was in bottles and didn't seem to be drugged. But I kept dumping the food in my jacket and pushing it into the corner of my cage."

"And this Igor didn't notice?" Leigh asked with interest.

"No, though he would have in another day or two; it was starting to stink." Valerie fell silent. She'd left out quite a bit, including the fact that the other women had told her they were sure Igor could read their minds. Because of that she'd made sure to recite song lyrics in her head every time he'd come around. It had been hard to concentrate enough to remember lyrics by the end. She'd been so hungry . . . and trying to figure a way to escape with one part of her mind while reciting lyrics with the other had been difficult. The only thing that had kept her going was Bethany and Janey. Their continued silence had worried her. But she'd also counted on their worsening state making Igor skip them that time around, and he had. He'd also skipped Laura, who wasn't as bad as the other two, but was starting to flag. That was probably the only reason her plan had worked. She wasn't sure if she'd have been strong enough to pull it off had she had to go another night without food.

"So you escaped by not eating the drugged food," Leigh said with a nod. "Very clever."

"That and taking him by surprise. And a lot of luck," Valerie said dryly, thinking that if that bench hadn't shattered under her, giving her a weapon, or if he'd tossed her just to the side of it, or if her aim had been off . . . Really, it had been a heck of a lot of luck and now she told them about shooting the shampoo into his face and using the broken bench leg to stab him.

"How did you end up in the bushes?" Anders asked when she fell quiet again.

Valerie glanced his way, noticing only then that while he'd brought food and drink for her and Leigh, he had neither. She was frowning over that as she answered, "I put down the phone and went out the window when Igor's boss came home. But I was injured and the best I could do was crawl ten feet or so away along the house and roll myself under the bushes before passing out."

"Okay, enough of this unpleasant business," Leigh announced abruptly. "It's time to relax and—" She cut herself off and frowned as she saw Valerie's soup bowl. "You didn't finish your soup."

"I'm afraid I'm full," Valerie said apologetically, and then quickly added, "But it was very good. Thank you."

Leigh nodded, but gestured to her barely touched milk. "Not a big fan of milk I take it?"

"No. Sorry. Never cared much for it. Even as a child," Valerie admitted.

Leigh nodded and stood. "Then let's go down and find you something else to drink. We need to replenish your fluids as much as we can and we can have it on the verandah. After being stuck in a cage all that time, some fresh air will do you a world of good and we have a lovely shaded verandah where we can enjoy this sunny day."

Valerie stood and reached out to collect her bowl and glass, but froze when her hands collided with Anders's as he reached out to do the same thing. She stood completely still for a moment as a strange sort of charge sparked through her hands from the point of contact, then sought out his eyes. But his head was bowed, his gaze focused firmly on the tabletop. She couldn't tell if he was experiencing what she was or not. Biting her lip, she withdrew her hands, breaking the contact, and he quickly set the items on the tray and picked it up.

"Come on," Leigh said cheerfully.

Valerie swallowed, and moved quickly to follow as the other woman led the way to the door.

"To tell you the truth, I could do with some fresh air myself," Leigh added dryly as she started into the hall. "My husband is fussing over the baby and hasn't let me out much the last three weeks. He's afraid I'll go into labor in the car or something."

She said it as if the idea were ridiculous, but as Valerie followed her up the hall, she decided she didn't blame the man for his worry. Leigh did look ready to pop. She didn't say as much though, but asked, "When are you due?"

"Last week," Leigh said dryly, one hand moving to her stomach. "Little one here is as stubborn as her daddy though, and taking her own sweet time."

"You know it's a girl?" Valerie asked with a smile.

"Yes," Leigh answered even as Anders said, "No," behind them.

When Valerie raised her eyebrows and glanced over her shoulder at the man following them, Leigh drew her attention back by admitting, "We didn't know what an ultrasound would do so didn't want to risk it, but I'm sure it's a girl."

"I've never heard that ultrasounds are bad for babies," Valerie said with surprise as they reached a set of stairs.

"Oh, I'm sure they aren't for mort—"

"Leigh." The warning growl came from Anders and stopped the woman abruptly.

She blinked once or twice, then forced a smile and said, "Oh dear, I forgot. The men insist I hold onto the rail when I go down the stairs," as if that was what the growling of her name had been about. She then made a show of grabbing the rail and started down the stairs saying, "I'm sure ultrasounds are fine, but you know how modern technology is. They say one thing is good or bad for you one minute, and then change their tune the next. Butter was bad and we should all eat margarine and then it turned out margarine was bad and we should use olive-oil-based spread and so on. And then there's that drug that was supposed to be fine and then got pulled off the market because pregnant mothers were miscarrying or having mutant babies or whatever. It's just better to be safe than sorry."

Valerie followed the woman, amusement curving her lips. Leigh had babbled that all out in one go and without taking a breath. Amazing, she thought.

In the next moment, her attention was diverted by her surroundings. The bedroom she'd woken up in had been nice, and the hallway had just been a hallway, but halfway down the stairs she noted that dead ahead of her was a two story wall of windows around a set of double doors. Beyond the glass was a huge yard with trees, ponds, pagodas, and gardens. It was gorgeous, and a far cry from the dark, dank basement she'd spent ten days in.

"It is beautiful, isn't it?" Leigh said, pausing two steps below her to look outside herself. "I'll never tire of this view."

"I don't imagine you will," Valerie said softly, noting that beyond the manicured lawn was what appeared to be a forest of trees. "Is this the back of the house?"

"No, the front," Leigh said. "The road is beyond those trees and the driveway is just out of sight to the right there." She gestured with her hand and then explained, "What looks like a forest is only about twenty or thirty feet deep. The true forest is behind the house. It goes for miles there." She continued down the stairs, adding, "There are trees lining the sides of the yard too, so you don't have to worry about the neighbors seeing you in my night-gown."

Valerie glanced down at herself, suddenly aware that she'd been sitting around in the thin cotton for the last half hour or so with two complete strangers. She should have been uncomfortable. She hadn't been. Although, now Valerie glanced self-consciously back at Anders and felt herself flush when she saw the way his eyes were skating over her figure in the thin material.

Turning abruptly forward, she hurried after Leigh, who was already stepping off the last step and turning right. Valerie had reached the bottom step herself when a doorbell suddenly chimed out, seeming to echo through the house. She stared at the large double doors before her, able to see a young man in black leather through the glass windows of the door.

Anders slipped past her with the tray. He set it down on a table beside the stairs, and then moved to unlock and open the door to the tall, smiling man carrying a suitcase and overnight bag that looked remarkably like hers.

"Justin!" Leigh returned to stand at the foot of the stairs beside her. "Are those Valerie's clothes?"

"Yes ma'am," he said cheerfully, stepping into the house and smiling at Valerie. His eyes traveled appreciatively over her in the nightgown as he set down the cases. "Everything from skivvies to shoes. Marguerite came along to do the actual packing," he added with a reassuring smile for Valerie as he straightened and looked her over again. "I'm just the beast of burden."

"Better known as an ass," Anders muttered and Valerie gave a startled laugh.

"Marguerite?" Leigh asked, moving to the door to look out. "Where is she?"

"Julius called as we pulled up. She stopped to speak to him and told me to come on in without her," Justin said. "She'll be along in a minute."

"Oh." Leigh turned to smile at Valerie. "I should make tea. Do you like tea?"

Valerie nodded.

"Good, we'll have tea then," she decided and headed toward the back of the house, adding, "You'll like Marguerite. She's my sister-in-law, well, Lucian's sister-in-law really, and just the loveliest lady. Oh, this will be nice . . . tea and a visit on the verandah."

"She doesn't get out much," Justin said with amusement when Valerie stared after her babbling host.

She glanced to him, noting the smile of appreciation was still on his face and he was looking her over again in the nightgown. Her gaze then shifted to Anders as he suddenly bent to pick up the bags Justin had put down.

"You'd probably like to dress," he said as he straightened.

"Oh, yes," Valerie said at once.

Nodding, he moved past her to the stairs with the bags. "I'll take these to your room."

As Valerie followed, he added over his shoulder, "Make yourself useful, Bricker. Help Leigh with the tea."

Four

"I'll wait in the hall," Anders said, setting her bags on the table they'd been seated at just moments ago.

Valerie almost said he needn't wait for her, but then realized that if he didn't she might have trouble finding the others when she was done. She didn't know this house, and judging by the length of the upper hallway she'd traveled twice now, it was huge. So she nodded and said, "Thank you," as Anders left her alone.

She had her suitcase and overnight bag open and was examining the contents before he'd pulled the door closed behind him. It was strange to see so many of her personal items neatly packed inside. Valerie recognized them, they were all hers, but they seemed somehow alien after her experiences. It made her wonder if everything would strike her that way.

Shaking her head, Valerie picked out underwear, a bra, a T-shirt, and jeans and began to dress. As she did, she recalled Leigh saying the man who went to fetch her clothes would check with her neighbors about Roxy, but the dog hadn't been with Justin. He hadn't found her with one of the neighbors then, Valerie realized, and frowned. She'd have to call about having Roxy's chip tracked. That thought uppermost in her mind, she finished dressing and then hurried out into the hall to find Anders waiting patiently, leaning against the wall, legs crossed at the ankles and arms crossed over his chest.

"That was fast." He complimented her as he straightened.

"Yes," Valerie agreed with distraction, starting up the hall. When he fell into step beside her, she said, "Roxy wasn't with that fellow Justin or Bricker or whatever his name is." Leigh had called him Justin, but Anders had called him Bricker. She wasn't sure how she should refer to him.

"His name is Justin Bricker," Anders said quietly. "But, no, he didn't have a dog with him. I'll ask him what he found when we get downstairs. If he's still here."

They were both frowning at that afterthought as they started down the stairs. But they needn't have worried, Justin Bricker was still there. Valerie could hear the murmur of a male voice as they started up a hall toward the back of the house.

"There they are," Leigh said brightly as Anders led Valerie into a combination kitchen/living room.

It was a large open area that appeared to take up the entire back half of the main floor. The kitchen was on the left, separated from the sitting area on the right by a long, granite covered island with chair-backed stools around it. Both sides were decorated in wood and earth tones. Like the front of the house, the outer wall here was more glass than anything else with French doors on both sides leading out onto a covered verandah. And Leigh hadn't been kidding about a nice shady verandah. Vines grew thick and healthy up the posts and along the edges, adding to the charm and providing more shade. The view beyond was as incredible as the view out the front of the house, only here there was also a pool.

"Come meet Marguerite, Valerie."

Tearing herself away from the view, she moved into the kitchen, where Leigh and a second woman were leaning against the counter on either side of a steaming teakettle. Valerie peered at the newcomer curiously as she approached. Marguerite was almost a head taller than Leigh, with a figure most women would kill for. She wore a summery red dress that looked lovely with her pale complexion and long flowing auburn hair, and she had quite the loveliest face Valerie had ever seen. Like Anders, the woman could have been a model. Also like Anders, she looked to be in her mid- to late twenties, but then so did Leigh and Justin.

"Hello, Valerie," Marguerite said smiling widely and offering her hand as Valerie came to a halt before the two women. "It's nice to meet you."

"Nice to meet you too," Valerie said politely, shaking the offered hand.

"I'm sorry we didn't find your dog," Marguerite said apologetically as they finished shaking and released each other's hands.

Valerie's shoulders slumped. It was what she'd expected, but was still disappointing. Forcing a crooked smile, she said, "Thank you for trying."

"Actually, I didn't," she admitted wryly. "That was Justin. I was packing your clothes while he checked with your neighbors. But not everyone was home. He's going to go back tonight, so he may yet find her," Marguerite said encouragingly.

"Actually, there were more people not home than home," Justin Bricker said, entering the kitchen through the French doors. "Middle of the afternoon, most people were working. The only people I found home were two houses close to the corner and—"

"And Mrs. Ribble next door," Valerie finished for him with a wry smile.

"No. The house across the street from yours," Bricker corrected.

Valerie's eyebrows rose at this news and she said, "But Mrs. Ribble is at least eighty years old. She's always home."

Bricker's pursed his lips thoughtfully. "Which next-door neighbor is she? The left or right side?"

"The right side if you're facing the house from the street," Valerie answered.

"There was no answer there," Bricker said firmly, and then added thoughtfully, "But a dog barked when I knocked."

"She doesn't have a dog," Valerie said with a frown.

"Bricker, I think you may have found Roxy after all," Anders commented.

Valerie glanced at him with surprise, but then realized he was probably right. He had to be . . . unless Mrs. Ribble had got herself a dog in the last two weeks, it was probably Roxy that Bricker had heard barking. Straightening, she said, "I have to go see if it's Roxy."

"No. You have to stay here," Anders said firmly. "Bricker will go back."

"She didn't open the door to him the first time, what makes you think she'll open it for him if he goes back?" she asked impatiently.

"What makes you think she'll answer to you?" Anders asked. "You only moved in next door a week or so before being kidnapped."

Valerie scowled. "I wasn't asking permission to go. I'm not a prisoner here . . . or am I?" she added grimly.

"No, of course not," Leigh said at once, moving to her side to add her support. "And I think we should all go see if it's Roxy."

"Oh, no," Anders said at once. "Lucian would have my hide if I let you out in your condition."

"So Valerie isn't a prisoner, but I am?" Leigh asked sweetly.

Anders scowled. "Neither of you are prisoners, but it's in your best interests to remain here. You, Leigh, because you could go into labor at any moment, and Valerie because—"

"I'm sure a quick drive to Valerie's house and back wouldn't be a problem," Marguerite interrupted soothingly.

"I'd believe that if I didn't know that Valerie lives in Cambridge, Marguerite," Anders said dryly. "That's a forty-five minute drive and if Lucian came back while we were gone—"

"He won't," Marguerite assured him. "A couple of new hunters flew in today and he's meeting with them. He told me to tell Leigh to call if anything happened, but otherwise he'd be a little late."

"We have new hunters?" Anders asked with surprise.

"Yeah," Bricker said with a grin. "Lucian said with his men dropping like flies we needed the extra support."

Valerie frowned. How dangerous was the job of hunting men like the one who had held her captive? Pretty dangerous, she guessed, but pushed that aside in favor of her worry over Roxy. The German shepherd was her responsibility . . . and she loved the dog. She wanted to know if she was all right and where she was. Shifting impatiently, she asked, "Leigh, can I use your phone?"

"Yes, of course, Valerie," she said at once. "But what for?"

"I'm calling a taxi to take me home," she answered, spotting the phone at the other end of the kitchen and heading for it.

"Oh." Leigh smiled uncertainly at her and then turned to Anders and snapped, "Well?"

Valerie was picking up the phone when she heard Anders release an exasperated sigh.

"Fine," he said curtly. "Hang up, Valerie. I'll take you."

Valerie hesitated, but then hung up and turned to face him. "Thank you," she said quietly.

"Great," Leigh said happily. "Maybe we can stop for ice cream on the way. I know this great place that sells Rocky Road sundaes with marshmallow topping and—"

"You're not going," Anders interrupted firmly. "I'll take Valerie, but you're staying here with Bricker. I'm not risking the wrath of Lucian so you can have ice cream."

"That's all right, Leigh," Marguerite said reassuringly. "We'll wait till they leave and then get Bricker to take us for ice cream . . . and maybe some shopping."

"All right," Leigh said, suddenly smiling, and then added excitedly, "Oooo, if Lucian's going to be late, dinner out would be nice too, don't you think?"

"Bricker is not taking you anywhere," Anders said firmly.

Marguerite shrugged. "Then we'll wait till he's busy and take Leigh's car and go ourselves." She smiled sweetly at Anders and added, "He can't watch us every minute. He'll have to go to the bathroom sooner or later."

Much to Valerie's amazement, Anders actually growled under his breath with frustration. But then he threw up his hands in defeat and turned to head out of the kitchen saying, "Fine. Come with us. But it's straight there and back. No stopping for ice cream. No lunch. No shopping. There and back and that's it."

"**M**mmm, this really is good," Valerie murmured, dipping her spoon into her ice cream and scooping out a large mouthful.

"I told you it was."

Valerie shifted around in the front seat and smiled at Leigh. The pregnant woman was seated between Bricker and Marguerite on the SUV's backseat where all three of them were each gobbling up their own Rocky Road sundae with marshmallow topping, nuts, and a cherry.

"You were right." Valerie assured her and then settled back in her seat, her gaze sliding to a scowling Anders in the driver's seat. The man had been scowling since leaving the house. Her gaze dropped to the sundae sitting on the floor between them and she said, "You really should pull over and eat yours before it completely melts, Anders. It will only take a couple minutes."

"I don't have a sundae," Anders said grimly. "That's Leigh's. She said she wanted two, so she has two."

"And I told you I lied so you could have one because I knew you were too annoyed to order one for yourself," Leigh said patiently. "Pull over and eat it, Anders. I promise you it's the best thing you've ever tasted."

When he didn't respond, Marguerite said, "Why don't you feed him, Valerie. That way he doesn't have to stop, but can still enjoy it."

Valerie's eyes widened. "Oh, I don't think—"

"Just pretend he's a sick and cranky child you have to feed," Marguerite said with amusement.

Valerie's eyes shot to Anders in time to catch him casting a dirty look into the rearview mirror, no doubt at Marguerite. Since the woman suddenly chuckled, she supposed Marguerite caught the look.

Valerie glanced down at the melting sundae. It did seem a shame for it to go to waste. It was good ice cream. And it hadn't been cheap.

"Just give him a taste, Valerie, so he'll stop and eat it," Leigh suggested.

Valerie hesitated, but they were pulling up to a red light and it wouldn't interfere with his driving, so she scooped up a healthy selection of her own ice cream and topping and leaned over to offer her spoon to him.

Anders eyed the offering, but didn't at first open his mouth. She was just about to give up, sit back and eat it herself when he suddenly did. Valerie moved the spoon between his open lips, watching silently as he closed his mouth around the spoon and ice cream. She could have sworn the gold flecks in his eyes flashed bigger and brighter in the black irises and then he closed his eyes on a long moan that sounded almost sexual.

Valerie stared wide-eyed as he savored the food, then withdrew the now clean spoon and sank back in her seat uncertainly.

"Told you you'd like it," Leigh said with amusement from the backseat.

When Anders didn't respond, but remained still, eyes closed, Bricker said, "Yo, A-man. The light's changed."

Anders blinked his eyes open, saw that Bricker was telling the truth, and urged the car forward again. He only drove half a block though, before pulling into a mall parking lot to finish his sundae.

"What kind of dog is Roxy?"
Valerie glanced around in surprise at that question from Leigh. She'd dozed off in her seat shortly after they'd finished their ice cream and continued on the drive. She hadn't meant to, but supposed she'd sleep a lot for the next little while as she healed. In truth, she was still tired and would no doubt still be asleep if her head hadn't fallen off the headrest and bumped into the side window. Clearing her throat, she shifted around so she could see the people in the backseat and answered, "She's a German shepherd."

"How old is she?" Marguerite asked with interest.

"About three," Valerie said, and then added, "She was a rescue animal. She's one of several dogs who were brought into my clinic after a raid on a puppy mill."

"Your clinic?" Anders asked, sparing her a glance before turning his eyes back to the road.

"Yes. I'm a vet," Valerie explained. "I have a clinic in Winnipeg."

"You have a clinic in Winnipeg, Manitoba, but live in Cambridge, Ontario?" Bricker asked, and before she could answer, commented, "That's one hell of a commute."

Valerie smiled faintly, but shook her head. "The house in Cambridge is a rental. I'm just staying there while I take some courses at the University of Guelph."

"Changing careers?" Anders asked curiously.

Valerie shook her head. "No,the courses are actually at the veterinary clinic at the university. I'm just brushing up on the career I already have," she said and when he raised an eyebrow in question, she explained, "I got my degree and training there. There have been advancements in the field the last couple of years and I wanted to get caught up on the latest techniques."

"Do all vets do that?" Leigh asked curiously.

"What about your clinic? Did you have to shut it down while you're away?" Bricker asked.

"And aren't there veterinary schools in Winnipeg?" Marguerite chimed in. "This seems a long way to go to brush up."

Valerie grimaced at the barrage of questions, but answered, "I don't know if other vets take courses to stay current. I have a partner, and two other vets work at the clinic; they're covering things till I get back. And Guelph is where I got my original degree.

It just seemed easier to return for these courses than to apply somewhere else."

Her answers were mostly true, and they were also the explanations she gave to everyone else. It was nobody's business that she'd chosen to brush up and to do so in Ontario because she'd wanted to be out of Winnipeg for a while.

"So were you born and raised in Winnipeg, or Ontario?" Anders asked.

"Cambridge, Ontario," Valerie answered reluctantly, knowing what question would come next.

It was Bricker who asked it. "Then how did you end up opening a clinic in Winnipeg?"

Valerie considered how best to answer, but really there was only one answer. "A man."

Silence filled the SUV briefly and then Anders said, "You aren't married."

It wasn't really phrased as a question, more like a command, she thought, and wondered about that, but said, "No. I've never been married. But I started dating another student my first year at university. We dated all seven years of school, but he was from Winnipeg. He wanted to go back when we graduated and he asked me to go." She shrugged. "I moved there with him and set up shop."

"But you didn't marry?" Anders asked and she glanced over to see that his eyes were narrowed on the road. There was a tension about him she didn't understand.

"No." She turned to stare out the window at the passing scenery and said, "We split up eventually, but by then the clinic was successful and I'd made friends there. I stayed."

They'd split up nine months ago after ten years

together. Ten years during which he'd claimed he never wanted to marry—a marriage certificate meant nothing to him. They didn't need one. Two weeks after they split up he was dating Susie; six weeks after that he asked Susie to marry him. It seemed it wasn't that he never wanted to marry, he'd just never wanted to marry Valerie. And she had no desire to be in town when he said I do to the woman he *did* want to marry. It wasn't that she wasn't over him. She'd been over him long before they'd got around to breaking up. It wasn't her heart that couldn't take it. It was her pride. It hurt that Larry had never wanted to marry her, yet had popped the question to his new girl within weeks. What the hell was up with that? Why hadn't she been the type he'd marry?

She had no idea and that bothered her.

"Oh, we're here," Marguerite said suddenly. "And now we're not."

Valerie blinked and focused on the view out the window to see that they . . . were driving past her house? She turned to Anders in question. "Why—?"

"Put this on," he interrupted, holding out a baseball cap and sweatshirt.

Valerie recognized them. He'd made a trip upstairs to fetch them before they'd left, and set them on the floor when they'd got in the vehicle.

When she didn't immediately accept the items, he asked, "Have you forgotten Igor and his boss already? They may be watching your house."

"Why would they do that?" she asked with a frown.

"Why did they take you in the first place?" he countered and then admitted, "They might not be watching, but they just as easily could be, and isn't it better to be safe than sorry?"

Valerie nodded, took the items, and quickly shrugged on the sweatshirt over her own clothes, then pulled the ball cap on her head.

"Tuck your hair under," Anders instructed as he cruised past her house again, his eyes scanning the area as they went.

Valerie took the hat off, caught her hair in a pony-tail, twisted it around into a bun on top of her head and then held it in place as she slid the hat over it. "Okay?"

He glanced over, nodded, then turned his attention back to the road, but made one more circuit around the block before pulling into Mrs. Ribble's driveway.

Valerie had the door open and was hurrying up the driveway almost before the SUV had fully stopped. She didn't head for the front door, however, but straight up the side of the house to the fence run-ning across the end of the driveway from the house and going around the backyard. She didn't need to go to the door and ask Mrs. Ribble if Roxy was there. She could see Roxy in the backyard.

She was halfway to the gate when the German shepherd spotted her and raced to the fence bark-ing excitedly. Grinning, Valerie ran the last few feet and reached over the gate to unhook the latch. She'd barely started to swing it open when Roxy burst through the narrow opening like a bullet. The dog circled Valerie, barking wildly, and then, tail wag-ging like a mad thing, she rubbed up against her legs and turned in circles in front of her. Roxy was happy and excited, but not so excited she'd forgotten that she wasn't supposed to jump up on people.

Laughing, Valerie dropped to her knees to hug the dog and ruffle her fur. Then she caught her face in her hands and massaged her cheeks and ears, saying, "Hi baby. Are you okay? I was worried about you. I missed you too," she cooed happily as the dog licked her face.

"Ewww. Seriously? You let her lick your face?"

Valerie glanced around at Bricker's words to see that he, Anders, Leigh, and Marguerite had followed her. While Anders looked tense and was dividing his attention between watching her greet her dog and the street, Leigh and Marguerite were smiling indulgently. Bricker, however, looked thoroughly disgusted. Chuckling at his expression, she said, "You obviously don't have a dog."

"No," he acknowledged. "But Anders has been looking into getting one."

"Really?" Valerie asked, glancing to Anders with interest.

"I've been researching breeds to see which would be a good fit for me," he said quietly, his eyes shifting briefly to Roxy before he glanced around the area again.

"Roxy? Roxy girl! Where'd you get to?"

Valerie glanced toward the backyard at that trembling old voice. She gave Roxy one last pet and stood up to walk to the gate and peer toward the back door of the house. "Hi, Mrs. Ribble."

"Valerie?" the woman said sourly, squinting to see her better.

"Yes. Thank you for looking after Roxy for me. I appreciate it," she said, glancing down and petting the dog as she leaned up against her side.

"Oh, well, she was sitting out on your stoop whining one night and I couldn't sleep so I brought her in," Mrs. Ribble said, and scowled at Valerie. "Not that you care. Two weeks you left the poor girl on her own. She could have died." The old woman scowled harder and added, "I don't think you should have her back if you can't take care of her."

"Valerie was gone two weeks and you didn't bother to call the police and report her missing?" Anders countered, suddenly behind Valerie. He sounded pretty angry.

"Well . . ." the woman scowled. "How did I know she wasn't just out partying or something?"

"You knew," Anders said with quiet certainty. "But you wanted the dog."

Valerie peered at him with surprise and then back to Mrs. Ribble as she suddenly shifted on the back stoop, guilt plain on her face before she turned away. "Just take her and go. And don't expect me to watch her the next time."

The door closed behind the old woman with a clack and Valerie raised an eyebrow in Anders's direction, saying carefully, "You were kind of tough on her."

Anders quit scowling at the now closed door and glanced to Valerie, but shook his head. "Not tough enough. She knew you were missing and that something must have happened, but didn't do a damned thing about it. She couldn't even be bothered to call the police. She was afraid they'd take Roxy away and she wanted the dog."

"You don't know that," she protested on a laugh.

"I do," he assured her.

"How?" Valerie challenged.

Anders opened his mouth, paused briefly, and

then said, "I drove around the block three times, each time her front curtain twitched and she looked out. I guarantee that woman sits in her front room watching the street. She probably sees everything that goes on, including the attack the night you took Roxy for a walk. It might have been slightly blurry for her at that distance, but she would have seen shapes and been able to tell enough to know that you were attacked and dragged off and Roxy came limping home."

"How did you know the attack took place on this street?" she asked with surprise.

Anders paused again, but then shrugged, "You're a woman. I imagine you'd stick to your street that late at night and circle it several times rather than venture farther away."

Valerie frowned. It all sounded likely enough. Common sense and logic really, but there was something about the way he was avoiding her eyes that suggested to her that there was more to it than that.

"We should go," Anders said suddenly, taking Valerie's arm and turning her back to the driveway.

She didn't protest, but allowed him to walk her back to the SUV. Roxy stuck to her other side like glue, bumping up against her with every step. The others fell into step behind them and they were almost to the vehicle when Valerie suddenly stopped.

"I should get Roxy's dog food while we're here," she announced when Anders paused and eyed her in question.

He frowned, his eyes traveling over the street and then to her house.

"It's a good idea, Anders. Roxy has to eat," Marguerite pointed out. "Besides, there may be things Valerie needs that I didn't think of when I packed her bag."

"My computer," Valerie announced at once. "I need it for classes. And I need my class notes and books."

"Right," Anders said grimly and turned to hand Bricker his keys. "Move the SUV to Valerie's driveway. It'll be easier for loading."

"Will do," the man answered as he withdrew another set of keys from his own pocket and held them out. "You'll need these."

"My keys," Valerie said as she recognized them.

"It's how we got in earlier to pick up your clothes," Bricker explained. "They were in your coat pocket at the house."

Valerie nodded, recalling Leigh mentioning that the men had found her wallet and keys in a coat in her cage at the house.

Anders took the keys and urged her in the direction of her rental.

"We'll come help," Leigh announced, trailing after them. When Anders slowed and glanced back, she added, "It will be quicker."

Sighing, he nodded and picked up speed again.

It was just as strange entering her rental as it had been going through the clothes they'd brought her. It all felt just a bit alien. Valerie shrugged that feeling aside and set about what she was there for. She headed for the kitchen first to gather Roxy's food dish and water dish, the big bag of her dry dog food, the spare leash, her bed and a couple of her favorite toys. Valerie set them on the kitchen table as she collected each item, but when she then found a grocery bag to stuff the smaller items in, Marguerite took it from her.

"Leigh and I will pack this. You go ahead and get your computer and whatever else you need," she suggested.

"Thanks," Valerie said and slid from the room, aware that Roxy and Anders were hard on her heels. She found her computer case and the back-pack with her notes and books for her courses in the living room. She started to pick them up, but Anders simply took them from her and slung both over his own shoulder.

"Anything else?" he asked.

She hesitated, but then headed for the bedroom to survey her wardrobe. Marguerite had done a good job of picking clothes for her, but there were a couple of items Valerie thought might come in handy. She pulled them out of the closet, and quickly rolled up and packed them into a duffel bag Anders pulled down from the closet's upper shelf for her.

The bathroom was last, and Valerie was very aware that Anders was standing a foot away, wait-ing patiently. She would have liked to ask him to leave, but she was a grown-up, he was a grown-up and old enough to know about the physiology of the female body, so she took a deep breath, knelt to open the cupboard under the sink and pulled out tam-pons and pads. Her period should come in the next week or so and she didn't know how long she'd have to stay at Leigh's house.

Valerie set the feminine items on the counter, and then moved to the other end of the cupboard to gather some makeup and moisturizer from a drawer there.

When she turned back with the new items, Anders was calmly packing her feminine hygiene products away in the duffel with her clothes.

"Thank you," she murmured self-consciously as she dumped the new items in. Valerie then moved to the medicine cabinet. Her birth control pills were still there. She didn't know if Marguerite had missed them or if she'd just thought that since Valerie had been without them for the last two weeks and was now in protective custody for an unknown length of time, she wouldn't need them, but Valerie took them and threw them on top of the other items in the duffel bag Anders was holding.

She zipped it shut with a cheerful, "All done," then bent to pet Roxy, who was nosing her side.

"Thank you for working quickly," Anders responded quietly, the words drawing a laugh from Valerie.

"That's the only speed I know," she admitted wryly as she led him out of the bathroom. The clinic was always busy and rush was the speed she'd become used to.

Leigh and Marguerite were waiting in the living room, Leigh holding the grocery bag with the smaller, lighter items. Marguerite had Roxy's bed under one arm, and was dangling the large bag of dog food from one hand as if it weighed nothing. Both women smiled at their arrival, but it was Leigh who asked, "All set?"

"All set," Valerie agreed. "We can go."

"Good. I'm dying for a cup of coffee," Leigh announced, leading the way to the door and out onto the porch.

"I thought you were avoiding coffee until you had

the baby," Anders said, following the women out of the house.

"I was. But the baby is overdue and mama wants a coffee," she said rebelliously, sailing across the porch. Pausing at the top of the stairs down to the sidewalk, she turned back with a grimace and said, "But I'll settle for decaf."

"Hmmm," Anders muttered as he locked the door with Valerie's keys. "I suppose that means you want to hit a coffee shop on the way out of Cambridge?"

"You suppose right," Leigh said cheerfully.

"I wouldn't mind a coffee myself," Valerie said apologetically. "That ice cream left me thirsty and—" She paused and glanced around as Roxy went suddenly stiff beside her and began to growl low in her throat. Noting that the dog was staring across the street, Valerie glanced that way herself as she put a soothing hand on the dog's neck, and then she froze. There was a man standing in the late-afternoon shadow cast by the house across the street and she was sure it was Igor. The shape and sheer size were his, but—

"Valerie?" Anders moved up beside her and took her arm. "What is it?"

She glanced to him briefly, and then back, eyes widening when she saw that Igor was gone. If he had ever really been there, Valerie thought and reminded herself that he was dead. She'd killed him. No man could survive a stake through the heart . . . and neither could a vampire, if that's what he'd been.

"Nothing," she said, letting her breath out slowly. She scanned the street, aware that Anders was doing the same, but there was nothing to see now. Literally. It wasn't quite three o'clock yet. Still early enough that the kids weren't yet home from school and the parents were still at work. Or, at least, most of them would be. So there were no cars, no people, and no pets, just silent houses and a couple of squirrels running about.

Actually, it was kind of spooky it was so still, she decided as a chill ran up her back. Giving Roxy one last pat, Valerie forced the feeling aside and lied, "Roxy probably saw a squirrel."

"Right," Anders agreed mildly, but she could tell he didn't believe that. He was now stiff with tension. So were Leigh and Marguerite.

"What's up?" Bricker asked, stepping out of the SUV now parked in the driveway of Valerie's rental.

"Nothing," she said, forcing a smile and starting down the three steps off the porch. "Roxy just caught a scent or saw something. Probably a squirrel or chipmunk."

"Hmmm." Bricker turned to peer across the street now too, but the others were following Valerie and Roxy as she led the dog to the SUV. They were all silent as they loaded her bags into the back of the SUV. Valerie was afraid Anders would want Roxy to ride back there too, but he closed the door without the dog inside and patted his leg to get her to follow as he led Valerie up to the front passenger door.

"I'll move your seat back to give her more room in front of you," Anders announced as he opened the door, and Valerie could have hugged him. She'd just got her dog back and didn't want to be parted even by a few feet. Judging by how close Roxy was sticking to her, she felt the same way, but Valerie was surprised Anders was sensitive enough to understand that. It was nice. For all his attempts to be stern, *he* was nice, Valerie thought as she watched him push the button to make the seat slide slowly back on its track. The proof was that they were all there despite his initial refusal to bring them. And the ice cream, she thought with amusement, recalling his undeniable pleasure when she'd given him a spoonful to taste. You'd have thought he'd never tasted ice cream before.

"That's as far as it will go," Anders said straightening and offering her a hand to help her in.

Valerie placed her fingers in his hand, and then stilled, her eyes shooting to his when a jolt of sensation shot from the point of contact and up her arm. This time there was no doubting that Anders felt it too. He met her gaze, his own eyes wide. They were also more golden than black, she noted with some confusion, then glanced down to Roxy when the dog suddenly nosed between them, whining.

"It's okay," Valerie told the dog, retrieving her hand from Anders to pet the German shepherd. Then she turned and got into the front seat unaided.

"Go on," Anders said to Roxy once Valerie was settled. The German shepherd immediately jumped up onto the floor in front of her mistress. She circled once in the confined space before settling between Valerie's legs and laying her head on her knee.

"Thank you," Valerie said, avoiding looking at Anders's eyes again by petting Roxy's head.

She saw him nod out of the corner of her eye. He closed the door, then opened the back door and helped Leigh step up inside. The pregnant woman settled in the seat with a little relieved sigh, her hands rubbing her stomach as if to soothe the little one inside as she muttered, "I can't wait for you to be born."

Valerie forced a smile and glanced around to ask, "Is this your first baby?"

She hadn't seen any signs of children at the house, but then she hadn't seen it all yet either. Besides, there may have been signs she just didn't recognize. Valerie had never had children herself and was beginning to think she never would. She was thirty years old, with a busy, successful career but no husband, or boyfriend, or even prospects in sight. She also had no social life to speak of. She had female friends, but little time to spend with them and even less to meet men. And she was only getting older and busier as the clinic continued to grow.

"Yes, this is baby number one," Leigh answered and then grimaced. "And he's already proving to be as stubborn as his father."

"*He* is?" Valerie teased gently. "I thought you were sure it's going to be a girl?"

"Oh, well, that was then. Now it's a boy," Leigh said with a touch of self-mockery and explained, "It changes twenty times a day."

Valerie chuckled at that and then did what she'd been avoiding doing and glanced around the street. Much to her relief there was nothing and no one of note. Letting out the breath she hadn't realized she'd been holding, she turned forward to see what was holding up the others. Marguerite, Bricker, and Anders were having a powwow a little distance from the van.

"They're debating whether they should check out what got Roxy upset," Leigh announced and when Valerie turned to her, eyebrows raised, she said, "I read lips."

"Hmmm." Valerie turned back to eye the others.

She could see their lips moving, but didn't have a clue what they were saying. She couldn't read lips.

"Anders wants to, but Marguerite thinks we should just go and keep an eye out for anyone following us. She figures since Roxy's calm now that whatever or whoever it is, is gone."

"She's probably right," Valerie said, shifting her gaze from the trio to the houses across the street again. Much to her relief, there was still nothing to see.

"Marguerite usually is right," Leigh said with amusement. "Oh, here they come. She must have won the argument."

Valerie peered back to the trio. It didn't look like anyone had won. They all had grim expressions and were scanning the area as they approached the vehicle. It seemed obvious they were pretty sure Roxy had picked up on a threat, but they'd agreed it was probably gone now. But gone where? And would it return?

"All right," Anders said as they all piled back into the SUV. "Direct us to the nearest coffee shop, Valerie, and we'll be on our way."

Five

"She's sleeping peacefully. No nightmares right now," Marguerite said from the backseat, and Anders tore his eyes away from Valerie to watch the road ahead.

The woman had pinpointed exactly what he'd been worrying about. Valerie had suffered nightmares while in her feverish state the last three days. He'd been able to hear her screams all over the house when he was there; they'd haunted his dreams as he'd slept, and every single one had made him want to soothe and reassure her that she was safe and all was well. But the women had been overseeing her—Leigh, Marguerite, and Marguerite's daughter Lissianna, as well as Marguerite's daughter-in-law Rachel. They had taken turns, and though he'd offered, he hadn't been needed.

The women had worried about Valerie coming out of the fever with her faculties intact. They'd said she was out of her head and there was no calming her.

So, when Anders had realized she'd fallen asleep in the passenger seat, he'd worried she might have more of those nightmares. Unfortunately, Valerie had nodded off with her head turned toward the window. He hadn't been able to see her face and read her expression to know if she was sleeping peacefully or having a nightmare from which he should wake her.

"I'm sure she'll sleep a lot for the next couple days while she heals," Leigh commented. "She's doing very well though. She hasn't once complained about the pain she's in."

"She's in pain?" Anders asked, glancing sharply to the rearview mirror to eye the woman in the backseat.

"She has a hole in her back, Anders," Leigh said dryly. "It's healed a lot the last couple days, but it's still sore."

"Valerie has a rather impressive ability to block pain," Marguerite commented. "It must be from all those years of martial arts she's taken."

"She's taken martial arts?" Anders asked with interest, his gaze switching to the reflection of the older woman.

He saw Marguerite and Leigh exchange a glance and then Marguerite said, "Yes. But I probably shouldn't tell you any more. Half the fun of finding a life mate is peeling back the layers and learning about them, and we've already taken a good deal of that away with our earlier questions on the ride out."

Anders didn't comment but shifted his attention to Roxy. The dog had remained seated between her mistress's legs, head on her knee, for the last forty-five minutes. Unlike her mistress, however, Roxy wasn't asleep. Her eyes were open and alert. Standing guard, he thought, and nodded at the animal. She was a good dog.

"Anders, we should stop for dinner on the way back," Leigh suggested suddenly.

"Oh yeah, dinner sounds good," Bricker said with enthusiasm.

Anders scowled at Leigh in the rearview mirror. "We are not stopping for supper. You are pregnant and I am not delivering Lucian Argeneau's baby on the side of a country road because you wanted a burger."

He saw her roll her eyes and then she said, "I promise I won't go into labor."

Anders snorted at the very words. That was a promise she couldn't keep. When the baby decided to pop out, it would, regardless of any promises she had made.

"Come on, Anders, have a heart," Marguerite chided. "Valerie was locked in a cage in a windowless basement for ten days. Dinner out will do her good."

Anders's gaze slid to the sleeping Valerie and he frowned. After delivering Valerie to Leigh and Lucian's, he'd been sent to collect the other women from the house of cages. The building had been an old farmhouse in the country, probably a good 150 years old, by his guess. The basement hadn't been finished. The floor had been concrete at the front and dirt at the back, the stone walls had been wet with mold growing in crevices, and the whole place had smelled like death thanks to the bodies they'd found piled up in a room behind the larger one where the cages were. The women they'd found in the cages weren't the first occupants. And the owners of the old farmhouse had been in that tiny back room along with previous tenants of the cages.

After her nightmare stay there, he had no doubt Valerie would enjoy dinner out. Certainly she deserved it. She was a hero. She'd saved herself and those other women. But if his long life had taught him one thing, it was that you don't always get what you want or deserve and he couldn't agree to dinner out . . . especially when he suspected Valerie had seen Igor across the street from her house. Marguerite had told him what Valerie hadn't when the three of them had powwowed in front of the van. She said Valerie had spotted Igor across the street, but convinced herself it was her imagination when he'd disappeared so swiftly. He'd wanted the three of them to spread out and search for the man when he'd heard the news, but it hadn't taken him long to realize that was a bad idea. Igor might have been bait to take him, Bricker, and Marguerite away to search while his master went after Valerie. Leigh would have been next to useless in her present state and both women would have been vulnerable. As much as he wanted to catch the bastard who had hurt Valerie, safety came first. He'd kept a sharp eye out on the way home though, but hadn't seen anything to indicate they were being followed.

"If we can't actually go eat in a restaurant, maybe we could just go through a drive-thru," Leigh suggested, her tone now wheedling. "Swiss Chalet is on the way home. It would only take a couple minutes and we can eat it out on the verandah. I'm sure Valerie would enjoy that almost as much."

"Christ," Anders muttered under his breath with frustration. Give him rogues to deal with any day. He had no problem saying no to them, and if they didn't listen, he could shoot them. But Leigh and Marguerite were a different matter altogether. They saw "no" as a challenge, and when they put their minds to it, they could be a real pain. Sadly, he couldn't shoot them.

Rather than say no, he tried reason. "Are you sure you want more junk food, Leigh? We've already had it twice today and you should be eating healthier. You have the baby to think of."

"Ice cream and coffee are not junk food," Leigh informed him stiffly.

"Then what are they?" he asked dryly.

"Necessities." That answer came from Valerie and drew his gaze her way as she straightened in her seat and ran her hands over her face to wipe the sleep away. Turning, she smiled at him sleepy-eyed and said, "Coffee is always a necessity. Ice cream less so. But coffee definitely is. And Swiss Chalet isn't really junk food. It's more like a Sunday-dinner-type meal. Chicken roasted over a spit, potatoes, and a bun." She shrugged. "It's relatively healthy, certainly healthier than a burger, and that way we don't have to cook."

The last part was the nail in the coffin of Anders's resistance. Valerie was injured and still recovering and Leigh was pregnant and had been complaining of swollen feet. Neither woman should be on her feet working in a kitchen. As for him, he didn't know a damned thing about cooking. It made stopping for dinner the logical solution. Anders liked logic.

"Very well. We'll stop for takeout at Swiss Chalet," he said and was rewarded with a smile from Valerie.

"Don't bother ordering meals for Bricker and me," Marguerite said moments later, putting away her phone as Anders pulled in to the Swiss Chalet drive-thru. "Bricker has to take me back to the Enforcer house to collect my car. Julius just texted and his plane lands in an hour. I want to go home and spruce myself up before he arrives."

"Julius is Marguerite's husband," Anders told Valerie as Bricker groaned in the backseat about missing out.

"Oh." She smiled at him and then turned to pet Roxy as the dog shifted restlessly and tried to look out the window as the SUV came to a halt.

"Not home yet," Valerie told the animal, rubbing her ears as she added, "Soon."

The dog settled back and eyed Anders balefully, as if blaming him for the delay in getting somewhere where she could get out and stretch her legs. Shaking his head at the thought, Anders glanced around. "What am I ordering?"

"A quarter-chicken dinner, white meat, for me," Leigh announced.

"Me too," Valerie said.

Nodding, Anders turned to the speaker box as a muffled voice asked what he'd like. Unsure what he'd like, he simply followed the ladies' lead and said, "Three quarter-chicken dinners. All white meat."

"Make it four, Anders," Leigh piped up suddenly. "Lucian will probably be hungry when he gets home."

He changed the order. If they were lucky, the food might mitigate some of Lucian's anger over his taking the women to Cambridge. He doubted it, but one could hope, Anders thought as he drove around to the window to pay and claim their order.

"Damn, that smells good," Bricker said as Anders set the bags of food on the floor between the front seats several moments later.

Anders didn't respond, but silently agreed. It smelled damned good and made his stomach tighten with what he suspected was hunger. That was something he hadn't felt in a long time. He wasn't sure he liked feeling it now. But he was beginning to understand how finding a life mate could mess with a man's instincts. Smells that he used to hardly notice now seemed to bring about physical reactions in him that were extremely distracting. And Valerie? He glanced to her to find her looking at him. When she smiled, he felt his own lips crack into a crooked smile in response, and then he quickly turned forward again.

This life mate business wasn't anything like he'd expected. In fact, he wasn't at all sure Valerie really was his life mate. His gaze slid to her again. She'd taken the sweatshirt off as they'd left Cambridge, leaving her in her own T-shirt and jeans. She had a good figure and he thought she was pretty, but he'd met thousands of prettier women in his life. And then there was the fact that Decker, Mortimer, and the others he'd witnessed with life mates couldn't seem to get enough of their women, but he didn't look at Valerie and have any great urge to "jump her bones," as Bricker would call it.

However, he *was* eating again, and when he'd taken her hand to help her into the truck earlier, he had felt a strange shock of awareness race up his arm and through his body. She'd felt it too. He was pretty sure about that. It hadn't been the first time either, and it made him want to touch her again and see what would happen.

Anders shook his head at his own confused thoughts. Was she a life mate or not?

"Of course, she is," Marguerite said softly behind him, and Anders grimaced at her being able to read his mind. Another sign of meeting a life mate. Damn.

"I'll help you bring Valerie's things in before I take Marguerite back," Bricker offered as Anders parked in front of Lucian and Leigh's house several minutes later.

"No need," Anders said, turning off the engine and opening his door. "I can handle it."

Leaving Bricker to open the side door and help the women out, Anders walked around to the back of the SUV to retrieve the backpack, computer case, and duffel bag they'd brought back. He slung those over one shoulder, then reached for the bag of dog food and the grocery bag holding dog dishes and other doggie accessories as well.

"You can't carry all that," Valerie protested, coming around the back of the SUV with the Swiss Chalet bags in hand and Roxy at her side. She grabbed the dog bed and tried to take a bag from him, but he shook his head.

"I'm fine," he assured her, nudging the SUV door closed with his elbow, and then nodding her toward the house.

Shaking her head at his stubbornness, she turned toward the house, but paused beside Leigh at the front of the SUV to say good-bye to Marguerite and Bricker and thank them for all their help today.

Anders waited patiently for the women to finish their nattering, and then followed Leigh and Valerie inside the house as Marguerite and Bricker got back in the SUV.

"Roxy might need to go out," Valerie said with a frown as Anders set down her bags and closed and locked the front door.

"That's okay. We're going out too," Leigh said cheerfully. "I thought we'd eat on the verandah."

"Oh, that sounds nice." Valerie smiled and followed Leigh toward the back of the house with Roxy trailing her.

Leaving Valerie's bags for later, Anders grabbed the dog food and the bag with Roxy's things and followed the women.

While the women headed out onto the verandah, Anders stopped in the kitchen to fill one of the dog dishes with water and the other with food before joining them.

"Oh, that was nice of you. Thank you," Valerie said with surprise when she turned from watching Roxy nose curiously around the backyard and saw that Anders had brought food and water for the dog. Grimacing, she added, "I should have thought of it myself."

"You were carrying the human food," Anders said with a shrug as he set the dishes on the edge of the covered verandah. Straightening, he glanced to Leigh, who was setting out the plastic containers on the patio table. "I'll get drinks. What would you ladies like?"

"Nothing for me," Leigh said, picking up the second bag of food containing the two meals she hadn't set out, and heading for the French doors.

"I'm going to put this in the fridge, take a nap, and heat it up to eat with Lucian when he returns. But there's a good selection of drinks inside, Valerie. You should take a look and see what you want. Anders can show you."

Anders stared after the woman with vexation. She was the one who'd wanted to stop to eat. Now she was going to wait for Lucian? She was up to something, and he didn't have to work hard to figure it out. What had started out as a simple dinner for three was quickly turning into a romantic dinner for two on the verandah in the setting sun.

"Oh, don't hesitate to use the candles," Leigh announced suddenly, popping her head back out the door. "The sun will be gone soon and you'll want to be able to see what you're eating."

"Thanks," Valerie said with a smile as the woman disappeared back inside. She obviously had no clue this was a setup, but then she didn't know the people she was dealing with here.

Shaking his head, Anders headed for the French doors. "Come. We'd best get our drinks and eat before the food cools."

Nodding, Valerie cast one last glance at Roxy before trailing him into the house.

"Will she be all right out there?" Anders asked as he led her to the refrigerator.

"Yes. She won't run off or anything. Roxy stays close. In fact, if she notices I've left the verandah, she'll probably come looking for me," Valerie assured him.

Nodding, he opened the fridge door and eyed the contents. There were juices, milk, and several varieties of pop . . . and he didn't have a clue what was good. He waited until she'd selected something called Dr. Pepper and then took one for himself as well.

"A glass and ice cubes?" Anders asked as he closed the door.

"Yes please. Just tell me where to find the glasses and I'll get them," she added.

Anders opened a cupboard door by the sink and they each took a glass. They then stopped at the refrigerator ice machine to get ice before heading back to the verandah. Roxy was just approaching the doors as they came out. She'd obviously noticed her mistress's absence and had been about to search for her as Valerie had said she would.

"Good girl," Valerie praised, holding both her glass and can precariously in one hand so she could pet the dog with the other in passing. Anders wasn't sure what she was praising the dog for, but the dog liked it and wagged her tail wildly, her butt moving with the action. Valerie chuckled, but said, "Go eat now."

Roxy immediately walked over to sniff the food he'd set out for her, and then settled down to eating with serious intent.

Shaking his head, Anders followed Valerie to the table and sat down across from her. As he opened his pop and poured it over the ice, he commented, "She listens well."

"Yeah. She's a good dog," Valerie said, glancing to Roxy as she poured her own pop.

"Well trained," he countered, turning his attention to opening the lid of his meal and surveying the contents. It smelled amazing.

"I'm lucky," Valerie said with a shrug, opening her

own meal. "I was able to take Roxy into the clinic and keep an eye on her full-time. And the other animals there helped socialize her as well."

Anders glanced to the dog and admitted, "That's one of the reasons I haven't got a dog yet. I want one, but my hours aren't exactly regular and I don't want to stick the poor thing in a cage for hours on end. And what would I do with it if I had to be away for days?" he added with a frown.

"You're thinking of the dog first. That's the sign of a good pet owner," Valerie said approvingly. "A lot of people don't consider things like that when they get a dog. They want one, so they get it. Then they're upset and think there's something wrong with the dog when it isn't easily trained or pees in the house." Opening the plastic bag her fork, knife, and napkin were in, she asked, "Have you considered a training nanny for the first six months to a year?"

Anders raised his eyebrows in question. "A training nanny?"

"You might not have anything like that here," she said with a frown and then explained, "We have a gal in Winnipeg who gets referrals from us. She takes puppies while the owners are working and helps train them. A dog sitter slash trainer ... puppy nanny." She pursed her lips and then admitted, "It can be a bit pricey, but it's worth it."

"I'll have to see if there's anyone like that here," he said thoughtfully and then they both fell silent as their attention turned to their food.

Anders's first bite of the chicken was a revelation. He'd thought the ice cream was the most delicious thing he'd ever tasted, but the chicken was easily its equal and he had to wonder if it was the food or this life mate business. Perhaps everything would be the most delicious thing he'd ever tasted now. He supposed he'd find out the answer to that as he sampled more and different foods.

As he ate, Anders thought perhaps he should stop being so hard on Bricker for his constant desire to stop for food here and there. He suddenly understood that desire. Although Bricker's hunger was only because he was young enough to still eat.

A satisfied sigh from Valerie drew his attention from his nearly empty container. His eyebrows rose when she pushed her half-finished meal away and sat back in her seat.

"All done?" he asked, eyeing the chicken and fries remaining in the container.

"I'm afraid so. My stomach really must have shrunk. I'm stuffed," she said, and then offered, "Do you want to finish it?"

When Anders nodded eagerly, she laughed and pushed the container across the table to him.

"Thank you," he said and quickly moved her left-over chicken and fries to his own container. He really shouldn't have room for the food either. His stomach had to be the size of a pea after centuries without solid food in it, and truth to tell, he was already past full himself, but he just couldn't seem to get enough of the tasty fare.

Valerie smiled indulgently as she watched him eat her food, but she began to yawn as he was finishing.

"You're tired," Anders commented as he returned both empty containers to the bag they'd come in.

"Yes." She grimaced. "I didn't use to be such a lightweight, but I've been falling asleep all over the place today."

"It's your body recovering. It'll pass," he assured her.

Valerie nodded and then glanced to Roxy as the dog returned from a trip to relieve herself and settled at her side. Petting the German shepherd, she asked, "How long do you think I'll be here?"

Anders hesitated. They had told her she was here because her captor had escaped, and that was partially true. There was a slim chance the man might come after her . . . if she'd seen anything and was able to identify him. But they weren't holding out much hope of that. None of the other women had been able to tell them much of use. If the rogue had half a brain, Anders thought he had probably moved far away to start over and was even now terrorizing others. The real reason Valerie was here and hadn't been moved to the Enforcer house was because Anders had been foolish enough to admit to Lucian that he hadn't been able to read or control her at the house. Lucian now suspected she was Anders's life mate and wanted to find out for sure if she was, and if she would agree to be a willing life mate to him, before deciding how to handle her.

If she couldn't accept what he was, and was unwilling to be his life mate, her memories of her captivity and her stay here would be wiped from her mind and she'd be returned to her life. But if she was willing . . .

Anders didn't allow himself to think about that. It would be too easy to imagine a whole life around this woman as his life mate. He could see it now, eating ice cream and other foods that didn't taste like sawdust, having a companion without having to constantly guard his thoughts . . . And then there was the supposedly hot life mate sex. He was very curious about that.

"Anders?"

Realizing he'd not answered her question, he finally said, "Probably not long."

"You think you'll capture him quickly, then?" Valerie asked, tilting her head. "Have you got a lead on him or something?"

"No," he answered honestly, and then gathered the remains of their meal together and stood. "Don't worry about that now. You need to relax and sleep to regain your strength. Let us worry about the rest. Come on, I'll carry your bags upstairs for you so you can go to bed."

Valerie hesitated, obviously wanting to ask more questions, but another yawn caught her. Covering her mouth, she stood and nodded. "Tomorrow is soon enough to worry about things like that I suppose."

"Tomorrow," Anders agreed and led her and Roxy into the house. He detoured to the kitchen to throw out the garbage, and then led her back to the bags waiting at the front door.

"I can help," Valerie said as he began to collect the bags. When he didn't respond, she moved to his side and picked up the computer case before he could, saying, "I'm not completely helpless, Anders."

It was the first time she'd actually spoken his name and Anders found himself stilling briefly at the sound of it on her lips.

"Is something wrong?" she asked.

"No." He straightened with the other bags and gestured for her to lead the way up the stairs.

Shrugging, Valerie turned and started up the

stairs. This time Roxy didn't follow, but sat at the foot of the stairs. Anders paused to look at her, but the German shepherd seemed confused and looked from him to Valerie and back without moving.

"She's waiting for you," Valerie announced, pausing halfway up the stairs to glance back when she realized he wasn't following. "She's been trained not to go up the stairs until the people have. It prevents her getting under your feet and tripping you up."

"Oh." He started up the stairs, marveling once again at how well trained the dog was. Once he reached the top, the jingle of Roxy's name tag and license clinking together told him she was following. Shaking his head, he trailed Valerie up the hall. It wasn't until she stopped to open her door that he realized he'd been staring at her derriere the whole way. The realization was rather startling. He'd never been an ass man, but the shift and sway of her behind had held his fascination all the way up the hall.

"You aren't expected to stand guard outside my room all night, are you?" Valerie asked curiously as she led him into her room.

"No. I'm in the room next door." Anders set her bags on the table by the window. "Close enough to hear you shout if you need me. But there shouldn't be any problems. The alarm system here is state of the art."

"Good," Valerie said with relief. "I would have felt horrible thinking you were stuck standing in the hall all night. I wouldn't have been able to sleep," she added with a smile.

Anders turned to peer at her and hesitated. He wanted to kiss her. More out of curiosity than any great desire. The more he got to know this woman, the more he liked her. He admired her courage and strength, and was impressed by how well she'd trained her dog. The loyalty the animal showed her mistress spoke well. And so far, he liked everything about her. But he wasn't lusting after her, and wanted to know if kissing her would bring on the life mate passion he'd heard so much about. Unfortunately, it had been a while since he'd wooed a woman and he wasn't sure how to go about it. Did he just grab and kiss her? Or was he expected to wait for some sign from her?

"Well, I should get ready and go to bed," Valerie said finally and Anders smiled wryly. That was definitely a sign, he supposed, but not one suggesting she would welcome his kissing her.

Nodding, he turned and headed for the door. "Yell if you need anything."

"Thank you," Valerie said softly as he opened the door.

Pausing, Anders glanced back, his gaze shifting to the dog. "Does Roxy sleep with you, or should I take her downstairs?"

"Oh, no. She sleeps with me," Valerie said, glancing to Roxy herself.

"Lucky dog," he murmured and caught her surprised glance before he stepped out and pulled the door closed.

Anders paused there briefly, silently kicking himself in the ass for not kissing her, but then shrugged and headed for the door to the room he'd been given for the duration of his stay here.

He'd kiss her tomorrow, he thought, and he wouldn't wait for a signal to do so. In the meantime, he was rather tired himself. He usually slept during the day, but Valerie's waking around noon had cut into his sleep. He'd been up all night and then all day. He suspected his hours were going to be all screwed up for the next little while. Valerie probably kept normal hours and he'd have to do so too to spend time with, and keep an eye on, her.

Roxy's whining woke Valerie. Opening her eyes to the dimly lit room, she took in the open bathroom door and the light spilling out of it. Despite Roxy being with her, she hadn't been willing to sleep in complete darkness. Valerie had been afraid she might wake up and think she was back in that cage.

Roxy whined again and Valerie shifted up onto her elbow to peer to the bottom right corner of the bed, but the German Shepherd wasn't there. She was standing on the floor beside the bed, whining unhappily. When Valerie glanced her way, she turned and moved to the door and then back.

"You have to go out, huh?" Valerie asked, recognizing the signal. Sighing with resignation, she tossed her covers aside and sat up, wincing as a shot of pain caught her by surprise. She'd forgotten about her back. Moving more carefully, Valerie stood up and glanced around for her robe, then recalled that it was still in the duffel bag. She'd been too tired to bother unpacking it, and had simply stripped off her clothes, pulled on the oversized T-shirt she slept in, and crawled between the sheets.

Valerie headed for the bags Anders had set on the table, but another, more urgent whine followed by a bark from Roxy made her change direction. Her T-shirt covered everything and the dog obviously really needed to go out. It made her wonder how long Roxy had been trying to wake her with her whines.

"Okay," she whispered as she reached the door. "But quietly. People are sleeping."

Roxy whined and wagged her tail and Valerie opened the door. The German shepherd was out the door at once, completely forgetting her manners. That said more about her urgency than anything else had and Valerie didn't waste time reprimanding her, but hurried up the hall after her, grateful for the night-lights in the plug sockets that lit her path.

Roxy remembered her manners at the stairs and paused to let Valerie go down first. There were no night-lights here, but they started again at the bottom of the steps and Valerie moved carefully down with one hand on the stair rail.

As she led Roxy toward the back of the house with the help of the night-lights, Valerie wondered what time it was. She glanced around for a clock as she crossed to the French doors and began to work the lock, but hadn't spotted one before she got the door unlocked. She pulled it open and Roxy bolted out just as an alarm suddenly started to blare. Valerie froze, only then remembering Anders saying something about a state-of-the-art alarm system. She'd just set it off.

Six

The sudden screech of the alarm had Anders abruptly awake. A wash of adrenaline pumping through him propelled him out of the bed. Before he even knew what he was doing, he was at the door and dragging it open. Movement at the end of the hall caught his attention as he started forward. Anders slowed when he saw that it was Lucian coming out of the master bedroom.

Like himself, Lucian was shirtless. However, he did have his pants on. Undone, but on. Either he had just been undressing to go to bed, or he had thought to pull his pants on before exiting his room. Something he hadn't thought to do, Anders realized, suddenly aware that he was wearing only his boxers.

"Valerie?" Lucian barked.

"On it," Anders shouted as he hurried forward, but he couldn't be sure the other man heard him. He himself hadn't really heard Lucian say Valerie's name so much as read it on his lips. But he didn't bother to clarify what he'd said. Moving swiftly again, he hurried to Valerie's door and thrust it open, only to find her bed empty. The bathroom door was open and that room appeared empty too. No Valerie and no Roxy.

Fear clutching at his chest, Anders didn't bother closing the door, but continued forward, shaking his head to tell Lucian she wasn't in her room. Anders got to the top of the stairs first and immediately started down, aware that Lucian was right behind him.

Groaning, Valerie leaned her forehead against the door and closed her eyes as she listened to the thud of feet overhead. She'd woken up everyone, of course.

Sighing, she straightened and turned to peer toward the stairs at the front of the house as she listened to the sounds coming from above. The thudding that had started out at opposite ends of the house was converging overhead, and then they started down the stairs.

Valerie really didn't want to stand there and wait for them, but had no choice. She'd accidentally set off the alarm. This was on her. Besides, what else could she do? Rush outside and hide in the bushes, then sleep on the lawn furniture till morning?

"Valerie!" Anders shouted, skidding to a halt as he rushed into the room and spotted her by the doors.

"I'm sorry," she yelled to be heard over the alarm as a second man, tall and blond, pushed past Anders to rush to the French doors on the living room side of the room and began to punch numbers on a panel there. "Roxy had to go out and I forgot about the alarm!"

The last word was shouted into sudden silence as the alarm died abruptly. Valerie hardly noticed, however; she was too busy gaping at Anders and what he was wearing. Or not wearing. The man was barefoot and barechested, in his boxers . . . and damn, he looked fine. He was also staring at her as if he'd never seen her before, she realized and bit her lip as she switched her gaze to the blond. The blond, though, was ignoring her entirely. He'd picked up a nearby cordless phone and was now punching numbers into that.

He was calling the security office, Valerie realized when he recited a seven-digit number and then growled that everything was fine, the alarm was set off accidentally. He set the phone down and turned to glare at her then, irritation in every line of his body.

Valerie was sure she was about to get a blistering reprimand, but Leigh's cheerful voice intervened.

"Well, thank goodness we weren't asleep yet," the pregnant woman said, drawing attention to her arrival as she hurried across the room in a long pink robe to the blond man's side. She patted his arm soothingly, and then stretched up to whisper something in the man's ear. Finally, she turned to Valerie and smiled. "And this works out well, because I was supposed to change your dressing before you went to bed, but you were sleeping when Lucian got home and I got up. I can do that now though."

"Anders will do it," the blond growled. "You're going back to bed."

"Oh, Lucian, it will only take me a minute. I can—" Leigh's protests died on a gasp when the blond picked her up and started across the room with her.

"See to it," the blond ordered as he passed Anders. "And make sure she doesn't set off the alarm again."

Anders grunted in response and watched his boss stride up the hall carrying Leigh. When the couple disappeared upstairs, he turned back to Valerie again.

"I really am sorry," she said quietly, trying to avoid looking directly at him. Honestly, no man should look that good, Valerie thought, but when he didn't respond, she risked a look. His shoulders had relaxed and he was running one weary hand over his short hair.

"Accidents happen," Anders said finally, his hand moving down to the back of his neck now, kneading as if trying to remove tension there. Then he gestured behind her. "Roxy's done her business I think."

Turning, she saw that the German shepherd had returned and now stood outside the door, peering in. Valerie hadn't even realized she'd closed the door, but opened it now and let Roxy in.

"I'd better see to your dressing," Anders muttered.

Valerie glanced around as she closed the door, but Anders had headed out of the room. She hesitated, but then followed, noting that he had very fine, muscular legs, and a nice rounded tush. Forcing that thought out of her head, she trailed him upstairs and to her room with Roxy on her heels. He had the bedside table drawer open when she entered and was removing items from it. He closed the drawer and turned to stride back to the door, but paused abruptly when he spotted her.

"Oh." He blinked at her. "I was going to do it downstairs."

"Okay," Valerie said at once, and spun to lead the way back downstairs. It seemed like a better idea than doing it there in her bedroom. Less personal. And there was no bed downstairs. Valerie wasn't sure why that made a difference, but didn't want to analyze it too much.

"The kitchen has better light," Anders said as he followed her into the open-concept kitchen/living room and hit a switch, lighting up both sides of the room.

Valerie headed for the kitchen. Roxy stuck to her side at first and then suddenly jogged ahead. Someone had brought in her food and water dishes and set them on the floor by the stove. Roxy had spotted them and now picked up the food dish and carried it back to drop at Valerie's feet, bringing her to a halt beside the island.

"What time is it?" Valerie asked with a frown as she bent to pick up the dish.

Anders glanced toward the microwave as he moved past her into the kitchen. "Six thirty."

Valerie followed his gaze, noting the digital time glowing green in the top right corner of the appliance and wondered how she'd missed that earlier. Not to mention how she'd thought it was the middle of the night when the sky was actually lightening outside. There was no sign of the sun yet, but the sky was blue gray rather than black.

"Feeding time I gather?" Anders asked with amusement when Roxy sat down in front of Valerie and whined pitifully.

"Yes," she admitted wryly, carrying the dog dish around the island. "Roxy's better than an alarm clock. Six thirty every morning she's up and outside and wants her breakfast."

Chuckling, Anders bent and retrieved the bag of dog food from a cupboard in the island and opened it, then poured it into Roxy's dish.

"Thank you," she said, when he'd finished and began to close the bag.

She carried the dish over and set it down beside the water dish someone had thoughtfully refilled. She straightened then, but it wasn't until she said, "Okay," that a hovering Roxy lunged forward. She was immediately snout deep in the food dish, gobbling up the colorful dry food.

"She has a healthy appetite," Anders said dryly.

"I swear she has a hollow leg." Valerie turned and moved back to lean against the island. It was a strategic move. It hid her bare legs from his view. She, herself, was steadfastly ignoring his bare legs . . . and bare chest . . . and bare belly. Well, trying to anyway. Sighing, she raised an eyebrow and asked, "Where did you want to do this?"

"The best light is here," Anders said, patting the island, and it was true, she acknowledged. The light was centered over the sink in the middle of the island and shone down bright and strong there.

After a hesitation, Valerie slid around the island and moved up beside him to lean over the sink, leaving her back under the light.

"Too low," he said, his voice gruff.

Valerie straightened and turned with a frown. "I don't know what I can do to—"

Her words ended on a gasp as Anders caught her by the waist and lifted her to sit on the island. He released her just as quickly as he'd picked her up, and had moved around to the other side of the island almost before she'd re-gathered her wits. Glancing over her shoulder, she saw him setting out the items he'd fetched from her room: a large gauze pad, white medical tape and antibiotic ointment.

Valerie turned forward again with a grimace as she realized she'd have to lift her shirt and she was presently sitting on it. Sighing, she leaned to one side, lifting one butt cheek off the island so that she could tug the cloth out there, then leaned the other way to do the same for that side. Then she tugged the cloth up and caught it under her arms so that it stopped just under her breasts in the front and—she hoped—at the same height in the back. She was extremely aware that it left her sitting there with only her pink panties covering her lower body. It made her wish she'd worn her black boy-cut panties. They at least looked more like shorts.

"Thank you," Anders said behind her and she wondered if he was catching a cold. His voice had been gruff earlier and now it was husky.

That worry fled as he began to remove the bandage presently covering her wound. He was working slowly, obviously trying to be as gentle as possible, but the tape was well adhered to her skin and it stung enough that she wondered if she had back hair there or something. Biting her lip, Valerie focused on the lit digits on the microwave and tried to ignore the pain he was inadvertently causing. She sagged with relief though, when it was done and the bandage was off.

"How's it look?" she asked.

"It's healing," Anders said.

That was good, she supposed. But "it's healing" didn't really tell her much. Was it a great gaping hole? Probably not, Valerie acknowledged. Leigh had said Dr. Dani had sewn her up, so it was probably a large, nasty puckered one. Lovely.

"I'm going to put the salve on now. It might sting," he warned quietly.

Valerie nodded, and braced herself.

Again, she could tell that Anders was trying to be gentle. His fingers barely feathered over her skin, but it was tender enough that even that stung. Grinding her teeth, she held her breath and waited, trying to keep her mind blank.

"Done," Anders announced and Valerie let her breath out on a sigh, only to suck it back in as he laid the gauze over the wound. The first brush of it was nasty, but after that it seemed fine and she was able to breathe normally as he taped the pad in place.

"All done," Anders said. "You can let go of your shirt."

Valerie immediately lifted her arms, allowing the cloth to drop back down. She would have slid off the island then, but Anders had come around and was standing in front of her.

"Oh. Hi," she said like a brainless twit.

"Hi," Anders responded and reached for her waist. She thought he was going to lift her down. She thought wrong. Instead, he clasped her waist, stepped between her legs and kissed her. It was just a gentle brushing of his lips at first, then firmer, and then his tongue slid out to nudge her lips open. It all got pretty fuzzy after that. Her brain seemed to shut down and give itself up to the rush of sensation that suddenly exploded through her. Honestly, the man could *kiss*. He did things to her lips and tongue that she'd never before experienced. Her ex, Larry, hadn't been much of a kisser. More a pecker. Frankly, if he had a tongue, she wouldn't know. Anders definitely had one and knew what to do with it.

When Roxy barked and they broke the kiss with a start, Valerie glanced down to see that she'd tried to climb the man like he was a tree trunk. Her legs were wrapped around his hips, her ankles hooked behind his legs, her arms around his shoulders, her hands cupping his neck and head, and her butt was off the counter and in his hands. Valerie stared at Anders, and said, "Mmmfph."

Anders's response was to let his lips curve into the sexiest damn smile she'd ever seen. Valerie stared back wide-eyed and bemused. She hadn't thought the man *could* smile. But then she hadn't known he could kiss either, Valerie thought as his mouth lowered toward hers again for another kiss, one that never landed because Roxy barked again, this time rearing up on her back paws to plant her front ones on them.

That was enough to get Valerie's attention. Roxy never jumped up on people.

"What is it, Rox?" Valerie gasped, pushing at Anders's chest to get him to set her down. He did, easing her to the floor as she swung her feet down from around his hips.

Now that she had her attention, Roxy immediately turned and ran to the door, where she barked and turned back to look at Valerie, legs shifting restlessly.

"Oh," Valerie sighed and hurried over to open the door. Roxy needed to go out . . . desperately, Valerie thought when the dog bolted across the verandah and barely reached the grass before squatting.

"I'm going to need to get some waste pick-up bags,"

Valerie muttered and then gave a start when Anders rested his hands on her shoulders from behind.

"We'll do that when the stores open," he promised, pulling her back against his chest and bending his head to press butterfly kisses to her ear. Valerie was melting into him when he started to move her hair aside to kiss her neck. She immediately stiffened and pulled away, one hand rising self-consciously to be sure her throat was covered.

"You don't have to hide it from me, Valerie," he said quietly. "I've seen your neck."

Finished with her business, Roxy returned then, nudging Valerie's hand with her nose. She glanced down at the dog and petted her, relieved at the excuse to look away from Anders. He may already have seen her neck, but it didn't make her less self-conscious about it.

"I'm still tired. I think I'll go sleep for a little longer," she lied, heading out of the room with Roxy at her side. He didn't say or do anything to stop her and Valerie walked calmly upstairs to her room. She stepped inside, waited for Roxy to clear the door, then shut it and leaned weakly back against it, her eyes closing.

The memory of those few moments, or maybe more than a few moments, in Anders's arms, immediately washed over her. The passion had been staggering . . . mind-blowing. Valerie hardly knew the man, but if Roxy hadn't needed to go out, she suspected she'd even now be riding that horse called sex. And where the hell had that passion come from? The guy was good-looking and everything, but until his lips had met hers, she hadn't really been thinking lusty thoughts about him. She'd admired his pretty face and trim figure like one would admire a well-designed dress or shoe, but there had been no real spark of sexual interest.

Well, except when their hands had met on the soup bowl . . . and when he'd taken her hand in Cambridge to help her back into the SUV, she acknowledged. Yeah, heated awareness had shot through her both times, but nothing like what had happened downstairs just now. That had been like a flash fire.

Roxy's wet nose against the palm of her hand stirred Valerie from her position. She glanced down at the dog, and gave her a pat, muttering, "I've lost my mind. You know that, don't you?"

Shaking her head, she walked over to the bed and lay down. It hadn't yet been nine P.M. last night when she'd lain down. She'd slept straight through to six in the morning. More than nine hours. Valerie didn't expect to sleep, but she did want to avoid Anders for a while. At least until she thought she could be around him without trying to climb him like a telephone pole again.

Anders dropped onto the sofa and leaned his head back with a sigh. He stared at the ceiling overhead, but he was seeing Valerie's face after Roxy had broken up their kiss. Her lips had been swollen from his kisses, her cheeks flushed, and her eyes heavy-lidded with passion and hunger. He didn't doubt he'd looked just as aroused. Just the memory of her lips under his, her body pressing eagerly against him, was making him hard again.

Damn, it had just been starting to go down, he thought with a grimace. On the bright side, there was now no question in his mind that Valerie was his life mate. Well, if there really had been before.

There shouldn't have been—he'd had all the other symptoms—but Anders had been hesitating about admitting it because of the lack of passion. It seemed he just had to touch her to ignite it. And he now understood the horn-dog type behavior of his comrades. Because now that he'd tasted it, he couldn't wait to taste more. So much so that it was a struggle not to follow her up to her room. One kiss and she'd melt in his arms like butter on a hot griddle.

"Amazing."

Anders glanced around with a start. He found Lucian leaning against the door frame, eyeing him with amusement.

"What?" he asked, sitting up straight.

"How everything can change so swiftly," Lucian said dryly, moving into the kitchen.

Anders watched him get a glass out of the cupboard before asking mildly, "And what is it you think is changing?"

"Three days ago when you first realized you couldn't read her and that she might possibly be your life mate, you weren't happy," Lucian said. He filled the glass with water, took a drink, and then continued, "You didn't like the idea of anyone stealing so much of your attention, of having something to lose, of becoming a mother hen like me, or of being led around by your dick. Now you want to follow that presently very evident dick upstairs and claim Valerie by any means necessary."

Anders glanced down to note that not only did he still have an erection, but it *was* very evident in his boxers. Grabbing one of the couch pillows, he dragged it over his lap and muttered, "You caught all that from reading my thoughts, did you?"

"Clear as glass," Lucian said.

"Right." Anders said and grimaced at the knowledge that Lucian had read his less than complimentary thoughts about his worry for Leigh and being led around by his dick. Raising an eyebrow, he asked, "Do I owe you an apology?"

"Nope. I can hardly complain when I was eavesdropping on your thoughts." He took another drink of his water. As Lucian lowered the glass, he swallowed, and added, "But I'd go softly with Valerie. I wouldn't want you to rush things and blow it."

"Thanks for the advice," Anders said dryly.

"I'm serious," Lucian said softly.

Anders stilled. As a rule, Lucian could be counted on to growl, grunt, or bark. His voice only got that soft, solemn sound on very rare occasions. When it did, you were smart to listen. Anders nodded. "I'm listening."

"She just experienced a nightmarish two weeks at the hands of what she thinks is a vampire. One of our kind," he pointed out. "Ten days and nights in the flesh and three in fever-driven nightmares."

"But we aren't vampires," Anders pointed out. "We're immortals."

"Semantics," Lucian said with a shrug. "It won't make any difference to her whether we are the mythological cursed and soulless beast Stoker wrote about, or scientifically evolved mortals turned nearly immortal by bio-engineered nanos that were introduced into our blood before the fall of Atlantis."

"Scientifically evolved mortals who need more blood than the human body can produce to power those nanos," Anders added wearily.

Lucian nodded. "We have fangs, we don't age, we are hard to kill and we need blood to survive. To her and many others, we *are* vampires."

"We drink bagged blood to survive now," Anders argued. "The immortal who kidnapped and held Valerie and the other women is a rogue."

"True," Lucian agreed. "Unfortunately, Valerie's first encounter with our kind was via that rogue. She, understandably, is not going to be very receptive to the possibility that there are good guys among our kind. She needs to get to know and trust us, you especially, before you reveal too much."

Anders nodded, seeing the wisdom in what he said. Then he cleared his throat and asked, "By don't reveal too much, you aren't including—"

"No," Lucian said, rare amusement curving his lips. "Bed her all you want, just keep your mouth shut while you do. At least until you think she can handle it. Otherwise," he warned, "you could lose the chance of a lifetime."

On that note, Lucian set the glass down and headed for the door.

Anders was just relaxing into the couch to contemplate what had been said when Lucian paused at the hallway and glanced back to add, "Of course, if you do something as stupid as take my very pregnant and overdue wife on another three-hour road trip, you won't live long enough to enjoy that chance of a lifetime anyway."

Lucian didn't wait for a response, but strode away, leaving the threat hanging in the air.

Grimacing, Anders closed his eyes. He wasn't surprised by Lucian's threat. He'd expected it to come eventually. When Valerie had retired, Anders had lain down too, stripping down to his boxers for comfort's sake. But he'd fully expected to wake up in an hour or so and come down to face the music if Lucian was back, or wait to face the music if he wasn't. However, he'd slept right through the night until the blaring house alarm had shaken him from sleep.

Christ, that had been an experience and a half. After all the panic and hurry, he'd charged downstairs only to find Valerie standing by the French doors in the kitchen looking guilty, mortified, and cute as a button in an overlarge T-shirt.

The memory brought a smile to his face that quickly faded as he considered Valerie and how to gain her trust enough that she wouldn't run screaming for the hills when he eventually risked explaining who and what he was. It wasn't going to be easy.

Seven

Valerie blinked her eyes open and found herself staring into Roxy's furry face. The dog immediately whined. It probably wasn't the first time. Grimacing, Valerie sat up and glanced to the bedside clock. It was a little after noon. She'd fallen asleep again. She hadn't intended to, and hadn't thought she would after sleeping so long already. Valerie had only intended to lie down for a bit until the others got up. It seemed to her that having others around might be a good thing if she didn't want another heated session with Anders.

"Sorry, girl," Valerie said, ruffling Roxy's fur. "You must be bored stiff and ready for a run. You probably haven't had one while I was gone. It's hard to imagine Mrs. Ribble walking you, let alone taking you for a run. But I'm afraid I'm in no shape to take you for one either right now. I'd probably flake out in five minutes," she added with a frown, and then suggested, "How about a game of fetch though?"

Roxy barked. Smiling, Valerie gave her another pat and then stood up. "Okay. Let's go see who's up and then I'll take you out in the backyard and throw the ball for you."

Roxy followed closely as Valerie walked to the door, bumping up against her leg repeatedly as if herding her along. It made Valerie smile and pat the dog's head as she walked. She didn't encounter anyone in the hall, or on the main floor. It looked like everyone else was still sleeping. But then it had been night when she'd called 911 and these men had been working. She supposed they worked nights and slept most of the day. Which was a bit worrisome. Did that mean the alarm was on again and would be every morning when Roxy needed out? She fretted over the possibility as she walked to the panel by the French doors in the living room. Much to her relief, the panel read "ready," which she knew from the alarm at her clinic meant it wasn't on.

Relaxing, she fetched Roxy's ball from the bag Anders had set next to the island last night, and then led the German shepherd outside to throw the ball for her to fetch. It turned out she wasn't in much better shape for that than running. Every time she threw the ball, the stitches in her back made their presence known. Even using her left hand didn't help much, and her throws were pretty lame.

Valerie was about to give up the game when she heard the French doors open behind her. She turned to look around at once, half relieved and half disappointed to see Leigh smiling at her from the kitchen.

"Morning," the brunette called cheerfully, stepping out onto the sheltered verandah.

"Morning," Valerie responded, offering a smile.

She threw the ball one last time for Roxy, and then turned to approach the other woman. "Sorry about waking you up this morning."

Leigh waved that away. "We'd just gone to bed. We weren't asleep."

Valerie raised her eyebrows. "Night owls?"

"Pretty much." Leigh laughed.

"I'm surprised you're up now if you only went to bed at six thirty," she commented.

"I napped earlier, remember?" she said with a shrug and rubbed her stomach as she admitted, "I find I'm having trouble sleeping for anything more than a couple hours. I can't get comfortable and tend to take a lot of short naps."

"Ah." Valerie nodded, her gaze dropping to Leigh's belly. She supposed it would be hard to find a comfortable position in her condition.

"Are you ready for breakfast?" Leigh asked suddenly, turning to lead the way back into the house.

"Actually, yes. I'm starved," Valerie admitted at once and whistled for Roxy as she followed her inside. As she waited by the open door for the dog to come in, she added, "But why don't you sit down and let me cook? Just tell me what you want and where to find it and I'll play chef."

When Leigh hesitated, looking tempted, she added, "It's the least I can do for your letting me stay here."

Leigh chuckled at the claim, and then heaved a sigh. "You're more than welcome here and don't have to work off your stay, Valerie." Grimacing, she added, "But I would appreciate some help with breakfast."

"My pleasure," Valerie assured her.

Nodding, Leigh walked over to a cupboard and opened it to survey the boxed and canned food inside.

"How do you feel about pancakes?" she asked as she pulled out a box of buttermilk pancake mix.

"Love them," Valerie said at once.

"Great." Leigh beamed and opened another cupboard to retrieve a big bowl. "Can you grab the eggs and milk out of the fridge while I start the coffee?"

They chatted amiably as they worked. Once they had the batter for the pancakes mixed, Leigh decided they should add sausages to the breakfast. She set the electric grill up on the island and sat in one of the chairs to cook the sausages while Valerie flipped pancakes at the range.

"Good Lord."

Valerie glanced around at that gasped comment from Leigh. "What's wrong?"

"I—nothing, I just—" She wrinkled her nose and then admitted, "I know you probably thought we had, but we never contacted your family to let them know you're okay, Valerie. They're probably worried sick."

"Oh." Valerie turned back to her pancakes and sighed. "It's okay. There's no one to contact or worry."

"No one?" Leigh asked and she could hear the frown in her voice.

Valerie shook her head. "I was an only child. My grandparents died one after another of heart attacks and cancer as I was growing up and my parents died three years ago in a car accident. There's just myself and an aunt who moved to Texas thirty years ago. I've only seen her twice since then. At her parents' funerals." She shrugged. "Other than Christmas cards, we don't stay in touch."

"Oh," Leigh said softly and fell silent.

"What about friends?" Anders asked, and Valerie nearly jumped out of her skin. Both at his sudden joining of the conversation and because of his chest brushing her back as he reached around her to set a small Petsmart bag on the counter.

"Waste pick-up bags," he murmured by her ear, his fingers drifting lightly over her bare upper arm as his hand withdrew. "Since Lucian was here to keep you safe, I popped out and picked them up for you."

Valerie stared blankly at the bag, aware that shivers were running down her spine and goose bumps were popping up on her skin where his breath and fingers had passed. She had to wonder how she could be staring at something so unsexy and be so turned on at the same time.

A muffled laugh drew Valerie's confused gaze to Leigh and the other woman grinned at her as she said, "That was sweet of you, Anders."

"Yes, it was," Valerie said and then paused to clear her throat when it came out froggy. "Thank you."

"Mind you," Leigh added. "Red roses might have been sweeter than red doggie pooh bags."

"I'll keep that in mind for next time," Anders responded.

Valerie flushed and turned back to the pancakes. What Leigh was suggesting would have been appropriate if they were dating or something, but they weren't, and she did appreciate his running out to get her the bags. She didn't want to repay Leigh for allowing her into her home by leaving little Roxy gifts all over their yard . . . And what did his response mean exactly?

"So, you have no family, but what about friends?" Anders asked, reminding her of his earlier question.

"I have friends, of course. But they're back in Winnipeg. They won't even know I went missing." She flipped the pancakes and added, "I only moved to Cambridge the week before I was kidnapped and I spent most of that week rushing around getting things I needed for the house and for classes. I hadn't made any friends here yet." She lifted the pancakes out of the frying pan and slid them onto a plate in the oven to keep warm, then poured two more onto the griddle before admitting, "Mrs. Ribble is the only person I'd even talked to besides store clerks and school officials and that was because she came out to say that Roxy better not be a barker or she'd call the police."

"And then the old bat goes and tries to steal her," Leigh muttered.

Valerie shook her head at the comment and glanced around with amusement. "I don't know why you guys have it in for the woman. She did look after Roxy."

"For purely selfish reasons," Leigh said grimly. "Trust me, that woman is the most selfish, bitter old biddy I've ever met."

Valerie turned to stare at her. "You didn't even talk to her. Have you met Mrs. Ribble before or something?"

Leigh opened her mouth, and then paused briefly before saying, "I know someone who knows her."

"Hmm." Valerie turned back to the pancakes. She wasn't terribly surprised to hear Mrs. Ribble was a mean-spirited old woman. She'd already developed that opinion herself even before the last encounter.

In the week that she'd been living next door to the woman, she'd heard or seen her giving hell to three neighbors for things that were none of her concern, and harass the local kids for infractions as small as accidentally stepping off the sidewalk onto her grass. The woman seemed to delight in making other people miserable. And she was good at it. Lots of practice, Valerie suspected.

"So, it could have been quite a while before anyone noticed you'd gone missing," Anders said thoughtfully, and Valerie glanced around to see that he was getting himself a cup of coffee.

"Yes, quite a while," she acknowledged, turning back to her pan. "None of the other women had family or friends in the area either. We figured that out pretty quick while talking. Not one of us had anyone to worry or raise a fuss over our going missing. We thought that was probably the reason he chose us."

"That's probably true," Leigh said solemnly. "And it was smart of him."

"It explains why we didn't get on to him sooner," Anders said, and then pointed out, "If he continues with that pattern it will be harder to track him down."

Valerie frowned at the thought of this monster out there somewhere preying on other women even as they spoke.

"It will take him a while to set up somewhere else," Leigh said, her thoughts apparently moving along the same line as Valerie's. "He needs to find a new home base, gather cages and whatnot . . ." She paused, and then asked, "Valerie, was there anything else you had in common with the other women?"

"Like what?" Valerie asked uncertainly, turning

sideways so she could keep one eye on her cooking and one on Leigh.

"Well, there has to be a way that he set his sights on each of you. It can't be a coincidence that none of you had family and friends. Likely he chose each of you because of that, but how did he find it out?" she asked. "Is there some welcoming organization or something? Did you all use the same realtor?"

"I don't know," Valerie admitted with a frown. They hadn't followed that line of questioning. After discovering each of them had that in common, they'd mostly talked about each other, their memories of better times, their lives, their regrets over things they hadn't yet done, their dreams for the future when they were free, and what foods they'd most like to eat. They'd even talked about books they'd read and movies they'd seen, anything to take them temporarily from their grim reality. Now she wished she'd thought of this and asked these questions of the others. It could be a way to find the man.

"Not to worry," Leigh said brightly, using her tongs to turn the sausages she was cooking. "We'll just have to do that now. We can get you all together and let you talk until we sort out what place or person you all have in common."

"I'm afraid that's not possible."

Valerie glanced beyond Leigh to see Lucian standing just inside the room. His hair was sleep ruffled, and he wore jeans, but was shirtless. However, a T-shirt dangled from his fingers and even as she looked his way he started to pull it on.

"Why isn't it possible, Lucian?" Leigh asked. "All we have to do is take Valerie to the Enforcer house to chat with them."

"Which would be nice except that the women have been returned to their lives," he said, moving forward to kiss his wife on the forehead.

"Oh," Leigh said with disappointment.

"Well, that doesn't mean we can't get them all together," Valerie said reasonably.

Leigh bit her lip as Lucian and Anders exchanged glances, and then Lucian said, "Of course, we can contact them and ask if they'd be willing, but I suspect they all just want to forget what happened and get on with their lives."

"Well, yes, I imagine they do. But surely they'll want the man who kidnapped us captured and off the streets," she pointed out with a frown.

Lucian made a noncommittal sound and moved around the island to fetch himself a cup of coffee. He fixed it sweet and white, took a gulp, and then turned to eye her. "Before they were returned to their lives, the other women were asked what this Igor of yours and his boss looked like. None of them seemed to be able to answer that."

Valerie grimaced and shook her head as she switched out the latest pancakes for fresh batter. "I'm not surprised. We were in the dark most of the time. Igor was just a large silhouette who delivered food and water and dragged one of us away every day. And whatever was in that oatmeal was some nasty stuff. The first time he took me upstairs I was under the influence and it was like a bad acid trip, faces coming out of the wall, their faces and bodies distorted as if looking through the bottom of a pop bottle, and the whole house spinning dizzily around me." She shook her head at the unpleasant memory.

"But the last time you weren't under the influence," Lucian said.

Valerie nodded, but concentrated on cooking for several moments, before saying, "I didn't see Igor's boss at all, and I'm afraid I didn't pay much attention to Igor himself. I was busy looking for a weapon or an escape route."

"Just do your best to describe him," Anders said quietly before Lucian could speak again.

Valerie sighed. She stared at the pancakes as she said, "He was big. Bigger than you two, even. And crazy strong. When he hit me it was like being hit by a train. He sent me flying right out of the bathroom."

"Okay," Anders said when she fell silent. "What color was his hair?"

"Dark brown," she answered as an image of him bent over the tub came to mind. "Short and dark brown."

"And his face? Was there anything notable about his features?"

Valerie frowned and tried to remember. She hadn't looked at him from the cage all the way up to the bathroom. Her eyes had been darting around looking for a way to escape. She pictured him turning to her in the bathroom, but all she saw was the shampoo squirting out over his face. But then she saw him coming out of the bathroom after her. There had still been shampoo on his face, but he'd wiped the worst of it away.

"I think he had a big nose," she said slowly. "And small mean eyes under a high forehead."

"And his mouth?" Anders asked.

"Thin lipped I think," she said uncertainly. "And he had big ears."

Silence fell briefly when she finished and then Lucian said, "We'll have to get Valerie together with a sketch artist."

"Do we know one?" Anders asked.

"We can borrow one, either from the local police or somewhere further afield," Lucian said. "I'll call Bastian after breakfast and see if he can arrange something."

"Speaking of breakfast, the sausages are done," Leigh announced. "Valerie, how are we doing on the pancakes?"

"The last two are in the pan," she answered.

"Good. Then I'll get plates and silverware—" Leigh began to get off her seat, but Lucian immediately put a hand on her shoulder to stop her.

"Anders and I will get plates and silverware. You just sit and relax," he said firmly.

"Valerie, do you have a coffee?" Anders asked as he retrieved plates from the cupboard.

"No. It only finished dripping just before you came in," she answered, turning the last two pancakes. "I haven't had a chance to grab one."

He didn't comment, but a moment later set a fresh cup of coffee down beside her.

"Thank you," Valerie murmured and picked it up to take a tentative sip. Her eyes widened as she tasted it.

"Cream and one sugar, right?" Anders asked uncertainly when he noted her expression.

"Yes," she said quietly. "It's good. I was just surprised you remembered how I ordered it yesterday."

"I was driving. I ordered it for you," he pointed out.

"Yes, but you had to order five different coffees. I'm just surprised you remembered how I take mine."

"I made a mental note of it," Anders said simply as he moved away.

Valerie stared after him as he retrieved maple syrup for the pancakes, and ketchup for the sausages under Leigh's instruction. He'd made a mental note of how she liked her coffee. What did that mean? Why had he gone to the trouble? For her? Did that mean he liked her? Was he interested in her? Well, okay, those kisses earlier suggested he was definitely interested, but that was just . . . well, chemistry. Physical. The consideration revealed in taking note of how she took her coffee was . . .

She didn't know what it was, but it had taken Larry years to remember how she took her coffee, and Anders had taken the trouble to remember it the first time out. It gave her something to think about.

Shaking her head, Valerie turned her attention to removing the last two pancakes from the pan. Breakfast was ready.

"For God's sake, Anders, your pacing is driving me wild," Leigh said with exasperation. "Sit down."

Anders paused with surprise and turned to peer at the brunette curled up in the corner of the couch with a book in her hands. "I'm not pacing, I'm . . ."

She arched her eyebrows, waiting, and he sighed.

"Pacing," he acknowledged and sank onto the nearest chair. He rested his elbows on his spread knees, allowing his hands to dangle between them, and stared out the window. After several minutes, he dropped back in the chair with a heavy sigh, then straightened and asked impatiently, "What the devil is she doing up there?"

"She's checking with her academic advisor to ensure that missing the first two weeks of classes won't bugger her up for the term," Leigh reminded him patiently.

"Yeah, but that should have been a five-minute conversation. She's been up there over an hour," he complained. Valerie had helped clean up the kitchen after breakfast, then had taken Roxy with her and escaped upstairs on the pretext of calling the veterinary college to be sure she was still welcome after missing the first two weeks of the semester.

"Yes, well, perhaps whoever she needs to speak to wasn't available and she's waiting for a call back," Leigh suggested. "Or maybe they had work for her to do to keep from falling behind and she's up their reading her textbooks and studying."

"Or maybe she's hiding," Anders said unhappily.

Leigh tsked with irritation. "Why would she be hiding?"

Anders didn't respond, but in his mind he was remembering their kiss that morning . . . well, kisses. Or maybe one kiss. He wasn't sure how to classify it. Did you have to come up for air to classify it as more than one kiss? Or was it counted in minutes or seconds? Because it had been a constant devouring of each other's mouths for several minutes.

"Oh my, yes. I see," Leigh murmured.

Anders glanced up at her murmur and noted her narrowed concentration on him. She'd read his damn mind.

"Yes, that might have made her want to hide out," she said sympathetically. "It wasn't that long ago when I had my first encounter with life mate passion. It was pretty terrifying. And she didn't have any idea what was happening. I mean, as an immortal you had heard about it, had some idea of what to expect, and yet you were still overwhelmed by it. Imagine how she must feel. She got hit by a nuclear explosion of passion out of nowhere."

Anders sighed and ran one hand wearily over his closely cropped hair. Leigh wasn't saying a damned thing he hadn't already thought of. Which was why he suspected Valerie was hiding out. The question was, how long would she hide? And how was he supposed to get her to know and trust him if she wouldn't come out of her room?

"All right." Leigh set aside the book she'd been reading, and uncurled her legs from under her to stand up. "I'll go see what I can do."

Anders was on his feet at once. "What are you going to do?"

"I don't know. I'll have to see what the situation is first," she pointed out patiently.

"Right." He nodded.

"Just sit down and try to stop looking like an expectant father. You're giving me contractions here."

Anders eyes widened. "You're—?"

"Joking, Anders," Leigh said with exasperation as she waddled out of the room.

He stared after her until she disappeared on the stairs, and then lifted his eyes to the ceiling, mentally following her journey to Valerie's room. When he heard her knock on the door, he stood frozen for a moment, then suddenly hurried to the bookshelf beside the television and grabbed a random book. Taking it back to his chair, Anders dropped to sit and opened the book to the middle so that he could pretend to be reading if Leigh lured Valerie back down.

Eight

"A swim?" Valerie said uncertainly.

"Yeah. I'm supposed to get exercise, but walking makes my ankles swell, and, frankly, carrying this baby around is like having a sack of potatoes strapped to your waist, but the water makes it all easier," Leigh explained. "However, Anders doesn't swim, and I don't want to be in the pool by myself in case I go into labor or something, so I thought maybe you'd like to join me?"

"Oh." Valerie hesitated. She really didn't have any excuse to say no. She'd made her phone call as soon as she'd got up here, and managed to get through to her advisor. The conversation hadn't lasted long, but afterward, Valerie had been self-conscious about facing Anders again. She maybe shouldn't be, she'd spent time with him since their kiss. But having him come into a room where she was, was different from her having to enter a room where he was. So, she'd made poor Roxy sit in this room for the last hour, and that after making her sleep in here for hours. The poor dog was probably sorry she was back. At least at Mrs. Ribble's she got to go out in the yard.

Now Valerie considered Leigh's words and shifted from one foot to the other. A swim. Being in a bathing suit in front of Anders. But with Leigh . . . who was afraid to swim and rightfully so in her state. And who had also been kind enough to allow Valerie into her home to help keep her safe.

"I can loan you a swimsuit if you—"

"It's okay. I actually picked up my swimsuit when we were at the house. I thought with the pool . . ." She shrugged.

"Great." Leigh beamed. "Well, I'll just go put mine on and meet you at the top of the stairs then. Okay?"

"Sure." Valerie smiled, and saw her out, then turned and went to dig her bathing suit out of the drawer. She'd finally unpacked the bags after coming up after breakfast. Now she pulled her swimsuit out and quickly changed. Once done, she then just stood there and stared at herself with alarm. Her body hadn't been anywhere near a razor in two weeks. She was a bloody gorilla!

Groaning, Valerie closed her eyes briefly, then moved to the makeup case Marguerite had packed for her. She hadn't checked inside when she'd taken it out of her suitcase and plunked it on the bathroom counter. Now, Valerie quickly unzipped the bag, silently praying that—

"Yes," she breathed when the first two items to spill out were her razor and a container of blades.

"Thank you, Marguerite," Valerie breathed. She was standing with one foot in the sink when a knock sounded at the door. Shouting, "Come in," she continued her work, scraping the razor swiftly over her skin.

"If you're grabbing a towel, don't bother. I have a couple of beach towels for us. They're bigger and— Oh." Leigh paused as she reached the bathroom door. "Gee, I hadn't thought about. Well . . ."

"Neither had I," Valerie admitted wryly, quickly drying the first leg before shifting positions to work on the other one. "It wasn't until I saw the koala bear legs I had developed that I remembered."

"Oh, they aren't that bad," Leigh said.

"Yes, they are, or were," Valerie countered, thinking Leigh really was a bad liar.

Apparently she agreed, because she suddenly grimaced and admitted, "Yes, they are. Girl, you could almost braid that hair."

"Thanks," Valerie said on a laugh as she soaped her second leg.

"Well, you didn't really have to shave. We'd have been a matching pair. I mean I haven't been able to even reach my legs in over a month."

Valerie chuckled at the suggestion as she shaved. "Yeah, but you have an excuse. I don't."

"Yeah," Leigh nodded. "I suppose being kidnapped and locked in a cage for ten days and then being unconscious for three days are no excuse for hairy legs."

Valerie blinked at her, and then felt a reluctant smile curve her lips before she agreed, "No excuse at all."

Finished with her second leg, Valerie grabbed the towel and quickly dried it, wiping away the remaining soap. She then paused and peered at herself, feeling a bit self-conscious in her swimsuit and T-shirt. Which was really just silly. She'd worn less at the beach. But then Anders hadn't been at the beach. The thought made her grimace. One kiss and she was suddenly shy of the man?

"Come on, beauty, you've vanquished the hairy beast. Now let's go get wet," Leigh said turning toward the door.

"Beast? Nice," Valerie said with amusement, and hurried to follow her from the room, patting her leg to command Roxy to follow.

"Here, let me take those." She relieved Leigh of the beach towels as they reached the stairs so the pregnant woman could hold the rail, and then followed her silently down.

Anders was sitting reading in the living room when Valerie followed Leigh into the room. She cast one nervous glance his way, then focused on the woman in front of her.

"Go ahead and go see how the temperature of the water is. I'm just going to grab some suntan lotion for us," Leigh said, suddenly veering toward the kitchen.

Valerie hesitated briefly, but then continued resolutely to the French doors and outside, Roxy on her heels. It was only as she closed the door and inhaled that she realized she'd been holding her breath since entering the kitchen/living room.

"You can quit pretending. She's outside."

Anders glanced up innocently from the book. "What makes you think I was pretending?"

"Well, it's that or you've taken a sudden interest in *The Joy of Pregnancy*," she said dryly, retrieving the suntan lotion from a kitchen drawer.

Anders flipped the book over with dismay to stare at the cover. It was indeed *The Joy of Pregnancy*.

Closing the drawer, Leigh added, "And you were reading it upside down."

Cursing under his breath, Anders tossed the book on the coffee table and stood up. "So, you're going swimming?"

"That's right. You can thank me later," she added, heading for the French doors.

"What for?" he asked with a frown.

"Go change into a swimsuit and come out in about ten minutes. I'm going to be exhausted and get out and you'll have to stay to watch Valerie." She put a hand on the doorknob, but paused and looked back. "But remember what I said and go easy with her."

Anders watched her leave, and then hurried upstairs to his room to change into his swim trunks, glad he'd thought to throw them in when he'd packed his bag. The house had come with the pool when Lucian bought it, and Anders knew he'd often used it at night, but after marrying Leigh he'd put an awning over it that blocked the UV rays and not the sun. It allowed her to swim in sunlight without having to ramp up the amount of blood she needed. It was an awesome experience and Anders had been seriously considering putting in a pool at his place with the same setup.

That wasn't why he was eagerly yanking off his clothes and dragging on his swim trunks though. He'd have risked the sun to swim with Valerie. Although, swimming wasn't what was on his mind. Holding her nearly nude and wet body in his arms in the sun-warmed water was what was making him as eager as a teenage boy.

Anders padded out of his room and back downstairs, but paused at the French doors. Leigh had said ten minutes. Did that mean he shouldn't go out before ten minutes had passed? Shifting impatiently, he glanced at his wristwatch, only to realize he hadn't checked it earlier. By his guess it had taken him thirty seconds to hurry upstairs, thirty seconds to hurry down, and maybe two minutes to change his clothes. Or three, he thought. So he maybe had another six minutes.

He patted his leg impatiently, eyes narrowing on the women. Both of them were already in the pool, only their heads visible as they talked and laughed. When Valerie turned and suddenly disappeared under the water, Anders checked his watch. Only two minutes had passed since he'd arrived at the door.

"Screw it," he muttered and headed out.

Leigh was mounting the steps out of the pool by the time he reached it. Snatching up one of the towels that lay neatly folded on the lawn chair closest to the steps, Anders carried it over to her.

"Perfect timing," Leigh announced as he took her arm to ensure she didn't lose her footing as she stepped onto the pool surround. "She's swimming laps, so can't protest my leaving or announce she's tired and escape with me."

"Marguerite's rubbing off on you," Anders said dryly.

"Flattery, Anders? Really?" she said, grinning as she accepted the towel he now held out. Leigh didn't bother drying herself, simply wrapped it around her torso and headed for the house. "Have fun. I'm lying down for a nap. All this fresh air has just exhausted me."

Anders smiled at her exaggerated tone of voice, glad Valerie didn't hear it. She would have known right away that the woman was just clearing the way for them to spend time alone. Speaking of which . . .

Turning, he eyed Valerie in the pool. She was on a return lap, swimming toward his end of the pool, her arms knifing through the water, legs kicking below the surface, and body beautiful in a royal blue two-piece swimsuit.

Anders had always liked women with some meat on them and Valerie had that. She'd never walk the runways in Paris, but she'd featured pretty constantly in the runways in his head since their kiss that morning. Constantly. Only she wasn't on a runway, and she wasn't wearing anything, let alone the latest fashions.

Damn. He was just as bad as the other immortal men he'd seen fall under the life mate spell, Anders acknowledged. He'd been pretty smug as he'd watched the others flounder at work, unable to concentrate and focus on anything but their life mate. It made him grateful no one was here to witness his own idiocy but Leigh and Lucian. Neither of them would tease or taunt him over this . . . much. But Bricker? Oh yeah. The young immortal would love to have something over him.

Valerie touched this end of the pool wall, took a breath, did a half somersault in the water and pushed off the pool to propel herself toward the opposite end. Anders watched her go, and then walked down the steps into the water, enjoying the cool liquid sliding up over his feet, calves, knees, thighs— Yeehaw! The pool was sun-warmed, but still cooler than his skin and the first splash of it against his groin was a shocking awakening. Damn. It was almost enough to dampen his hunger for Valerie. *Almost* being the key word in that thought, Anders acknowledged with a wry, self-deprecating smile as he moved through the water to stand where she had turned at the end of her last lap. He then simply stood and waited as she did her flipping thing at the other end and started back.

Anders was actually disappointed when Valerie paused little more than halfway back and surfaced. Pushing the hair and water off her face, she glanced around, no doubt in search of Leigh as she laughed and said, "Geez, two weeks makes a difference. I can't do half the laps I used t—"

Her voice died, her smile fading as she noted that Leigh was missing and Anders was now submerged in the water ahead of her. Swallowing noticeably, she asked, "Where—?"

"Leigh tires easily right now," Anders answered, interrupting the question. He started to move toward her through the water, adding, "She asked me to spot you."

"Oh." Her expression growing wary, Valerie moved sideways toward the side of the pool. "Well, I should probably get out too then."

"There's no need," Anders said, stopping where he was and giving her space. "Besides, if you get out, who's going to spot me?"

Valerie paused, looking uncertain. "Leigh said you don't swim."

"Well she was wrong, and I'd like a couple laps myself if you're willing to stick around and keep an eye on me. It's never good to swim alone, and I need the exercise or I get flabby." It was a bald-faced lie.

Nothing he did would ever make him flabby, but his words had the effect he'd hope for. Her eyes widened and dropped over what was visible of his chest above the water line.

"You? Flabby? Yeah right," Valerie said with a snort of derision. "How many hours a day do you work out to get that twelve pack? Ten, fifteen hours?"

Anders chuckled and shook his head. "I'm afraid I can't take much credit. Just lucky enough to have an extraordinary metabolism." That wasn't entirely true. He did work out some to improve on the lean and mean body the nanos gave him.

"Really?" Valerie asked with disgust. "Mind loaning me that metabolism for a while?"

Anders grinned. He'd like to give it to her for life, a very long life, but didn't say so. Instead he said, "Why? You have a beautiful body."

Valerie grimaced. "No one mentioned you had vision problems."

"And no one told me you had body image problems," he countered gently.

She smiled wryly. "I don't think there's a woman on the planet who doesn't. If they aren't skinny and wanting to be bigger, they're bigger wanting to be smaller. The ones in between want bigger breasts, or think they don't have hips, or they have a fat butt, or, or, or." She sighed. "Truly, we are in an era of women made neurotic about our bodies."

Anders could have told her she was right. He'd read enough female minds to know there were a very few who didn't have some complaint about their figure. At least mortal women did. Immortal women, on the other hand, were a different creature. They knew the nanos made them their optimal self, with a body in peak condition. It took away the possibility of self-criticism. It was rather like scoring high on an IQ test. With scientific results saying you were smart, it was hard to feel stupid. In the same way, knowing that you had a perfect body made it hard to imagine you were fat, or imperfect physically. Of course, it didn't stop them thinking they had a big nose, or thin lips or a myriad other imperfections, but at least it cut out a portion of the self-flagellation humans seemed determined to torment themselves with.

"What's 'Anders' short for?"

He blinked his thoughts away and glanced to Valerie. She was looking more relaxed now that he wasn't approaching, and her head was tipped curiously as she waited for his answer.

Apparently he wasn't quick enough answering, because she went on, "Or is it your last name like you call Justin by his last name Bricker?"

"It's a short form of my last name," he answered.

Her eyebrows rose. "Which is?"

"Andronnikov."

That made her eyes widen. "What's your first name?"

He was silent for a moment, but suspected now that she knew she didn't even know his first name, Valerie would hardly be willing to kiss him again, let alone anything else if he didn't tell her. Women could be funny about wanting to know the name of the guy sticking their tongue down her throat while groping her. "My first name is Semen."

She blinked several times at this news, and then simply breathed, "Oh dear."

At least she wasn't laughing, Anders thought wryly, and explained, "It's Basque in origin. Based on the word for son."

"I see," she murmured.

"Everyone just calls me Anders."

"Yes, I can see why," she muttered, and then cleared her throat and said, "So your father was Russian, and your mother Basque and neither of them spoke English?"

"What makes you think that?"

"Well it's that or they had a sick sense of humor," she said dryly. "That's like naming a daughter Ova. Worse even. I'm surprised you survived high school with a name like that."

"Actually, I've met a couple of women named Ova over the years," Anders said with amusement.

"Dear God," she muttered.

Anders chuckled and moved sideways, not drawing any closer, but moving to grip the edge of the pool as she was doing so that they faced each other with their sides to the pool rim.

Valerie smiled, and then said, "So were you raised in Basque Country or Russia or Canada?"

"Russia to start," he answered solemnly, easing a step closer in the water.

She nodded, seemingly unsurprised and said, "You have a bit of an accent. Not a thick one, but a bit of it. I figured you weren't raised here from birth."

"No, I came here later," Anders acknowledged. Much later, but he kept that to himself for now and eased another step closer.

"And is there a Mrs. Andronnikov?"

The question startled him, and made him pause mid-step. Affronted by the very question, he said stiffly, "I would hardly have kissed you earlier if I was married."

"Good to know," she said and glanced away almost shyly.

Anders took advantage of her lack of attention and closed the distance between them. When Valerie turned back, he was only inches away. Close enough to grab her arm and pull her into his embrace, but he didn't. This was him trying not to rush and scare her off. His best behavior. It was damned hard. He really just wanted to kiss her, rip her bathing suit off, and take her there in the water up against the side of the pool.

Of course, he couldn't do that without endangering her life. She'd surely drown at the end when they both went into the life mate post-coital faint. That knowledge was enough to make Anders behave himself.

"What made you decide to be a vet?" he asked to distract her from his nearness.

Valerie smiled faintly, some of the tension that had gripped her when she saw how close he was, easing. "I think every girl wants to be a vet and take care of sick and injured animals when she's little," she said wryly and then shrugged. "I just never grew out of it."

"So, still a child at heart?" Anders suggested quietly.

"Maybe," she acknowledged and then tilted her head and asked, "Why did you join law enforcement?"

"Every little boy wants to save the damsel in distress and be a hero when he's growing up. I guess I just never outgrew that," Anders said lightly.

She wasn't amused as intended; instead, Valerie frowned. "Is that how you see me? As a damsel in distress?"

The question surprised a bark of laughter from Anders and he shook his head. "Hardly. I see you as incredibly brave and strong. You rescued yourself from that house. You didn't need a hero. You are one."

Valerie lowered her head as he spoke, and didn't look back up. It made him frown and ask, "Should I not have brought it up? Does it upset you to talk about it?"

She was silent for a moment, and then raised and shook her head. Her cheeks were a bit pink and he realized she'd ducked her head to hide a blush.

"No. Surprisingly enough, it doesn't." She glanced to the side, checking on her dog, he realized when he followed her gaze and noted Roxy was sleeping by the chair with Valerie's towel on it. He supposed the dog had been roaming the yard when he'd come out, but he hadn't noted her absence then. He'd been too eager to get to Valerie.

"I'm not sure why it doesn't bother me," Valerie acknowledged wryly, drawing his attention back to her. "I guess maybe because I was drugged and slept through most of it. I mean, the kidnapping was pretty traumatizing, and the first night out too, but the last night . . ." She hesitated and then admitted, "It felt good to fight back."

Anders nodded in understanding.

"Mind you, if I hadn't managed to escape it would have been a different story," she added wryly.

"You didn't just escape, Valerie," he said quietly. "You saved those other women too. Each of them owes you her life. You *are* a heroine."

She looked uncomfortable and shifted in the water, and then asked, "Do you think Lucian's right and the other women won't agree to a meeting?"

Anders hesitated. He didn't want to lie to his life mate, but didn't know how not to. Lucian wouldn't ask the other women to get together. He couldn't. When he'd said the women had returned to their old lives and probably wanted to forget, he'd meant they had been returned to their old lives after they'd been *made* to forget. Their memories had been wiped. They wouldn't recall anything of what had happened. Bringing them back together would probably undo all of that, but that was risky. They'd wiped them because more than one wasn't as strong as Valerie and had been ready to crumble. Wiping their memories had been the kindest thing to do. Lucian wouldn't reverse it unless it was absolutely necessary.

"You don't think they'll agree to meet either, do you?" Valerie asked when he remained silent, lost in thought.

Deciding distraction was the best tactic in this situation, Anders pulled her into his arms and kissed her. That was all he'd intended for it to be. A kiss, maybe two, to distract her from a question he couldn't answer honestly.

He was an idiot, Anders acknowledged seconds later when, after an initial hesitation, Valerie opened her mouth to him. Any thought of stopping at one or two kisses flew out the window the moment she began to kiss him back. He was hardly aware of her arms twining around his neck, his senses were rocking under the impact of what their mouths were doing, and the feel of her body pressing against his in the water.

Groaning, Anders turned her and pressed her back up against the cold tiles of the pool, holding her there with his body as his hands began to roam down her sides.

Had he thought the water was cool when he'd entered? It seemed to be warm now, hot even, as if their bodies were heating it, Anders thought as his hands found her breasts through her swimsuit top and Valerie moaned into his mouth. A sound he echoed as her pleasure rolled through him as well. Eager for more, Anders tugged the cups of her bathing suit top aside and covered her breasts with his hands. The moment he did, Valerie broke their kiss on a gasp of excitement, her legs wrapping around his hips, and fingers scraping over his short hair as he squeezed and kneaded the soft globes. When he removed his hands to clasp her by the waist, she moaned in disappointment, then cried out as he lifted her out of the water enough to clamp his lips on one rosy nipple.

Anders groaned as her excitement shot through him, a punch to the gut. He suckled eagerly at one breast, then the other, then couldn't stand it anymore and lowered her back down enough to claim her mouth again. Their kiss this time was almost violent, a battle of tongues as he ground his hips forward, rubbing his groin against her. She ground right back and this time he was hit with a double whammy of excitement and need as their pleasure commingled, vibrating through him in growing waves.

Clasping the cheeks of her behind in both hands, Anders squeezed and pressed her even tighter to him, then slipped one hand down to find her hot core. He'd nearly reached that sweet spot and his body was throbbing with the anticipation of it, when he heard his name barked in an unmistakable voice.

Anders froze, torn between groaning and cursing. Then, he slowly withdrew his hand and eased some space between himself and Valerie.

"Sorry," he whispered when she moaned at the loss. Sighing with regret, he tugged her bathing suit top back into place and glanced past her toward the house. Lucian stood in the open French doors, face expressionless.

"Bring Valerie. The sketch artist is here," he said simply. He didn't shout. He didn't have to. Anders heard him just fine.

Sighing, he nodded, then lowered his forehead to Valerie's and briefly closed his eyes.

"What did he say?" she asked, her voice shaky.

"The sketch artist is here," Anders answered solemnly.

"Oh," Valerie breathed.

"We have to go in," he added gently.

"Yes, of course," she murmured, but didn't move. It was Anders who gently unwrapped her legs from around his hips.

"Sorry," Valerie muttered, seeming only then to become aware of where her legs had been. She removed her arms then too, grabbing for the side of the pool as if unsure her legs would take her weight, and Anders understood thoroughly. His own legs were a little shaky at that point. He was also sporting one hell of an erection.

"Let me just take one lap and I'll see you out," he said, backing away from her and hoping the distance and one lap would give his erection a chance to dissipate enough that it wouldn't look like he had a tent pole in his swim trunks when he got out.

Nodding, Valerie turned away and pulled herself up and out of the water enough to rest her chin on her crossed arms on the pool rim. It was then that Anders spotted the bandage on her back and recalled her wound.

"I didn't hurt you when I pressed you up against the side of the pool, did I?" he asked with concern.

"What?" She glanced over her shoulder with confusion, and then seemed to recall her back wound and shook her head. "No. It's okay, I—oh crap!"

Anders started back with concern. "What is it?"

"I wasn't supposed to get it wet," she said with vexation, trying to twist around enough to see her wound. "I forgot all about that when Leigh suggested a swim today."

"Apparently, so did she," Anders said quietly, moving up beside her to pull himself out of the water. He stood and turned back, caught her under the arms and quickly lifted her out as well. Valerie's eyes were wide when he set her on her feet and for a moment he thought it was the strength he'd revealed with the action, but then he realized her eyes were locked on his groin.

Glancing down, he viewed the pop-tent in his trunks and grimaced. Even he was impressed by the size of it. Christ, she'd inspired a small Eiffel tower down there. Sadly, she looked more worried than impressed.

Sighing, Anders moved past her to grab her towel, only then realizing he hadn't thought to grab one. Shaking his head, he turned to open it for her, but she shook her own head.

"I think you need it more," Valerie said, biting her lip as she continued to eye his erection.

Mouth tightening, Anders wrapped it around her shoulders and then physically turned her, pointing her toward the house. "Go. I'll follow in a minute. I just want to swim a couple laps."

Valerie hesitated, but started to walk when he gave her a gentle push. Anders watched until she reached the French doors with the faithful Roxy following, then turned and dove into the water. He suspected it was going to take more than a couple laps to rid himself of the hardness presently acting like a rudder in the water.

Nine

"His ears were a little bigger, and his eyes a little smaller," Valerie said, leaning forward and watching Bryan, the sketch artist, do his thing.

"Better?" Bryan asked, turning the picture toward her after making the corrections.

Valerie peered silently at the image for several minutes, but then nodded her head. The sketch lacked the personality and terror-inducing life of the real man, but she suspected it was as close as they were going to get with a drawing.

The moment she nodded, Lucian leaned over and took the drawing from the sketch artist. He stared at it with a frown and then turned it toward Anders. "Do you recognize him?"

Valerie glanced to Anders, her eyes automatically dropping to his now dry swim trunks. He'd managed to rid himself of the telltale tent in his swimming trunks before coming inside, but it had taken him several minutes and she suspected a heck of a lot of laps to accomplish it. But the fact that it was no longer there didn't eradicate the image from her memory. Dear God, the man was huge. Or at least he'd looked huge to her out there, but then it wasn't as if she had a lot of people to compare him to; a boyfriend in high school and Larry were the extent of her experience.

God, she was lame, Valerie thought unhappily. Most women her age had more experience. Didn't they? She had no idea. Certainly they did if you could believe *Sex and the City* and some of the other shows, past and present, on television. The female characters seemed to change men almost weekly on those shows.

"No," Anders said finally and Valerie managed to drag her gaze and mind up to his face as he shook his head. "I don't recognize him."

"Hmm." Lucian peered at the picture for another moment, then let the hand holding it drop. "Well, I'll have Mortimer make copies and circulate it. I'll have him fax it to Bastien in New York too. He can have it distributed there. Someone should recognize him." His gaze moved to Bryan as he finished packing away his things. "If you're ready I'll take you back to the airport first."

Bryan nodded and stood. "All set." He turned to Valerie and held out a hand. "Ms. Moyer."

"Thank you," Valerie responded, shaking his hand. When he then turned to Leigh, she stood up, wincing at the pulling sensation in her back. It was the first bit of discomfort she'd felt since coming in from the pool, but then she'd been sitting in one spot and one position since coming in, her attention focused on the image growing on the sketch pad.

"I'm going to go change," Valerie said to no one in particular as she slipped away from the distracted foursome and headed out of the room. The bathing suit had dried on her. It would be nice to put on clean clothes that didn't smell of chlorine. But she also wanted to try to look at her back and see if the swim had done any damage to her wound. Valerie was hoping a fresh application of ointment and a clean bandage would set things right, but if not, it was better to take care of it than leave it any longer.

She had reached her room and just pushed the door closed behind her when someone knocked. Frowning, Valerie swung back and opened it, her eyes widening when Roxy slipped inside leaving Anders on the threshold with ointment and gauze in hand. She was less surprised at Anders's presence than the fact that she'd forgotten all about her dog.

"I need to take a look at your back," Anders said apologetically, drawing her attention back from the German shepherd, who had walked over to the bed and dropped to lie beside it.

Valerie hesitated briefly, but then nodded. It had to be taken care of. She knew what could happen to wounds that weren't cared for properly and she'd be damned if she'd risk dying of an infected wound after surviving that hell house.

"The bathroom?" she asked as she turned away.

"Fine," Anders said and she was aware of him on her heels as she crossed the room. When the German shepherd started to get up to follow, she put her hand out and shook her head. "Stay Roxy."

The dog settled back down and Valerie led Anders into the bathroom. Once there, she watched him set down the gauze, tape, and ointment.

"Right," he said, glancing her way.

Valerie turned her back to him and let her towel drop. She'd worn it sarong style since entering the house and being introduced to the sketch artist, Bryan. She'd wanted to go get dressed, but Lucian had said she was fine and didn't want her to take the time.

"Fast or slow?" Anders asked and when Valerie glanced over her shoulder he explained, "It seemed pretty painful for you when I did it slowly this morning. One quick yank might be better."

Valerie bit her lip, but nodded and then turned to face away from him again.

"Deep breath," he said.

Valerie started to suck in a slow deep breath, but halfway through, it became a sharp inhale as he ripped the bandage from her back.

"Okay?" Anders asked with concern.

Valerie nodded, letting her breath out slowly. It really had been better than the slow way. It had hurt, but had been one quick jolt of pain rather than the long drawn-out constant pulling pain from that morning.

"How does it look?" she asked, raising her arm and craning her head around to try to see her wound.

"Less red than it was this morning," he added. "I'm going to put the salve on."

Valerie gave up trying to look at it and nodded as she turned forward again. She felt him brush the ointment on. It was cool, but not cold, and didn't sting quite as much as it had that morning, which made her wonder if the chlorine from the pool had dried out the wound a bit. The swim may even have done it some good, she thought as he pressed the gauze over it.

She waited patiently as he taped the gauze in place, barely restraining a shiver as his warm fingers moved over her skin. His touch, as methodical as it was, sent shafts of pleasure through her that were hard to ignore. It was actually a relief when he said, "Finished." Until his hands settled on her shoulder and he pulled her back against his chest.

Valerie closed her eyes, stealing herself against the warmth that seeped through her. It radiated from where his chest pressed against her back, but seemed to then gather and slide to pool low in her belly.

"Your skin is so soft," Anders whispered by her ear, his breath stirring her hair, his fingers sliding down and then up her arms.

When she felt his lips brush her ear, Valerie tilted her head slightly to the side and then moaned as he pressed a kiss to her neck and then her earlobe. They were soft caresses, light as a butterfly's wings, and the brush of his fingers over her arms was just as light, but it all made her body tremble in his hold.

Hungry for his kiss, Valerie turned her head back and up toward Anders and was rewarded with his mouth closing over hers. It was an awkward angle, but she didn't care as his tongue thrust between her lips. She cared even less about the angle when his hands shifted from her arms to close over her breasts through her swimsuit.

Moaning into his mouth, Valerie turned in his arms, momentarily dislodging his hands. As she'd hoped, though, they were quickly back. Even as she slid her arms around his shoulders and pressed close to him, his hands found and covered her breasts. Squeezing her eager flesh through the thin cloth, he was able to kiss her properly.

Valerie moaned and sucked on his tongue, her fingers following the muscles and lines of his back, kneading and urging him closer against her. She was vaguely aware of one of his hands drifting away from one breast, but didn't realize why until the front of her bathing suit top came loose and fell to catch between their bodies, barely cresting her nipples. He released her other breast then and caught her by the waist to lift her onto the sink counter. Valerie instinctively spread her legs and drew him between them as he quickly undid the lower fastening of her bathing suit top and removed it entirely.

Anders broke the kiss and pulled back to peer down then.

"God," he breathed and lowered his head to claim one nipple.

Valerie cried out, feet pressing against the cupboard door and her butt lifting off the counter as she arched into the caress. He immediately slid one hand beneath her, holding her up and urging her tight against him as he suckled at first one breast and then the other.

"Semmy," she moaned and pressed her open mouth to the top of his head as their lower bodies ground together.

Anders immediately stilled and lifted his head. Meeting her gaze, he raised his eyebrows. "Semmy?"

Valerie felt the blush that claimed her. "Well, calling you by your last name at a time like this seems . . . er . . . wrong," she said awkwardly, and then admitted, "But I just can't call you Semen." She shrugged helplessly. "But Semmy sounds like a good nickname. If you don't mind it," she added and then bit her lip and waited.

Anders stared at her for several minutes and then suddenly grinned. "I like it."

"Do you?" she asked with relief.

"Oh, yeah," he said, and raised a hand to brush his fingers lightly over her cheek. Valerie turned her head to kiss his fingers and he smiled, and then let his fingers drop to brush lightly over one nipple and added, "I like everything about you."

Valerie gasped at the shafts of excitement the light caress sent through her, and raised her own hand to clasp his neck to draw his mouth back to hers. Their lips had barely touched when a knock sounded at her bedroom door. They both froze. When a second knock sounded, Valerie urged Anders away and slid off the counter to grab her towel and quickly wrap it around herself as she headed for the door.

She wasn't terribly surprised to open it and find Leigh there. Lucian had been talking about taking the sketch artist to the airport and heading to the Enforcer house when she'd left. If he'd done that, Leigh was probably looking for company.

"I thought I'd better see how your back is," Leigh admitted with a grimace. "I just remembered that you weren't suppose to get it wet. Yet big dummy me, I suggested a swim."

"It's all right," Anders said behind her and Valerie glanced around to see that he'd followed her out of the bathroom. "I changed her dressing. It actually looks better than it did this morning. I don't think any harm was done."

"Oh good." Leigh looked relieved. "But I'll still feel better once Dani has a look."

"She's coming by after work tonight, isn't she?" Anders asked.

Leigh nodded. "She should be here at about four thirty, and Lucian said he'd be back about then as well." She smiled wryly. "I guess I should start thinking about making dinner in case we need to do some shopping or it's a meal that needs a lot of prep time. I wonder if Dani and Decker would like to stay to eat?"

"Decker?" Valerie asked.

"Dani's husband," Anders answered behind her. "He's Lucian's nephew."

Valerie's eyebrows rose and she glanced back at Anders. "Lucian has a nephew old enough to be married?"

"He has several nephews old enough to be married. And a couple nieces," he said simply.

Valerie nodded slowly. Her best friend in school had been the niece of one of their classmates. It was unusual, but certainly not unheard of. She supposed Lucian had been the youngest of his parents' brood.

"I'll help with supper," she offered. "I just need to change out of my swimsuit first."

"Oh, thank you," Leigh said with a smile and then glanced at Anders. "And are you going to change too? Or do you plan to just hang around half naked and looking studly to make Lucian and Decker jealous?"

Anders snorted at the suggestion. "Those two wouldn't even understand the word jealous. They know they have you and Dani locked down," he said, stepping around Valerie. He gave her arm a squeeze in passing and murmured, "I'll see you downstairs?"

"Yes," she said softly, then flushed when Leigh grinned from one to the other. Grimacing at the matchmaking gleam in the woman's eye, she added, "Oh go on, I'll be down in a minute."

"Okay," Leigh said cheerfully and slid her arm through Anders's, saying, "I'll walk you to your door."

"You will, will you?" he asked dryly.

"Of course. I wouldn't want you to get lost," she said lightly.

Shaking her head, Valerie closed her door and turned to cross the room. Leigh obviously realized something more had been going on than his changing her dressing. Her lack of a bathing suit top might have helped with that, Valerie supposed, glancing down at herself as she removed the towel she'd wrapped around her chest.

"Oh well, *c'est la vie*. Right Roxy?" she said, glancing to the dog lying beside the bed. At the sound of her name, Roxy stood and moved to her side, tail wagging.

"Good girl," Valerie murmured, giving her a pet. "Want to help me decide what to wear?"

Roxy barked, tail wagging more furiously, and Valerie grinned. She didn't for a moment think the dog understood what she'd asked her. She just understood her name and the tone of voice was a question, so she responded. Still, it was nice to have someone to talk to. It made a gal feel less crazy than talking to herself.

Valerie debated what she should wear briefly and settled on a pale peach halter dress that left most of her back and her sides bare. It would make it easier for Dr. Dani Pimms to look at her wound without her having to disrobe.

She changed quickly, switching the swimsuit bottoms for a pair of peach panties and slipping the dress on. Valerie then ran a brush through her hair, applied some lipstick and headed downstairs with Roxy on her heels.

"Oh, hello. That was quick." Leigh smiled at her from her seat at the island. Anders was there as well, retrieving a large pot from the cupboard under the range. He straightened at Leigh's words and nodded in greeting, his gaze appreciative as it slid over her.

"Hello. Did you decide on what we're making?" Valerie asked as she led Roxy to the French doors and let her out.

"How does chili sound?" Leigh asked. "If we start now it can simmer till everyone gets here. Then we just have to throw some fries in the oven and have Anders throw some hot dogs on the barbecue before we can eat. We can have Coney Island hot dogs and chili fries."

"Cravings?" Valerie guessed, closing the French doors and turning to peer at her.

"Serious cravings," Leigh admitted on a sigh. "And they keep changing. First it was sweets: ice cream and chocolate. Now it's chili dogs and fries."

"Then I think it sounds yummy," she assured her, moving around the island into the kitchen. "How can I help?"

Valerie sat back in her seat and sipped at her wine, doing her best to ignore the way Anders's leg was pressing against her own under the table. He had been touching, brushing up against, or sneaking caresses all night. First under cover of their working together in the kitchen and then under cover of the table as they'd eaten. He was driving her wild.

"Thank you, Leigh. That was good," Dani said, sitting back in her own seat with a satisfied little sigh. "I haven't had chili dogs since I was a teenager."

Valerie smiled at Dani. She liked the good doctor. They'd finished making the chili and it was bubbling away on the stove when the woman had arrived with her husband, Decker. While Anders had offered Decker a beer, the three women had all gone upstairs to Valerie's room so that the doctor could check her wound. Dani had examined it, announced that it was healing nicely, and then redressed it.

One would expect that it would have been a quick trip. It hadn't. The women had begun chatting about this and that as they mounted the stairs, and continued that chat throughout the examination. Afterward, they had simply stood there in her room, talking for several minutes more before heading down to rejoin the men.

Dani and Decker had kissed and hugged as if she'd been gone for days instead of the hour the women had dallied upstairs. They'd then cuddled up on the couch, his arm around her and her hand on his leg as the group had chatted. The two had seemed as connected mentally as they had been physically; finishing each other's sentences and exchanging loving smiles and the occasional affectionate caress of the cheek or hair. It was enough to make Valerie envious.

By the time Lucian had returned home and they'd sat down to dinner, Valerie had come to the conclusion that Dani and Decker were great. They were also perfect for each other.

"Hmm," Decker said now as he finished and sat back as well. Reaching for his wife's hand, he drew it onto the arm of his chair and caressed it absently with thumb and fingers. "I've actually never had them before at all. But they were good. My compliments to the chef."

"Chefs," Leigh corrected with a laugh. "Valerie and Anders did most of the work. I just cut the onions. And I apologize for not offering you something fancier. You can blame the menu on Lucian."

The blond male paused with a chili dog halfway to his mouth and glanced to his wife with amazement. "What? Why blame me for chili dogs? I'd never heard of them before tonight either."

"Yes, but it was your son who gave me the bizarre craving for chili dogs and fries," she said as if that should be obvious.

Lucian stared at her briefly, and then shrugged. "Well, at least he has good taste. I agree with Dani. It was good."

Leigh chuckled and squeezed his arm as he popped the last half of his chili dog in his mouth and chewed away. "You think everything is good."

"Everything you serve me *is* good," he said after swallowing. "Fortunately, we appear to have similar taste in food."

"So do we," Dani commented. "I wonder if that's why the nanos—"

"Oh dear," Leigh interrupted, her drink suddenly crashing over on the table.

There was only a bit of water left in it, but it seemed to run everywhere, and Valerie quickly grabbed up her napkin to help soak up the liquid even as Lucian did on Leigh's other side.

"Thank you," Leigh said.

"No harm done. It was only water and there wasn't much of it," Valerie pointed out and set her wet napkin on her plate. She then stood up and started gathering plates. Everyone seemed to be done, and the clutter was only likely to lead to more accidents.

"You don't have to do that," Leigh protested, getting up as well. "You and Anders did all the cooking. I'll—"

"Sit down and relax while the rest of us fill the dishwasher," Lucian said firmly, standing up as well.

"He's right, Leigh," Dani said, getting up. "With all of us helping it will only take us a minute. Put your feet up and relax."

They were quick about clearing the table and filling the dishwasher. Valerie then put coffee on before joining the others at the table. As she sat down, Dani said, "Leigh mentioned that you're a vet in Winnipeg, here to take some courses to update your skills?"

"Yes." Valerie grimaced. "That was the idea, but if they don't catch this guy in the next day or two, I'll have to give up the courses until next semester and if that happens, I might as well head home."

"What?" Anders turned on her sharply.

Valerie bit her lip, not very happy at the thought herself. She would have liked to get to know him better, but if she couldn't do the course now, she'd have to do it next term and it wouldn't be fair to be away from the clinic that long. Sighing at the very thought, she said, "That's what my academic advisor said when I talked to him today. I've missed the first two weeks of class already. He said if I'm not back by Monday, then I might as well give it up and reapply for next term."

Anders frowned, his gaze shooting to Lucian.

It was Leigh who said worriedly, "You can't go home, Valerie. Not with him still out there."

"Actually, it's probably better if I did," Valerie said and pointed out, "He can't know I'm from Winnipeg, so I'd be safe there, and Anders wouldn't have to waste his time playing babysitter so he could help hunt for him."

Dead silence met this announcement as the others all exchanged glances.

"But your courses," Anders said finally. "You wanted to upgrade."

"And I still do, but I can't do that if I can't attend classes," she pointed out reasonably.

Another moment of silence passed with everyone exchanging glances she didn't understand and then Lucian said abruptly, "Then you'll have to attend classes."

When Valerie stared at him with surprise, he added, "Anders will accompany you."

"Oh." She hesitated briefly and then shook her head. "I don't think they'll let him attend with me."

"They might," Dani said slowly. "I've heard of people auditing classes. I even knew someone who audited a couple of mine. She had to get permission from the instructor, and the department chair, and I think her program counselor first though."

"Then he'll get permission," Lucian said as if it were the simplest thing in the world. When Anders frowned at this news, he added solemnly, "It's that or we put her and Roxy on a plane home to Winnipeg."

For some reason, those words sounded ominous to Valerie, and certainly Anders reacted as if they were. His mouth tightened grimly, and he nodded once. It was Friday now, but apparently come Monday, she was attending class and Anders was coming with her. The thought made her smile. She didn't really want to go home, and not because she wanted to avoid her ex anymore. But because she didn't want to leave Anders. He made her feel things she'd never experienced before, and she wanted more of that.

She wanted him.

Ten

Anders finished sucking back his second pint of blood and glanced to the clock on the bedside table as he threw out the empty bag. A frown claimed his lips when he noted that it was six thirty. Despite staying up late to visit with Dani and Decker last night, he'd set his alarm for 6:15 this morning to be sure he was awake and downstairs before Roxy woke Valerie to go out. He'd hoped to prevent another incident like the morning before with the alarm blaring and rousing Lucian and Leigh. But apparently it had taken longer than he'd expected to jump in and out of the shower and don jeans and a black T-shirt. Hopefully he'd still beat them down there though.

Padding barefoot to the door, Anders stepped out and started up the hall, slowing when he approached Valerie's door and saw that it was cracked open. Pausing, he knocked lightly. When there was no answer, he slid it open and peered inside. The bed was empty, as was the bedroom itself, and through the open bathroom door he could see that it, too, was empty.

Cursing under his breath, Anders rushed for the stairs, desperate to get to Valerie before she opened the French doors. With every step he took, he kept expecting the sudden blare of the alarm going off. But he made it all the way to the living room without it happening. He spotted Roxy first. The German shepherd was in the kitchen, gobbling down her food. Valerie was at the French doors, staring at the security panel with slumped shoulders. Anders exhaled a relieved breath and said, "I'll get that."

Valerie glanced over her shoulder with surprise as he crossed the room toward her.

"You said Roxy goes out at six thirty, so I set my alarm," he explained, pausing beside her.

"Oh, I'm so sorry you had to get up. Grateful, but sorry," Valerie said softly, keeping her voice low to avoid disturbing anyone's sleep as he reached past her to punch the numbers into the security panel that would turn off the alarm.

"It's no problem," he assured her. Finished with the panel, he turned back and glanced toward Roxy who was now licking the empty bowl in search of any leftover crumbs. "I see you found a way to distract Roxy from going outside."

"I had to do something, she was whining most pitiably until I produced food. That made her briefly forget she needed to go out," Valerie said wryly.

"She *is* a dog who likes her food," Anders said dryly as the dog turned and headed toward them. He reached down to open the door, but paused when he spotted the leash hanging from Valerie's hand.

Seeing the direction his eyes had taken, Valerie smiled and raised the leash. "I promised Roxy a walk after she does her business and eats," Valerie explained. "She hasn't had one since . . . well, in a while."

Nodding, he opened the door to let Roxy slip out. "Just let me grab my shoes and we'll do that."

"Oh, I didn't want to bother you," she protested at once. "You don't have to—"

"Bodyguard, remember?" Anders said gently. " I have to be with you to guard your body."

"Right," Valerie muttered, blushing as she slipped past him to follow Roxy out of the house. "We'll wait in the backyard."

Anders nodded, then pulled the door closed behind her, his gaze finding Roxy's hunched shape beside the pool. His eyes narrowed as they moved back to Valerie. He hadn't seen any bags in her hands. Knowing she'd need them, he swiftly crossed to the kitchen and retrieved a roll of them from the kitchen drawer where they'd been stored. He got back to the door just as Valerie suddenly turned and headed toward it. Opening the door, he reached out, roll of bags on the palm of his extended hand.

"Thanks," Valerie said with a small laugh as she reached for the roll. "I just remembered them."

The moment her fingers touched the bags, Anders's closed his over hers. He immediately drew her forward even as he slid the door wider and leaned out to kiss her. It was just a swift brush of his lips over hers, he couldn't risk any more than that. As powerful as the life mate shared pleasure was, they could end up rolling around naked on the verandah if he risked more than that. Even just the brushing of lips stirred the desire for more in him, but he managed to break the kiss and pull back to utter a husky, "Good morning."

Her voice was weak and breathy as she responded, "Good morning."

Anders smiled slowly, then withdrew inside and closed the door between them again. He was aware that Valerie didn't turn away, but stood and watched him walk away. He could feel her eyes on him as he left the room.

Valerie glanced around at the sound of the door opening and offered a shy smile when Anders reappeared, running shoes on. He'd been fast about getting his shoes on, but Roxy had been faster. She was done, leash on and standing by Valerie when he stepped out to join them.

"The road or the woods?" Anders asked as he approached.

Valerie didn't need to ask what he meant. Did she want to walk Roxy along the street, or through the woods? She debated the matter briefly. The woods would be more interesting, but she had no idea if there were trails through it, and while the sun was just making its appearance, it wouldn't be able to penetrate the trees. It would be darker in there, maybe dark as night.

"Is it safe to walk on the road?" she asked finally.

"Safe enough," he said quietly.

"Okay. Road it is then."

Nodding, Anders took her arm and started her walking, steering her around the house to the front yard. Roxy immediately fell into step beside Valerie.

"What time did Dani and Decker leave last night?" she asked, to fill the silence as they walked.

"Late," he said dryly, which made Valerie smile.

"Anders, it was late when I went to bed and they weren't showing signs of moving. How much later is late?"

"An hour or so after you went to bed," he answered and then added, "They, like Leigh and Lucian, are night owls."

"Geez, so you've had even less sleep than me," Valerie said apologetically. "I'm sorry, but I appreciate it. I don't know what I would have done with Roxy once she'd finished eating if you hadn't been here to unlock the door. She would have been desperate then."

Anders shrugged. "It's all right. I can always take a nap later."

"I'll probably do that too," she murmured as they started up the driveway to the road, and then asked suddenly, "How old are you?"

It was a question she'd begun to ponder last night when she'd gone to bed. Everyone she'd met since waking up here appeared to be twenty-five to thirty years old. Most of them closer to twenty-five by her guess. Anders, though, seemed closer to thirty, but perhaps that was just wishful thinking on her part since she was thirty herself. Valerie had never dated anyone younger than herself. Although, she supposed a couple years difference wouldn't be that big a deal. Her grandmother on her mother's side had been four years older than her grandfather, and her mother had been two years older than her father. It seemed to be a trend in her family. She could handle a couple years' age difference, if that was all it was.

"Older than you," Anders said finally, regaining her attention.

"I'm thirty," she said, just in case he thought she was younger.

"I know. Your driver's license was in your wallet," he pointed out.

"Oh right," Valerie said wryly, and then asked dubiously, "And you're older?" When Anders nodded, she peered closely at his face, but just didn't see it. "How much older?"

"Why is it rude to ask a lady her age, but not rude to ask a man?" he queried rather than answer and Valerie considered the question.

"I suppose because men aren't usually sensitive about their age," she said after a moment.

"I am."

Valerie turned to him with surprise. "Seriously?"

"Seriously," he confirmed.

"So you won't tell me your age?" she asked with disbelief.

"Not right now. But I will later," he said.

"Later when?" she asked with interest.

"When we know each other better."

"Huh," Valerie muttered, falling silent for a moment and glancing around as they reached the end of the trees lining the drive and stepped out onto the road. They were in a rural area: the nearest house was the one across the road and that was half a field to the right of them. The next house over on this side of the road was a full field away, and by her guess that field was about the size of two football fields.

"Well, now I know why it's so quiet when we're sitting outside," she commented as they started up the road.

Anders smiled, but didn't comment.

"All right, if you won't tell me your age, tell me how many brothers and sisters you have," she suggested.

"Why?" Anders asked with amusement.

"Because as much as I enjoy your kisses, I don't like being kissed by people I know nothing about," Valerie said bluntly, and then stopped to turn to him in question when she realized his steps had faltered and he'd come to a dead halt. His expression was priceless, she had to say. It briefly looked like he'd swallowed his tongue.

Raising her eyebrows, she asked, "What? Like it was a big surprise that I like your kisses?"

For some reason that made a slow smile creep over Anders's face. "No, I guess not," he acknowledged. "I suppose I'm just surprised you're willing to admit it."

Valerie snorted and turned to continue walking. "It's not like I didn't make it obvious. I mean, I was all over you the last two times you kissed me."

"Yes, you were," Anders agreed with a grin.

"Gloat much?" she asked with dry amusement, and then prompted, "So? Brothers and sisters?"

"None," he answered at once.

"Oh dear, an only child," she said with an exaggerated wince.

"What's wrong with that?" Anders asked with surprise.

"The only child is spoiled rotten. They get all the attention, all the focus, all the toys, all the everything that is normally doled out between multiple siblings," she answered simply, and then added, "I ought to know. I was an only child too."

Anders chuckled, but then said, "Well perhaps

that's true of yourself and most only children. But there isn't much spoiling when you're an orphan."

"Were you orphaned?" Valerie asked with surprise.

"Yes."

Valerie peered at him silently and then turned forward again, muttering, "Well, that is an entirely different kettle of fish."

"Why does that sound bad?" he asked with a frown.

"Not bad, just . . ."

"Not good?" he suggested and Valerie grinned at his disgruntlement. For some reason she enjoyed ruffling his feathers. Perhaps because she suspected his feathers weren't often ruffled.

Being more serious, she asked, "How old were you when your parents died?"

Anders was silent for a minute, debating how to answer that, and how to answer all the questions that would follow. He didn't want to lie to her. He wanted her for a life mate and lying wasn't a good way to start, but he couldn't tell her the full truth right now. She'd either think he was mad, or he'd then have to explain about immortals, and he didn't think she was ready for that explanation yet. She may never be.

Sighing over the depressing thought, Anders decided the best thing to do was to tell her as much of the truth as he could and just leave out any details that might need explanations . . . like the fact that he'd been born in 1357.

"My father, Ilom, died before I was born," he said quietly, thinking that was safe enough to tell. "And my mother, Leta, when I was twelve."

"I'm sorry," Valerie said quietly, and then asked, "Will you tell me about them?"

"My father was from Sofala," he said, leaving out that his father had been a Zanj slave.

"Sofala?" she asked uncertainly.

"It's a province of Mozambique. South of Pemba on the coast of East Africa," he explained, not mentioning that it was Nova Sofala now and had been for a while. Continuing on with what he *could* tell her, he said, "My father's father was an Arab. His mother was a local Bantu woman."

"And your mother? Leta?"

"Basque."

"Spanish?"

He nodded, and then frowned. That wasn't completely true. She had come from Atlantis originally, but she'd settled in the Basque country and considered it her home for centuries. It had been her home when she'd met his father.

"How did they meet?" Valerie asked curiously.

"My mother traveled a great deal. She was visiting a friend my father . . . worked for," Anders finished, and Valerie peered at him curiously. He supposed she suspected he had been about to say something else, and she would be right. He'd almost said that his father had been a slave of this friend of his mother's, but had caught himself in time.

"So she met him through this friend?" she asked. "Were they in love?"

"They were life mates," he said solemnly. "They planned to spend their lives together."

"How did your father die?"

That question made him hesitate, but finally he said, "He was killed for choosing my mother."

Valerie blinked. "What?"

Anders grimaced. It was getting a bit tricky now to not lie. His father, Ilom, had been the slave of another immortal, Alecto. She had been a friend of his mother's for some centuries. His mother had gone to visit her during one of the periods when she'd had to leave her home so that no one would notice her not aging. Had things not gone as they had, his mother would have returned ten or twenty years later, claiming to be the daughter, or a niece of herself, who had inherited everything. It was how most of them had handled the not aging issue in the old days.

However, his mother had met his father and realized he was her life mate. The problem was that he was one of the slaves belonging to Alecto's family and when his father was brought to her attention, Alecto, who had apparently never bothered much with the slaves before that, claimed not to be able to read or control him either. She'd claimed he was a possible life mate to her as well, and as he was her family's slave, Alecto wanted him for herself. His father, though, had already given himself over to his mother and chosen her over his mistress.

That had not gone over at all well. Alecto had tried to keep his parents apart, and Ilom and Leta had fled. And had been hunted for it.

Speaking slowly and carefully, he said, "There were those who didn't think my parents should be together. My father and mother were hunted. They planned to escape on a ship. My mother managed to, but my father was killed before they reached it."

He glanced to Valerie to see how she was taking this part of the story and found her deep in thought, a frown on her face. Anders suspected she was

thinking the problem had been the color difference, his father being a black man and his mother
a white woman. And that might have been a problem among other people of that era, but it had never
been an issue amongst Atlanteans. However, it was
handy if she thought it was the problem. But only if
she didn't ask about it and force him to either evade
the question or lie, which he wouldn't do.

Much to his relief, she let the issue lie and simply
asked, "If your father was African and your mother
Spanish, how is it that your last name is Androni-
kov? Was that the name of the family who adopted
you after your mother died?"

He shook his head. "No, it was the name of the
man who gave my mother a safe haven to give birth
to me when she landed in Russia. She had to change
her name and hide out after they killed my father.
She chose his name for us to live under."

"Oh," she said softly. "Did he raise you after your
mother's death?"

Anders smiled at the thought. Andronik, now
known as Saint Andronik, had been the hegumen
of a monastery. The Russian equivalent of an abbot.
Anders had not been raised in a monastery. He
hadn't even been born in one. Andronik had given
his mother safe haven in a small cabin near the monastery and had taken her food. But neither of them
had ever set foot in the monastery.

"No. He was long gone by then," Anders said finally. "Or I should say, we were. My mother only
accepted his aid until she'd given birth to me. Once
she'd recovered enough, we moved on."

"Then who raised you from twelve on after she
died?" Valerie asked with a frown.

"We should turn back," Anders said rather than answer.

Valerie glanced around, noting how far they were from the house, and then nodded, and swung back the way they'd come. After a few steps, she repeated, "So, who raised you from twelve on?"

"I was adopted by the family of a friend I'd made," he answered truthfully, his voice growing gruff. The memory was a painful one for him.

"Why the family of a friend? Did you have no family?" Valerie asked with a frown.

"No," he said simply.

Valerie frowned over that and asked, "How did your mother die?"

Anders hesitated, but then sighed and admitted, "The same people who killed my father killed my mother."

Valerie stopped walking with dismay. "Your mother was murdered too? And twelve years after your father . . . by the same people? Dear God, who does that?"

"Determined people who have nothing better to do?" he suggested, trying for a light tone that failed miserably. What he said was true, or at least part of the truth. Time wasn't the same for an immortal, twelve years was a paltry amount of time when you lived centuries. Even so, there was more to it than that Alecto was determined and had nothing better to do. The way she saw it, she'd been robbed of a possible life mate and wanted to punish someone for it. That had become her obsession. She had hunted them high and low with the help of her family, forcing them to move often and repeatedly. His childhood with his mother had been a series of different homes and constant running and hiding. Unlike Alecto, Leta hadn't had a large support network. She had come out of Atlantis alone except for friends, and her best friend had become her worst enemy. She'd been on her own.

In truth, his mother hadn't had a chance and the fact that she'd survived so long was a combination of dumb luck and sheer determination to see her son survive. And he had. She'd managed to keep them both alive until he was twelve. On his twelfth birthday, she'd sent him out on his first solo hunt for a blood donor. They had been practicing for the last couple months, with his going out on his own and her following in case there was trouble. But that night she'd sent him completely on his own, warning that she wouldn't be there to watch his back so he must be very careful. And he had been; he'd returned that night full of pride and triumph only to find she had been less careful, or perhaps less lucky.

Anders had seen the wagon and several horses as he'd neared the cabin. They'd only been living there for a couple weeks. They hadn't made friends, they never did. He and his mother had only once dared stay in one place long enough for things like that and this hadn't been that time.

Using the cover of the woods, he'd slipped around to the back of the cabin and snuck up to a window. His mother's body was sprawled on the floor; her head, however, had been set on the table and Alecto was ordering her men to ride into the village so the horses wouldn't scare him off when he returned. One of the men had suggested she just leave Anders alone. Leta had paid, there was no need to carry on Alecto's vendetta with the son, but she'd refused.

The boy, as she'd called him, would replace his father as her slave.

Anders had slipped away and managed to evade them. He'd returned to that cabin some weeks later to find they'd burned it to the ground. There was nothing left of his life with his mother, not even a trinket or keepsake to carry with him. He'd left again then and had wandered briefly, but memories of the happy summer he'd spent in a small village in Spain the summer before had led him back there. It was the only place they'd stayed more than a handful of weeks and he knew the only reason they'd stayed there so long was that his mother hadn't had the heart to drag him away from the only friend he'd managed to make during his lonely childhood of running and hiding.

Pedro Alvarez had been eleven like himself that summer. He'd also had a bit of the devil in him, as they'd called it then. Now they would have called him a troublemaker or hell raiser. Pedro was forever escaping his nanny and tutors and slipping away from the castle his family inhabited. Which was what he'd done the night Anders had encountered him. Anders himself had been sent out to find wood for their campfire while his mother was on the hunt. She'd taken him out earlier in the evening to oversee his feeding, and then had returned him to their camp, suggesting he find some firewood while she went out to find her own meal.

He'd barely begun his task when Anders came across Pedro fishing perhaps a quarter mile along the lakeshore from their camp. After an initial start at his sudden appearance, Pedro had greeted him fearlessly and cheerfully and invited him to share in the cheese, bread, and wine he'd smuggled with him from the castle kitchens.

It had been the start of a firm friendship. The two had quickly become as close as brothers. Pedro would sneak out of the castle every night and Anders would be waiting for him. The two would then run through the forest and fields, always ending at the waterside, where they lay in the grass, stared up at the stars, and shared their dreams for the future. Pedro planned to be a brave knight and lord to his people, and Anders dreamed of a day when he would slay the evil Alecto, avenging his father and ensuring his mother wouldn't have to run and hide anymore and they could stay in one place at least for more than a matter of weeks. Pedro was the only person Anders had ever revealed his history to. Not all of it, of course. He hadn't told him he was immortal. Just that the jealous Alecto had killed his father and now hunted him and his mother as punishment for his father loving his mother. Pedro had solemnly vowed to help him slay Alecto.

Every night when Pedro had left, Anders had returned to the camp he shared with his mother, terrified it would be the night she'd say they had to break camp and move on. In the end, nearly an entire summer had passed before she'd made the dreaded announcement. When he'd instinctively tried to protest and convince her to stay, she'd revealed that she knew about his friend, knew it would be hard to leave him, but they'd stayed too long as it was and their pursuers had caught up. She'd spotted one of Alecto's men in the village that night. They had to move on. Anders hadn't even got the chance to say good-bye to his friend. They'd left at once.

Looking back, Anders suspected that his mother's kindness in letting him have a friend for that summer had been the beginning of the end for them. For all of them, including Pedro and his family. Alecto and her people had caught their scent in that village and had been on them like a pack of hounds, constantly nipping at their heels over the following six months until she'd caught up to them on his birthday and butchered his mother. Six weeks later, Anders had found himself back by that lake in Spain, waiting for Pedro.

On hearing of his mother's death, Pedro had insisted he come home to the castle with him. He'd been sure his parents would welcome him as his friend. Anders had been less certain. Kindness hadn't been a commodity he'd much experienced in his life, but Pedro's mother had felt sorry for him being orphaned, and on learning that his mother had taught him to read and write, Pedro's father had decided he would make a fine page after some intensive personal combat training to catch him up to other pages of his age. He could then squire for him and eventually become one of his knights, Pedro's father had assured him.

What had followed was the most wonderful six months of Anders's life. With a little mind control he'd managed to arrange his training so that he had as little exposure to sunlight as possible. But he'd also worked hard to please Pedro's father as page, and had been treated with kindness and affection . . . right up until the night Alecto and her men had tracked him there, slid into the castle during the night and butchered the entire family, including Pedro's three younger sisters.

Anders and Pedro had been out running, playing at battle and then fishing as they did most nights when it happened. It wasn't until they were slipping back into the castle that they realized anything was amiss. It was the blood. Anders had smelled it the moment Pedro had pushed open the stone door from the secret tunnels into the upstairs hall where the bedchambers were. His mortal friend hadn't caught the scent, but Anders, with the exceptional olfactory sense immortals possessed, had, and the scent had made him stop abruptly in the opening and sniff the air with sudden alarm.

It wasn't until Pedro had hissed, "Come on, or we'll be caught," that Anders had realized while he'd stopped to scent the air, Pedro had continued and was now at his bedchamber door. Even as Anders had opened his mouth to hiss a warning and call him back to the safety of the tunnels until they knew what was about, Pedro's bedchamber door had opened and one of Alecto's men had been on his friend. There had been no questions, no threats, no warning. The bastard had caught the startled Pedro by the scruff, lifted him, and ripped out his throat in one blurred motion.

Anders had frozen in shock and horror. While he'd spent his entire life running and hiding from these people, he'd never actually seen Alecto and her men in action. Even with his mother, the attack had been over and she'd been dead by the time he'd crept up on the cabin. The cruelty and violence of this attack was unfathomable to him, breathtaking. It had left him shaking and unable to move . . . until another door had opened and Alecto had led several men out of the bedchamber of Pedro's mother

and father. He'd barely counted six men pouring out
of the room when a thump had drawn his wide eyes
to where Pedro's lifeless body had been dropped on
the hall floor like so much trash. One of the men
had spotted him then and shouted, and Anders had
jumped back, letting the stone door slide closed between them.

He'd begun to run then, taking the stairs in the
secret passage two at a time until he burst out into
the tunnel under the castle. It led out to a cave on the
edge of a clearing far beyond the castle walls and
Anders had fled through it, his mind in utter chaos.
Fear, fury, and loss had battled in his brain, leaving
him unable to hold on to any one of the emotions.
He'd run until he couldn't run anymore, and then
he'd collapsed in the woods and lay weeping until
the sun had risen.

Somewhat dazed and completely uncaring of the
damage the sun might cause him then, Anders had
returned the way he'd come. He'd known Alecto
and her men would be gone by then and he'd hoped
to find that Pedro had somehow survived. He'd also
wanted, needed to know what had happened to the
rest of the family who had welcomed him to their
bosom.

He hadn't even had to leave the tunnels. The hall
had been crammed with weeping servants when
he'd unlocked the opening to the secret passage
and a quick read of the nearest one had told him
all he needed to know. Alecto and her men had
slaughtered every member of the family down to
their three-year-old daughter, and even some of
the servants.

Anders had let the stone door slip closed and then

simply sank to sit in the dust and cobwebs of the tunnel, overwhelmed with loss and guilt. He had brought this on Pedro and his family by being here. It had been a hard lesson. He'd learned that no one would be safe near him so long as Alecto hunted him, and he'd realized that Alecto would never stop hunting him so long as she lived. The woman was obsessed to the point of madness.

After two days and nights huddled in that dark, cold passage with his grief, Anders had descended to the tunnels and made his way out into the clearing, reborn with a purpose. He would never again let anyone close to him. He would never stay anywhere long enough for Alecto and her people to catch up to him. He would grow, and train in combat, and when he was strong enough and had learned enough, he would kill that bitch and every one of the bastards who rode with her.

"I'm sorry."

Anders glanced to Valerie then, and managed a smile. "It was a long time ago."

"Not that long," she said sounding incredibly solemn, but then she was thinking that it had only been a decade or two when in reality it had been centuries. More than 644 years. A lot had happened since then, including his sending Alecto and every one of her men to join his father and mother in death. That had happened ten years to the day after his mother's death, and in the clearing where the cabin his mother had been killed in had once stood. He'd chosen the place and date, and simply allowed Alecto and her men to catch up with him.

Anders doubted Alecto had even recognized the clearing or its significance. Finding his horse in the clearing where he'd left it, she'd sent her men out to search the woods for him and he'd taken them out one at a time until there was only her left.

Anders had dreamed about that day so often over the years . . . He'd thought he would feel relief or vindication when it came. But in the end he hadn't felt anything at all once he'd confronted, fought, and beheaded the bitch. It hadn't brought back his mother, or Pedro and his family, and had taken away the only purpose he'd had for the last decade. He'd left there feeling like a hollow man, only half alive and going through the motions. He'd continued to feel that way for a very long time. For centuries he traveled around, joining various groups of mercenaries and spending his life knee-deep in blood and corpses, hiring himself out for the coin, and never really caring much about the cause or his comrades. That had gone on right up until he'd encountered Lucian.

Lucian Argeneau had a way about him. When he looked at you he seemed to see right down into your soul, and he'd looked into Anders's soul and offered him what he needed: a purpose. Lucian had convinced him to become an Enforcer and help not only to keep mortals like Pedro and his family safe, but to prevent what had happened to his mother and father from happening to other unfortunate immortals. That purpose had helped him begin to feel human again. He was still reticent and careful about opening himself up much to others, but he counted Lucian as much a friend as a boss, and there were others he worked with that he called friend . . . And then there was Valerie. He thought he could open up to her. He wanted to. Certainly, he'd told her more than most knew about his history. The problem was that once again someone he cared for was in danger. The only difference was that this time he didn't bring the danger.

"We need to change the subject," Valerie announced.

Anders glanced her way at those words, smiled wryly, and arched one eyebrow. "Too depressing for you?"

"Yes," she admitted, and then patted his arm, adding, "But thank you for sharing."

For some reason that made Anders want to laugh, which wasn't something he often did. But then he'd found himself amused and smiling a great deal since Valerie's arrival in his life . . . which he liked . . . and didn't want to lose. He had to succeed where he'd failed with his mother and Pedro and his family. He had to keep her safe.

Eleven

"I suppose it will be a while before Leigh and Lucian get up," Valerie commented as they approached the house.

"No doubt. They usually sleep through the morning," Anders said. "I suppose we're on our own for breakfast."

"You don't think Leigh would mind if we helped ourselves?" she asked.

Anders shook his head and reached out to open one of the French doors into the kitchen for her. "She said we were welcome to whatever we like."

Valerie let out a little relieved breath as she stepped through the door. The walk had made her hungry, and she'd worried that they would have to wait to eat until Leigh and Lucian got up.

"What do you feel like for breakfast?" Anders asked, closing the door once Roxy trotted in.

Valerie shrugged. "I'm not sure what's available. I guess some toast will do."

"Toast? After that walk?" Anders asked with raised eyebrows, pausing in front of her. As Roxy walked around him, sniffing the floor, he asked, "We have more choices than toast. There's bacon, eggs, sausage, cereal, grapefruit, or toast, if you like. But I liked those sausages we had with the pancakes yesterday and I was thinking of having those."

"Those sausages *were* good," she agreed with a grin, and then stumbled a step forward, putting her hands up to Anders's chest to catch herself as something pressed into the back of her knees, throwing her off balance. Glancing down and around, Valerie saw that it was the leash. Roxy had walked around both of them and then back behind Anders to get to her dish.

"Did you train her to do that?" Anders asked, hands clasping her waist to steady her.

"No! Of course not," Valerie gasped, horrified that he might even think that. She relaxed though, when she saw the teasing twinkle in his eyes.

"Well you did say you like my kisses," he pointed out, his voice a husky taunt as his hands crept around her back and urged her closer. "Perhaps you were hoping for more."

Valerie could feel the heat flushing her cheeks. It was partially from his teasing and partially because her body was tingling everywhere they touched. Lowering her eyes to his chest where her fingers were now nervously plucking at the black cotton of his T-shirt, she murmured, "Perhaps I was."

"As you wish," Anders whispered and when she glanced up wide-eyed, his lips settled on hers. Valerie had thought she must have imagined the passion that had exploded between them the last two times they'd kissed. That somehow her memory had made it seem better or stronger than it really had been. But if anything, her memory had been like a faded picture, unable to hold onto the vibrancy and sheer strength of the heat and need that erupted inside Valerie as his lips met hers. She was a grown woman, it wasn't the first time she'd been kissed, but damn, no one had ever brought about as violent a reaction inside her as he did. She melted and imploded all at the same time.

When he broke the kiss to trail his mouth across her cheek, Valerie regained enough sense to become aware that she'd dropped Roxy's leash and wrapped herself about him like clinging ivy . . . and he was just as wrapped around her. His arms were around her, his hands trailing over her back and sides, one leg between hers, the other hugging the outside of her leg as his lips found her ear and began to drive her wild. She withstood that briefly, but then twisted her head back in search of his again.

Anders responded to her silent request and kissed her again, his tongue thrusting into her mouth aggressively as one of his hands drifted around to find a breast. They both moaned into each other's mouths as his hand cupped her breast. When the leg between both of hers rose up then and rubbed against her, Valerie thought the three-pronged assault of pleasure might kill her. It was incredibly overwhelming, seeming to come from everywhere, bouncing through her in wave after building wave.

Valerie wasn't aware of his pushing her T-shirt up until he tugged the cup of her bra aside and cool air reached her nipple. Groaning into his mouth, she pressed into his caress as he squeezed and kneaded the soft flesh, and then began to pluck at the nipple.

"Semmy," she pleaded when he broke their kiss, then gasped when he bent her back over one arm and lowered his head to claim her nipple, drawing it into his mouth and sending a whole new riot of sensation through her. Valerie dug her fingers into his shoulders and groaned, a sound echoed by Anders. Both of his hands were at her back now, one supporting her while the other . . . worked at her bra, she realized when it suddenly loosened around her.

Anders immediately raised his head and claimed her mouth again. Valerie returned his kisses eagerly, gasping as she felt the cool leather of the couch against her back and realized he'd lowered her onto it. In the next moment, his body covered hers and he broke their kiss. Raising himself on one arm, he used the other hand to push the silky cloth of her bra up over her breasts. His eyes then slid over her heated skin. Valerie squirmed under his gaze, then moaned as his mouth bent to claim one nipple.

When his free hand then covered the other, Valerie gasped and arched her back, one hand sliding around his neck, and the other covering his hand and squeezing even as he squeezed her. She was so overwhelmed by the sensations he was stirring in her that Valerie was slow to realize she wasn't doing anything in return. She had never been a selfish lover, but right now she was taking and not giving. And that right there spoke to the effect he was having on her. Cripes, all she was doing was holding on for dear life to keep from drowning in the passion washing over her.

Releasing the hand she'd been clutching, Valerie slid her hand to his back and ran it down to his behind. She squeezed one cheek, urging him harder against her and then started to slide her hand around between them. She had reached the top of his jeans when Anders immediately stopped what he was doing and reached down to catch her hand.

"But—" Valerie's protest ended when his mouth covered hers.

Anders's kiss was determined and hard as he caught both of her wrists in one hand and raised them above her head, holding them in place so that she couldn't touch him. Meanwhile, his other hand slid down her cheek, over her chest, down her belly and inside her jeans. It was only then that she realized that he'd apparently undone her jeans at some point while she was distracted, allowing his hand to slide easily between her skin and panties and slip between her legs.

Valerie jerked beneath him, gasping and making little whimpering sounds into his mouth as his fingers brushed over her sensitive skin. She also eased her legs apart, giving him better access. Anders accepted the invitation at once, his fingers dipping into her moist center.

His touch set off an explosion of pleasure inside Valerie that built and rushed over her wave after wave under his caress. It was incredible, overwhelming, all encompassing and terrifying. She wanted him to stop and she never wanted it to end. She wanted to drown in the pleasure he was creating in her and was afraid she would.

Valerie's body was arched like a bow, taut and trembling. Her eyes were squeezed tightly closed and while she had been sucking desperately at his tongue when he first covered her mouth with his, now she couldn't find the wherewithal to do even that. Her mouth was just open to him as she panted little puffs of breath into his that grew faster and shallower with each brush of his fingers over her.

When he suddenly pressed one finger into her while continuing to caress her, the tension inside her snapped like a thread. Valerie cried out into his mouth and bucked violently, and then she finally drowned under the pleasure assaulting her and sank into darkness.

When Valerie murmured sleepily and shifted, drawing her leg up along his, Anders opened his eyes to peer down at her. She was curled on her side, one arm and leg cast over him and her head on his chest. She shifted again, her leg now sliding down his. Damn. Even that small, unintentional caress in her sleep sent shivers of pleasure through him. But then his body was still sensitized after what had happened downstairs.

Anders had enjoyed every second of pleasure he'd given Valerie, experiencing every ripple and wave of excitement and pleasure that had traveled through her, including the end orgasm that had overwhelmed them both. Valerie wasn't the only one who had passed out downstairs. But Anders had woken up first.

Aware that Valerie would be embarrassed if they were found on the couch by Leigh or Lucian, and unsure how long she'd stay unconscious, Anders had scooped her up and carried her up here to her room. He'd removed her jeans, T-shirt, and the al-ready undone bra so that she would be more com-fortable. Then he'd stripped down to his boxers and climbed into bed with her. He wanted to be there when she woke up, to be sure that she hadn't been too freaked out by what had happened.

Intimacy between life mates just wasn't your everyday sexual experience. Anders had bedded hundreds, perhaps even thousands of women during the first century or two of his life, and had never experienced anything like it. Nothing even close.

His thoughts fled as Valerie shifted again and wiped a hand over her face. The action made him smile. She'd been drooling on him for the last half hour while she slept. Apparently, she was waking up enough to feel the liquid that dribbled across her own skin before dropping onto his chest.

Lifting his head, Anders peered at her face in time to see her eyes blink open. A heartbeat later, she stiffened in his hold, and then jerked up, banging him in the chin with the top of her head. Wincing, Anders let his head drop back on the bed.

"Ow," Valerie muttered, following closely with, "Sorry."

"It's all right," Anders said with a wry smile, rubbing his chin with the hand not presently wrapped around her back.

"We're in my room," she noted with surprise.

"I carried you up here," Anders explained, and when she raised the sheet covering them both to peer down at herself, added, "And took your jeans and stuff off so you'd sleep more comfortably."

"You left my panties on," she said, blushing.

"Yes. I didn't want to make you uncomfortable."

"Thank you," she whispered, and then gave an embarrassed laugh. "I suppose it's silly that I would have been embarrassed if you hadn't left them on, but . . ."

"But you would have," Anders finished with understanding.

Valerie nodded, and then tipped her head back, carefully this time, and eyed him uncertainly. "I fainted, didn't I? I've never fainted before. Ever."

Anders hesitated and then said, "Your system is weaker than normal right now, and you were on your back, putting pressure on your wound." All of that was true of course, but it wasn't the reason she'd fainted.

"I didn't feel any pain," she said with a frown.

"You were rather distracted," he pointed out delicately.

Valerie flushed and lowered her head again briefly. When she raised it a moment later, there was a determined expression on her face. "Yes, I was definitely rather distracted. And selfish. You didn't get to—"

"It's fine," Anders interrupted, knowing where her thoughts were headed. She felt like it had all been one-sided and that he had given her pleasure while not enjoying it himself. She couldn't be further from the truth, but he couldn't tell her that, or explain how he could have enjoyed her pleasure with her.

"That's sweet, Anders, but it's not fine," Valerie said on a sigh, and raised herself up enough to look him in the face. She began to slide her hand down his stomach as she said, "I could do for you what you—"

She stopped abruptly when Anders caught the hand that had nearly reached the top of his boxers. As tempted as he was, he couldn't let her touch him. While it would certainly give him pleasure, Valerie, too, would experience that pleasure with him and he couldn't explain that without explaining everything. She wasn't ready to hear the truth of his origins yet.

Raising her fingers to his lips he pressed a kiss to them, then released her hand to slide his around her neck and draw her face down to his. His kiss was as light and gentle as it had been on her fingers. At least, he'd intended it to be, but the moment their lips met, the passion came roaring back like a freight train. Reeling under the blow, Anders rolled in the bed, pressing Valerie into the mattress as his body covered hers. The feel of her flesh against his was exhilarating, her naked chest to his, her naked legs entwining with his . . . It all started a clamoring in his body it was impossible to ignore.

"Semmy," Valerie gasped when he tore his mouth from hers to follow a trail down her neck.

Anders smiled against her throat at the nickname. No one had ever called him that. His mother had only ever called him Semen, and to everyone else he had given the name Anders and nothing else. But he liked Semmy. On Valerie's lips it sounded like an endearment or a prayer.

Valerie shifted beneath him, sliding her heels down the backs of his calves and then digging them in so that she could arch her pelvis into him. The action had an immediate effect. Blood rushed to his groin, turning the semi-hardness that had been building there into a full-on, raging hard-on.

Growling, deep in his throat, Anders caught the fingers of one hand in her hair and pulled, drawing her head back and elongating her throat as he thrust back. Both of them groaned at the passion that rushed through them, and Anders felt his fangs slide out. He froze briefly, and then allowed them to gently scrape across her flesh, shivering along with her before forcing them back where they belonged and continuing down to crest one breast and close over her nipple.

"Oh, God, Semmy, Semmy, Semmy," Valerie breathed, cradling his head as he suckled.

Anders nipped at her flesh lightly, then raised his head to claim her lips again before sliding further down her body, his lips and tongue tasting her upper stomach, her belly, dipping into her belly button . . .

"Semmy?" She shuddered under his teasing, her legs shifting restlessly. When he hooked his fingers in the waistband of her panties and began to draw them down, Valerie lifted her behind to help. He slid them down her legs and off, then let them drop to the floor as he stood to remove his boxers. The moment he stood, Valerie rose up and reached to help him. Anders didn't think there was any harm in that until she reached for his erection while his boxers were still around his knees.

Anders sucked in a sharp breath at the shock of pleasure, but was almost immediately distracted by the gasp she released as she experienced that pleasure with him. When she raised confused eyes to him, Anders brushed her hand away and cupped her head to kiss her. It was a quick, hard kiss intended to distract her from the shared pleasure, but he knew before he raised his head that it hadn't worked, and wasn't surprised when she immediately frowned and said, "Anders, I—"

That's as far as he allowed her to get. Catching her legs beneath each knee, he tugged her to the edge of the bed, dropped to his knees between her legs and sought out a more effective way to distract her.

The moment his lips pressed against her warm core, Anders knew he'd found the perfect way to make her forget what she'd experienced. Heck, he was having trouble remembering what he was trying to distract her from himself as her pleasure began to course through him in growing waves.

Anders nearly pushed them both over the edge with his mouth; certainly, they were both teetering on that edge when Valerie suddenly cried his name and tugged at his ears almost painfully. He immediately recalled what had started all this. Her feeling that it had been unfair that he'd pleasured her earlier without, she thought, gaining any pleasure himself.

Cursing, Anders stood at once, caught her legs in both hands again and thrust into her. He froze then, hardly aware of the long groan both he and Valerie issued together. All he was aware of for a moment was how damned good it felt to be buried in her, to have her warm, wet heat closing around him like a glove, squeezing and pulsing around him. Nothing in his life had ever felt this good and for a moment, he couldn't move, didn't want to. But then Valerie shifted, wrapping her legs behind his butt and arching against him.

Anders began to move then, withdrawing and thrusting in again. But as far along as they were, it was only a few thrusts before they were both crying out and then sinking into the dark well of pleasure.

Twelve

Valerie opened her eyes and found herself staring at Roxy's furry face. She smiled wryly at the sight of her pitiful eyes, and then Roxy shifted and twisted a bit so that she could scratch her ear with her back paw.

"Damn," Valerie breathed.

"What is it?"

Glancing around at Anders's question, Valerie smiled shyly when she saw that she was lying on her back with her head on his arm while he lay on his side, peering at her sleepily. The last thing she remembered was being splayed across the bed sideways with him between her legs. She supposed he'd moved her again after she'd—"I fainted again."

Anders smiled slowly. "Would that be due to my superior skill as a lover?"

Valerie chuckled at the smug look on his face, but said, "I guess it must be . . . that and my wound. Maybe I haven't built my blood back up yet."

"Maybe," he said mildly.

A whine from Roxy drew her attention again and Valerie began to shift the sheets and blankets aside with a sigh, but paused when she recalled that she was naked.

"Shy?" Anders teased lightly as he got up, completely, gloriously, and unabashedly nude.

"A little," Valerie admitted, her eyes roaming over his body. Damn, the man was beautiful. He was like a Greek god, muscles rippling under unblemished mocha skin. How did she dare show her own less-than-perfect body to him?

"Here."

Valerie managed to drag her eyes up to his face, but paused along the way as she noted the clothes he was holding out.

"You go ahead and dress. I need to use the bathroom," he said.

Valerie watched him cross the room, her eyes fused to his tight tush as he walked. Damn. This just wasn't fair. The man had a nicer behind than she did. And those legs? Wow. When the bathroom door closed, cutting off her view, Valerie gave her head a small shake and turned her attention to dressing as quickly as she could. She had no idea how long he'd be in the bathroom.

Anders took long enough that Valerie had dressed, brushed her hair and was hooking Roxy's leash to her when he came out of the bathroom. Much to her amazement, he too was dressed. He must have taken his clothes into the bathroom with him earlier. How had she missed that? She didn't have to wonder hard about it. She'd been so busy ogling his butt, he could have been wearing a moose head and she wouldn't have noticed, Valerie acknowledged wryly.

"I imagine Roxy has to go out," Anders commented as he approached.

"Yes. Unfortunately, so do I," Valerie said as he paused in front of her.

"I can take her out while you use the bathroom," he offered, taking the lead from her.

"Thank you," she said with sincere gratitude. She really had to go. "I'll be down in just a minute."

"No hurry," he assured her, heading for the door with Roxy trotting dutifully behind him. "Take a shower if you want."

Valerie didn't wait to see him leave, but immediately headed for the bathroom. She hadn't originally intended to shower, but after taking care of other matters, she noted the still dripping showerhead, realized Anders must have had a quick shower before dressing, and decided maybe she wanted one after all. But a quick one.

With her long hair to shampoo and rinse and the need to shave, Valerie wasn't as quick as Anders, but she was still pretty quick. When she got out, she brushed out her hair, put it back in a ponytail and then went out into her bedroom to find fresh clothes. A glance out her window showed another hot and sunny day, so rather than the jeans she'd worn that morning when it was cooler, Valerie donned a pair of red shorts and a white T-shirt.

Anders and Roxy were still outside when she got downstairs, so she headed out to join them, frowning and muttering another, "Damn," when Roxy sat down to scratch herself.

"What's wrong?" Anders asked, moving toward her.

"Roxy should have had her flea pill three days ago," Valerie answered.

Anders paused and glanced back to a still scratching Roxy. Frowning, he said, "Well, surely fleas couldn't have infested her already?"

Valerie smiled. "No. She's probably just scratching because of dry skin or something, but if I don't get her her pill, she could get fleas."

"I suppose her pills are in Cambridge?" he asked with a grimace.

"Yes," she admitted, but quickly added, "The nearest vet should be able to supply them, though. There's no need to drive all the way to Cambridge."

"Good," Anders said, obviously relieved. He glanced to the house, then to Roxy and finally to Valerie and said, "Well, we could pick them up now. Maybe grab some breakfast out."

"Or brunch," Valerie said wryly with a glance at her watch. It was after 11 now. They'd been up for hours. Well, not really up, she supposed. More like up and down, she thought and then said, "I guess we'll have to take Roxy with us. I wouldn't want to leave her here alone. She might get up to mischief."

"You can leave her with me," Leigh announced, drawing their attention to her presence in the open French doors.

"Good morning," Valerie said, offering a smile and wondering why she was suddenly blushing. It wasn't like the woman knew what had happened between she and Anders while Leigh and her husband were sleeping just up the hall. They hadn't been that loud. Had they?

"Good morning," Leigh responded, reaching out to squeeze her hand. "You two go ahead and get the pills. I'm happy to look after Roxy while you're gone."

"Are you sure?" Valerie asked.

"Positive," Leigh assured her. "Roxy's a sweet-heart, and she'll keep me company until Lucian wakes up."

"Thank you," Anders said. "Is there anything you need while we're out?"

Leigh hesitated, and then asked, "Would you mind making a stop at the grocery store on the way back?"

"Not at all," he assured her. "What do you need?"

She glanced back toward the house, and then said, "I know we need bread and milk, but there may be a couple more things. I'll check and text you a list if that's all right?"

"Of course," Anders said with amusement and then took Valerie's arm to urge her into the house. As he walked her through the living room and up the hall he said, "Go grab your shoes and purse. I'll pull the car out of the garage and around to the door."

"Okay," Valerie agreed and started to turn for the stairs, only to have Anders swing her back and claim her lips. She hesitated under the caress, but then slid her arms around his neck and kissed him back when he deepened it. Damn, one kiss and she was ready to drag him up to her room again.

She'd barely had the thought when Anders broke the kiss and smiled at her. "Go, or we'll end up back in your bed and Roxy and Leigh will have to do without."

A bit dazed still from the kiss, Valerie nodded si-lently and turned to the stairs, flushing bright red

when she glanced up the hall and spotted a grinning Leigh watching them from the kitchen.

Shaking her head, Valerie hurried quickly upstairs, trying to remember what she was going there
for. It was damned embarrassing, but just one kiss
from Anders left her a blithering idiot.

"Geez, there isn't a single parking spot," Anders
muttered, scanning the crammed parking lot of the
veterinary clinic. "I'll have to look for a spot on the
street."

"Or you could just double-park here and I could
run in," Valerie suggested. When he frowned at the
suggestion, she rolled her eyes. "You can see everyone coming and going from here and I should only
be a minute. I'll be fine."

He pursed his lips, then let his breath out on a
sigh and nodded, "Okay, but scream my name if you
need me. I'll hear you."

"Sure you will," Valerie said with amusement, and
then leaned forward to kiss him, but caught herself
at the last minute. It was just too risky. His kisses
sent her up in flames. Besides, she wasn't sure she
had the right. Valerie wasn't really sure what was
happening between them yet. They'd had sex, sure,
really hot, mind-blowing sex, but that didn't mean
she had the right to kiss him when she wanted to,
or to treat him like a boyfriend. Heck, they hadn't
even been on a date yet, and she had no idea if they
would, or if he wanted to. Maybe she was just a fling
to him.

Sighing at the situation she'd managed to get herself into, Valerie forced a smile and slid quickly out
of the car, saying, "I'll be right back."

The clinic was as busy inside as the parking lot suggested. Every seat in the place was taken and the floor was littered with dogs, cat carriers, and cages with smaller animals. There were also three people in line, waiting to register their animals.

Valerie took her place at the end of the line and glanced around as she waited. There was a Doberman pinscher with an injured paw, a sheltie lying down and looking miserable, a Lab who appeared to be losing its hair, a cat who was meowing nonstop . . . She mentally noted each animal, doing a quick assessment, and working out what treatment was required. It was a mental exercise to pass the time, but made her miss her own clinic quite a bit. Valerie loved being a vet, always had. You didn't go to school all that time for a career you didn't love and Valerie loved animals. Taking care of them was her dream job.

"Ma'am?"

Valerie glanced forward, surprised to see that it was her turn at the counter. Either the two women running the desk here were particularly efficient, or she'd spent more time analyzing the animals than she'd realized.

Smiling, she stepped up to the counter and explained the situation. It turned out to be a little more involved than she'd expected. This clinic was pretty strict and made her fill out a patient form for Roxy, listing her birthday, full name, date of last shots, etc. Valerie shifted along the counter to make way for the next person while she quickly filled out the pertinent information. She was half listening to the pet owners who stepped up to the counter after her, and had just finished filling out the form when a woman's voice caught her ear.

Pausing, Valerie lifted her head and glanced over, peering curiously at the petit, short-haired blond chatting easily with the receptionist. Her voice was familiar. She sounded an awfully lot like one of the women who had been caged in the house of horror with her, Cindy—

"Sorry, Miss MacVicar," a man in a doctor's coat, one of the vets she supposed, said, appearing on the other side of the counter. "I had to write up the file."

Valerie froze, her eyes running over the woman again. It *was* her: Cindy MacVicar. Her eyes slid to the cat carrier the woman carried. Cindy had told them she had a cat named Mittens.

"That's all right, Doc," the blond said with a smile. "Mittens and I are in no hurry."

Nodding, the man turned to the receptionist and began to give instructions and Valerie immediately stepped closer along the counter, saying, "Cindy?"

"Yes?" The blond turned, a small scar by the corner of her mouth puckering as she smiled at her uncertainly. Tilting her head as she peered at Valerie, she frowned. "I'm sorry. Do I know you?"

"Yes," she said at once, and then admitted, "Well, not by sight. I'm sorry, it's me, Valerie Moyer," she explained and when the woman's expression remained blank, she added, "From the house?"

Cindy shook her head with bewilderment. "What house?"

The question made Valerie frown, but she explained, "The house with Igor and his boss?"

"Igor?" Cindy echoed with amusement, but shook her head again. "I'm sorry. I don't know what you're talking about."

Valerie stared at her with bewilderment. She knew

it was her. Her voice was somewhat distinct, sharp and quick. She sounded like the Cindy MacVicar from the house. And how many Cindy MacVicars could have a cat named Mittens?

Determined, Valerie stepped closer still and said, "The cages? You were kidnapped a week and a half before me. You were there for at least three weeks. You have to remember."

"I'm sorry. I think you have me mixed up with someone else," Cindy said gently. Actually she said it as if unsure Valerie were quite mentally stable, and then added, "I was on a month long vacation up until the day before yesterday. I just got back."

"Here are the pills, Dr. Moyer. Are you done with the form?"

Valerie turned with confusion as the receptionist set a packet on the counter. She stared at it blankly, and then nodded and handed over the form with Roxy's information. She started to take the pills, already turning back to Cindy, but the receptionist said, "Do you want to pay in cash or debit?"

Valerie grimaced. She'd almost forgotten to pay. Opening her purse, she took out her wallet and retrieved the necessary cash.

"Thank you. I'll just get your change," the receptionist said when she handed it over. She then glanced to Cindy. "Ms. MacVicar, the doctor forgot to weigh Mittens. If you follow Joan, she'll do it now for the file."

"Of course."

Valerie watched Cindy follow the second receptionist from the room, bewilderment uppermost in her mind. Lucian had said the women wanted to get on with their lives and forget about what had happened to them, but this was ridiculous. It was as if Cindy really didn't have a clue what she was talking about. Maybe she wasn't the right Cindy, Valerie thought with a frown. But the voice . . . She was sure it was the same. However, she'd never seen Cindy and couldn't be 100 percent sure.

"Here you are," the receptionist said, recapturing her attention. She was holding out her change.

Valerie accepted her change with a small sigh, murmured, "Thank you," and turned to head out of the clinic.

"Ms. Moyer?"

Pausing, she glanced back.

"Roxy's pills." The receptionist held them up.

Valerie returned quickly to collect them, very aware that the room had gone quiet, everyone eyeing her with speculation now, including the receptionist. She supposed blurting out the bit about being kidnapped hadn't been too smart. And Cindy's complete denial hadn't helped. They were all wondering about her state of mind, she supposed. Look out for the crazy lady.

Forcing a smile, Valerie accepted the packet of pills and turned to hurry out.

"Everything all right?" Anders asked as she got back into the car a moment later.

"Yes," Valerie muttered, shoving the packet in her purse and quickly doing up her seat belt. But then she asked, "Did you see the house where we were kept?"

"Yes," he answered, frowning a bit.

"The cages?"

He nodded, looking perplexed by the question.

"Did you meet the other women?"

Anders frowned. "Valerie, why—?"

"Cindy MacVicar?"

"Short, blond?" he asked uncertainly. "Scar by her mouth?"

Valerie sank back in her seat without responding. It *had* been her. It had to be. Why hadn't she seemed to recall anything about their misadventure? Or was she just an excellent actress?

"Valerie?" Anders asked.

She could hear the frown in his voice without looking at him, but didn't at first react. Her mind was racing. She was recalling how certain Lucian had sounded when he'd said the women wouldn't want to meet again, and wondering if that was because he knew they didn't even recall it? Had Lucian and the other Enforcers somehow erased their memories? But how and why would they do that?

"Valerie?" Anders repeated, sounding concerned now. "Did something happen inside the vet's clinic?"

She shook her head at once, instinctively keeping what had happened to herself for now . . . at least until she could figure out why Cindy didn't remember anything. Realizing that he was staring at her suspiciously, Valerie cleared her throat and lied, "I was just thinking while I waited in line and wondering about the other women. I never saw them, you know. I wouldn't recognize them on the street if I bumped into them."

Much to her relief, that seemed to make him relax, which, in turn, made her suspicious. Why would he be relieved that she wouldn't recognize the other women? Fretting over that, she straightened her shoulders and lied again. "I just recalled that there's a book I need for class on Monday."

"Oh." Anders turned forward in his seat and switched on the engine. "Well, the campus isn't far from here. We could swing by on the way to the grocery store."

"Yes, please," Valerie said and closed her eyes briefly. She'd been about to suggest that, but he'd done it for her. Billie had said she worked at the coffee shop in the bookstore and Valerie intended to find and talk to her. If she could find her.

Valerie tightened her hands around her purse. She had to find her. Billie was the only other woman Valerie had a chance of finding. Laura worked in a realtor's office, but hadn't said which one or where, and Kathy was unemployed and hadn't said anything that would lead to her.

"So," Anders said, peering around as they entered the bookstore twenty minutes later. "What book are we looking for?"

"Let's have a coffee first," Valerie said determinedly.

"Coffee?" Anders asked, picking up speed to keep up with her as she hurried forward. "Where?"

"There's a Tim Hortons in Pages on the upper level," Valerie announced. She had no intention of buying a book. Heck, she *couldn't* buy a book here for her courses. This was the university bookstore in the MacNaughton Building. To get books for any of her classes, she'd have to go to the Ontario Veterinary College Book Barn in the OVC Lifetime Learning Centre. Fortunately, Anders didn't know a thing about the Ontario Veterinary College at Guelph University.

"Isn't it kind of hot for coffee?" Anders asked as Valerie led him to the Tim Hortons counter.

She grimaced. He was right. The walk here from the car had left her hot and sweaty. "We can have iced capps then."

"Iced capps?"

"Iced cappuccinos," she explained.

"Which are?"

"You've never had them?" Valerie asked with surprise as she turned back to scan the name tags of the workers behind the counter. She didn't have a clue what Billie would look like. Just that she'd had a high, sweet voice. She'd sounded about twelve, though she'd said she was twenty-two.

"No. Are they good?" Anders asked.

"Yeah," she answered absently. "They're kind of like drinkable ice cream. They're made of coffee, sugar, cream, and ice cubes all put through a blender."

"Hmmm. Drinkable ice cream sounds good," Anders said cheerfully.

Valerie smiled absently and urged him toward the counter. "Why don't you order us a couple. Two iced capps large," she added when he looked uncertain.

Anders nodded and headed for the counter, and Valerie returned to searching the name tags. She had read every the name of every worker behind the counter without spotting anything close to Billie and was about to give up when a tall, slender brunette with her hair in a ponytail came from the back of the store. She was pulling a hat on as she approached the sandwich station. Her name tag read BILLIE.

Valerie moved to the far end of the counter at once. "Excuse me."

The brunette glanced up and offered a polite smile. Her voice was the high and sweet one Valerie recalled when she said, "I'm sorry. You have to place your order at the other end of the counter by the tills."

It was her. That voice was just too recognizable. There couldn't be two Billies with that voice working at this Tim Hortons. Valerie smiled. "I'm not placing an order, my . . . er . . . friend is," she said, unsure whether she had the right to call Anders her boyfriend or not. Though, really, at thirty, were they even called boyfriends? She supposed she could have said *lover*, but that was just giving away too much information.

Putting aside the issue of what to call Anders, she said solemnly, "My name is Valerie Moyer . . . from the house of cages."

Billie tilted her head. "Is that a bar or a band or something?"

"No." Frowning, she shook her head. "Billie, I'm talking about the house where we were held captive in cages in the basement. Remember?" Valerie coaxed when Billie just stared at her. "The cages we couldn't stretch out or stand in? Oatmeal once a day. The crazy guy and his boss who thought he was a—"

"Valerie!"

Pausing at Anders's sharp voice, she glanced around with surprise when he took her arm and steered her away. "Wait. I wasn't done talking to her."

"Yes, you are," he said firmly, forcing her forward.

"But Semmy, she was one of the girls. Maybe we can figure out how he picked us all."

"She can't help us. She doesn't remember."

Valerie jerked her arm out of his hold and turned

on him. "Why?" she asked grimly. She knew he was right. She'd watched Billie's face the whole time she was talking and there hadn't been a lick of recognition or recall in her face. She hadn't remembered anything. Just like Cindy. And while that shocked her, Anders wasn't the least bit surprised.

Mouth tightening, she asked, "What do you know that you aren't telling me?"

Anders's gaze slid back to Billie, who was watching them curiously. Turning back, he urged the cardboard drink tray toward Valerie. When she automatically took one of the iced capps in it, he turned to urge her forward again and said, "Not here."

Valerie didn't protest or fight. She walked silently beside him until he paused on the main floor of the bookstore and glanced to her. "Did you really have a book you needed to buy?"

She hesitated, but then shook her head guiltily. Anders didn't seem surprised, but merely sipped at his drink as they started walking again. They were silent all the way to the car, but once there, Valerie turned on him. "So?" she said. "Would you care to explain why Billie and Cindy don't recall what happened to us?"

"Cindy?" he asked sharply.

"She happened to be in the vet clinic," Valerie said grimly. "She didn't recall me either, or the house and Igor. She didn't remember anything. And neither did Billie." Valerie paused briefly, and then asked, "What's going on?"

"Not here," Anders repeated, and when she opened her mouth to protest, he added, "I need to concentrate on driving . . . at least until we get somewhere we won't be interrupted."

Blowing out a breath, Valerie sank back in the passenger seat and did up her seat belt. She then turned her attention to her iced capp, sipping at it slowly to avoid a brain freeze. She thought he'd take them back to Leigh and Lucian's, but when he stopped the car some time later it was at a farmhouse. It looked new, built during the last ten years by her guess, a large, red brick house with a couple of outbuildings, including a stable and paddock with half a dozen horses in it.

"Where are we?"

"My place," he said and got out of the car, leaving her to follow.

Valerie stared after him, unsure what to do. She was no longer certain she could trust him. She had no doubt he could explain, but that was because he was probably involved in whatever had happened to make the other women forget.

Should she be worried? Her gaze traveled over the man in front of the car as she tried to work out if he could be a threat to her or not. Valerie wanted to think no, but she had so many questions that had not yet been answered. What was this enforcement team Anders, Bricker, and Lucian worked on? Why had she been treated in a private home rather than in a hospital? They'd said to keep her safe because their kidnapper had escaped, but surely a police guard would have kept her safe? And besides, if it was so dangerous, why had Anders suggested coming out to pick up the pills? Why hadn't Leigh protested? Hell, not only had she not protested, but she'd requested they make an additional stop.

So, Valerie thought unhappily, was she in danger or not? And if she wasn't, why was she the only one at Leigh and Lucian's house? And the only one who still retained her memory? Well, if she *was* the only one. It was possible Laura and Kathy still retained theirs, but she suspected they didn't.

Valerie stared at Anders as her mind twisted itself in loops trying to sort things out, but in the end she had to acknowledge that the only way to get any answers was to let Anders explain. And the only way to do that was to have enough trust in the man to get out of this vehicle and ask him the questions. That shouldn't be so hard. She'd been naked, with this man inside her body, just hours ago. She had trusted him with her body, surely she could trust him with her well-being, for God's sake?

Anders sipped at the last of his iced cappuccino while he waited for Valerie to decide if she trusted him enough to get out or not. Whether she did or not was important. He needed her trust, and knew that right now it was a bit shaken. But Anders needed to know just how shaken . . . and if he could regain it.

Sighing, he pushed away from the truck and moved the ten feet to the paddock fence he'd parked in front of.

The day had started so well and with such promise. He'd thought he had more time, but Valerie's encounter with Billie was forcing his hand. Well, her encounter with both Billie and Cindy. His mouth tightened as he thought of Cindy. He had suspected something had happened when Valerie had come out of the clinic. She'd seemed . . . off. Different. He couldn't have guessed, though, that one of her cage mates from the house had been inside the clinic. What were the chances?

The sound of the SUV door opening reached his ears and Anders sighed with relief. She still trusted him a bit, now he just had to hope it was enough.

"I'm surprised you live on a farm," Valerie said quietly as she reached the fence and leaned against it next to him.

"Most people are," he acknowledged with a faint smile. "For some reason everyone seems to expect me to have a condo in the city or something."

Valerie nodded. "I can see that. It's because you're so sleek and sexy."

Anders blinked and glanced to her sharply. "Sleek and sexy?"

"Like you didn't know?" she asked with amusement. "I'm sure I'm not the first gal who threw herself at you."

"You didn't throw yourself at me," he said solemnly.

"Hmm," Valerie murmured.

Anders watched a small smile claim her lips and then just as quickly fade.

"Why don't they remember what happened to us?"

Straight to the point, he thought wryly and said, "A couple of the women were traumatized badly by their time in that house. Lucian thought it was in their best interests to remove those experiences from their memory and allow them to live a normal life without those experiences haunting them."

"And they were willing to let that happen?" Valerie asked.

"They weren't asked for permission," Anders admitted reluctantly. He just knew that wouldn't go over well and wasn't surprised when her voice turned cold and hard.

"So, he just stole the memories without asking them if it was all right?"

Sighing wearily, he turned to face her and asked, "Do you really think they would have wanted to hold on to those memories? Do you enjoy the nightmares they give you?"

Valerie frowned and turned away, her face flushing.

Anders presumed she hadn't thought he knew about those, but he'd held her in his arms through them just that morning in her room.

"So why didn't they take my memories?" she asked sounding tired.

"They could, if you want them to," he said quietly.

Valerie hesitated, biting her lip, and then asked, "What do they do? Hypnosis?"

"No. It's more in-depth than that. They'd have to wipe out your memory of what happened in that house . . . and everything since," he added solemnly.

"*Every*thing since?" she asked, turning on him with amazement.

Anders nodded. "Everything. Leigh, Lucian, their house . . . me. They'd put new memories in their place."

"Why?" Valerie asked. "I mean, sure, remove the memories of Igor and the house of horror, but why you guys?"

"Because remembering us might lead to your reclaiming the other memories," he said gently. "After all, you were brought to the house to heal and recover from the injuries you got there. And we hunt people like Igor and his boss."

"Oh." She was silent, working it out in her head. Valerie was a clever woman, he wasn't surprised when she said, "So would that mean you and I . . ."

"We couldn't see each other again," he said what he was pretty sure she wanted to ask, but just couldn't. "Seeing me might bring back the other memories."

"But seeing me didn't bring back Cindy and Billie's memories," she protested. "Maybe—"

"Cindy and Billie never saw you," he interrupted gently. "From what I understand, none of you saw each other except as shadows and silhouettes in that dark basement. And, fortunately, your voice is normal so unlikely to spark a memory for them."

She raised an eyebrow. "Normal?"

"I mean it isn't unusually high like Billie's, or sharp and measured like Cindy's. It isn't unusual enough to be memorable."

"Thank you," Valerie said dryly.

"You have a lovely voice," he assured her.

"Just not a memorable one," she said and before he could assure her that it was most memorable to him, Valerie continued, "So, Lucian called in the quacks to wipe the memories of the other women and then set them back in their lives. What happened to those supposed worries about the guy who kidnapped us? I thought that was why I was at Leigh and Lucian's place?"

"We don't really expect further trouble from the rogue who kidnapped you and the other women. If he's smart, he's moved on rather than risk our catching up with him," Anders admitted.

"Then why am I at Leigh and Lucian's?"

"You're there to heal," he said carefully.

"Ahh." Valerie nodded. "Of course you couldn't place me back in my old life minus the memories. The wound I gained in the house of horrors might spark my memory."

Actually, they could. They simply would have had to give her memories of an accident to explain them, but she didn't give Anders the chance to say as much.

"So I suppose they are waiting until I heal and then they'll wipe my memory and place me back in my life. I'll forget every moment of my time since being kidnapped."

She was scowling and obviously angry, but he didn't understand why until she added, "And all of this . . . whatever this is that's going on between us won't even have happened in my mind?" Valerie turned on him and accused, "So this is all just a short-term bang for you? No emotional entanglement, no clingy woman demanding to know what she means to you or expecting a relationship?"

Anders's eyes widened as he realized where her thoughts were going, but again she didn't give him the chance to respond, and barked, "Nice. How many women have you enjoyed such short-term affairs with? How many women have there been? Is half the female population of the GTA running around without a clue that they had mind-blowing sex with a hot hunk who—"

Anders shut her up by kissing her. It was the easiest way. Besides, he liked kissing her, and he really didn't want to hear any more accusations of his having bedded half the Greater Toronto Area, or GTA, as it was called by locals. Especially when it had been centuries since he'd had sex before her. Ironically, he supposed it was fitting that his last name was taken from a monk.

The moment Valerie stopped fighting and kissed him back, Anders broke the kiss. He had to. Much more kissing and they'd be rolling around naked on the ground rather than talking, and right now, talking was more important.

Releasing her slowly, he set her a step away and waited for the dazed look to fade from her face. But the moment it did and he saw her memory and anger returning, he said, "I do not make a practice of making love to injured victims of the rogues we hunt. I have not bedded any other women in the GTA. In fact, it has been a very, very long time since I have been intimate with anyone. You are special, and I will explain just how special and answer all your other questions if you will give me the chance."

Much to his relief, Valerie relaxed slowly and then nodded her head. "Okay."

"Okay," he agreed, letting out a slow breath, and then taking her arm, he led her toward the house. "Come on. I'll show you my home and then we'll sit down and talk."

Thirteen

"And this is the kitchen."

Valerie glanced around the cozy room, noting the bright yellow walls and warm wood cupboards. It was as surprising to her as the rest of the house. While Anders's wardrobe seemed to consist of nothing but cold, lifeless black, his home was a plethora of color. The living room had been cream with red accents, his dining room had been burnt umber, his bedroom a vibrant maroon and gold. The guest bedrooms and bathrooms had all been bright blues, greens, and aquas. If his home revealed his personality, there was a lot of depth and passion to the often silent and almost stern man. But then she'd already tasted that passion and knew it existed. There was nothing cold about this man.

"What would you like to drink?" Anders asked, moving to the refrigerator, only to pause without opening it. When he turned back with a frown, she raised her eyebrows.

"Is something wrong?"

"I— No," he said with a grimace. "I just remembered that I don't have anything here for you to drink."

She nodded slowly. "I suppose you didn't bother with groceries since you were staying at Leigh and Lucian's."

"Right," Anders glanced around before offering, "Would you like some water?"

Valerie smiled faintly. "Sure. Water is fine."

Nodding, he moved toward the sink and then paused and turned slowly, his gaze sliding over the cupboards as if trying to recall where the glasses might be. After a moment, he muttered, "I'll be right back," and headed for the kitchen's back door.

Valerie watched with amazement as he walked out of the house. Moving to the window over the sink, she watched him cross the yard and head for what looked like a guest house partially hidden by trees on the opposite side from the stables and paddock. Frowning, she waited until he disappeared from sight, then turned and surveyed the kitchen. The counters were spic-and-span, with nothing to clutter their sparkling granite surface, and the refrigerator and stove looked brand new, without a speck of grease or food drippings on them. It certainly didn't look like the average bachelor pad.

Reaching for the nearest cupboard, Valerie opened it and then froze. It was completely empty. She let it swing closed and moved to the next cupboard and then the next before starting on the drawers and lower cupboards. Every single one was completely and utterly empty. There wasn't a dish, cup, glass, pot or pan, or even a can or box of food in the cupboards.

Her gaze swung to the refrigerator and Valerie crossed to it and pulled it open, fully expecting to find the same situation there. Instead, she found the shelves lined with row after row of neatly stacked bags of blood.

The sound of the back door opening had her quickly slamming the door closed and whirling as Anders froze just inside the kitchen door, two steaming cups in hand. Neither of them moved or spoke for a moment, and then Anders said quietly, "I can explain. Please trust me enough to let me."

Valerie stared, his words running through her mind. *Please trust me enough to let me.* It felt like an awful lot for him to ask when her heart was pounding like a mad thing in her chest and her mind was a riot of confusion and fear. The empty cupboards had confused her, but the sight of all that blood in the fridge had shaken her up. For some reason it made her think of the house of horrors, though she hadn't seen any bagged blood there. And there could be at least a dozen perfectly reasonable explanations for him to have bagged blood in his fridge. At least, that's what she wanted to believe. Unfortunately, she couldn't think of even one at the moment.

"Please," Anders repeated, and then held up the cups he carried. "I have coffee."

A short bark of laughter escaped her and Valerie slapped her hand over her mouth. It might just be her, but it had sounded almost hysterical to her ears. Taking a deep breath, she nodded and moved silently to the kitchen table. It was a counter height table with barstool-type chairs. Valerie settled in one and then glanced to Anders.

There was no doubting his relief at her decision. Anders's shoulders actually sagged under the weight of it as he moved to set the cups down on the table and sat down across from her.

"Right," he said, pushing one of the cups toward her. "My caretaker had a fresh pot of coffee on."

"Thank you." Valerie accepted the cup, and even wrapped her cold hands around it, but didn't drink any.

"Right," Anders repeated, and then sighed. "I don't know where to start."

"Try at the beginning," she suggested and for some reason that brought a short laugh from him.

"The beginning. Right," he said dryly, and then straightened his shoulders. "Okay, but you have to let me finish all my explanations before you freak out and run. Okay?"

She blinked. That was one hell of an encouraging way to start.

"Valerie, I promise I won't hurt you. I would never hurt you," he added solemnly. "But what I'm about to tell you might seem surreal, or crazy, or even scary. So, just promise me that you'll let me finish explaining everything before you react and you'll sit right there in that chair until I'm done."

Valerie didn't immediately agree. She did take a moment to consider the promise, but really she was sitting there looking at a man who had not only found her and saved her from the house of horrors, but who had treated her with gentle respect ever since, and had given her so much pleasure she'd actually fainted from it. He was a man she liked, enjoyed spending time with, in and out of bed, and who she really, even then, just wanted to climb like a telephone pole. All of that was enough to trump what she'd found in his kitchen now that she'd got over the first shock of it . . . which made it hard not to make that promise. Valerie just wanted him to explain everything away and make it all better so that she could get on with lusting after the man, which she was doing anyway.

"I am truly pathetic," she said under her breath.

"No you're not," Anders said at once and she glanced at him with a start, amazed that he'd heard her whispered words.

Shaking her head, she waved her hand. "I promise. Go on. Explain."

"Right." Anders nodded and then paused, and stared at the dark wood tabletop briefly before shaking his head and saying, "Okay, I guess I can start with what I told you about my family this morning. My father being killed, my mother raising me to twelve and so on."

Valerie raised an eyebrow, half suspecting that he was going to tell her those were all lies.

"It was all true," he assured her. "But I left out a couple of pertinent details."

"What details?" she asked warily.

Anders struggled briefly, and then admitted, "That it all took place in the fourteenth century. I was born in 1357."

Valerie blinked as her brain tried to accept what he'd said, and then she stood abruptly.

Anders immediately caught her hand. "You promised."

"Well, and I would keep my promise if you'd care to tell the truth, but you can't expect me to sit here and listen to some nonsense about—" Her voice died abruptly when he opened his mouth and his canines suddenly slid forward and down forming two very long, pointy fangs.

Valerie sat, not because she wanted to, but because her legs suddenly gave out on her. Memories were suddenly flashing through her head; cruel laughter, flashing fangs, excruciating pain . . .

"Breathe," Anders said grimly, rubbing his thumb over her wrist and Valerie realized she was starting to hyperventilate. Trying to drive off the panic gripping her, she forced herself to take several slow deep, steady breaths. Once the threat of hyperventilating passed, she became aware that he was talking in a calm, soothing voice.

"You are safe with me. You saw the bagged blood in the refrigerator. I will never hurt you. I am not like the man who kidnapped you. He's a rogue. Lucian, myself, and the others hunt his kind. I would never hurt you. You are safe with me."

Valerie suspected he'd said those things more than once, repeating them like a mantra until she'd calmed enough to hear and accept them. And she did find herself accepting them. He had no need to bite and hurt her, there was a fridge full of blood behind her. Besides, if he'd wanted to hurt her, he could have done that a gazillion times over since she'd woken up in Leigh's house.

"Where did the blood come from?" she asked abruptly.

"A blood bank." His answer came swift and without hesitation. She suspected it was true.

"So, you're a vampire and so was my kidnapper, but you're a good vampire who hunts bad vampires, and he's one of the bad vampires you hunt?" Valerie asked, trying to wrap her brain around the situation.

It *did* sound surreal, she thought grimly. Cripes, was she really going to now believe in vampires just because Anders flashed some fang? They could be as fake as she'd assured herself her kidnapper's were. Of course, she hadn't really believed they were fake. It had just been reassuring to think so. It had helped her not feel so crazy.

"We prefer the term *immortals* to *vampire*," Anders said with a wince. "But essentially, yes, that's the situation."

"So this enforcement team Leigh mentioned—?"

"A collection of immortals who enforce our laws and hunt down rogue immortals who break them."

"Enforce your laws," Valerie muttered, rather startled to think vampires would have laws. She didn't know why. It just seemed weird. But then a thought struck her and she glanced at him sharply. "Leigh isn't—"

"She wasn't born immortal, but she is immortal now," Anders answered the unfinished question.

Valerie stared at him blankly. Sweet, very pregnant and girl-next-door Leigh was a vampire . . . but she hadn't been. Frowning, she asked, "How did she become a vampire?"

"She was attacked and turned by a rogue. A different one than yours," he added quickly. "Lucian rescued her when he and some of our other men raided the nest where she was being held."

"But she's pregnant," Valerie protested. "Vampires can't have babies, can they? Was she pregnant when she was attacked? So will she be pregnant forever? And are she and Lucian really a couple, or was that all just—"

"Leigh was turned several years ago now," Anders

interrupted. "She was not pregnant at the time. Yes, our women can get pregnant. Her baby is Lucian's, and yes they are definitely a couple. They are life mates."

Valerie stilled. He'd used that term before when talking about his parents. She'd thought it was just a quaint way of saying life partners, or soul mates or something. But vampires didn't have souls. "What is a life mate?"

"A life mate is . . ." He paused and then sighed and shook his head. "They are the most valued treasure one of our kind can find."

"Why? How?" she asked at once.

"To understand that, I need to explain some other things first," Anders said quietly.

Realizing he was asking permission, Valerie nodded.

Anders said, "We are as human as you are."

A snort slid from her before she could stop it and Valerie covered her nose and mouth, and then muttered, "Sorry. Go ahead."

Anders was frowning, but after a moment explained, "We have the same ancestors as non-immortals. As yourself. However, ours were somewhat isolated for many centuries and developed much more quickly, technologically, than the rest of the planet." He paused to take a sip of coffee, probably as much to let her digest what he'd said as because he was thirsty, and then continued, "They developed bio-engineered nanos that could be injected into the body to repair damage and fight infection and illness. These nanos had the added benefit of greatly extending our lives."

Valerie's eyes widened. She'd read an article recently on research being done to use nanos to fight cancer. He was suggesting his ancestors had come up with them long ago. She supposed it wasn't completely impossible, but he was saying they didn't just fight cancer. He'd said they repair damage and fight infection and illness. That covered a rather broad spectrum, which she supposed was possible.

"Extending your lives for how long?" she asked. "Surely you weren't really born in 1357?"

"Yes, I was. I haven't, and won't lie to you, Valerie," Anders said solemnly, and then said, "As for how long our lives are extended for . . ." He shrugged helplessly. "No one knows. Barring an accident that results in beheading or burning up the immortal in question, I suppose we might live indefinitely."

"Indefinitely," she echoed weakly. That was a bit harder to accept. The fountain of youth was a nano?

Anders remained silent and simply sipped at his coffee as she digested that. He waited until Valerie sighed and said, "Go on," before continuing.

"These nanos were a miraculous development. But they had one drawback—well, two, I suppose, since our elders at the time didn't think that near immortality was necessarily a good thing," Anders said dryly. Shaking his head, he said, "The other flaw was that the nanos used their host's blood to perform their work and as a propellant or energy source. Unfortunately, they use more blood than a human body can produce."

"So your scientists gave you fangs and turned you all into vampires?" Valerie asked with disbelief.

Anders shook his head. "No. Our scientists gave us blood transfusions. The fangs didn't develop until after the fall of Atlantis. Then the—"

"Atlantis?" she squawked with disbelief.

"I take it you've heard of it?" he said, his tone dry.

"Well, yes, of course. But Atlantis was mythical and existed like a gazillion years ago," she protested.

"A gazillion is a bit of an exaggeration, but it was thousands of years ago. However, it wasn't mythical," Anders assured her.

Valerie frowned, but after a moment nodded. "Okay. So you had blood transfusions in Atlantis, but it fell, and *then* your scientists developed fangs for you?"

"No. The nanos did," he corrected. "The scientists all died when Atlantis fell; only their guinea pigs, the patients who had been given the nanos, survived. None of them were from the scientific or medical field, so they had no way to get their transfusions anymore. They crawled out of the ruins of Atlantis to join a world much less developed than Atlantis had been. Without the transfusions, many of them died, but in others, the nanos forced a sort of evolution that gave their hosts fangs to get the blood the nanos needed to continue their work and ensure their hosts' survival."

"Fangs and what else?" Valerie asked, remembering how scary-strong and fast her kidnapper and Igor had been. And the other women had been sure they could read their minds, she recalled.

"Fangs, strength, speed, better night vision . . ." He shrugged. "Anything that would make them better predators to get what they needed."

"Things like mind reading?" she asked tersely.

When Anders nodded, Valerie cursed and tried to stand again.

"You promised," he repeated, catching her hand so swiftly the movement of his own hand was just a blur to her.

"I'm sorry. I know I did. But I'm not very comfortable knowing that you can read my thoughts, and I—"

"I can't," Anders said firmly.

Valerie hesitated, and eyed him narrowly. "You just admitted that one of the abilities the nanos gave you was mind reading."

"It is," he acknowledged. "But I can't read your mind."

She frowned now. "Why? Does that skill skip a generation or something?"

"No," Anders said with a faint smile. "I can read most mortals and even most immortals younger than myself."

"Than why wouldn't you be able to read me?" she asked suspiciously.

Anders swallowed and then said, "Because you are my life mate."

Valerie stared at him blankly as that word struck her again. His parents had been life mates. Leigh was Lucian's life mate . . . and she was his? "What is a life mate?"

"If you would care to sit down, I'll explain," Anders said quietly.

Valerie sat down. She could hardly do anything else. She had to know what a life mate was. She suspected it was important. Vital, even. She just didn't know why.

"Mind reading is one of the skills that evolved through the nanos. Immortals can read most immortals younger than them, and occasionally even immortals older than themselves. But they can read *all* mortals unless they are mentally ill or suffering some sort of ailment like a tumor that might block the part of the brain where thoughts are processed."

"I'm not crazy," Valerie denied, eyes wide.

"No, of course not," he said quickly.

"Then I have a tumor?" she asked with horror. The news was devastating. Dear God, she was only thirty. Too young to—

"Breathe," Anders repeated, capturing her hands and chafing them between both of his. "You don't have a tumor, Valerie. That's not why I can't read you. Leigh, Lucian, and—hell, everyone who has encountered you—has been able to read your thoughts like a book. You are not ill."

"Oh, good," Valerie let her breath out on a sigh and then frowned. Really it wasn't that good. While she was glad she wasn't ill, it was rather disturbing to think every one she'd met since waking in Leigh and Lucian's house had been able to read her mind. Pushing that worry away for now, she asked, "Why can't you read my mind?"

"Because you're my—"

"Life mate," she finished for him, recalling his saying that earlier.

"Yes. And a life mate is that one person, mortal or immortal, that an immortal can neither read nor control, and who cannot read or control them."

"And that makes them a life mate?" Valerie asked uncertainly.

Anders nodded. "It is a special gift to us. With the rest of the world we have to constantly guard our minds to prevent our thoughts from being read, which can be exhausting. It's that, or restrict ourselves to a solitary existence." He paused and then said, "But with a life mate we don't have to do that. We can let our guards down around them, and just enjoy the company of another without fear that they'll read our thoughts."

"And I'm that for you?"

"Yes, you are," Anders assured her as if it was a good thing.

Valerie frowned. Being a peaceful haven didn't sound all that sexy or exciting. And she simply didn't see how the passion that exploded between them every time they touched or kissed could be peaceful. He did experience that passion too, didn't he? She thought he did, and then there was—"I don't think we're life mates."

Anders stiffened. "You don't?"

Valerie shook her head, actually sorry to have to disillusion him. "I'm sorry, but when we were . . . er . . . earlier in my room when I . . . er . . . touched you," she grimaced, but continued, "I think I actually might have read your mind or something. When I touched you it sent a jolt of physical pleasure through me that, well, it must have been yours that I was picking up on and reading. I mean while I enjoy and want to touch you, I shouldn't actually experience the excitement you do."

Much to her surprise, rather than look devastated, Anders relaxed, a slow smile crossing his face. "That's called shared pleasure."

"It is?" she asked dubiously.

"Yes. It's a sign of life mates. When they mate, they share and experience each other's pleasure."

"Oh," Valerie said faintly. Life mates. The words echoed in her head.

"That shared pleasure is something that you will not experience with anyone who is not a life mate," he said quietly. "And it is . . . rather overwhelming. It's the reason we both lost consciousness."

"You fainted too?" Valerie asked with surprise.

She'd just assumed that she alone had fainted. He always seemed awake and fine when she woke up.

Anders nodded, "Yes. I lost consciousness both times as well. But I woke up before you."

"Hmmm." Valerie fell silent. She was sorting through everything she'd learned, trying to think what to ask. She knew there were things that hadn't been covered and that she would wonder about later. For instance—"So, you aren't dead?"

He smiled faintly. "No. Just old."

"Oh yeah," she muttered, shaking her head. He was born in 1357? The man was ancient. But he looked damned good for ancient, and he wasn't dead, so he presumably still had a soul. An old one, but a soul just the same. Valerie hadn't been to church since her parents had been taken from her, but was still glad she wasn't pissing off the big guy by getting tangled up with some soulless bloodsucker. Surely a bloodsucker with a soul was better than a bloodsucker without one, right?

"And you don't bite us mortals to get the blood you need?" she asked, eyes narrowed.

"Not anymore. We are restricted to bagged blood now," he assured her.

"Not *anymore*?" Valerie asked, managing not to wince. "But you did at one time?"

Anders shrugged apologetically. "Blood banks have only been around since the twentieth century. Before that, we were all forced to feed off the hoof."

"Off the hoof?" she echoed with disbelief. "Seriously? You call it that?"

He raised his hands in a helpless gesture. "I didn't make up the term. We just all used it."

Valerie rolled her eyes and shook her head. "Nice."

"My apologies," Anders said solemnly. "I will try to remember not to use the term in front of you again."

"Hmm," she muttered, only slightly mollified. Off the hoof? Like they were cows or something, which she supposed they were to his kind. The idea was a bit lowering. Valerie stared at him silently for a moment and then asked what she really wanted to know. "What does my being your life mate mean exactly?"

Anders stared at her blankly, and then said, "I told you, a life mate is a rare and precious treasure. They are someone an immortal can live with happily and in peace."

"Yes, but—" Valerie hesitated, a bit frustrated in her effort to verbalize what she wanted to know. Finally, she just asked, "What do you want from me, Anders?"

"You," he said simply, and reached out to take her hands gently in his. "I realize that your experiences in that house were horrible and traumatizing, and most likely turned you against my kind, Valerie. But I would remind you there are evil and bad mortals as well. All immortals are not like the one who attacked and took you from the street that night, then kept you in a cage to feed on."

Valerie stared at him silently, memories of the house running through her head. They were quickly followed by the memories she'd made with this man. The drive to Cambridge and back, the pool, their walk, the shared meals, cooking together, the overwhelming passion, waking up cradled in his arms . . . Oddly enough, the horror and trauma from the house had paled somewhat next to the vibrancy of the memories she'd started to make with Anders. They were like sepia photos next to new, modern, color ones.

Anders continued, "And I also know that as a mortal you are more used to a long and slow court-ship before making such an important decision. But for my kind it is different. A life mate is a gift to us and knowing we cannot read or control them, that we share pleasure, and that our other appetites are returning is enough in our minds to tell us that this is the one we are meant to be with. That this is the one who suits us in all ways. So, what I want is to spend the rest of my very long life with you at my side and in my bed. And if you agree to that, I promise I will never hurt or bring harm to you. I would sooner hurt myself." He squeezed her fingers gently. "I would give my life for you, Valerie. Be-cause having experienced the vibrancy and tasted the spice of life with you, returning to the dull, cold existence I had before you is unbearable to even con-sider."

Anders stared solemnly into her wide eyes as he said that, and then released her hands and sat back, adding, "However, I know you may need more time to make up your mind about whether you are will-ing to be my life mate. And that is the real reason you were moved to Leigh and Lucian's home, to give you the chance to get to know me, to see if you could accept being my life mate."

"And if I can't?" Valerie asked quietly.

"Then your memories will be erased like the other women and you too, will be returned to your life to live it out as you choose without your experiences to haunt you."

Valerie stared at him. In that moment, she didn't know what she wanted. Or perhaps she did, but was afraid to admit it. She wanted this man. All she had to do was look at him and she began to salivate like one of Pavlov's dogs. Even right then she wanted to jump up, rip his clothes off and experience some more of that mind-blowing shared pleasure that made her faint. Seriously, she was like a druggie jonesing for a fix, in that regard. So the lust factor was there. But she also liked him.

So far, Anders had proven himself thoughtful and considerate and a man who paid attention to details. He'd set his alarm to get up just hours after retiring to turn off the alarm so that she could let Roxy out. When she had commented on needing doggie bags, he'd gone out and got them for her without being asked. He was always fetching her coffee, or refilling her glass at meals . . . He listened to what she said and was attentive to her needs. To Roxy's needs as well. And at mealtimes, he didn't sit around expecting to be waited on, like her ex, Larry, had, either, but pitched in to help cook and set the table, etc.

Aside from that, he was intelligent, and seemed to have a good sense of humor. She had noticed he didn't talk much in the presence of others, but he could say more with a quirk of an eyebrow and a twist of the lips than Bricker could say in an hour of jokes and babbling, and from what she could tell, his opinions and beliefs seemed to line up with her own. While chatting with Dani, Decker, Leigh, and Lucian the other night, she'd often found herself nodding at something one of the others said and glanced to him to see him nodding as well. And more than once she'd heard her own words coming from his mouth, opinions she'd stated in the past to others, verbalized succinctly by him.

All of that was enough to tempt her to throw caution to the wind, jump in with both feet and agree to be his life mate. However, one simply didn't jump into something like this. From what she could tell, agreeing to be his life mate was tantamount to agreeing to marry the man, and no one would consider making such an important decision after knowing someone less than a handful of days. They got to know the other person, learned how they handled day-to-day life, how they reacted in a crisis, if they were moody and hard to live with, or easygoing and dealt with life head-on. It was the smart thing to do.

Anders had said she had time, Valerie reminded herself. She suspected it wasn't a lot of time, but she would take what she could get and try to be more rational about all of this than her instincts were urging her to be. If for no other reason than because she suspected that what he'd told her hadn't all sunk in yet. Otherwise, Valerie suspected she wouldn't be so calm. The man was telling her that vampires existed, or immortals did, as he called them. Atlantis and souls aside, they had fangs and sucked blood and that was a vampire. And according to him, Igor's boss, and probably Igor himself, had been a vampire, as the others had suggested in whispers in that dark basement. He'd also told her that he was one too, though a good one, and that he wanted to spend his long life with her . . .

But there had been no mention of love. Not that there should be, she thought quickly. They hadn't known each other long enough to love each other. Still, when one was talking about forever, love was a word usually included. So did she wish he'd mentioned love or not?

Sighing, Valerie rubbed her face, trying to clear her thoughts. They were a bit confused at the moment, but other than that . . . well, she suspected she shouldn't be as calm as she felt right now. But rather than being terrified, she was wondering if his giving her time to make up her mind meant no more of that wondrous passion they'd shared so far, because, damn, she could use some of it right now. In fact, she wanted to drown in it again, and suspected part of that was a desire not to have to think about everything right now.

Reaching out, Valerie took one of his hands in hers and ran her fingers gently over it, then raised it to her mouth and kissed first the back of his hand and then his palm. She slid her tongue out and ran it between his first two fingers, barely repressing a smile when a shiver of pleasure drifted through her. This time he didn't stop her, but remained completely still. There was no need to prevent her experiencing the shared pleasure.

Standing, Valerie walked around the table to stand beside him. Anders immediately tipped his head back to watch her and she raised her free hand to run her fingers lightly down his throat, then bent to press her lips to his. That's when his stillness ended. Fingers tightening around hers, Anders turned in his seat and drew her forward between his legs as he began to kiss her back.

Valerie sighed into his mouth, and caressed his chest. When he reached for her, this time it was Valerie who caught his hands and stopped him.

"My turn," she muttered against his mouth and

pushed him away. She'd got a brief taste of this "experiencing the other's pleasure business" earlier that morning, but she wanted to experience it properly, without his stopping her.

The tall chairs put Anders at just the right height that Valerie could slip her hands beneath his T-shirt and push it up to bare the taut flesh beneath. Little tremors of pleasure shot through her as she caressed him, squeezing his pecs before running over his belly. But when Valerie then let one hand drop to cup him through his jeans, she nearly cried out at the shock of pleasure that shot through her.

Damn. He liked that, she guessed, and continued to caress him through the heavy cloth, feeling both his pleasure as well as the way he hardened beneath her touch. The combination was like a road map, telling her exactly where and how to caress him, and how much pressure to apply. It made her the perfect lover, she realized, and made him the perfect lover too.

Soon, touching him through his clothes wasn't enough, and Valerie turned her attention to quickly undoing his belt and the button of his jeans. The zipper was next. It slid down easily, allowing her to slide her hand inside both his jeans and his boxers and find that hot hardness to caress.

Her first touch made them both gasp as his body reacted. Valerie felt his stomach ripple with pleasure, but her own stomach was doing the same, jumping under the skin with excitement.

"Valerie." Anders's voice was a rasp of sound.

Her response was to drop to her knees and take him into her mouth. She damned near bit into him with shock at the roar of sensation that was sent rushing through her body, but caught herself at the last moment.

Wow, this shared pleasure rocked, Valerie thought as she slid her tongue around his tip and began to move her mouth along his shaft. Anders's pleasure was her pleasure as she worked, excitement rolling over her in waves and centering at her core where it turned liquid. She was so caught up in what she was doing and the sensations it was causing that Valerie was taken completely by surprise when Anders suddenly caught her under the arms and lifted her up.

She actually growled with frustration at being forced to stop, but then Anders covered her mouth with his and began to tear at her clothes. He wasn't doing so carefully either. Valerie heard cloth tearing, but didn't care. She simply helped him strip herself and then him, though he only allowed her to lift his T-shirt off over his head. When she reached for his jeans, he pushed her hands away, shoved them off his hips, raised her onto the table and stepped between her legs.

"Christ," Anders growled against her mouth as he slid home. He paused then and glanced briefly around.

"What?" she gasped, digging her fingers into his behind to urge him to move.

Anders shook his head, and then lifted her off the table and lowered them both to the floor.

Valerie felt the cold tile press into her back and almost protested, but then recalled the fainting that would follow the pleasure. The floor was probably better, she acknowledged and then didn't care as he began to move.

Fourteen

Valerie frowned at the empty cupboard she'd just opened in search of a water glass, and asked, "Why don't you have any dishes or food here? You eat."

"Eating is a very recent occurrence for me," Anders said quietly as he tugged his T-shirt on over his head. "I ate for the first hundred years or two, but food lost its interest after that. As did sex and many other things. Your arrival in my life has re-awakened those old appetites though," he admitted. "That, by the way, is another sign of a life mate."

"Oh." Her mind tried to consider the fact that she was his life mate, but Valerie wasn't ready for that yet and pushed it away. Closing the door, she turned to face him and commented, "I suppose that explains how you've never had a Tim Hortons iced capp then."

"Yes." He smiled faintly. "They're very good. Everything I've tasted so far has been good."

Valerie eyed him silently. He was rubbing his stomach and licking his lips. She suspected they were both subconscious actions he wasn't aware of, but it made her ask a little nervously, "When did you last have blood?"

Anders blinked, but answered, "This morning. I'm good for a while. I *am* hungry for food though. We never did stop for brunch."

Valerie's eyebrows flew up. Her stomach had been gnawing at her since leaving the bookstore. She'd assumed it was just a symptom of her anxiety and fear, but most of her fear had dissipated now, yet the gnawing remained. Hunger, she realized.

"I'm sure you have many questions," Anders said quietly, almost stiltedly. "But do you feel safe enough with me to go have that brunch we planned on, and then hit the grocery store?"

"You're kidding, right?" she asked with disbelief.

He looked uncertain. "No."

"Geez," Valerie muttered and pointed out, "I just woke up from passing out after jumping your bones. I think you can take it that I feel pretty safe around you."

"Oh." Anders grinned, but then said, "Well, one doesn't necessarily mean the other. The shared pleasure is pretty addictive. You might not have been able to help yourself."

"Because of your superior lovemaking skills?" she teased, remembering his words from earlier that morning in her bedroom.

"Exactly," he said and walked over to pull her against his chest with a chuckle.

"Oh no," Valerie said, ducking the kiss he tried to grace her with. "That leads right back to getting naked which is awesome, but I need food. My stomach is killing me."

Concern crossed Anders's face. "I'm sorry. I should have realized. Come. We'll leave right away."

Valerie smiled crookedly as he urged her toward the door. She liked his caring and concern. She could get used to it, she thought as they walked out to the SUV and got in.

They stopped at literally the first restaurant they saw. It was a little diner in the middle of nowhere with bench seats and a surly waitress, but the food was actually amazing. Valerie and Anders chatted amiably as they ate, but stayed away from the topic of her kidnapping, and his origins entirely. She was glad they did. It allowed her to pretend they were just a normal couple out for brunch . . . well, a very late brunch, she supposed since it was after one in the afternoon.

They didn't talk about anything immortal related until they were walking back out to the SUV and then it was Valerie who brought up the subject, asking, "So, I take it that whole business about crosses and sunlight hurting vampires is bogus?"

"Crosses have no effect at all and we can go into churches," he assured her. "But sunlight is something we generally try to avoid."

"Why?" she asked with a frown, her gaze sliding up to the sunny sky they were walking under and then to his bare arms. "Does it hurt when the sunlight touches your skin or something?"

"No. If it did I wouldn't be walking in it right now. "But sunlight does damage to the human body, both mine and yours. The difference is that the nanos will repair the damage my skin takes, which means they need more blood. We quickly learned to avoid anything that does damage to reduce the amount of blood we need," Anders explained, walking her around to her side of the SUV. He saw her in, kissed her on the nose, closed the door and walked around to get in on his side, before adding, "The more blood needed, the more often one needs to feed, and the more risk of discovery. So we've habitually avoided the sun."

"But you use blood bank blood now so can go out in it again," she guessed as he started the engine.

"True we can," Anders agreed as he pulled out of their parking space. "But we try to avoid putting too much unnecessary demand on the blood bank. Most of us don't spend much time in the sun. Walking to and from a car is one thing, but you won't catch an immortal sunbathing."

"But Leigh, and even you, were swimming in the pool in bright sunlight," Valerie recalled with a frown.

"Lucian had a special awning installed over it so that he and Leigh could swim during the day."

"That barely there awning?" Valerie asked with a snort as she recalled the tinted glass awning over the pool.

"It may not look like much, but while it lets the light in, it blocks the damaging rays," Anders assured her.

"Really?" she asked with interest.

He nodded. "Most immortals have their windows treated with a similar coating as well. In fact, the windows of this SUV are treated with it." Anders smiled at her. "We no longer need to live in the dark."

"Oh." Valerie found herself examining the windows now. They looked like normal windows with a coating of that anti-glare stuff. Nice to know she was avoiding UVs though, she thought and then asked,

"So do you all sleep during the day from habit then? I mean, I noticed that Leigh and Lucian tend to sleep late, and I'm guessing you would too if you didn't have to be up with me."

Anders hesitated and then said, "Some immortals keep bankers' hours. Those who have jobs where they need to deal with mortals have to work mortal hours. But they still avoid sunlight as much as possible with treated windows and underground parking and whatnot."

"And the others?" she asked. "Like you. If you hunt bad vampires, you aren't dealing much with mortals."

Anders narrowed his eyes and tilted his head from side to side briefly. "That's not completely true. We do deal with mortals, yourself and the other women for instance. But we also have to question mortals when hunting a rogue. To try to find your kidnapper, we have Hunters out questioning people in the pet shops all over the Greater Toronto Area, asking about purchases of three or more large dog cages."

She nodded and said, "So you have to have workers who work during the day."

"Yes, but there are more Enforcers on the night shift than the day shift," Anders said. "Most rogues revert to the Stoker version of vampires, feeding off the hoof, stalking the night . . . Some even turn a large number of mortals to make themselves a small army of adoring underlings."

"Charming," Valerie said dryly, and then asked, "But you prefer to work nights?"

Anders shrugged. "It doesn't make much difference to me. I work when I'm needed and I've been needed a lot lately."

"Right, you've been short-handed," she murmured, recalling Bricker saying new recruits had arrived because their hunters had been dropping like
flies. The memory made her nibble her lip worriedly.
"I suppose hunting these rogues is dangerous?"

"It can be," he said with a shrug as he turned off
the engine. Then he smiled at her and undid his seat
belt. "We're here."

Valerie glanced out the window to see that they'd
arrived at a grocery store. "Did Leigh send you a list
of what she wanted besides bread and milk?"

"I forgot to check," Anders admitted and pulled
out his phone. It was an iPhone, she saw, as he began
to run his fingers over the face and punch icons.
"Geez."

"What?" Valerie asked, leaning toward him to try
to see what had brought on the dismayed sound.
Anders turned the phone toward her and she stared
blankly at it, slow to realize she was looking at a text
from Leigh. A text of a grocery list. A long grocery
list, she realized, reaching out to run one finger over
the screen so that she could find the bottom of it.
Cripes, the woman had about fifty entries on it. She
supposed Leigh's shopping had been a bit restricted
what with Lucian acting so protective. He'd probably refused to let her shop and merely picked up a
few things himself here and there on his way home.
Valerie had noticed that the cupboards and refrigerator didn't hold all that much.

Giving a soft laugh, she reached for the door.
"Guess we'd better get started."

"Dear God, I thought we'd never get out of there,"
Anders muttered, opening the back of the SUV to

begin transferring the grocery bags from their shopping cart.

Valerie grinned at his exasperation. "It was pretty bad, but I've seen worse. You should see the stores at Christmastime."

"You mean that wasn't the worst?" he asked with disbelief, pulling bags from the cart and tossing them in the back of the SUV. "There seemed to be half a dozen shoppers in every aisle we went down, and each one seemed to delight in blocking the aisle with their carts. Does no one have the good sense to leave room for people to maneuver around them? And what the hell is Leigh going to do with all this food?"

Valerie burst out laughing at his griping as she helped transfer the bags. Her amusement was mostly because she could sympathize. They had hit the late-afternoon crowd, which seemed to be made up of people who had nothing better to do than stand about chatting. It hadn't helped that neither of them had been familiar with this particular grocery store's setup and that Leigh hadn't listed her grocery items in order so that they'd had to backtrack and crisscross the store several times to get all the items.

"Sorry," Anders muttered, looking chagrined. "I'm bitching."

"Don't apologize on my account," she said with amusement. "I wanted to smack that old lady with the blue hair and orange top. I think she deliberately blocked us every time we came across her."

"Which was at least five times. I swear if we'd had to go back to the dairy aisle one more time . . ." He didn't finish the thought, and Valerie grinned. They'd had to visit the dairy aisle for milk, butter, cheese, liquid creamer, and eggs, and each item had been separated by meat, baked goods, canned goods, and veggies stuck between them. Leigh had listed the groceries by meals as she'd come up with them. The list went eggs, bread, bacon, potatoes, butter, steak, tomatoes, and so on. Most inconvenient, especially since only five items showed on the small screen at a time and they had to go down the list item by item to be sure they didn't miss anything.

"Well, at least it's done," Valerie pointed out with a smile. "And we got to contribute so I don't have to feel bad about Leigh and Lucian putting us up." They'd split the bill, each paying half. Valerie had wanted to pay for them herself, but Anders had been equally intent on paying, so in the end they'd compromised and split the bill. She liked that he had compromised rather than be bullheaded and macho about footing the bill.

"You know, now that you know about us, there's really no reason that we have to stay at Leigh and Lucian's," Anders said quietly as he set the last bags in the truck. Turning to her, he added, "Lucian originally suggested that so that you could get to know me. My being your bodyguard and your not being able to go home were just his attempt to allow you that chance. But now that you know about us, we could stay at my place. You'd get to know me better there without others around to distract us."

Valerie didn't respond at first. She was kind of feeling a bit alarmed. He was suggesting she move in with him. Cripes, they hadn't even been on a date yet. Oh wait, maybe brunch would be considered a date. Still, it was only one.

On the other hand, staying at his place would have some benefits. For instance, they wouldn't have to be worried about being overwhelmed by that shared pleasure business and doing something as stupid as having sex and passing out on the living room couch where anyone might have come across them. Not that they'd made love that time, she acknowledged. Though, they may as well have, and no doubt would in the future, which could lead to embarrassing situations.

"You don't have to decide right now," Anders said, closing the SUV's door. "Just think about it."

Nodding, Valerie took the grocery cart in hand and started to steer it away.

"I'll take that back inside," Anders said moving up beside her. "You go ahead and get in the car."

"It doesn't go inside," Valerie said. "It just goes over here. You go ahead and get the engine started and the air conditioner going. I'll be right back."

He glanced to the cart corral she'd gestured to and frowned. She knew he wanted to protest, but hurried off without giving him the chance. Valerie could feel him watching her though and suspected he wouldn't get in the SUV until she returned. Smiling faintly at his courtly behavior, she reached the corral just as a tall platinum blond did with his own cart. Valerie slowed to allow him to put his cart away first. However, he stopped too and waved her toward the lined-up carts.

"Go ahead," he said with a wide smile.

"Thanks." Valerie smiled back as she pushed forward again and nosed her cart into the end one. Turning back, she nodded at the man, offering another smile as she passed. She suspected they'd passed him about a dozen times in the grocery store during their back and forth. He looked vaguely familiar, and his smile was almost flirty, which was something Anders had apparently noticed, if she were to judge by the scowl presently on his face. Goodness, Anders looked almost jealous, Valerie thought, her smile unintentionally widening as she passed the man, which made his smile widen appreciatively.

The whole thing made her feel pretty darned good and she walked straight back to Anders, grinned, and went up on her toes to kiss him on the cheek.

"Smile. Life is good," she said lightly before moving to the passenger door.

"Cheeky," Anders muttered, opening it for her before she could.

Grinning, Valerie stepped up into her seat. She reached for her seat belt, and then gave a start when Anders leaned in, his face suddenly in front of hers.

"That wasn't a kiss," he informed her when she stared at him wide-eyed. "This is."

His mouth covered hers, his tongue moving out aggressively to urge her lips open. Valerie moaned as he stirred the passion that seemed to rest just below the surface in her now. All this man had to do was look at her and her body seemed to awaken and unfurl like a flower opening under the sun. Touching or kissing her, however, brought a tidal wave of heat and need and she instinctively reached for him, one hand raising to caress the back of his neck, the other moving to cup him between the legs.

Anders growled into her mouth, his excitement and need shooting through her body to mingle with her own. But then he tore his mouth from hers and stepped abruptly back, breaking all contact.

"Home," he said, his voice a husky rasp.

Valerie stared at him uncomprehending for a second, then glanced around and recalled that they were in a busy parking lot. Letting her breath out on a sigh, she sagged in her seat as he closed the door and then just sat there taking deep breaths and trying to regain some semblance of calm as he walked around and got in the driver's side.

Neither of them spoke on the ride home. Valerie was too busy trying to get control of herself. Her entire body was screaming with need, every nerve ending sensitized, and her mind clamoring, all for one thing . . . Anders.

Dear God, she really was like a drug addict when it came to him, Valerie acknowledged with concern. She just couldn't get enough and it didn't matter where they were. While they'd been in the brightly lit and thoroughly unromantic grocery store she'd watched him, wishing he'd kiss or touch her. His every glance, every brush of his hand or body against hers, even if unintentional, had stirred hunger in her. It was like a beast inside of her, barely asleep and rousing at the least provocation, but it had become fully awake and ravenous the moment he kissed her. She'd wanted to pull him on top of her and ride the pleasure that had awoken until they were both blissfully unconscious again. And she hadn't cared in the least that they were in a public parking lot.

Actually, perhaps it was more correct to say that she'd forgotten where they were. The moment his mouth had covered hers, all that had existed was the two of them in her mind. There hadn't been room for anything else in her brain with all that passion filling it.

How on earth were they going to manage at Leigh and Lucian's like this? Valerie wanted to believe that she could control herself with others around, but she wasn't at all sure that was true.

"Lucian's still home."

Valerie glanced around at that comment and saw that they were cruising up the driveway to Leigh and Lucian's house. Her gaze slid over the van parked in front of the house and then to the door as it opened and the tall, blond Lucian stepped out with Leigh just behind him.

"They just look like a normal young married couple," she whispered, watching Leigh waddle around to her husband's side. Lucian glanced down, apparently surprised that she'd followed, and then scowled and gestured to the house as he said something which Leigh ignored. Ordering her back inside, no doubt, Valerie thought with amusement.

"There is nothing normal about Lucian Argeneau," Anders said wryly as he pulled to a halt in front of the couple, and then he added seriously, "But they are the same people who opened their home to us and who you've spent the last two days with."

"Right," Valerie said and knew it was true. They hadn't crawled out of coffins and donned capes. Lucian wore his usually stern expression, along with jeans and a T-shirt that stretched over his muscular chest, and Leigh was . . . well, Leigh. She wore a pretty black summer dress with big red flowers on it that did little to hide her overlarge pregnancy bump. She also wore a wide welcoming smile that was hard to resist. Valerie found herself smiling in return as she got out of the SUV. Her smile turned into a grin of amusement, however, when Leigh called out a cheery "hello" and waddled quickly to the back of the truck.

"Go inside and rest, Leigh," Lucian growled, trying to usher her away from the vehicle as Valerie followed them.

"I'm pregnant, not disabled. I can help," Leigh protested, shaking off his hold as Anders opened the SUV's back doors. Eyeing the bags of groceries, she smiled widely and rubbed her hands together like a child faced with a truckload of gifts. Before the men could start unloading, she grabbed the nearest bag, tugged it out and opened the handles to peer eagerly inside. "Ooh, look, Lucian. Lemon coffee cake. That wasn't on my list."

"No, but Anders thought it looked good," Valerie said with amusement.

"It does," Leigh agreed, closing the handles to hold the bag in one hand.

"Why don't you take it inside and start coffee while we get the rest of this," Lucian suggested hopefully. "We can have a slice of cake and coffee while we decide what to have for supper once we get everything unpacked and put away."

"Okay," she agreed cheerfully and Lucian started to relax, but then scowled when she grabbed two more bags to take with her.

"Stubborn woman," Lucian muttered as he watched his wife walk away.

Valerie smiled to herself as she stepped up to the truck to grab a couple bags, but glanced around with surprise when Lucian suddenly said, "So you told her about us."

He was speaking to Anders and added, "She appears to have handled it better than I expected."

"How do you know?" she asked, eyes narrowing. When he simply arched one eyebrow, Valerie recalled that Anders had said immortals could read mortals, and muttered, "Oh."

Lucian nodded, and then stepped up to the truck to grab several bags himself, adding, "But you're not staying at Anders's, so get the thought out of your head."

"You decided to stay at my place?" Anders asked Valerie with a crooked smile, obviously pleased. That crooked smile faded though, as he turned to Lucian and announced in hard tones, "She'll stay in my home if she likes, Lucian. There's no reason she shouldn't."

"Kathy's gone missing," Lucian said calmly as he turned away from the truck loaded up with bags. "I think you'll agree Valerie shouldn't go anywhere until we know where her cage mate has got to."

He walked away then, carrying the groceries he'd collected into the house. Valerie stared after him with a frown. Kathy had gone missing? She turned to Anders. He was frowning too.

"Come on," he said, taking the rest of the bags out of the back of the truck and elbowing the door closed. "We'd better go find out what's happened."

Valerie nodded and followed him inside, but didn't find out what was going on at first. Roxy was waiting for her just inside the door, all excited at her return. By the time Valerie finished greeting her and led the German shepherd into the kitchen, Leigh was happily pulling groceries out of the bags, oohing and aahing over each item as she and Anders put them away. Lucian was nowhere in sight.

"Lucian's in the office taking a call," Anders said when she glanced his way.

Valerie nodded in understanding and helped put away the rest of the groceries, knowing they'd have to wait for the man's return before finding out what he'd meant about Kathy going missing. After putting away the last item, she and Anders gathered plates, forks, and coffees for everyone and joined Leigh at the island, where she was already slicing up the coffee cake.

Lucian returned as Leigh set the last slice of cake on a plate for him and announced abruptly, "Kathy went missing at some point during the night."

"Who was watching her?" Anders asked.

"Nicholas and Jo."

"Nicholas is Lucian's nephew and Jo is his life mate," Leigh said quietly to Valerie as Lucian took a break to eat several bites of cake in a row. "Nicholas was an Enforcer, then was considered rogue for fifty years. Everyone thought he'd killed a mortal woman, but that was all cleared up a little while ago and he's back in the fold again."

"And this Joe, he's Nicholas's life mate?" Valerie asked with interest. Gay vampires. Who would have thought?

"Jo is a girl," Leigh said with amusement. "Her name is Josephine. Although there *are* same-sex life mates," she added.

"Hmm," Valerie murmured and then turned her attention back to the men as Anders asked, "How was she taken if they were watching her?"

"They were just supposed to keep an eye on her and make sure there were no problems with her returning to her life. They could control and influence anyone with questions, that sort of thing. We weren't expecting any problems other than that, so there was no need to stay too close when she was home alone," Lucian said.

Anders nodded with understanding.

"Kathy rents a house on her own. Nicholas and Jo followed her there at the end of the day and parked out front to watch. It was just a safeguard, in case she went somewhere in the evening and talked to someone who might be a problem. So they settled in and watched the front of the house."

"No one was watching the back," Anders said solemnly.

"No," Lucian agreed. He pushed his plate away and stood to get himself another coffee as he continued, "Bricker took over from Nicholas and Jo this morning. When Kathy didn't come out by noon, he thought she was just sleeping in on a Saturday morning. But by mid-afternoon he started to worry, and went in. The house was empty, but her bedroom window was wide open."

"The bedroom was at the back of the house?" Anders guessed. Gathering his and Lucian's plates, as well as his own coffee cup, he stood up. He rinsed the plates and set them in the dishwasher as Lucian answered.

"The bed apparently looks slept in, so she was taken sometime after retiring, but probably before getting up."

Anders finished at the sink and moved to join him at the coffeepot with his own empty cup. Frowning, he asked, "He's sure she was taken? She didn't just go out using her back door or something?"

"Her purse, keys, and cell phone were all still

there, and the back door was locked. She went out the window. I'm guessing not willingly," Lucian added dryly as he led Anders back to the table.

Valerie noted that Anders didn't look happy at this news, but then neither was she. She also wasn't hungry anymore, and pushed her unfinished cake away.

"And that's not all," Lucian added.

"Great," Valerie muttered under her breath as the men reclaimed their seats.

"I got that news just before you returned," Lucian said, and then added, "My stop in the office after you got back was to call the other watchers to check on the status of the women each were watching."

"And?" Anders asked.

"Everyone was accounted for but one," Lucian said, sounding weary. "Decker was on Laura Kennedy and said she hadn't left the house yet and he was about to go check on her when I called. I told him to call after he checked. I'm waiting to hear back from him."

"So we might have two missing women," Anders said slowly and blew out a long breath. Shoulders sagging, he shook his head and stared into his coffee, saying, "I thought for sure he'd leave them alone and move on to somewhere else. Only an idiot would stay in this area now that we know he's here."

"Or someone who wants to be caught and put down," Lucian said grimly.

"Caught and put down?" Valerie asked with surprise.

"Most rogues are pretty suicidal," Anders said quietly, and then glanced to Lucian and said, "But this guy wasn't acting like a typical rogue. He was careful. He chose women who wouldn't be missed, picked a country house out in the middle of nowhere, with owners who were old with no kids or friends to check on them." Anders shook his head. "The suicidal ones aren't careful to avoid drawing notice like that. They do things that attract attention to themselves."

"Like what?" Valerie asked curiously.

"Like buying coffins by the dozen and filling them with new turns," Leigh said dryly. "That's how they got on to the rogue who took me. His purchasing coffins in bulk."

Valerie's eyes widened incredulously. "Coffins? You guys don't really sleep in coffins, do you?" she asked with dismay. After Anders's explanation of a scientific basis for their vampirism, she had been sure that whole coffins, capes, and garlic image was wrong.

"No," Leigh assured her, even as Anders and Lucian said, "Not anymore," in unison.

She stared at the three of them, one after another. "Not *anymore*?"

"Oh, well . . ." Leigh grimaced and waved one hand. "I guess in the old days when houses weren't as well built as now, some of them slept in coffins to ensure no sunlight got in at them through cracks in the walls, or roof, or via poor window coverings." She shrugged. "Most of them just use blackout curtains and such now, but rogues tend to sink into living the horror-movie version of vampires for the benefit of their followers. I know Morgan—the rogue who turned me," she explained, "He did it to keep his turns in line. They all thought he was their sire and lord and all that nonsense and were as obsequious as Dracula's Renfield."

"Most rogues do it for precisely that reason," Lucian said dryly. "It engenders fear and obedience."

"My rogue didn't do that," Valerie said. "I never saw a coffin and he didn't turn Janey or Bethany, he just let them die."

"Yes. Your rogue was careful to avoid drawing attention to himself," Anders agreed. "Which is why we thought he was just old-school. Preferring to feed off the—er . . . from the source," he corrected himself with a grimace. Then he sighed and ran a hand around the back of his neck, adding, "We were wrong."

"You might not be," Leigh said. "Perhaps Kathy's disappearance has nothing to do with the rogue. Maybe a mortal took her. Or maybe she noticed Nicholas and Jo out front in the van, got nervous, thought they were watching her for some nefarious purpose, and snuck out her window to go somewhere safe or something," Leigh suggested. Unfortunately, neither her words nor her tone of voice were very convincing. She obviously didn't for a minute believe what she was saying might really be true.

Judging by the expressions on Anders's and Lucian's faces, they didn't believe it either, but before either man could comment, muffled music began to play.

Valerie glanced to Lucian when he reached for his pocket and pulled out a cell phone. The music immediately grew louder and she tilted her head slightly and said, "That sounds like 'Ridin' Dirty' by Chamillionaire."

Lucian growled under his breath, and then barked, "Speak!" as he pressed the phone to his ear. But Leigh smiled brightly and exclaimed, "You know the song!"

"Yeah." Valerie smiled faintly. "I loved playing it in the car on the way to work."

"I listened to it in the car too," Leigh said with a nod. "But it's just called 'Ridin',' not 'Ridin' Dirty,' and that's not it."

Valerie blinked. "I'm sure it is. It sounds like—"

"It does sound like 'Ridin','" Leigh acknowledged. "But it's Weird Al Yankovic's 'White and Nerdy.'"

"'White and Nerdy'?" Valerie echoed, eyes wide. Lucian just didn't seem the sort to be able to laugh at himself . . . or anything else really. The man was mostly stern and grim-faced. But he had to have a good sense of humor to make that his ring tone.

"Oh, Lucian has a wonderful sense of humor," Leigh assured her cheerfully. "But I'm the one who put it on his phone. I did it last week when I was annoyed with him."

"Oh," Valerie said uncertainly and then glanced to Anders to see that his lips were tightly compressed. She suspected he was trying not to laugh.

"I'll change it eventually," Leigh added serenely. "But probably not until I have the baby and he stops acting like an overprotective dictating ass."

Valerie's eyes went wide and round, but Anders released a bark of laughter he quickly tried to cover with a cough.

"Call and update the others. Tell them I want 'eyes on' from here on out," Lucian suddenly barked into the phone.

Valerie stilled, her head turning slowly to the man. This was obviously the call he'd been waiting for, and she guessed that by "eyes on" he meant there would be no more just watching the homes of the other women and following at a distance. They were to keep the women in sight at all times. Laura must be gone then, she thought. He'd hardly make that order otherwise. Would he?

Lucian's next words confirmed that fear for Valerie as he said, "And double the watchers. I want two teams on each of the remaining women around the clock. We aren't losing another one."

Valerie sagged back in her seat. Laura was gone too. That left Cindy, Billie, and herself.

"Has Beth already headed to Port Henry?" Lucian asked.

"Beth is an Enforcer from Europe," Leigh explained to Valerie, her expression solemn now. "She and Lucian's niece, Drina, were partners there. But Drina came to Canada to help out with a situation and found her life mate, Harper. She stayed here. So when Lucian sent out the call that our Enforcers' numbers were getting too low and we needed help, Beth volunteered. She and another new recruit, Paolo, arrived the day you woke up."

Valerie nodded and asked curiously, "Was she headed to Port Henry on another Enforcer job?"

Leigh shook her head. "Beth wanted to visit Drina before she started to work. She was going down to Port Henry to stay with Drina and Harper for the weekend and then starting here in Toronto Monday."

"Oh," Valerie murmured, thinking it would be a shame if the woman's visit was halted before it began.

"Niagara Falls? Why the hell were they taking her there?" Lucian squawked, and then muttered, "sightseeing," under his breath with disgust. "Well, why the hell didn't they take their cell phones at least?"

Probably so they couldn't be contacted and dragged from their vacation to be pressed into work, Valerie thought.

"Call the hotels around Niagara Falls and find them," Lucian growled.

Valerie bit her lip. Lucian obviously didn't realize how many hotels there were in Niagara Falls. If they were in a hotel . . . they might have rented a cottage, or could even have checked into a bed and breakfast. And it was possible that they weren't even on the Canadian side, but had gone over to the American side of Niagara Falls. Finding them could turn out to be harder than finding the rogue, she thought, but then paid attention as Lucian spoke again.

"Just do your best," he barked. "In the meantime, Christian and his band are at Marguerite's right now. Every one of them have spent some time as Enforcers at one point or another over the centuries. I'll call there and see if a couple of them would be willing to help until we can get Beth and Drina here."

"Christian is Marguerite's son, and Lucian's nephew," Leigh explained and then frowned. "Well, technically, I guess he isn't his nephew. At least not by blood, but Marguerite is Lucian's sister-in-law, so he's family."

Valerie nodded, and then glanced back to Lucian as he said, "No, you needn't arrange anything for her. Anders and I have that covered. You just concentrate on the other two."

She didn't have to think hard to know he was talking about her when Lucian said he and Anders had that covered. She was definitely in protective custody now. But then Valerie had thought she was from the start.

Lucian hung up then, but immediately stood and walked to the phone at the end of the counter. Picking it up, he began punching in numbers, and then held the phone between his ear and shoulder while he plugged his cell phone into the wall socket charger. He'd barely managed to get the task done before dropping the cell phone on the counter and grabbing the other phone to bark, "Marguerite?"

Valerie was distracted from the latest conversation when Roxy nudged her arm with a wet nose.

Glancing down, she petted the dog's head. "Do you have to go outside?"

Roxy whined, then turned and headed for the nearest set of French doors.

"That would be a yes," Leigh said with amusement.

Smiling wryly, Valerie nodded and stood to cross to the doors. Roxy waited for her to step out first and then followed and rushed ahead to find a patch of grass. Valerie started to close the door behind her, but paused and glanced around when it wouldn't close. Anders was following her out of the house.

Fifteen

"I'll keep you company," Anders said as he stopped Valerie from closing the door on him.

"Thank you," she murmured, and turned to walk to the edge of the porch to watch Roxy.

Anders closed the door and followed. He too looked out over the yard, but he wasn't watching Roxy. He was taking in the forest backing onto the house and the trees on either side of it. Hell, he realized, there were even trees ten or twenty feet deep along the front of the house. The whole place was surrounded by woods that would make for a great hiding place for anyone who wanted to sneak up on the house. What the hell had Lucian been thinking when he'd bought this home in the middle of the bloody woods?

"I suppose this means our rogue is suicidal," Valerie commented suddenly.

Anders frowned. "Yeah, it's looking that way."

"Does that make him more, or less, dangerous?" she asked unhappily.

"More," he admitted reluctantly.

Valerie nodded as if that had been exactly what she'd expected him to say. Then she turned to face him. Arms crossed over her chest, she asked quietly, "Just how dangerous is your job, Anders? I mean I know being a mortal cop is dangerous, but how much worse is being an immortal cop in comparison?"

"It can be dangerous at times, but we're very careful," Anders said. He had hoped to reassure her, but she didn't look much reassured, so he added, "When all is said and done, it's probably safer for us than a mortal law-enforcement officer, if only because we're harder to kill."

Valerie still didn't look reassured, he noted. In fact, she looked pissed.

"Really?" she said grimly. "You're going to lie to me after you said you wouldn't?"

"I'm not lying," he said with affront.

"No?" she asked dubiously. "That's funny, because I'm pretty sure I remember Justin saying something the other day about you guys dropping like flies. And Leigh said not ten minutes ago that a Beth and Paolo had come to help fill the ranks because your numbers were getting so low."

"Oh." Anders smiled and clasped her upper arms, rubbing them as he said, "You misunderstood, Valerie. Drina, Beth, and Paolo are here because so many of my co-workers have found their life mates," he explained gently.

"What?" she gasped with disbelief. "Why would they need to replace people who found their life mates?" Frowning, she added, "You guys aren't like praying mantises, are you? You don't have a mate-and-die kind of deal going on, do you?"

The suggestion was so ridiculous it startled a laugh out of Anders, but he sobered quickly under her scowl and assured her, "No, of course not. It's nothing like that."

"So? What is it?" Valerie asked, sounding a bit belligerent now.

Anders found her attitude kind of sexy. Mind you, he suspected Valerie could blow her nose and he'd find it sexy at this point in their relationship. Grimacing at that bit of self-awareness, he decided to show rather than tell and simply pulled her into his arms for a kiss.

It wasn't the most brilliant idea, Anders acknowledged some time later. He wasn't sure how many minutes had passed when Lucian's voice pierced the heated fog cloaking his brain. It brought Anders around enough to realize what he was doing. And what he was doing was dry humping Valerie up against the porch rail while simultaneously trying to examine her tonsils with his tongue, touch and squeeze her breasts and behind, and undo his jeans all at the same time.

Groaning, Anders disentangled himself from Valerie's clinging arms and took a step back. He paused to take several breaths, attempting to give his brain a chance to recover before turning toward Lucian. Once he faced the man, he simply asked, "What did you say?"

"I said I'd rather my wife not look out our French doors and see your bare ass if you don't mind," Lucian said succinctly.

Anders glanced down at himself, relieved to see that, as he'd thought, he hadn't yet achieved undoing and dropping his drawers. Trying for dignity he straightened his shoulders and said, "I assure you my self-control would have kicked in before things went that far."

"Yeah right," Lucian snorted. "One more minute and you would have been bare-assed and giving Valerie a good seeing to right there on the porch rail." Grimacing, he added, "For future reference, I don't recommend it. Leigh got some nasty slivers off that rail some months ago. It's too rough for such endeavors."

Anders glanced over his shoulder to Valerie with concern at this news. The shorts she was wearing weren't especially long and he had no doubt her upper legs at least had been ground into the wood as he'd dry humped her. "Are you all right?"

Blushing brightly, she nodded. "I think so."

"I'll check later." Anders had meant that to be reassuring, but Valerie's blush went from a becoming rosy color to the red of a tomato and her wide eyes shot to Lucian with embarrassment.

"And that is precisely why we need help at the moment," Lucian said dryly to Valerie, obviously having read enough of their minds to know that was what Anders had been trying to show her. He clarified, however, by adding, "I've lost most of my best Enforcers to life mate brain . . . which means more often than not, they're as brainless as cats in heat. Even I suffer from it on occasion. We'll need help for the next year or so until the worst of it passes."

"Oh," Valerie breathed.

Apparently satisfied that she understood, Lucian turned back to Anders. "Christian and his cousins from the band are all going to help out for the next day or two and perhaps even longer. They've agreed to meet us at the Enforcer house."

"Why the Enforcer house?" Anders asked. "Why not just have them come here?"

"We need to discuss a plan of action for hunting down this rogue and doing so quickly. I want those women back safe. I've called Greg to get his insights and I want Mortimer and Justin there as well, but they can't leave the house unmanned. Someone has to be there to ensure things run smoothly. So the boys are meeting us there."

"But what about the women?" Anders asked with a frown. "I'm not leaving Valerie—"

"They're coming with us," Lucian interrupted, and then turned to head back into the house, adding, "Leigh wants to take some food to cook up over there for everyone. She's getting it together now, and then we're leaving. You have about ten minutes at most."

Anders turned back to Valerie just as she asked, "Who is Greg?"

"Oh." It took a minute for his mind to backtrack, but then he explained, "Greg Hewitt. He's married to Lucian's niece, Lissianna. He's a psychologist. He's helped a time or two in the past when cases weren't following a normal pattern."

"Like this one," Valerie suggested.

"Yes. Like this one," he agreed grimly. Really, this rogue wasn't making any sense at all. Anders had been sure that he was just an older immortal who refused to give up feeding off the hoof. There were many old ones who still thought of mortals as nothing but walking feedbags to be used and used up as desired. Most of them just stayed in Europe, however, where feeding off the hoof was still tolerated.

Although, feeding from the source to the point of death wasn't tolerated anywhere anymore, so the man would have been rogue there as well.

Still, Anders hadn't thought this particular immortal was suicidal so much as selfish and lacking a conscience. But staying in the area, and even re-kidnapping his previous victims when he must know they were being watched . . . well, that *was* suicidal.

"I better take Roxy up to my room," Valerie said quietly. "She can stay there while we're gone."

Valerie's comment drew Anders's attention from his thoughts and he glanced down as the German shepherd crossed the patio to stand between them. Reaching down to pet the dog, he said, "I'll check with Lucian, but I'm sure it will be fine to bring her along if you like. Actually, Mortimer has been thinking of getting some guard dogs at the Enforcer house to help with security and free up some manpower, so I know he won't mind her being there."

"I don't have her travel cage," Valerie pointed out.

"She's a pretty well-behaved dog. She should be okay without a cage. She rode here from Cambridge on the floor in the front seat without a problem."

"I know, but I'd rather not just show up with her," Valerie said with a frown. "And as long as we aren't gone too, too long she should be fine here."

Anders hesitated, but then shrugged and nodded. "We shouldn't be too long. A couple hours at most," he guessed, giving Roxy a last pat. Taking Valerie's arm, he then urged her toward the door, saying, "We should head in then."

"Yes, it looks like Leigh is almost done," Valerie pointed out, and Anders glanced inside as he reached to open the door. It did indeed look like Leigh was almost done. At least he hoped so. It looked like she'd nearly repacked everything they'd just bought and unpacked. How many people did she think she was feeding?

"My count is nineteen," Justin announced, entering the kitchen at the Enforcer house. "Twenty-four if you plan to feed the guys at the gate and on guard duty."

"Thanks," Valerie said, glancing at Justin Bricker as he opened the refrigerator, and then just staring with amazement when he pulled out a bag of blood, and popped it to his teeth.

"Twenty-four then," Leigh said with a nod, setting down the ladle she'd been using to stir the big pot of chili and bending slightly to open the oven door and check on the lasagna. "Valerie, how's the garlic bread coming? Almost ready to go in the oven? Valerie?"

Blinking, Valerie tried to tear her eyes away from watching Justin, but just couldn't. She wasn't even sure what Leigh had said to her, so just muttered, "Huh?"

"Valerie, I— Jesus, Justin, what are you doing?" Leigh gasped with amazement, apparently noting where her attention was.

"What?" the man cried, tearing the bag from his mouth, and then rushing to the sink with it as the punctured bag began to squirt blood everywhere. Dropping the bag in the sink, Justin glanced from Leigh to Valerie as he began to pull streams of paper towel from the roll. "I thought she knew about us?"

"Well, yes, she does. But she just found out today. She's never seen us feed or anything," Leigh said with exasperation.

"Oh. Sorry," he muttered, quickly wiping up the mess on his shirtfront and then turning his attention to the floor. There was a blood trail on the white tile from the fridge to the sink.

"Valerie?" Leigh asked gently, moving to her side. "Are you all right?"

She tore her eyes away from the quickly disappearing blood trail, and nodded weakly. "Yes. Sure. I was just . . ."

"A little startled by seeing Justin pop a bag of blood to his teeth," she finished for her on a sigh. Leigh patted her arm. "It takes some getting used to, I know. Here I can see you're done with the garlic bread. I'll pop it in ten minutes before we eat, but maybe you can start on a salad for me?"

"Sure," Valerie murmured and moved to the refrigerator to get the necessary ingredients. But when she opened the door, she found herself staring at the neatly stacked bags of blood on the bottom shelf, just above the fruit and vegetable crisper. And while she bent to reach for lettuce, she straightened holding a bag of blood.

Valerie turned with it in hand just as Justin straightened beside her from cleaning up the mess he'd made.

He glanced from her face to the bag and back. "What are you doing?"

"Do it again," she said, surprising even herself with the request.

"Which part?" he asked with amusement. "Feeding or making a mess when Leigh yells at me again?"

His words made Valerie glance to Leigh to see that she was watching her worriedly. Turning back, she held the bag out to Justin. "Put it on your mouth again."

He hesitated, his gaze shifting to Leigh, but when she nodded, he took the bag, and then, eyeing Valerie warily, opened his mouth, let his fangs slide out and simply popped the full bag onto them.

Valerie watched with fascination for a moment, and then moved to the side of him to try to see what was happening. "Are you swallowing the blood or is it—"

Justin tightened his lips, pulling them back to reveal his teeth. She could see that there was no liquid gathering in his mouth. The fangs were sunk into the bag and appeared to be draining the liquid from the bag themselves as if they had little pumps drawing in the blood.

"Interesting," she murmured, moving closer.

"He's not the usual rogue, though," Anders said, his eyes drifting toward the doorway as he wondered what Valerie was doing. She had headed off with Leigh, Lissianna, and Dani to help cook while Jo, Carolyn, and the men had come to the living room to come up with a plan of action for this rogue. Unfortunately, they couldn't agree on one because they couldn't sort out what kind of rogue they were dealing with.

"You may be right," Greg said. "He doesn't seem suicidal. Or he didn't," he added thoughtfully. "He was careful not to be caught in the beginning. If Valerie hadn't managed to knock out Igor and call 911, he may never have come to your attention."

And I never would have met her. She would have died alone in the dark in a cold, dirty cage, Anders thought, mouth tightening.

"Knocked him out?" Christian asked. "So you don't think she killed Igor when she staked him?"

"His boss arrived right afterward, he probably removed the stake, and if a stake is removed quickly enough the immortal lives. We figure he's alive," Anders said. They'd had to explain the whole story from beginning to end for Christian, his life mate, Carolyn, and his band mates. They could hardly send them into a situation where they didn't know what was going on and what they were up against.

"Right," Christian said with a frown. "So we're really on the lookout for two rogues."

"We have a picture of the one they called Igor," Lucian announced and Mortimer immediately handed out copies of the sketch artist's rendition of Igor.

"And the other guy?" Christian asked.

"None of them saw him when not under the influence of drugs," Anders said.

"I thought they weren't given drugged food the night they were taken upstairs?" Carolyn said with a frown. "Surely it should have been wearing off by the time they saw him?"

"They weren't and it should have," Lucian agreed. "But we think Igor was administering a drug during, or after, the bath."

"A different drug than the one in their food," Greg clarified. "One that didn't make them docile, but screwed up their perceptions. Valerie and the other women all recall fighting him on their nights out and his enjoying it. But for each, their memories of their surroundings as well as what he looked like were just too distorted to have been the result of coming down off drugs administered the night before in their meal."

"None of them mentioned being drugged on their night out," Anders said with a frown. He wasn't sure who the "we" were Lucian was talking about. He hadn't been in on this conversation.

"Igor could have controlled them to prevent their remembering," Lucian said with a shrug. "He didn't seem as sadistic as his boss."

"Well, if we have no idea what the head guy looks like, that's not why he's risking taking the same women again," Greg muttered, and then asked, "And you didn't find any stores with large purchases of cages?"

Anders shook his head. "No. We didn't even find a store where anyone bought more than one large cage at a time."

"If he was suicidal and looking to be caught, subconsciously, he'd be leaving a bread crumb. But he hasn't left any trail at all," Greg said with a frown. "I really don't think he's suicidal."

"Then why risk grabbing his prior victims again?" Anders asked with frustration. "He had to know we'd be watching them to be sure there were no problems placing them back in their lives, and it wouldn't have taken more than a glance at the street to spot our SUVs. Those are well known as Enforcer vehicles by immortals."

"The first two women weren't that risky," Mortimer commented. "His taking them wasn't expected. We weren't watching for him."

"Billie was risky, though," Anders pointed out, his

mouth tight. Mortimer had got the call just before they'd arrived. Billie had been snatched from work. They were waiting for their man to get to the house to explain, but it sounded like she'd gone into the "employees only" section to change and had never come out. Why their Enforcer hadn't followed her in, Anders couldn't say. Lucian had ordered "eyes on." Eyes on did not mean letting her leave your sight to change. Privacy took a backseat to safety, or should have.

"Yes, Billie should have been more risky," Lucian said, voice cold. Anders didn't envy whichever one of the men had been on Billie. The guy was in some serious shit.

"So, why take the risk?" Carolyn asked.

"I don't know," Greg admitted wearily. "Unless he's afraid they may have seen *something* in that house that could give away who he is."

Mortimer shook his head. "We checked all of them. In each case their memories were distorted. Their recollections of his face are like images through the bottom of an old glass pop bottle or in a funhouse mirror. There is absolutely nothing of use in their memories."

"It may not be his face he's worried about," Greg pointed out. "There could have been a piece of mail on the bedside table with his name on it, or his wallet may have fallen out, open to show his driver's license during one of their struggles, maybe even when they were kidnapped. Or during their kidnapping they might have caught a glimpse of his face in the reflection of a window or something. It could be anything."

Anders cursed. He wasn't the only one, both

Lucian and Mortimer echoed the sound as they realized that they might have missed something important.

"Valerie's in the kitchen, isn't she?" Greg asked.

Anders nodded and headed for the door. "Yes, I'll get her and—"

"No, don't," Greg's words brought him to an abrupt halt. "We'll go to her. It will be more natural. She'll be relaxed, more likely to remember things than if we drag her in here and make her feel like she's being grilled."

"She's going to know what you're doing and tense up the minute you ask her to return to her memories anyway," Jo said sensibly.

"Yes," Greg agreed. "But I want to ask her some other questions first and see if we can't sort out what the women may have had in common. How he came across each of them. That might tell us something about him that would lead us to where he would go now."

Anders nodded. "Let's go."

Everyone in the room began to move as Anders turned away. It made him shake his head. They weren't all going to fit in the kitchen. Aside from himself, there was Christian, his life mate, Carolyn, and his four bandmates, and then Greg, Lucian, Mortimer, Nicholas, Jo, and Decker. Lissianna, Dani, and Sam had opted to help Leigh and Valerie with the cooking. There was simply no way they were all going to fit into the kitchen.

Sixteen

Okay, so maybe they would all fit in the kitchen, Anders thought as he stepped into the large bright room. It was a lot bigger in reality than in his memory, but then he wasn't often in here.

Anders thoughts died as he came to a halt just inside the kitchen. It was the sight of Valerie over by the refrigerator, examining Justin like he was a horse up for sale that made him stop. The young Enforcer stood completely still, a quickly dwindling blood bag in his mouth, and eyes wide as Valerie stood beside him, pulling his upper lip back and poking at his teeth.

"There must be a direct path into the bloodstream via the fangs," she was saying thoughtfully. "But I don't see how. Or how they can draw in the blood without some sort of pump system or something . . . unless the nanos do the actual work of drawing in the blood. Hmmm."

The blood bag was empty now, and Justin removed it with relief, muttering, "Yeah. Well, I don't know how it works. I just enjoy the benefits."

"Can I see your fangs again?" Valerie asked.

"Er . . ." Justin said, then spotted Anders and smiled with relief. "Anders, buddy. Show your woman your fangs."

"Shy, Bricker? You?" Anders asked dryly, moving forward again as Valerie glanced around to smile at him.

"Nah. I just don't want to show you up by letting her see how much bigger my fangs are than yours," Justin responded.

"Actually, I saw Anders's fangs at his house this afternoon and they're bigger than yours," Valerie said at once, and then as Anders reached her side, she glanced at him and asked, "Why? Is it like big fangs, big feet, big—?"

Anders put an end to her question by kissing her naughty mouth. God, he loved this woman. Justin had tried to embarrass him and she had slapped him back with so little effort that—

His thoughts died as Anders's brain caught and held on to one particular sentence that had run through his mind. God, he loved this woman? Breaking their kiss, he lifted his head and stared down into her sweet face. She was like a ray of sunshine. Golden hair, porcelain skin, bright green eyes, luscious red lips. She was as beautiful as the sun to him, and he'd always thought the sun the most beautiful thing in the world. Perhaps because he could never really enjoy it, and he'd only allowed himself brief glimpses of it, or enjoyed it second-hand from the memories of mortals he fed off. It was only the last decade or so that he'd been able to enjoy it properly with the help of the window coating that blocked UV rays.

Valerie rivaled the sun in his eyes. And won. If given the choice of seeing her every day but never seeing the sun again, or never seeing her again and getting to enjoy the sun, Valerie would win hands down, he acknowledged.

Anders had always understood that the nanos got it right when they chose a life mate for an immortal. He just hadn't realized how right it could be. When he was with Valerie, he felt at peace. He enjoyed her smile, her laughter, her chatter, her sense of humor, her everything. He enjoyed just being with her, even if they were saying nothing. And he definitely enjoyed their passion.

"Anders?" Greg's deep voice interrupted his musings.

Straightening, he turned and stared at Greg for one blank moment, and then nodded. "Valerie, this is Greg Hewitt. He's—"

"Lissianna's husband," Valerie said with a smile, holding her hand out to Greg. "Nice to meet you. Lissianna is lovely."

"Nice to meet you as well," Greg said with a smile, then raised an eyebrow and glanced around. "Speaking of my wife, where is she?"

"Outside," Valerie answered. "She was in here helping us, but Luciana got fussy, so she took her out to let her run around the yard while she checked with Sam and Dani to see if they were good at the barbecue or needed anything."

"Sam and Dani are manning the barbecue?" Decker asked with a frown. "Why didn't they call one of us to handle that?"

"Because you all were busy," Valerie said with a shrug. "Besides, there was no need. As Sam said, she's a lawyer and Dani's a doctor, between the two of them they should be able to get the barbecue going without blowing up the place."

"Christ," Mortimer muttered and hurried out of the room with Decker on his heels.

Anders tightened the arm he still had around Valerie, giving her a little squeeze. He'd caught the twinkle in her eye, even if the other two men hadn't.

"You have a beautiful daughter," Valerie said now to Greg. "She's a little wingless cherub with her golden curls, chubby little rosy cheeks and those gorgeous big, silver-blue eyes. Speaking of which," she added, turning back to Anders. "You guys all have kind of metallic eyes. They're either silver-blue, silver-green, or black and gold like yours. Is that because of the nanos?"

"Yes," Anders answered.

Before she could ask why the nanos had that effect on the eyes, which Anders suspected would be the next question, Greg asked one of his own, "I hear you're a vet here to take some upgrade courses at the Veterinary College at the University of Guelph?"

Valerie nodded. "And I hear you're a psychologist? That must make for an interesting job."

"At times," he agreed wryly, and then said, "I gather one of the other women taken by your kidnapper worked at the university? Billie?"

"Yes, she—" Valerie stopped abruptly, her eyebrows drawing together. "Wait. Did you say worked?"

"Sorry, I meant works. She works there," Greg corrected himself quickly.

Valerie stared at him for a minute and then turned to Anders. "Is Billie all right?"

Anders could feel all eyes on him. He knew everyone wanted him to lie and say Billie was fine so they could get on with questioning Valerie, but he just couldn't do it. He wouldn't lie to Valerie. But before he could tell her Billie had been taken, Lucian spoke up, drawing Valerie's attention his way.

"She still works at the university coffee shop and will be fine," Lucian said.

Anders was just relaxing when Valerie turned back to him and asked, "Is Billie fine *right now*?"

Grimacing, he shook his head. "She was taken from her workplace just before we got here." Her eyes widened with horror and she opened her mouth to say something, but he rushed on, saying, "We don't know the details yet, Valerie. As soon as I know, you'll know. In the meantime, Greg has some questions for you. They'll help us help her."

Valerie was silent for a moment, and then nodded and turned to Greg. "Go ahead."

Greg glanced from Anders to Valerie and then said, "You and Billie have a connection to the Guelph University. Did any of the others? Could the college or university be where he found all of you?"

Valerie considered the possibility, but shook her head. "I don't think so. Laura was a realtor and Cindy was a teacher. Kathy was unemployed. Billie was the only one who mentioned a connection to the university or college."

Greg looked disappointed, but then said, "All right, you saw Cindy at the vet's. Perhaps he is connected to the vet clinic and that's how he got onto you all."

Valerie shook her head at once. "The day I saw Cindy at the clinic was the first time I ever went there. I only did that because I needed flea pills for Roxy and didn't want to waste Anders's time driving to Cambridge. It just happened to be the closest clinic. I had no connection to it before that."

Greg was silent for a moment, but then sighed and said, "Tell us about the house."

Valerie glanced from him to Anders uncertainly. "Tell you what about the house?"

"Whatever you can remember," Greg said. "I understand most of your time was spent in a cage in the dark in the basement?"

Valerie nodded and moved closer to Anders. He suspected it was a subconscious action. She was seeking comfort. He tightened the arm he had around her and rubbed his hand soothingly up and down her upper arm.

"But you were taken upstairs twice," Greg continued. "I'd like you to close your eyes and go back there in your memory for us and tell us everything you see. Can you do that?"

Valerie hesitated, obviously not eager to do so, but then she grimaced, nodded, and closed her eyes.

"Good," Greg said. "It's the last night you were in your cage. Igor has let you out of your cage and is leading you upstairs. The first room at the top of the stairs is what?"

"A kitchen," she said quietly.

"Can you describe everything you see in that kitchen?" Greg asked.

Valerie was silent for a moment, but Anders could see her eyelids twitching as if she were looking around. He suspected she was seeing the kitchen again.

"I was looking for a weapon," she said suddenly. "I had my head down and was using my hair for cover. The floor was black and white checker tile, the kitchen table an old aluminum job with that speckled top, circa 'really old.' The cupboards were plain rectangles, that bright blue they used fifty years ago, and the countertops were completely bare. It was like it was an empty house they'd taken over or something."

Anders continued to rub her arm. It hadn't been an empty house. Igor and his boss must have emptied out the rooms they wouldn't be using. But they hadn't told Valerie that the old couple who owned the place had been killed and left to rot in the room behind the room where her cage had been. There was no need to give her worse nightmares.

"Nothing at all on the countertops?" Greg questioned with a frown. "What about on the fridge? Were there any magnets with notes, or mail, or—"

"No. There was nothing," Valerie assured him.

"Okay," Greg said. "You're leaving the kitchen. Now what do you see?"

"A hall as empty as the kitchen, and then we're heading up the stairs."

"You must have passed rooms on the way to the stairs. Did you see anything in the rooms?"

"Nothing near the doorways and that's all I saw," she said and reminded him, "My head was down."

"Okay, you're mounting the stairs. What do you see at the top?"

"I raised my head as we mounted the stairs, and then we were in another hallway. There's a blue shag carpet—God I hate shag," she added in a disgusted mutter. "It gets all gross and matted."

Greg smiled faintly. "Anything else?"

"Paneled walls, a cheap, fake Renaissance portrait, and he turns me to the left and—"

"A Renaissance portrait?" Greg interrupted sharply.

Valerie opened her eyes curiously. "Yeah. But it was a bad knockoff, ugly and dirty-looking."

Greg's eyes narrowed. "Marguerite has portraits of herself and her children down through the ages. She has them taken care of, has them cleaned and touched up regularly and so forth when the paint begins to darken or crack, but if your rogue didn't, the painting might look dirty and cheap."

Her eyebrows rose. "You think the portrait might be of him?"

Rather than answer, Greg glanced to Lucian in question. "Do most immortals keep portraits of themselves?"

"Some," he acknowledged. "There were no cameras back then and portraits were the only way to capture memories. But it could just as easily be a cheap knockoff, as Valerie thought. Something the previous owners had put up."

"They took everything out of the kitchen that belonged to the previous owners. What makes you think they left anything in the rest of the house?" Greg asked.

Lucian raised his eyebrows. "Good point. I suppose it could be of him. That would explain why he'd want the women back. They might have been able to describe his portrait."

"But none of the others mentioned it, did they?" Anders asked. No one had mentioned the portrait to him prior to this.

"No," Lucian acknowledged.

"But the others were drugged, probably unsteady on their feet and watching their step because of it. Valerie wasn't drugged and was looking for a weapon to facilitate her escape," Greg pointed out. "However, he couldn't be sure that one of them might not have glanced up. At least not without searching their memories. To do that, he needed to recapture them."

Anders frowned. That didn't bode well for the women that had been recaptured. If he'd only taken them to search their memories and ensure they didn't tell anyone about the portrait, then he had no reason to keep them alive. His plan might actually be to capture and kill each of the women and then move on to new, safer pastures.

"True," Greg said.

Anders glanced up to see that the psychologist was speaking to him. He'd read his mind, he realized with irritation.

"But that means there's good news," Greg continued. "If he's worried about that portrait, it's because someone might recognize him from it."

"Maybe, but no one has recognized Igor yet," Anders pointed out.

Greg shrugged. "He may be new. A newer turn that the rogue took on to tend to the women and do the more unpleasant or heavy work he doesn't want to do." He paused to let that sink in and then added, "But he himself may be more recognizable . . . especially if he's been around a while and had enough wealth and power to be able to afford a portrait. I suspect those didn't come cheap."

"No, they didn't," Lucian agreed and glanced to

Valerie. "Describe the portrait. You said Renaissance. Are you sure, or was that just a guess?"

"He was wearing one of those fluffy collar things around his neck like Queen Elizabeth wore," she said.

"Ruffs," Lucian said. "They were around near the end of the Renaissance. Sixteenth century. What else?"

Valerie hesitated, and then bit her lip and closed her eyes. "A fur collar, dark clothes, maybe a robe or something, but it's only from the shoulders up."

"The face, Valerie," Anders said gently.

She sighed with resignation and then her face screwed up. He couldn't tell if she was in pain or thinking really hard. "A beard and mustache, big ears, a miserable expression."

"Everyone looked miserable back then," Anders said with amusement.

"Yeah, but I don't remember facial hair on Count Rip-Out-Your-Throat," she said raising a hand self-consciously to her neck as she opened her eyes.

Anders reached for her hand and drew it away from her neck to kiss her knuckles. She was struggling with this and he wished she didn't have to go through it, but she wouldn't be safe until they found this man.

"He may have removed the facial hair since then," Greg said soothingly. "Just try to remember his eyes and nose and what color his hair was."

"Right," she muttered, and closed her eyes. "Eyes and nose and hair color. Well, the painting was dirty, but it looked like his hair was terribly fair."

"Blond?" Anders asked.

"Fairer than blond. Almost white, but his face

wasn't old-looking. He had a straight nose and his eyes were kind of like— Oh," she interrupted herself with surprise.

"What is it?" Anders asked and could feel the way everyone in the room had suddenly stilled and were leaning forward with anticipation.

"I just realized why he looked so familiar," she said with wonder. "He looked like the man in the portrait."

"Who did?" Anders asked with alarm. "You've seen the man from the portrait since leaving the house?"

"Yes." She opened her eyes and turned to him. "In the grocery store parking lot. The man at the cart corral."

"Damn," Anders growled, recalling exactly who she meant. The greasy bastard he'd thought was giving her the eye when she took the cart back. "I knew there was something wrong with that guy."

"You saw him too?" Lucian asked sharply.

Anders nodded. "I didn't recognize him though. But then I didn't see much of his face. He kept his back and side to me."

"Then he *is* after Valerie too," Greg said with a nod and when Anders turned on him, he said, "Well, you don't think his being in the parking lot was a coincidence, do you? He must have been following you."

"How?" Anders asked with a frown. "He couldn't know Valerie was at Lucian's so couldn't have followed us from there."

"Perhaps he was after Billie earlier in the day and spotted Valerie when she was talking to her. Or he might have been following Cindy and just awaiting his chance but followed the two of you instead because Valerie isn't at her home anymore," he suggested. Pursing his lips, he added, "I suspect if you hadn't watched Valerie so closely the whole way, and had got into the SUV to start it as she'd suggested, he'd probably have her even now."

"How did you know—?" Valerie began and then muttered, "Oh right. Mind reading." She scowled, and added, "It's kind of rude of you to read my mind, don't you think? I'd appreciate it if you'd all stop that. If you don't, I might just put some nasty thoughts in there for you to find."

"Nasty thoughts?" Justin asked with amusement.

"Things you won't enjoy finding," she assured him.

"Oh, now you just have me curious," he said, focusing on her forehead.

Valerie's eyes narrowed on the young immortal, and then she tightened her lips and closed her eyes. A heartbeat later, Justin gasped and stepped back, his expression horrified.

"Eww, that's disgusting," he exclaimed, giving his head a shake as if trying to get an image out of it.

"Anytime you want a refresher, give my brain a go," Valerie said sweetly, and then added grimly, "I'm a vet. There's plenty more where that came from."

Anders had been about to ask what she'd thought of, but her words were explanation enough. He had a farm. He could imagine an unpleasant thing or two himself. He'd just never thought to bombard the others with it for reading his mind. But Valerie had, the clever little minx. Damn, he did love her.

"All right," Leigh said suddenly, clapping her hands. "Dinner will be ready in ten minutes. Lucian,

that gives you just enough time to call Bastien and
have him send back that nice sketch artist who
did the picture of Igor. That way we can get Count
Rip-Your-Throat-Out's picture without traipsing
through images of puppy guts and Doberman di-
arrhea in Valerie's mind," she added with a grin
for her. "Everyone else go wash up so you can help
fetch plates, condiments, and whatnot."

"I don't think I can eat after what Valerie showed
me," Justin muttered with disgust.

"That's a shame," Leigh said, not sounding terribly concerned as she bent to peer in at something
she had in the oven. "We have lasagna, chili, garlic
bread, salad, potato salad, and then hamburgers and
hot dogs on the barbecue. I was hoping everyone
would find something they like in that collection."

"Your lasagna? Homemade?" Justin asked, his interest and appetite apparently returning. But then it
was only to be expected. Justin was always hungry,
Anders thought.

"Go wash up," Leigh said with a laugh, one hand
rubbing her belly and the other her back as she
straightened.

"Are you all right, Leigh?" Valerie asked, giving
Anders's waist a squeeze before slipping free of his
arm and moving toward the other woman.

"Oh, fine," she said sounding tired. "I think I've
just been on my feet too long."

"Sit down," Valerie said at once, taking the woman's arm and ushering her to one of the stools around
the island in the center of the long room. "I'll take
over from here."

"Take over?" Leigh asked with amusement. "You
did most of it to begin with."

Valerie shrugged and grabbed a ladle to give the chili a stir, saying lightly, "You can return the favor when I'm pregnant."

Anders stared at Valerie, her words reverberating in his head. When she was pregnant? He immediately started to imagine just that, Valerie glowing and beautiful, her belly rounded with his child.

"Has she agreed to be your life mate?"

Anders glanced to Greg at that soft question and then turned back to look at Valerie as he shook his head.

"Well, whether she realizes it or not, she's accepted what we are and isn't afraid of us. I think you can thank Leigh for that," Greg added.

"Leigh?" he asked with surprise. He'd been rather hoping it was him.

"Sorry, Anders, but that's not how a woman's mind works. You're a dark, mysterious, and sexy vampire to her, and none of those words are equated with trust and feeling safe," he pointed out dryly, and then added, "But Leigh . . ." Greg glanced to the woman and smiled crookedly. "She's the most non-threatening vampire on the planet right now. Valerie can see herself in Leigh. It will help you that they are becoming good friends. I think she'll choose you in the end."

Anders grunted. He hoped Greg was right. He'd been alone a long time and never really minded until she'd come into his life. Now he didn't even want to contemplate a future without her in it.

Seventeen

"You look tired."

Valerie grimaced at Anders's comment as she approached the couch where he sat. He was alone in the living room of the Enforcer house, which looked like a normal house to her. Well, a normal, huge, expensive house with loads of bedrooms upstairs, high-tech security, and guards at the entry gate as well as walking the perimeter, not to mention a big outbuilding that was half prison cells and half garage, although she hadn't yet seen that.

She gathered Mortimer, who was in charge of the Enforcers under Lucian, lived here with his life mate, Sam, a lawyer who now worked at his side as well as helped out with legal matters that came up. However, she'd been told that the spare bedrooms were often used by either Enforcers from other areas, or mortals and immortals who needed a safehouse.

"I'm a little tired," she admitted as she settled on the couch beside him. "But I'm not the only one."

"Leigh?" Anders asked.

"Yeah, she's lying down upstairs. She says she can't get comfortable enough to sleep through the day, so ends up taking several naps."

Anders nodded. "She's all right though?"

"She says she is," Valerie said with a frown.

"You don't think so?" Anders asked.

Valerie hesitated, but then sighed and shrugged. "What do I know? I'm just a vet. If she says she's fine, she probably is."

Anders was silent for a minute, and then reached out and took her hand in his. "And how are you?"

"Me?" she asked with surprise. "I'm fine."

"So you haven't been avoiding me for the last hour since we finished cleaning the kitchen?" he asked solemnly.

"Has it been an hour?" Valerie asked with surprise. Everyone had stayed to help after eating, but then Lucian had taken Christian, his life mate, and his band members with him and left. He was taking the band members to replace the two teams presently watching Cindy and getting them settled, then taking Christian and Carolyn home before bringing back the men the band members were replacing. The band members didn't have vehicles here to use, so Lucian and Mortimer had come up with just swapping out the teams.

After Lucian had left with them, everyone else had cleared out pretty quickly, the couples all heading home. No one was expecting any activity until tomorrow. They didn't think they'd be able to get the sketch artist back till then. Once they had pictures of the rogue, they would be out showing it around . . . if one of them didn't recognize the man.

Once the last of them had left, Leigh had announced that she needed to lie down. Sam had shown her to a room and Valerie had followed to be sure the woman was all right. She couldn't explain why, but she was just getting the sense that Leigh wasn't feeling well. But Leigh had assured her she was fine and then had started talking to distract her and it appeared Valerie had been up there for an hour chatting with the woman.

"Leigh and I talked for a bit," Valerie admitted. "But I didn't think it was an hour. I'm sorry."

"There's no need to apologize. Leigh's a good person, well worth talking to."

"She *is* nice," Valerie said with a smile. "Nothing like I would have imagined a vampire would be like . . . if I'd have even imagined vampires existed," she added wryly. "But then you're all nice. Well, all of you that I've met since escaping Count Rip-Your-Throat-Out."

"We're just people, Valerie. We have good ones and bad ones and some in between," Anders said quietly.

She shook her head, a crooked smile on her face. "And you're delusional if you think that, Anders."

When alarm crossed his face, she patted his hand soothingly. "I believe you want to believe that. But you aren't 'just people.' 'Just people' don't live centuries or even millennia. They can't see in the dark, or lift a small car with little effort, or read the minds of, and control others. And 'just people' don't need to feed on other 'just people' to survive."

"I—"

"It's all right. You were born this way, so you don't have a clue that you're like a fricking superhero. You probably don't even realize how differently you see things. That your perception of time is so much different than non-immortals because it has so little hold on you," Leigh had mentioned that to her. That one of the things she'd noticed about immortals since becoming one herself was that the old ones had a different concept of time. That what she considered a long time, was a mere twinkling of time to them. Valerie supposed if you lived thousands of years, a day was a blink in time and a week wasn't much more.

Grimacing, she added, "You probably don't realize that you have so many fewer fears and worries than mortals because cancer, and heart disease, and all those other nasty little life stealers can't claim you. And you've surely never been afraid of a mortal doing you harm."

Valerie paused and glanced down at their entwined hands. "Leigh said that to be your life mate I'd have to be turned."

"Yes." His voice was husky. Clearing it, he added, "Though not necessarily right away. Sam didn't turn right away after agreeing to be Mortimer's life mate."

"Leigh told me that too, but said that Mortimer was a mess, constantly worried that Sam would be killed in an accident or something before she agreed to the turn."

"But she wasn't," Anders said. "And I'd be willing to go through that if you needed me to."

Valerie smiled faintly and shook her head. She didn't really want to make him suffer, but she was having trouble with this situation. She hadn't considered that she would have to become a vampire to be with one. Stupid, she supposed. He had told her that Leigh used to be mortal. He'd also told her that he wanted to spend the rest of his life with her. The rest of his life could be a hell of a long time. Certainly, it was longer than the fifty or so years she had left in her. But she hadn't considered that his wanting her to be his life mate included turning her into an immortal until her talk with Leigh. Now the decision to be his life mate was that much bigger.

It wasn't like just saying, "Ah heck, let's give it a go," and then moving in with him, knowing she could always move out. It wasn't even like taking a risk and marrying him. That could be reversed through divorce if it was a mistake. But this was not reversible. She would have to become one of them. And from her talk with Leigh, Valerie knew that wasn't reversible. She had a decision to make that would affect the rest of her life.

Did she want to become a vampire and spend forever with this man?

Cripes, marriages nowadays were lucky to last ten or fifteen years. There were exceptions, of course. The newspaper and the news occasionally ran articles or items on couples who had been together for fifty years or more. But that was the exception, not the rule, and he was asking her to spend a heck of a lot more than fifty years. Try adding a zero or two to that number. Surely even that incredible life mate sex cooled after a millennia or two?

"Leigh said that being turned was the most terrible experience of her life, but turned out to be the best thing that had ever happened to her," Valerie said quietly.

"She's Lucian's life mate. They were meant to be

together. You've seen how perfect they are together and how much they love each other," he said encouragingly.

"But they've only been together less than a handful of years. They're still newlyweds, for heaven's sake," she pointed out.

Anders sighed. "You're right, of course. They haven't been together long," he acknowledged. "But I could take you to meet life mates who have been together millennia if it would help you make your decision."

She glanced to him with surprise. "You know life mates who have been together that long?"

He nodded.

"Are they still happy?" she asked.

"Yes," he assured her, and then frowned and said, "I am not saying they have never argued or fought. But—" He paused when Valerie put one hand up.

Smiling, she tilted her head and simply said, "'White and Nerdy'?" She then assured him, "I understand that a healthy relationship includes disagreements."

Anders smiled, and then squeezed her hand and said, "I know this is a big decision, and I won't put pressure on you to make it quickly. There is no need. I have waited centuries, and I can wait a little longer. However, you can never tell anyone about us."

"Like anyone would believe me," she said with a snort, and then assured him, "Your people and their secrets are safe with me."

"Thank you," Anders said, and leaned forward.

Valerie was sure he was about to kiss her, but at the last moment, he paused, and turned toward the door. She followed his gaze curiously, just in time to see Mortimer appear in the hall outside the door. Leigh had mentioned that immortals had incredible hearing. Obviously that was true. She hadn't heard Mortimer approaching. Heck, she couldn't hear him walking now as he entered and crossed the room, toward them.

"Anders, I need you to go to the airport," the man announced as he paused before them. "I just got word that Bastien put the sketch artist on a United flight and it lands in forty-five minutes, but Sam is out getting groceries and Nicholas and Jo's SUV needed maintenance so I had Justin drive them home. I don't have anyone else to send at the moment but you."

"The sketch artist is on his way already?" Anders asked with surprise. "We didn't expect him until tomorrow."

"Apparently he was available immediately," Mortimer said with a shrug. "But all the company planes were busy, so Bastien sent him on a commercial flight."

"That lands in forty-five minutes," Anders said dryly, standing up. "He couldn't give us any more of a heads-up than that?"

"He said he put the man on the plane himself so he could tend to any mortals who might cause a problem about such a last-minute flight addition. He's been calling Lucian for the last forty-five minutes since successfully getting him on the flight, but Lucian hasn't been answering so he finally called the house."

"Lucian was here an hour ago," Anders said with a frown. "I didn't hear his phone ring."

"His phone is on the kitchen counter at the house, charging," Valerie said, recalling watching him plug in the item as he'd called Marguerite on the house phone.

"Well that explains why Bastien couldn't reach him," Mortimer said with annoyance, and then waved away the irritation. "Whatever. At least I got the message in enough time to get someone there to meet him. At this hour and with Toronto traffic, it will be close, but you should be able to get there just before the flight lands . . . If you leave right away."

"Right," Anders murmured, but turned to look worriedly at Valerie.

"She's safe here," Mortimer said quietly.

"Of course she is." Anders nodded, and then bent and kissed her quickly. Releasing her, he said, "I'll be back as soon as I can."

Valerie nodded, and watched him follow Mortimer out of the room as the other man listed the flight number and gate Anders should go to at the airport. She continued to stand even when they moved out of sight, and didn't sit until she heard the front door close behind them. Sighing, Valerie dropped to sit on the couch then, her thoughts immediately going to the decision she had to make. Spend a lifetime—well, several hundred lifetimes—with the man who had just left, or give him up and go back to her boring, lonely life?

That last part made her frown. She had never thought of her life as boring before this. And she shouldn't now. Normally, she was hip deep in animals, working to heal and cure them. Animals were rarely boring. Or hadn't seemed boring before. But then she supposed it was hard for life as a local vet to compare with the idea of several lifetimes with a vampire. Never aging, never needing to worry about getting sick, never having to watch her diet . . . That last part made her grin.

Leigh was the one who had pointed that out during their hour-long conversation upstairs and it had fascinated Valerie. She had a pretty okay figure, not supermodel skinny or anything. She had a few jiggles and some cellulite, but all in all she didn't hate her body. But she also worked to keep it that way. She wasn't constantly on a diet, but she did diet every couple of months and generally watched what she ate, and refused herself a lot to keep the figure she had. Her eating habits since waking up in Leigh's house had been the worst she'd ever behaved, food-wise. So, the idea of never having to diet again was not an unpleasant one. However, that was not a good excuse to become Anders's life mate.

And, with the opposing factor that her diet would then have to include daily doses of blood . . . Well, that thought wasn't very appealing. It was kind of gross actually, despite Leigh's assurances that she didn't even have to taste it. Just plunk the bag on her teeth like she'd seen Justin do and let the fangs do the work.

Fangs. Valerie grimaced, and then reached up to run a finger across her teeth. How would she look with fangs?

Valerie let her hand drop to her lap at the sound of the front door opening and closing, and watched the hall until Mortimer reappeared.

"He's on his way. He should be back in an hour, or hour and a half," Mortimer announced with a smile.

She nodded, and when Mortimer hesitated, glancing up the hall toward where she knew his office was, she smiled faintly and said, "If you have things you need to do, I can entertain myself."

"Yeah, I do," Mortimer said apologetically. "But there's a television in that cupboard there at the far end of the room. The remote is in the end table drawer. If you'd rather read, there's a library just up the hall with a load of books, and you're welcome to whatever is in the kitchen if you get hungry or thirsty."

"Great," Valerie said lightly. When he still hesitated, she smiled and said gently, "I'll be fine. Go on and get back to work. You don't have to babysit me."

Mortimer let his breath out on a long exhalation and nodded. "Thanks. Shout if you need anything."

"I will," she assured him, and he finally turned and headed out.

The moment he was gone, Valerie sagged back on the couch and closed her eyes. Silence immediately crowded in on her and she blinked her eyes open.

"It's like living with Larry," she muttered, staring at the ceiling and then grimaced at the thought.

Valerie didn't normally mind being alone. After a rushed and busy day in the crush at the clinic, she generally looked forward to getting home to some peace and quiet, but it hadn't always been like that. While she and Larry had lived together . . .

She frowned at the ceiling and sat up. Valerie was uncomfortable because she was in someone else's home. Despite its use as a safe house and headquarters, it was also Mortimer and Sam's home, and one where she didn't even have a room temporarily her own to retreat to. Valerie felt like an inconvenient guest, there due to circumstance. It was how she'd felt with Larry too, she realized now. She'd had this same discomfort the entire time she'd lived with him.

In truth, Valerie suspected that if her parents hadn't died, she and Larry would have split up before they'd finished getting their degrees. But Larry was a nice guy, and his family had welcomed her into their bosom when her parents died, inviting her to Winnipeg for the holidays and so on. She'd become family, and he hadn't had any real reason or motivation to break up with her.

Valerie supposed the life insurance and her inheritance being there to help them start a clinic when they graduated hadn't hurt either. Not that she thought Larry was a gold digger and had consciously stayed with her for that, but, like it or not, it had no doubt been a factor, if only subconsciously.

As for herself, Valerie had clung to Larry like he was a life raft in a storm after losing her parents. She hadn't been madly in love with him, or even infatuated, but she'd liked him well enough and had adored his family . . . and wanted them for her own. It had been enough for the relationship to limp along while they were busy getting their degrees and then starting a clinic. It hadn't been enough once the clinic was up and running.

Valerie supposed she'd known that would be the case all along. She'd known it would end and she'd eventually be on her own in this big scary world. That was probably why she'd always felt uncomfortable. She'd known she was on borrowed time in a way.

She didn't feel like that around Anders. She felt wanted and truly liked by him. She enjoyed his company whether they were just shopping, or chatting over a meal. She felt—

"Damn, trying to get out of that bed made me feel like a beached whale."

Valerie glanced around with surprise at that comment, to see Leigh waddling into the room, holding her stomach as if to keep it from swaying from side to side as she moved. Smiling sympathetically, Valerie stood as she approached. "Couldn't you sleep?"

Leigh grimaced and reached for Valerie's hand when she offered it, clutching it as a counterweight as she lowered herself to sit on the couch. "I'm bloated, gassy, my ankles are crazy swollen, and I'm beyond exhausted, but I can't sleep in a strange bed."

"I'm usually like that too," Valerie admitted. "Although I haven't seemed to have that problem at your house."

Leigh smiled faintly. "Thank you. But you're healing from an injury. You could probably sleep in a doghouse right now."

Valerie chuckled at the words and then eyed Leigh with concern when she shifted on the couch, trying to find a more comfortable position.

"Is there something I can get you?" she offered. "Something to drink, or—?"

"My own bed and Roxy to warm my feet," Leigh interrupted, and when Valerie's eyes widened in shock, she said apologetically, "I'm sorry, is she not allowed on the bed? I didn't think you'd mind, and my feet were cold and she seemed to know it and plopped right on top of them on the blanket. Honestly, she's the best foot warmer ever."

"No, I— She's not normally allowed on the bed, but that's okay. I'm just— I forgot all about her," Valerie admitted with dismay. "The poor thing has been stuck in my room for hours without any food or water or a chance to go outside," she explained guiltily. "How could I forget about her like that?"

"We were busy," Leigh said soothingly, beginning to rock where she sat. "We can fix that right now . . . and get me to my bed so I can rest," she added, rocking forward again.

Valerie stared at her blankly, wondering what on earth she was doing, and then she suddenly realized the woman was trying to get up, but finding it difficult with her stomach in the way.

"Here," she said, taking her arm to help her to her feet. Once she had her upright, Valerie frowned and shook her head. "But I'm afraid we can't go home. Lucian isn't back from dropping everyone off, and Anders just left for the airport."

"Justin can take us," Leigh said, starting across the room.

"He's on an errand for Mortimer. That's why Anders went to the airport. There was no one else to go," Valerie told her, following her to the door.

"Well, hell," Leigh muttered, pausing in the doorway. She pursed her lips with displeasure, and then suggested, "We could always call a taxi."

Valerie grinned at the suggestion, but shook her head. "I somehow don't think the men would like that much."

"No," Leigh agreed on a sigh. "And there's still the rogue to worry about. Having Justin drive us home and hang out until the men get back would be one thing, but I'm in no shape to keep you safe right now and a mortal taxi driver would be less than useless."

"Do you want to try to lie down again?" Valerie suggested. "I could make you a cup of cocoa or hot milk. It might help you fall asleep."

"No, I—" Leigh paused and glanced toward the door as it opened. A wide smile claimed her lips when she saw Justin entering. "Just the man I wanted to see."

Justin paused with the door half open, his expression going wary. "Why?"

"Mortimer has another errand for you," Leigh announced, waddling toward the young immortal at speed.

"What's that?" Justin asked with a frown.

"Taking Valerie and me home," Leigh announced, catching his arm and turning him in the doorway. Using his arm as a crutch, she shuffled down the steps, dragging him with her as she added, "Valerie needs to feed and let Roxy out, and I need to lie down, but the men are both busy, so you're to take us home and stay until they can get there."

"Okay," Justin said, trying to disentangle his arm from her hold. "Just let me talk to Mortimer first."

"You can call him once we're on the road," Leigh announced, hanging on to him tightly.

"But—" he protested dragging his feet.

"Justin, I'm overdue, exhausted, and have to pee. Get me home," Leigh demanded, sounding incredibly cranky.

"Well, for heaven's sake. Let's go back inside so you can pee," he said at once. "I can talk to Mortimer while you're in the bathroom."

"No," Leigh said at once.

"Why?" he asked with exasperation.

Leigh sighed, but then admitted, "I had a devil of a time getting up from the toilet here earlier. I thought I'd have to ask for help. I managed it, but just barely, and I'm not sure I'll be so lucky next time. At home the counter is right beside the toilet to hold on to and help me get up. I want to go home and pee in comfort without the fear of not being able to get up," she admitted, looking miserable.

Valerie bit her lip, now understanding why Leigh seemed so uncomfortable and unhappy. She'd been following them up until then, but now moved up beside her and said gently, "Leigh, I can help you go to the bathroom if you want to go before we head out."

Leigh grimaced. "Thank you, but it's humiliating enough that I'm having trouble getting up and down. I'd really rather not have to resort to having help getting on and off the toilet when we can just go home." Turning to Justin then, she threatened, "And I swear if you don't get me there in ten minutes, I'll either pee on the seat of your SUV, or make *you* come into the washroom of whatever gas station or coffee shop is closest and help me on and off the toilet . . . and then I'll tell Lucian you did."

Justin actually turned green at the threat. He also started moving again. Rushing Leigh forward, he muttered, "I'll call Mortimer on the way."

Valerie bit her lip to keep from laughing and simply followed the pair to a van parked in front of the house.

"My SUV is being serviced along with a couple others, so we're stuck with the van," Justin said apologetically as he helped Leigh into the front seat.

"I'm sure that's fine," Valerie said when Leigh didn't comment. She slid the side door open and climbed in, pulling it closed behind her. Valerie then settled on the backseat on the driver's side. It would allow her to see and talk to Leigh, she thought as she did up her seat belt.

"Sorry," Leigh muttered as Justin closed her door

and rushed around the front of the vehicle. "I know I'm being cranky and difficult."

"No apology necessary," Valerie assured her. "I'd be cranky too if I was bloated, gassy, exhausted, and had to pee."

Leigh smiled faintly, and then sighed. "I've also got terrible heartburn and I've been having Braxton Hicks contractions all afternoon."

Valerie peered at her with concern and asked, "Braxton Hicks are the false alarm labor pains, right?"

"Yes," Leigh said.

Valerie nodded slowly, but then asked, "You're sure they're Braxton Hicks and not the real thing? I mean you *are* overdue."

"Yes," Leigh said, and then frowned. "Well, I'm pretty sure they are. They don't hurt much and have been going on for hours, but haven't gotten any worse than when they started on our way to the Enforcer house."

"You've been having them all evening?" Valerie asked with amazement. It had been three thirty when they'd set out for the Enforcer house. It was now after seven. Leaning forward in her seat, she asked, "Why didn't you say something?"

Leigh clucked impatiently. "You've seen how overprotective and mother-hen-like Lucian is acting. I didn't want him freaking out and making a big deal about it. I'm pretty sure they're just Braxton Hicks. It'll be fine."

"What are Braxton Hicks?" Justin asked, catching the tail end of the conversation as he got into the driver's seat.

"Nothing," Leigh said. "Just get us home. I really have to go."

Justin nodded and started the van to send it cruising down the driveway toward the gate. He then reached into his pocket and pulled out his cell phone.

"Give me that. I'll call," Leigh said at once. "You concentrate on driving."

Justin handed over the phone and Leigh quickly placed the call.

"The answering machine picked up," she said as they waited for the gates to open.

"Mortimer must be on another call," Justin muttered.

"Hmm, I'll leave a message," Leigh said as Justin steered them through the gates and onto the road and immediately laid on the gas. The man was definitely eager to get them back to the house and out of the vehicle, Valerie thought with amusement as he sped up the road.

"Hi Mortimer," Leigh sang out cheerfully. "Just letting you know Justin got back from his errand and is taking us home. I wanted to lie down and Valerie needed to tend to Roxy, so we told him you wanted him to take us. Send Lucian and Anders home when they get back. 'Kay? Later."

"He did want me to take you, didn't he?" Justin asked suspiciously as Leigh pulled the phone away from her ear.

"I'm sure he—oh crap!" she muttered as she went to hit the button to end the call and dropped the phone. Valerie saw it bounce off the woman's knee and then disappear somewhere on the floor in front of her.

"Just leave it," she suggested when Leigh began trying to bend forward to grab it. There was no way she was going to reach it in her condition.

"Oh crap!" Leigh gasped suddenly.

"What is it?" Justin asked, glancing sideways at her with alarm. "Is my phone broken?"

"No, my water is," Leigh muttered.

"What?" he and Valerie said together.

"I guess they weren't Braxton Hicks after all," she muttered. "Damn."

"I—you—are you sure your water broke?" Justin got out finally, his voice high with alarm and his eyes repeatedly moving from the road to her.

"Well, I still have to pee, so I'm guessing the puddle I'm sitting in is amniotic fluid," Leigh said dryly.

"Watch the road, Justin," Valerie said, undoing her seat belt and shifting out of her seat to kneel between the front seats.

"I'm turning around. We're going back to the house," Justin warned, slowing.

"Well, why the heck would you do that?" Leigh asked with irritation. "I need Rachel or Dani. Neither of them are at the house. So who's going to deliver this baby? You?"

"Oh God," Justin muttered, hitting the gas again. "Rachel and Etienne's house is closer. I can have you there in twenty minutes. No, fifteen. Just hang on and don't push or anything."

Valerie grabbed for Leigh's seat, to keep from toppling over as the SUV jerked forward, and then glanced at Leigh with surprise when she began shifting about in her seat, trying to get her legs to the side rather than the front.

"What are you doing?" she asked with alarm.

"I want to move to the backseat," Leigh explained. "I can spread out more. And the seat won't be wet."

"Well, here, let me help," Valerie said, shifting at

once to get out of the way and taking her arm to help her. Much to her relief, they managed the move to the backseat without being tossed about unduly or thrown through the front windshield by Justin stopping abruptly. She then helped Leigh with her seat belt before doing up her own. After that, all she could do was hold Leigh's hand and try not to whimper as her fingers were crushed with each contraction. She was alarmingly aware that the crushing seemed to be coming at rather regular and quickly decreasing intervals as they traveled. But she didn't hit panic mode until Leigh began to groan and cry out along with the crushing.

Valerie didn't think she'd heard words more beautiful than, "We're here," when Justin uttered them. She glanced out the window at the house he stopped in front of, and then glanced quickly to Leigh as the woman gasped and crushed her fingers again.

"Oh God!" Leigh cried out with pain, and then snapped bitterly, "Why do we women have to have the babies? Men should have them. What did we ever do to deserve this?"

"Eve ate the apple," Justin responded, braking and shifting the van into park.

"Shut up, Justin, or I swear I'll shove an apple up your—"

"Ow, ow, ow," Valerie cried out as Leigh nearly pulverized the bones in her fingers.

"Sorry," Leigh muttered, releasing her fingers. "I was trying not to squeeze too tight."

"That's okay," Valerie said weakly.

"I'll go get Etienne and Rachel," Justin announced, opening the door. "I don't think we're going to be able to get Leigh in the house without help."

"That's because I'm a beached whale," Leigh moaned, suddenly sounding teary.

"No, honey," Valerie said quickly. "He's just worried about you having a contraction while we're walking you in. It's better if we have someone to help us carry you in."

Leigh snorted with disbelief, all sign of tears gone and irritation in their place again. "Justin could carry me with one hand. He's just scared I'll bite him or something."

"I'm sure, he—" Valerie didn't bother finishing. Leigh had gasped in pain again and was now hunched forward, head bowed as she clutched desperately at her stomach. Undoing her seat belt, she shifted to kneel in front of her, ready to help when the men got back.

"Breathe," she said, rubbing Leigh's upper arm and shoulder, but she frowned when the front door opened again. Continuing to rub Leigh's shoulder, she said, "I thought you were getting Etienne?"

When the engine started, Valerie joined Leigh in groaning. Etienne and Rachel must not be home, she thought with dismay and said, "Maybe we should just go to the hospital."

"We can't go to the hospital. Nanos," Leigh gasped between pants.

"Right," Valerie muttered. Turning, on her knees so she could look at Justin, she said, "How far is Dani and Decker's from here? Dani—"

Her voice died as she stared at the driver. It wasn't Justin.

"Oh crap," Valerie breathed.

Eighteen

"What?" Anders stared at Mortimer, his brain completely blank as he tried to accept the news he'd just been given.

"Valerie and Leigh told Justin that he was supposed to take them home—"

"Yeah, yeah, I caught that," Anders interrupted tersely, his brain kicking back into gear. "Skip forward to the part where some white-haired guy drives away with my life mate and Leigh. Who the hell is he?"

"We think it's the rogue." Mortimer steered the SUV through the gates and onto the road.

"Of course," he muttered, and then asked grimly, "How long ago?"

"Justin called me from Etienne's phone the minute it happened. That was at almost twenty minutes after seven. I checked the clock," he added dryly, and then muttered, "Although I don't know why."

Anders shook his head at how quickly life could

change. All had been right with his world just moments ago when he'd arrived back at the house with the sketch artist. He'd thought Valerie was safe, and that things were going well there. He'd had great hope that the sketch would be done, they'd identify and collect the rogue, and that with a little time Valerie would agree to be his life mate. But as he'd got out of the SUV, Mortimer had strode out, headed for another SUV waiting in front of the house. The head of the Enforcers hadn't even slowed. He'd barked at Sam to take care of the sketch artist, and then ordered Anders into the truck and had headed out the moment his butt had hit the seat. Anders hadn't even had his door closed yet. He'd known then that there was trouble, but certainly hadn't expected this. He'd left Valerie safe and secure at the Enforcer house. She should still be there. She wasn't. He was still trying to wrap his mind around that.

"They're in the van, and all our vehicles have GPS," Mortimer pointed out, eyes on the road they were racing down. "There's a tracking program in the computer on the floor between us. They were headed south when I left the house. Check it and see where they are now, then call Justin and Lucian and tell them where to go."

"Lucian knows?" Anders asked, reaching for the open computer on the floor.

"He'd just left Marguerite's when I called there. He didn't have his cell phone," Mortimer reminded him. "Christian and Carolyn chased him down and are riding with him. It's Christian's number you'll have to call. Use my phone. It's programmed in there," he added, pulling his phone from his pocket and passing it over.

Anders took the phone, but his attention was on the computer on his lap. It had gone into standby mode. As he waited impatiently for it to start up again, he muttered, "I should have told her."

"Told who what?" Mortimer asked, distractedly.

"Valerie, I should have told her I love her. But I figured she'd think it was too soon and—" He didn't bother finishing. The computer was back on line. He stared at the moving dots on the screen. "Which one is the van?"

"The green one," Mortimer answered.

"Still heading south. He's on the 401," Anders announced, and then started punching numbers on the phone to let the others know.

"**W**hat are you doing? Both of you back in your seats now."

Valerie ignored that order from the man who had hijacked the van, and continued to help Leigh around the bench seat to the open area in the back. "She's in labor. She needs to lie down."

"Get back in your seats or I'll take control of you and make you get back in your seats," came the steely response.

"Oh, stuff it," Leigh snapped. "I have a beach ball trying to squeeze its way out of me. I'm lying down and there isn't a damned thing you can do about it. You can't control her and drive too, and you can't control me at all . . . I hope," she muttered under her breath.

The rogue didn't respond, but Valerie hardly noticed. She was glancing at Leigh worriedly as they moved to the back in a crouch. She whispered, "Can immortals control each other?"

"I think really old ones can control younger ones sometimes," Leigh admitted reluctantly in a whisper of her own. "At least, Marguerite's first husband controlled her."

"Oh," Valerie murmured unhappily and glanced around for something to lay on the floor of the van. Spotting a blanket and first aid kit strapped under the backseat, she grabbed both and quickly opened and spread out the blanket.

"Here, Leigh, let me help you," Valerie said, moving to take her arm to help her lower herself onto the blanket.

"Don't worry, Lucian and the boys will come for us," Leigh reassured her as Valerie then knelt beside her.

"What if they don't come in time?" Valerie asked.

"They will," she said firmly.

"Well, just in case they don't, I think we should come up with a plan of our own," Valerie suggested, crouching next to her and glancing around for a possible weapon.

"Yeah," Leigh agreed through gritted teeth. "Just don't think about it much in case he reads your mind."

"Right," Valerie muttered and began to recite song lyrics in her head. The first song to come to mind was "Ridin'." Only instead of *Ridin' dirty*, the chorus kept turning into *White and nerdy* in her head. It was kind of annoying.

"I wish Dani or Rachel were here," Leigh said on a sigh as her contraction ended.

"Sorry," Valerie murmured, and then to distract her, she asked, "Who is Rachel?"

"She's Etienne's life mate. He's Lucian's nephew. She works in the morgue, but she's a doctor too," Leigh explained.

Valerie nodded, but commented, "Lucian seems to have loads of nieces and nephews."

"Yes, he—ahhhhh!" Leigh shrieked and grabbed Valerie's shoulder, fingers digging in so hard, it made her cry out in pain too and fear they would punch right through her skin. Dear God, she was strong.

"Breathe," Valerie said in a strained voice once the worst of the contraction ended and the fingers in her shoulder eased.

"I *am* breathing," Leigh gasped.

"Of course you are," Valerie said soothingly, her eyes shifting around the van again. She didn't see anything they could use as a weapon, but she had an idea she was trying hard not to think about. If she could just find an excuse to go back to the front of the van—

"We should . . . time the . . . contractions," Leigh panted.

"Good idea," Valerie agreed absently. If nothing else it would keep Leigh busy. And then glancing to her sharply, she asked, "Do you have a watch?"

"No."

"Neither do I." She tried not to sound too happy about that as she peered over her shoulder to the front of the van. Their kidnapper probably had one.

"Valerie?"

"Hmm?" She turned back and leaned closer when Leigh tugged on her hand.

"Scream," she whispered, staring her in the eye. Leigh then let out a long, agonized shriek again. She didn't, however, grab for Valerie's shoulder or hand again, but simply met her gaze calmly and began to beetle her eyebrows up and down until Valerie caught on and began to shriek along with her.

"Shut up back there," their hijacker growled.

Leigh let her shriek die off slowly, and when Valerie too fell silent, snapped out a suggestion to their hijacker that was really physically impossible.

"I'm in labor," she barked. "It hurts. I'm going to scream my head off. If you don't like it, let us go."

She then let out another howl of pain. This one was real though. Valerie could tell by the fact that Leigh had latched on to and was crushing her wrist. Damn, she was going to be lucky to get out of this without broken bones, and not from their kidnapper, Valerie thought, shrieking along with the woman.

The van immediately filled with loud music. Classical, and cranked all the way up, to try to drown out the racket they were making, Valerie supposed. And that had been exactly what Leigh had been hoping for, she realized when Leigh's shriek ended a moment later on a grunt of satisfaction and she pulled Valerie closer to hiss, "We need to get out of here."

Valerie nodded. She was pretty sure the rogue hadn't kidnapped them to return her to her cage and feed off her slowly again. He was probably worried about her having seen the portrait. So worried that he'd risked taking Leigh. He couldn't let either of them go now.

"He must plan on killing both of us," Leigh added. "I've seen him."

"I know," Valerie agreed, not at all sure Leigh could hear her over the music. She was hardly able to hear Leigh and was mostly reading her lips.

"And the baby," Leigh added, glancing down and rubbing her stomach. "We can't let him kill the baby."

"No, of course not," she said soothingly.

Valerie was just thinking how amazing it was that mothers bonded with their child even before birth, when Leigh added grimly, "Not after I've gone through all this crap to carry it to term."

"Ah," Valerie murmured and wondered if it was the hormones talking right now, or Leigh was possessed. Honestly, this was not the woman who had been her host since she'd woken up from her fever. But whether it was hormones or possession, Valerie couldn't say. She didn't have a lot of experience with pregnant mothers, at least not of the two-legged variety. Dogs, cats, horses, and cows just didn't act like this.

"The SUVs all have weapons and blood cases," Leigh hissed. "Maybe the van does too."

"I don't see anything," Valerie muttered, glancing around again.

"Check the floor and side panels. They hide them in case the vehicles are stolen by mortals."

"Smart," Valerie commented and began to crawl around the floor, tapping here and there and then feeling along the wall. She was about to give up, when she noted a seam in the side panel on the side of the van where she was feeling around. Valerie peered at it briefly, and then pressed along the edges. When that had no effect, she instinctively pressed her fingers in and dragged them to the left. A little puff of relief slid through her when the panel moved, opening a couple of inches.

Valerie glanced nervously toward the front of the van, but the bench seat was offering her cover, so she slid the panel further open and bit her lip as she stared at what she'd revealed. Under the thin panel was a toolboard, a panel with rows of small holes in it where tools were clipped into place: screwdrivers, wrenches, hacksaws, hammers, mallets, tape . . .

"Take the saw," Leigh advised, crawling up beside her. "You can hack off his head."

Valerie cast her a look of disbelief, and then took down a mallet and the duct tape instead. Setting them both on the floor, she slid the panel shut and turned back to Leigh. "We need to find a way to brace you in case we swerve or something."

Both of them considered the space, and then Valerie suggested, "Turn sideways and brace yourself between the wheel wells."

Leigh shifted to do as suggested, bracing her feet against one wheel well, but it wasn't wide enough for her to lie flat. It was only about four feet and four or five inches by Valerie's guess. The other wheel well came up an inch or two below the base of Leigh's neck.

Valerie leaned over her and suggested, "Bend your legs and lay your back and head flat."

She hadn't been sure Leigh would hear her over the music, but apparently she could. That or she was reading lips too, because Leigh did as instructed.

"Do you think you can brace yourself like that?" Valerie asked uncertainly.

Leigh hesitated, and then raised her hands, placing them against the van wall on either side of her head. She followed that up by pressing her feet against the metal above the wheel wells on the opposite wall. She tensed briefly, pushing into both surfaces and then relaxed and nodded at Valerie.

"Right." Valerie managed an encouraging smile and then glanced toward the front of the van, but turned back when Leigh suddenly grabbed her arm just below the elbow. She understood why when Leigh began to shriek and squeeze.

Valerie groaned and waited for the latest contraction to end, then quickly stuffed the duct tape and mallet down the front of her jeans and said, "We really need to time these. I'll see if Count Rip-Your-Throat-Out has a watch."

Not wanting to sound like she was up to something, she said it in a normal speaking voice, hoping their hijacker's immortal hearing would pick it up despite the loud music. Then she exchanged a glance with Leigh and shifted to a crouch, bending forward to hide the lumps in the front of her pants as she started back up toward the front of the van again. The whole way she just kept thinking, "I need a watch, I need a watch, we have to time these contractions, I need a watch," over and over in the hopes that there wouldn't be any vestiges of her plan in her surface thoughts.

Valerie didn't know if he caught a glimpse of her in the rearview mirror, or just sensed her approach, but she was just moving around the bench seat when the rogue shouted something at her.

She couldn't hear him over the loud music, but suspected he was telling her to get back in the back. Ironic, since just moments ago he'd wanted them to stay in their seats, she thought, but simply yelled, "I can't hear you. We need a watch."

He shouted again and turned to glare at her as she continued forward, but she shook her head, pointed at her ear, and yelled, "Can't hear you! We need a watch! I have to time her contractions!"

Jerking impatiently forward, he snapped off the

music and began to yell again, just as Leigh began to shriek.

Pausing, Valerie turned and leaned over the back-seat, resting one knee on it as she peered back at Leigh. Relief coursed through her when she saw her expression and realized she was faking it. A moment later though, that relief died when Leigh's eyes suddenly widened and the shriek grew louder as a real contraction hit her.

Damn, I am never having babies, Valerie thought with dismay as Leigh clutched at her stomach and began to almost writhe on the floor in agony.

"There's something wrong," Leigh gasped as soon as she could speak.

Valerie hesitated, torn between hurrying back to the woman and continuing forward. But forward was the only answer. He'd kill them all while she was busy trying to deliver the baby if she went back now. When Leigh relaxed again with a moan as the contraction ended, and then immediately braced herself again, Valerie felt every muscle in her own body tighten. It was a go.

"Get in the back!"

Valerie grabbed the center seat belt with her left hand and weaved it around to wrap the belt twice around her wrist as she slid the mallet out of the top of her pants. She then pushed herself off the bench seat and swung back toward the driver's seat, keeping the mallet down, and, she hoped, out of his sight.

"I need to borrow your watch to time the contractions," she said grimly as her gaze slid over the road ahead. They were on the highway, but he was slowing and steering onto an off-ramp, she saw. Her eyes shifted to the speedometer as it dropped from one hundred kilometers an hour to ninety . . . eighty . . . seventy . . .

They were in the curve, still going too fast, but the speed was still dropping when he suddenly turned his head toward her. For some reason, that seemed ominous to Valerie. Afraid that he was going to read her, or—even worse—take control of her, she tightened her hold on the seat belt and swung the mallet at his head.

You'd have thought she'd hit the steering wheel and spun it herself with the mallet rather than slamming it into his temple. His head whipped to the left, but so did the steering wheel. Valerie cried out and dropped the mallet, grabbing for the front passenger seat instead to keep from flying around as the van shot off the road, and toward a line of trees ten feet to the side of it.

Despite the burning pain in her wrist and along her left arm as the seat belt jerked at her hold, Valerie was glad she'd had the forethought to entangle her wrist in it. Otherwise, she surely would have flown out the front window. As it was, she bounced around between the seats, slamming into one padded surface and then another as they careened over the grassy veldt, and then they slammed into a tree.

Valerie screamed as she was thrown forward on impact, sure her arm had been dislocated. She then nearly bit off her tongue as she fell backward onto the bench seat. She didn't stay there long once they came to a halt. She knew she couldn't afford to and pushed herself forward off the seat, crashing to her knees on the floor as she reached for the dropped mallet.

She wanted to check on Leigh. Valerie thought she'd heard the other woman scream during the accident, but had been screaming herself so couldn't be sure. However, there was no time to check on her just then. Count Rip-Your-Throat-Out appeared a little dazed from her blow, but the airbag had prevented his gaining any more injuries, and he was stirring.

Grabbing the mallet, Valerie straightened and hit him with it again, this time on top of his head. Much to her relief, he moaned and collapsed against the deflated airbag and steering wheel.

"Leigh?" she shouted, pulling out the duct tape. "Are you all right?"

A groan sounded from the back and Valerie frowned, but quickly began duct taping the driver to his seat, drawing the tape across his chest, around the back of the seat, and then across his chest over and over again in quick succession as she shouted, "Hang on. I'll be right there . . . Okay?" she added worriedly.

Another groan sounded, and Valerie bit her lip, but ran the tape around a dozen more times before deciding it was good. Leaving the tape hanging down the back of the seat, she then braced herself on both the driver's seat and the backseat for leverage as she staggered half upright.

Much to her surprise, Valerie's legs nearly gave out beneath her. Gritting her teeth, she forced them straight and began to move around the bench seat in a crouch.

Leigh was lying on the floor clutching her stomach, but it looked like she hadn't been banged around too terribly badly. At least Valerie didn't see any lacerations or bumps or bruises.

"The rogue?" Leigh gasped with concern as Valerie knelt beside her.

"I duct taped him to his seat," she assured her. "How are you doing?"

Leigh's eyes went wide with alarm. "That won't hold him. He's immortal."

Valerie frowned and glanced toward the front of the van, but couldn't see him past the bench seat from that angle. Biting her lip, she rose up on her knees to get a better view, relieved to see that he wasn't moving. Turning back, she said, "I knocked him out first."

"He won't stay unconscious long and the tape won't hold him when he wakes up," Leigh said. "Go check that he isn't awake already."

"He doesn't look to be," Valerie assured her turning away for another look anyway.

"He could be faking it. If he wakes up, he'll kill us all," the last was said in almost a scream as she clutched at her stomach.

Another contraction, Valerie realized with concern.

Grinding her teeth a moment later as the contraction apparently began to ease, Leigh growled, "There's something wrong with the baby. I need you here, but not if he isn't out of commission. Go cut his head off or something."

"What?" Valerie asked with disbelief. "Who do you think I am? The Queen of Hearts?"

"No, if you were you'd already have cut his head off," Leigh snapped and then groaned in agony.

Valerie hesitated, her gaze shooting from Leigh to the driver, and then she sighed and shifted to her feet, muttering, "Hang on."

Mallet in hand, she moved quickly back around the bench seat to peer worriedly at the rogue. He appeared to be just as she'd left him, but then Valerie thought she saw one eyelid twitch. Afraid he was faking still being unconscious as Leigh had said, she slammed the mallet into his head again. She was satisfied that she'd been right when a little sigh slipped from his lips and his head sagged further forward. He had been faking it. Crap. What was she supposed to do here? She couldn't cut off his head. That was just—

"Damn," Valerie muttered, and then glanced sharply toward the back of the van when Leigh cried out again. This was ridiculous. She couldn't watch the rogue and Leigh too with the seat in the way. And she couldn't cut off an unconscious man's head, rogue or not.

Cursing, she peered at the bench seat, noting the latching legs. Valerie then peered to the sliding side door. They'd crashed head-on into the tree, hitting it with the front driver's side. There was nothing blocking the door. Moving to it, she grabbed the handle and opened it, sliding it back until it locked into place, then she moved back in front of the bench seat.

Valerie started to kneel, but then turned to the rogue and smashed the mallet into his skull again just to be safe. Satisfied that she had a couple minutes at least, she then knelt and quickly pulled up the handles to free the seat.

"What are you doing?" Leigh gasped out as the contractions ended.

"The best I can," Valerie said simply as she began to maneuver the seat toward the door. She managed to get it to the mouth of the door with some effort, and then just shoved it out to somersault across the grass.

Leaving the door open, Valerie then turned back to hammer the rogue in the head again. She didn't feel bad for doing it. He was immortal. They healed. Besides, it was better than trying to cut his head off with a hacksaw. The very thought made her shudder as she turned to head back to Leigh in a crouch.

"Okay, I'm going to pull you up behind the seats," she announced, bending to grab the corners of the blanket Leigh lay on. As she dragged her up the van, she added, "That way I can keep hitting him while trying to help you."

For some reason, her words made Leigh laugh. Mind you, the sound was a bit hysterical, Valerie noted.

Once she had Leigh directly behind the front seats, Valerie released the blanket, and then turned, and smacked the rogue over the head again, which just made Leigh laugh harder. Shaking her head, Valerie quickly leaned over the front passenger seat to look for the phone Leigh had dropped earlier.

"What are you doing now?" Leigh asked through her laughter.

"Looking for Justin's phone to call for help. It should be here somewhere. You— Ah ha!" she exclaimed as she spotted it.

"Christ!" Anders cursed into the phone as he spotted the crashed van in the trees beside the curve. Mortimer had driven like the wind to catch up to the other vehicle. Anders had been on the phone with Lucian when he'd seen the van's blinker come on, and had immediately told him the exit number for the off-ramp they were taking. He'd then hung up to call Justin on Etienne's phone and give him the same information.

"What is it?" Justin asked with concern on the other end of the line.

Anders didn't explain. "Get Rachel here as quickly as you can," he barked, and ended the call.

"Is that the bench seat?" Mortimer asked, a frown in his voice. "Why the hell is he throwing it out?"

"Who cares? Hurry up, dammit. They need us." Anders snapped, dumping the computer on the floor and climbing out of his seat. He grunted and dropped to his knees on the backseat when Mortimer steered the SUV off the road and began to bump quickly across the uneven grass. Leaning over the seat then, he reached down to open the weapons locker. Anders had just retrieved two guns when his phone began to ring. Shifting the guns to one hand, he pulled his phone out and frowned when he saw Justin's name on the caller I.D.

"What?" he barked impatiently.

"Semmy?"

No one had ever called him that but Valerie. If he hadn't recognized her voice, that would have told him who it was, but he did recognize her voice, as well as the stress in it. He heard a muffled, "Who's Semmy?" in a voice he suspected was Leigh's.

"Valerie, honey?" he said, before she could answer. "Are you okay?"

Turning on the seat, he peered toward the van as Mortimer came to a halt behind it.

"Yes," Valerie said, and then blurted, "We were carjacked by the rogue."

"I know, honey," Anders said, wishing he could somehow pull her through the phone to safety. No doubt the rogue had spotted their approach and made her call to tell them to back off. Mortimer must suspect as much as well. He'd put the SUV in park, but then had turned in the seat to listen to his side of the conversation, waiting to hear what the situation was.

"You do?" she sounded surprised. "Well—"

"Valerie!" Leigh cried in the background.

"Damn," Valerie cursed, and then there was a clatter as the phone was dropped and sounds in the background, including a loud thwack that made Anders peer desperately at the van, trying to see what was happening through the small, blackened back windows.

"Sorry," Valerie muttered a moment later.

"I swear I saw his eyelid twitch," Leigh's voice came faintly, and Anders frowned. He didn't understand what she was talking about, but it was more the sound of her voice that bothered him. It was like she was talking through gritted teeth, and then either she or Valerie began to shriek and there was another clatter as the phone was dropped again.

"Valerie?" Anders shouted.

"Who's screaming?" Mortimer asked, able to hear it from where he sat.

Cursing, Anders handed Mortimer one of the guns, shoved the other into the top of his jeans and then turned and pulled the door beside him open. He still had the phone pressed to his ear and was shouting Valerie's name as he climbed out of the SUV. Anders pulled his gun as he ran toward the van, vaguely aware that Mortimer had jumped out of the SUV and was following.

Anders saw that the sliding side door was still open as he neared it and ran right up to it; phone still to his ear, terror in his heart, and gun in his hand . . . and then he just stood there, staring. Inside, Leigh was hunched on the van floor, clutching Valerie's hand and shrieking. Valerie was on her knees, howling along with the woman, but even as he looked in, she turned and thumped the driver's seat with what appeared to be a mallet.

Not the driver's seat, he realized as she lowered the mallet and sank to sit on her heels. It was the rogue she'd thumped.

"Well, hell," Mortimer muttered beside him. "Looks like the girls saved themselves."

Nineteen

"**I** need my phone."

Anders barely heard the words over the screams coming from the van, but turned blankly to glance at Mortimer, who was holding out his hand.

"It's stuck to your ear," Mortimer said helpfully. "I want to call Lucian and let him know we've caught up to the women and they're alive."

"Right." Anders lowered the phone and handed it over. He then watched Mortimer walk around the van toward the driver's side, punching in numbers.

Sighing with relief as the shrieks from the women began to slow and grow less vociferous, Anders shoved the gun down the back of his pants and stepped up to the open side door of the van. But he waited for it to end altogether before asking, "Are you both all right?"

Valerie's head jerked his way, her eyes wide and mouth open. Obviously she hadn't realized they were right behind the van when she'd called him.

But then the back windows of the van were high and she wouldn't have been able to see through them, kneeling as she was.

"How did you get here so fast?" she asked, retrieving her hand from Leigh's now loose grip and wincing as she rubbed it. Spotting the impressions in her hand from Leigh's squeezing, Anders began to understand why she'd been shrieking. He *had* wondered. Leigh's screaming he'd understood, but he hadn't been sure if Valerie was just screaming in sympathy with her or what.

"We were right behind you when you called," Anders explained, his gaze shooting to the driver's side window when Mortimer appeared there. Apparently, he'd finished his call. Now, the man reached through the window to grab the rogue's head and turn it his way so he could examine him. In the next moment, he jerked his arm back out the window with a shouted, "Whoa!" as Valerie suddenly grabbed up the mallet and turned to whack the rogue again, nearly pulverizing Mortimer's hand in the process.

"Oh," Valerie said, sounding surprised. "Sorry, I heard movement and thought he was stirring again."

Anders bit his lip and leaned into the van. "Maybe you should give me that."

Valerie handed over the mallet with apparent relief, and then said, "We have to get Leigh to either Rachel or Dani. She's in labor and it's not going well."

"Etienne and Justin are bringing Rachel right now. They should be here soon," he assured her, his gaze finally moving to Leigh. The woman lay shaking on the van floor, her face pale and sweaty. He'd smelled blood since moving up to the open door and had at first assumed it was from the rogue's head wound, but he was beginning to think perhaps it was coming from Leigh as well. The smell was strong when he leaned in to peer at her.

"Leigh? Are you all right?" he asked.

Leigh moaned and shook her head weakly where she lay. "I think something's wrong. It hurts too much."

Anders frowned, but kept his concern out of his voice as he said, "Hang on. Rachel will be here soon."

When she didn't respond, he shifted where he stood, feeling useless. It was Valerie who bent over the woman and asked, "Is there any way we can make you more comfortable until she gets here?"

"You can get that bastard out of the front seat and cut his head off," Leigh said weakly.

Valerie grimaced and glanced to Anders, saying, "She's delirious. She keeps thinking I'm Jeffrey Dahmer or something."

"No. It's the Queen of Hearts, remember?" Leigh said on a weak laugh, and then added wearily, "Just get him out of here and make sure he doesn't escape or rise up and kill us all while you three are distracted watching me try to squeeze out Lucian's humongous progeny."

"On it," Mortimer announced, opening the driver's side door when Anders glanced his way.

"Need a hand?" Anders asked hopefully.

"No, I— Jesus, you wrapped him up in duct tape," Mortimer said with disgust, and began ripping at the silver tape, muttering the whole time about the job being worse than Justin's gift wrapping.

Shaking his head, Anders turned his attention back to the women as Valerie urged Leigh to the opposite side of the van so she could lean up against the side panel. His gaze dropped to the spot where she'd been lying and he frowned and leaned in, feeling the darker patch in the middle of the blanket. It was huge, and glistening, and his hand came away red with blood.

"Mortimer!" he barked, straightening.

The Enforcer paused with the rogue half out of his seat and raised an eyebrow. "Problem?"

Anders turned his hand for him to see. "Is there blood in the SUV?"

Mortimer's mouth tightened and he shook his head. "This was all unexpected. The only thing I grabbed was the computer on the way out." He dumped the rogue back in his seat, and pulled his phone back out of his pocket. "I'll call Lucian and see if he has blood. If he doesn't, maybe Rachel will have thought to grab some."

"Don't bother. You can ask Lucian in person," Anders said as the sound of a slowing engine drew his gaze toward the road in time to see an SUV steer onto the grass, heading their way. Lucian was at the wheel.

Grunting, Mortimer put his phone away and dragged the rogue out to heft him over his shoulder. He then carried his burden out of view as he headed for the arriving vehicle. Anders watched until Mortimer appeared at the back of the van, and then turned his attention to the interior of the van as Valerie left Leigh and crawled across the van to him.

"How long until Rachel gets here?" she asked worriedly. "There's something really wrong and Leigh's losing strength fast."

"Can you help her?" Anders asked with a frown. He knew Justin, Etienne, and Rachel were a good ten minutes behind Lucian. Rachel had insisted on taking the time to get a medical kit of everything she might need together before leaving the house. Justin had mentioned that in one of the calls.

"I don't know. I might be able to help her," Valerie said cautiously. "And I was going to offer, but she keeps saying she wishes Rachel or Dani were here and I'm not sure she'd be comfortable with my examining her."

"Rachel and Dani aren't here," Anders said quietly. "You are."

"Where is she?" Lucian suddenly loomed beside them, worry knitting his brow.

"Inside," Anders said, and caught Valerie by the waist to lift her out of the van and out of the way. He'd barely set her feet on the ground when Leigh screamed out again and began to writhe in the van.

Lucian was inside and at her side in the blink of an eye, his face almost as bloodless as Leigh's as he scooped her into his lap and held her through the pain.

"Valerie," Lucian barked the minute Leigh's shrieks ended and she sank into an exhausted heap in his arms.

Anders lifted Valerie back into the van, and followed to kneel on one side of Lucian as Valerie knelt on the other.

"Something's wrong," Lucian growled. "Leigh's in too much pain."

Despite the concerns she'd mentioned to Anders, Valerie tried to soothe the man, saying, "Leigh is in labor, Lucian. It's painful."

"Not this painful," he said firmly.

"She's lost a lot of blood, Valerie," Anders said quietly. "There shouldn't be this much blood."

"Blood?" Valerie glanced to him with surprise and he realized that she hadn't noticed the blood. He should have realized, of course. Her senses weren't as acute as his and the blanket was dark, as was the black and red maternity dress Leigh wore.

Anders gestured to the large slightly darker spot on the blanket and she stared at it blankly, and then turned back to Lucian. "Where is Rachel?"

"Too far away to help right now," Lucian said grimly. "Help her."

Valerie glanced to Leigh uncertainly and asked, "Is it all right if I examine you?"

"Just make it stop," Leigh begged.

That was enough for Valerie. Shoulders straightening, she glanced to Anders and said, "Check the first-aid kit and see if you can find hand sanitzers, or wound cleaners or something."

Anders nodded and moved to do as she asked, but his attention was on her as she then turned to Lucian and said, "Remove her panties and turn her to sit between your legs. You can support her back and comfort her while I examine her."

Lucian did as instructed, quickly tugging down Leigh's panties and then settling her on the blanket on the van floor between his legs. He then wrapped his arms around her gently, resting them over her stomach as he pressed a kiss to the side of her temple and murmured encouragingly to her.

"Anders, have you found anything I can use to clean my hands?" Valerie asked, as she knelt at Leigh's feet and arranged her legs, setting her feet outside of Lucian's legs so that her knees were bent and his legs acted like stirrups of a sort, keeping her from closing her legs.

"Don't worry about cleaning your hands," Lucian growled.

"But she could get an infection and—" Valerie paused and shook her head. "Right. Immortal. The nanos will take care of any infection," she muttered.

Anders turned his attention back to the first-aid kit as Valerie began her examination. He rifled through the contents in search of anything that might be useful, but didn't expect to find anything. Mostly, he wanted to give Leigh some semblance of privacy.

"The baby is sideways," Valerie announced suddenly, her voice grim. "Christ, she's bleeding badly. Where the hell is Rachel?"

"Get the baby out," Lucian barked and Valerie jerked her head up to peer at him.

"She needs a cesarean section, Lucian. I don't have the equipment to do that."

"Can't you turn the baby yourself?" Anders asked.

Valerie frowned. "Maybe if her water hadn't broken, and I had the right drugs to make her uterus relax . . . and an epidural to ease her discomfort. But . . ."

"She's already in agony, Valerie. You can't hurt her any more than she's already suffering," Lucian said grimly. "And you have to get the baby out now if it is to live."

"What?" Valerie stared at him in shock. "But he's an immortal baby. I thought that meant survival would be a sure thing?"

"It usually is," Anders said quietly, dragging the first-aid kit with him as he moved over to join them.

"Fetuses with any genetic anomalies are aborted by the nanos during the first trimester, but after that, so long as the mother takes in enough blood, the baby is fine."

"Well then—" Valerie began.

"She's losing too much blood," Lucian interrupted. "And if the nanos see the baby as a threat to Leigh's well-being, they will attack and try to kill the baby. The baby's nanos will fight back. If enough damage is done and the nanos kill each other off we could lose one or even both of them."

When Valerie stared at Lucian with incomprehension, Anders said, "Think of it like a nuclear war inside the body. So long as no one launches, everything is peachy. But if the nukes are launched, or in this case, the nanos start attacking each other, no one gets out alive."

"Jesus," Valerie breathed, going pale.

"Can you get the baby out?" Anders asked quietly.

Valerie hesitated. "We could try a cesarean section, but I'd need a knife and—"

"That would increase the blood loss and raise the risk of the nanos attacking before you can get the baby out," Lucian interrupted. "We need to turn the baby and get it out now."

Valerie stared at him silently, but then said, "She's fully dilated. I can try to turn the baby manually, but it's risky and you'll need to hold her still."

Lucian nodded once.

Sighing, Valerie hesitated and then turned and crawled out of the van. Standing in the open door, she patted the floor of the van. "Bring her forward."

When Lucian moved both himself and Leigh to the edge of the van, Valerie nodded and knelt in the grass, but before she could do anything, another contraction hit Leigh and she arched in Lucian's arms, shrieking her head off.

"Help her!" Lucian shouted.

"I have to wait for the contraction to end," Valerie said helplessly and they all waited. It seemed to Anders to go on forever, but finally, Leigh's screaming ended on a moan and she passed out in Lucian's arms.

"Spread her legs more and keep them open," Valerie said at once and then set to work the moment Lucian complied.

Anders held his breath as he waited behind the couple. He knew exactly what Valerie was doing, she was using a technique he'd seen used ages ago on a mare in trouble. She was physically easing her hand in to try to turn the baby's head down so it could be born. He also knew that if another contraction hit Leigh while Valerie's hand was inside her . . . well, immortal muscles crushing down around a mortal's bones was never a good thing, Anders thought grimly and then glanced past her when Mortimer appeared.

"Justin's just pulling— Whoa!" Mortimer interrupted himself and turned abruptly away as he realized what he'd walked up on.

"See if they have blood," Lucian barked and then turned his attention to Valerie when she frowned and said, "There's something pressing down on . . ."

"Pressing down on what?" Anders asked, when she paused a semi-perplexed look on her face. In the next moment, her eyes suddenly widened and she exclaimed, "There's a second baby pressing down on the first. It's why the baby couldn't turn."

"Twins!" Mortimer exclaimed, forgetting himself and turning back, only to turn green and swing abruptly away. "I'll fetch the blood if they have any."

Valerie's face was scrunched up with concentration. "I think I can—that should do it," she muttered and leaned back slightly.

"What did you do and did it work?" Anders asked. Valerie didn't bother to answer, Leigh's sudden shriek would have drowned it out anyway. In the next moment, Lucian and Leigh's first child was lying silent and still in Valerie's hands.

"Is he all right?" Lucian asked anxiously, cradling Leigh and rocking her gently from side to side as she sank back against him.

"She's alive," Valerie said, holding her to her chest and rubbing her back until the baby coughed and began to breathe normally, her little arms beginning to wave now.

Anders saw the relief on Valerie's face and knew the baby's stillness had worried her.

"I need something to cut the cord," she said.

"I can help with that," Rachel announced, appearing behind her and frowning as she peered at Leigh.

"Valerie, this is Rachel," Anders announced, reaching past Lucian's shoulder to take the blood bags she was holding out. He passed the first one to Lucian, and held the second one while Lucian popped the first bag to Leigh's teeth. She didn't even appear to be conscious, he noted.

"Nice to meet you, Rachel. If you have something to cut the cord, we should do it quickly," Valerie said. "I don't think the second baby is going to wait long to join us."

"Twins?" Rachel asked, a smile claiming her lips.

But she didn't react at once to Valerie's suggestion. Instead, she watched Lucian tear the now empty bag from Leigh's teeth and replace it with a fresh one. Anders didn't know what she was looking for, but after a moment, she relaxed and turned to gesture to someone Anders couldn't see. Etienne, he realized when the man appeared in the opening, a large duffel bag in hand that he opened for Rachel to dig through. After a moment, she turned back with surgical scissors and clamps.

Valerie held the baby as Rachel made quick work of the umbilical cord, and then offered, "I can take the baby if you want to take over here."

Rachel grinned, but shook her head. "Are you kidding? You've done all the hard work. This is the fun stuff. I wouldn't take that away from you," she said, taking the baby and using a wet nap to clean her up as much as possible before wrapping her in a blanket.

Valerie watched silently, but turned back to Leigh when she groaned around the blood bag in her mouth.

"Bear down, Leigh," Valerie ordered. "Push."

Within moments, the second baby emerged to join the world. This one began to squawl and wriggle about at once, arms and legs flailing as Valerie sat back on her heels with it in her hands.

"A boy," she announced and met his gaze with a smile.

When canine whining roused Valerie from a deep sleep, she eased one eyelid open and scowled at the furry face in front of her.

"You're kidding, right?" she muttered with disgust. "You couldn't let me sleep in this one time? Just this once? I mean it was only four A.M. when I finally crawled into bed last night. But you can't let me sleep?"

Roxy whined again, shifting on the spot, and Valerie sighed.

"Fine," she said, pushing herself wearily to her hands and knees to get up. She then froze as she took note of the man in bed beside her. Anders. Damn. He wasn't there when she'd crawled into bed last night. He hadn't even been at the house. Once the second baby was born and Leigh had been fed three or four bags of blood, they'd deemed it time to move and everyone had come back to the house. Well, everyone but Mortimer, who had taken the rogue back to the Enforcer house to be locked up. He'd returned later with Sam, though, so she could see the babies.

It seemed like half of Toronto had arrived at the house last night to see the babies. Valerie had been introduced to at least two dozen new people, all related in some way or another to Lucian and Leigh. And those people had stayed hours, trying to help as Leigh and Lucian had debated on the babies' names.

It seemed Leigh had refused to pick names before the baby was born. She'd miscarried a previous child and had gained some superstitions from the loss. One of those superstitions was a fear that if she picked names before the baby was born, it wouldn't be born. Or they wouldn't, since the baby had turned out to be two.

No decisions had been made, though there had been a couple of suggestions Leigh and Lucian were considering. The party had finally broken up at four

A.M., when Lucian and Anders had decided it was time to go question their rogue.

Before joining everyone at casa bambino, Mortimer had tried to get answers out of the man as to where Laura, Billie, and Kathy were, or if they were even still alive, but the rogue hadn't been very forthcoming, refusing even to give his name. So after relaxing for a bit, and enjoying his new family, Lucian had decided it was time to get those answers. Anders, Mortimer, Sam, and Justin, as well as a couple of the other men, had gone with him.

Much to Valerie's relief, everyone else but Rachel and Etienne had left then. But the doctor and her game-creator husband were going to stay for a day or two to help Leigh with the babies, so Valerie had felt it was all right to finally find her bed. It had been an extremely long day and she'd been exhausted, so after letting Roxy out to take care of business, she'd tripped upstairs, stripped off her clothes and fallen into bed. Alone.

Valerie stared at Anders now, taking in the fact that he was fully clothed and on top of the blankets. But when Roxy whined again, she shushed her, and eased carefully out of bed.

Rather than hunt around in her drawers in the dark room or risk turning on a light and waking Anders, Valerie felt around for her clothes from the day before and then tugged them on one at a time. She was so tired, she didn't even care if they were on inside out. She also didn't bother brushing her hair or teeth and simply led Roxy out of the room. Valerie had every intention of climbing back into bed the minute Roxy had eaten and done her business. Two hours of sleep just was not enough for her system to function with any kind of clarity. Besides, she deserved a sleep in. She'd bested a bad guy and delivered two babies the day before.

The thought made her smile. The babies were adorable little bundles, and Lucian had been strutting about like the prize bull at the fair as everyone had fawned over them last night. As for Leigh, once she'd been given a couple more bags of blood at the house, all signs of the "off with his head" woman had vanished. She was back to her sweet laughing self. Valerie had been rather relieved by that.

Speak of the devil, Valerie thought as she entered the kitchen/living room and spotted Leigh by the island with one of her little bundles of joy. Baby girl, she realized, noting the pink baby blanket.

"Feeding time?" Valerie asked as she approached.

"Burping time," Leigh corrected wryly. "Feeding time ended fifteen minutes ago, but she hasn't burped and won't settle."

Valerie nodded, but frowned. "Should you be up and about already? Do you want me to take her?"

"I'm fine," Leigh assured her with a laugh, and then added wryly, "Immortal, remember? Half a dozen bags of blood and the nanos fixed me right up. I'm good as new."

Valerie raised her eyebrows. "Impressive."

"Yeah." Leigh smiled.

"But you must be tired," Valerie said.

Leigh shook her head. "We can do without sleep if we pump up the blood consumption."

"Really?" Valerie asked with amazement and not a little envy.

Leigh nodded. "Of course we try not to do that much. It means more blood, and it's always best to be conservative on blood use. But sometimes, like now, it's hard to avoid."

"Hmmm. Well, that will make motherhood a lot less painful. The lack of sleep is the thing most new mothers and fathers complain about," Valerie commented and then glanced down to Roxy when she nudged her hand with a wet nose.

"You can let her out," Leigh said, smiling at Roxy. "I turned off the alarm when I heard you moving around upstairs."

"Thanks." Valerie moved to the French doors and opened one to let Roxy out, then closed and leaned against it as she asked Leigh, "Decided on names yet?"

"No," Leigh admitted with a sigh and cuddled her little girl close briefly. Easing her hold, she admitted, "I really didn't think it would be this hard. Shouldn't you just look at them and know what their name should be?"

Valerie chuckled at the suggestion. "Sure. That's how the seven dwarfs became Sneezy, Bashful, Grumpy, Happy, Dopey, Sleepy, and Doc, isn't it?"

Leigh grinned, but then wrinkled her nose. "In that case, this little girl should be called Smelly . . . or Poopy. I think it's diaper-change time."

"Hmmm. Speaking of . . . I guess I'd better find the waste pick-up bags and go tend to *my* little girl," Valerie said, pushing herself away from the door to move into the kitchen and fetch the bags.

"Have fun," Leigh said, heading for the door.

"You too," Valerie called out with a laugh as she grabbed the bags from the drawer and headed outside.

Roxy hurried eagerly to her side as Valerie stepped

out onto the covered porch. Giving the German shepherd a pet, she promised, "I'll feed you in a minute. Just let me collect all your little gifts from last night and this morning first."

Roxy barked and pressed against her side, eliciting a smile and another pet from Valerie. She didn't think the dog understood what she'd said. Well, except perhaps for feed. She was pretty sure Roxy understood that word. But her not understanding had never stopped Valerie talking to her before. She'd had whole conversations with the German shepherd, pouring out her troubles and cares to the dog. Roxy always watched her, bright-eyed, and tongue lolling, giving the occasional bark. She appeared just happy to have her attention. It was part of her charm.

"So," Valerie said, starting across the yard in search of Roxy treasures. "What do you think of Anders? Should I agree to be his life mate or not?"

Roxy barked and raced a little ahead before stopping to peer back at her.

Eyebrows rising, Valerie followed and paused when she saw that the dog had stopped beside one of her treasures.

"Is that a yes I should, or no I shouldn't?" she asked as she collected the doggy deposit, and Roxy barked and moved away, sniffing the ground as she went and then she paused again and looked back at her expectantly.

"Good of you to be so helpful," Valerie said dryly as she reached her and bent to scoop up the deposit in front of the dog. She spent the next couple of minutes following Roxy around, cleaning up after her. She was pretty sure they were on the last one, when

Roxy suddenly paused, head up, ears pricked, and then she charged forward and around the house.

"Squirrel," Valerie muttered and shook her head. That was usually the only thing that made the dog react like that. Tying the top of the bag, she whistled for her, and then started around the house. She turned the corner just in time to see Roxy jogging around the front of the house in hot pursuit of whatever furry little critter had caught her attention.

"Dumb dog," Valerie said with exasperation, hurrying after her. She was exhausted and eager to get back to bed, so of course that's the day that Roxy decides she's a hunting dog.

Roxy had nosed the garage door open and was slipping inside by the time Valerie came around the front of the house. Cursing, Valerie rushed to the door and pulled it open.

"Roxy?" she called, frowning into the dark garage. Tossing the bag of dog waste in the garbage pail just inside the door, Valerie felt around for a light switch on the walls on either side of the door. If one of the big, automatic garage doors for the cars had been open it would have offered more light, this door merely cast shadows everywhere.

"Dammit, Roxy where are you?" Valerie said testily giving up on a light switch. She couldn't even hear the German shepherd moving around and the dark and silence was starting to spook her. If she knew where the panel was to open the big doors, she'd be opening them both at that moment.

Sighing into the silence, Valerie eased back a step, considering closing the garage door and then opening it and calling Roxy again. Perhaps the fear that she might be left here would lure the dog out, Valerie thought and was about to step outside when there was a tinny clang in the back corner of the garage. Roxy had knocked over a can of something. Valerie took a couple steps forward, calling her again.

Impatient to get back inside and go to bed, Valerie walked further into the garage, moving carefully between Lucian's van on her right and the shelves lined with tools, pool cleaner, paint, and various other miscellaneous items on her left. She was halfway along the van when the garage door suddenly closed behind her.

Freezing, Valerie turned slowly toward the van in the darkness, ears straining.

"It was the wind," she assured herself in a whisper.

"No it wasn't."

The voice came from her right and very close. It startled a gasp out of Valerie and sent her heart pounding. It also made her whirl and run blindly in the opposite direction. Valerie had only taken half a dozen steps when she was caught by the hair and jerked back against a very wide, very hard chest. She immediately caught a whiff of a musky scent she'd forgotten but immediately recalled.

"Igor," she breathed, horror washing over her. He was alive.

"Igor?" he asked, sounding nonplussed.

"Where's Roxy?" Valerie asked grimly.

"Dead," he barked, and countered, "Where is Ambrose?"

Valerie didn't answer, she couldn't have if she'd wanted to. His announcement sent a shaft of pain shooting through her chest that had left her gasping for breath.

"Where is Ambrose?" he repeated, shaking her furiously by his hold on her hair to get her attention.

"I don't know who Ambrose is!" Valerie cried out, grabbing at the hair on the sides of her head to try to ease the pain. His shaking her certainly regained her attention. He'd pulled her out of her haze of grief, but rage replaced it as Valerie thought of her poor Roxy, lying dead somewhere there in the dark garage. She reacted without stopping to think about it, raising her foot and shooting it back at his legs with force. Score! Valerie thought grimly as he bellowed in pain and stumbled back, dragging her with him.

Growling as he regained his footing, Igor turned and slammed her into the van, his weight crashing into her from behind to add to the assault. Valerie groaned as the wind was knocked out of her and shock waves of pain vibrated from her breasts down to her knees.

"Who do you think I mean?" he asked furiously by her ear.

"Your boss," she gasped almost soundlessly. She simply didn't have the breath in her to speak.

"Where is he?" Igor demanded, easing his weight from hers enough to allow her some air. As he did, Valerie heard a very faint bark. It sounded far away, or muffled as if coming from outside, but it was definitely a bark. Roxy wasn't dead. She'd barely had the thought when Igor cursed and dragged her away from the van by her hair.

"Where is he?" he growled, pulling her several feet, presumably, toward the garage door.

Valerie hesitated, but when he stopped and caught her by the throat, she quickly answered, "At the Enforcer house."

There was no reason not to tell him. It wasn't like Igor could break him out. Although, if he tried, it would give them a chance to catch him. Savoring that thought, she asked, "What did you do with Billie, Laura, and Kathy?"

"You'll see soon enough," he assured her. "Where is the Enforcer house?"

"I don't know the address," Valerie said. When he started to lift her off the ground by her hair, she added quickly, "I don't. They took me there, they didn't tell me the address."

"Then I guess you'll have to show me," he said grimly, releasing her throat and continuing the way he'd been dragging her before stopping.

"I'd really rather not," Valerie said honestly and then frowned and asked, "Why aren't you just reading my mind and controlling me?"

"Why bother?" he asked dryly.

"Because then you wouldn't have to drag me around by my hair and hurt me," she pointed out in an arid tone of her own.

"But I like hurting you. It eases the pain you caused me when you staked me."

Valerie bit her lip. He sounded testy, even resentful. Imagine! Like he hadn't deserved it and she was the bad guy or something. Mouth tightening, she said, "Or maybe you're a new turn and haven't learned to control or read us mere mortals yet."

Her talk with Leigh at the Enforcer house was what had given her that idea. Leigh had mentioned that she was still learning both skills, but was getting pretty good at them and Valerie had wondered if Igor was a relatively new turn and hadn't yet learned those skills. Otherwise, why hadn't he just taken control of her in the bathroom when she'd squirted the shampoo at him? Or after, when he'd come out of the bathroom to get her?

She suspected she'd hit the nail on the head when Igor's step faltered and he snapped, "Shut up."

"Make me," Valerie muttered, blinking rapidly when he suddenly pushed the door open and dragged her out into bright sunlight. Half-blinded by the sudden light, Valerie was taken by surprise and stumbled to her knees when she was suddenly free. She was so startled that she almost missed the grunt Igor let loose as he released her, but she definitely heard the sounds of the short fight that followed. Turning her head, she watched with amazement as Anders thrust a wooden sunflower stake from the garden into Igor's chest. The man fell like a ton of bricks, crashing onto his back beside her on the concrete driveway.

"Well, that felt good," Anders said grimly and when she glanced to him with surprise, he shrugged and admitted, "It's nice to be able to actually save you for a change, rather than just showing up after you've already saved yourself."

Valerie released a startled laugh that ended in a gasp when he caught her by the arms and raised her to her feet.

"Thank you," she sighed, sliding her arms around his waist and resting her head on his chest. "You're my hero."

"Hmm," Anders said dubiously, and then eased her back so he could kiss her nose. Smiling crookedly, he then commented, "You seem to have a tendency to find trouble."

"It wasn't me this time. I was just following Roxy.

She— Roxy!" Valerie stiffened, her eyes wide and worried. "He said he killed her but I thought I heard her bark."

"She's fine," Anders assured her quickly. "She's in the house. She came up to the bedroom and woke me up. It's how I knew you were in trouble. You weren't with her. So I came looking for you."

"Oh," Valerie sagged against him, but shook her head. "I don't know how she got in the house. I saw her go into the garage, but when I got there she wasn't there and he grabbed me."

"There's a door between the garage and the laundry room. He must have opened it and lured her into the garage and then the house somehow, and then closed it behind her to wait for you to catch up," Anders said.

"Oh," Valerie sighed, and then followed Anders's gaze when he suddenly stiffened and glanced toward the house. The front door was opening, she saw, and then Roxy rushed out. Lucian and Leigh followed more slowly as Roxy hurried toward them, tale wagging happily. Valerie slid free of Anders and crouched to greet the dog as she ran up.

"Good girl," she said, massaging her cheeks and the sides of her neck. "Good girl for getting Anders. Yes," she praised, and then straightened as the other couple reached them.

"Igor?" Lucian asked on a yawn, rubbing his hand across his very wide, bare chest. The man had obviously just rolled out of bed. He wore only a pair of green plaid pajama bottoms, and his hair was standing on end.

Anders nodded.

Lucian peered at the large man with the wooden

sunflower sticking out of his chest, and commented, "Well this makes a change from the old pushing up daisies."

Leigh tsked at the comment and slipped past Lucian to get a better look at the man. Shaking her head, she said, "Did you have to use the sunflower? I loved that tomato stake and it's the only one I have. You should have used one of the frog stakes. I have three of them."

"I'll remember that for next time," Anders said with amusement.

Lucian slid his arm around Leigh and hugged her briefly. "I'll call the boys to come collect him. They can take out your sunflower before they take him away . . . I'll have them clean off the blood for you too," he added, when Leigh screwed up her face with disgust.

"Maybe we should take it out now," Anders suggested. "If we leave it in too long he might not come back and we still need information. We haven't even been able to get a name out of his boss."

"Ambrose," Valerie announced.

Anders glanced at her with surprise and shook his head. "Damn, woman, you were only in the garage with him for a matter of minutes. How did you get that out of him?"

"My natural charm?" she suggested with a grin.

"You didn't happen to find out what they did with the women too, did you?" Lucian asked.

Valerie's grin faded and she shook her head. "No. I'm afraid not."

"I guess you'd better take it out now then," Lucian suggested, not sounding pleased that they had to.

Anders didn't look any happier about having to

do it as he bent to grab the wooden sunflower and pull it from the man's chest. When Leigh grimaced at the bloody tip, he said, "I'll rinse it off with the garden hose. It will be good as new."

"Good thinking," Lucian said. "I'll watch Igor while you do that."

Anders raised his eyebrows. Apparently, he'd meant later, but he nodded and headed around the garage saying, "I'll only be a minute."

Shaking her head, Leigh turned to lean up and kiss Lucian's cheek. "I'll call Mortimer for you. I have to go check on the twins anyway."

"Thank you, love," Lucian said, watching her go. Once she disappeared into the house, he turned back and eyed Valerie. "So? When do you want to be turned?"

"I didn't agree to turn," Valerie squawked with amazement.

"You haven't, but you will," he said with a shrug.

"What makes you think that?" she asked warily.

"Because if you don't, I'm going to have to wipe your memories and have you returned to your life and neither of us wants that," he said simply.

"Anders said I could have time to decide," Valerie protested, and then frowned and added, "And what do you mean, neither of us wants that? Why would you care?"

"You saved my wife and children, Valerie. And Leigh adores you. You're family now."

"Oh." She stared at him nonplussed, wondering if he meant that.

"I mean it," he said firmly. "Leigh has decided it's so, so it's so. She'd be disappointed if you didn't become one of us and I won't have her disappointed."

Valerie scowled slightly. The last part sounded like a threat.

"As for Anders saying you could have time to decide," Lucian continued. "What do you need time for? The nanos have paired you, you're meant to be together."

"You make it sound so simple," she said wearily.

"It is simple. Don't make it hard."

"Great, the nanos paired us. But what about love?" she asked.

Lucian shifted impatiently. "Do you like him?"

"Yes," she admitted.

"Respect him?"

She nodded.

"Trust him?"

"Of course," she said without hesitation.

Lucian nodded and said dryly, "I don't need to ask if you want him sexually."

Valerie flushed and raised her chin.

"All those things combined make up love," Lucian assured her. "Whether you realize it or not, you already do love him."

Valerie swallowed, knowing in her heart he was right. She bit her lip, and then blurted, "But does he love me?"

"Ah." Lucian nodded. "So that's the holdup, is it? He hasn't said it yet."

Valerie sighed and looked away, muttering, "When he asked me to be his life mate he went on about finding peace and being able to relax and be at peace. It was all peace, peace, peace," she added with frustration and glanced to Lucian, eyes narrowing when she caught his lips twitching. If he laughed at her, she would—

"Don't you feel at peace with him?" he asked, and then added, "When you're not hot and bothered, I mean."

"Well, yeah, but—"

"But you want to hear that he loves you," Lucian said and shrugged. "I guess you'll have to ask him then."

"Ask him if he loves me?" she asked with dismay.

Lucian sighed with exasperation. "You took on Igor and staked him, saving yourself and six other women in the process—"

"Four," she corrected unhappily. "Two died, remember."

"And then," he continued heavily, ignoring her interruption. "You took on Ambrose and saved my wife and unborn twins by crashing the van you were all in and repeatedly bashing the man over the head until help got there. You are not a coward, Valerie, so stop acting like one. Ask him. And when he says yes he loves you, I will personally oversee the turning and pay for the wedding." On that note, he turned and strode toward the house.

Valerie stared after him with amazement, then turned and glanced at Igor, and back. "Hey! What about—?"

"Anders will watch him," Lucian responded, not slowing.

Valerie glanced around just in time to see Anders coming around the garage. Lucian had heard him approaching, she realized.

"Most of it came out," Anders said as he approached her. "I'll take it home with me tonight and give it a quick sanding and repaint for Leigh. It should be fine."

"We're going to your place tonight?" she asked with surprise.

Anders lowered his hand to his side, the stake dangling from his fingers. Expression solemn, he said, "I am. But I think you should stay here. I think that's probably best until you make your decision."

Valerie frowned. "What do you mean?"

Anders grimaced and glanced away, "Well, I've been thinking that life mate sex is pretty mind-blowing and addictive."

"I've noticed," she admitted wryly, bending slightly to pat Roxy, who had been lying down beside her, but now stood and pressed against her leg.

"That being the case," he continued gently, "I thought perhaps it might be best if we abstain until you've made your decision."

Valerie straightened slowly to stare at him. "Abstain?"

"Yes," he said solemnly, and then added, "You need to have a clear head to make a decision as big as this and constantly being bombarded with pleasure, your body and mind crying out with it . . . well, it will just muddy your thinking and delay your decision."

Valerie frowned. "But—"

"It's for the best," he added solemnly.

Valerie narrowed her eyes. "How long are we supposed to abstain?"

"Like I said, until you've made your decision," Anders answered.

"But what if it takes a while?" she asked.

"Then we'll wait a while. Years if we have to," he

assured her. "Honey, I want you happy and you're
worth waiting for."

"But I'm happy when we—" Flushing, she cut herself off and said instead, "And if I decide I'm willing
to be your life mate?"

"Then I'll rip your clothes off and make love to
you until you can't stand," he said as if they were
discussing the weather.

"And if I decide I'm not willing to risk being your
life mate?" she asked.

Frustration filled his expression. "Valerie, there is
no risk here. The nanos don't make mistakes. This is
a sure bet. The only game where you can't lose. All
you have to do is be willing to accept the gift they're
offering us."

Valerie stared at him silently. Like Lucian, he
made it sound so simple. The nanos had decided. It
was a fait accompli. Blah blah blah. Men were such
twits sometimes. She needed more than—

A moan from Igor caught her attention and she
glanced down, then gasped in surprise when
Anders plunged the stake into him again.

"Anders, we need him alive," she protested, reaching for the swaying sunflower sticking out of the
man's chest.

"I'll take it out in a minute," he said, brushing her
hand away. "If he's moaning, he's recovering. I just
want to slow him down a little. At least until the
men get here."

As if his words had conjured them up, the sound
of a vehicle drew Valerie's gaze to a dark SUV
coming up the driveway. Mortimer and Bricker had
arrived to collect Igor, she guessed as they parked
the vehicle beside Anders's and got out.

"We finally got our rogue's name out of him," Mortimer announced with a smile as he led Bricker toward them.

"Ambrose," Anders said at once.

Mortimer's smile faded, his mouth making an "o" of surprise. "How the hell do you know that?"

"Valerie got the name from Igor," Anders said with amusement.

"Ah." Mortimer glanced toward the man lying in the driveway, then glanced back, his gaze meeting Valerie's, "So . . . did you find out about the girls?"

"No." Valerie admitted with a frown. "Did you?"

"Yes, indeed." Mortimer's smile was back. "They're alive and well in a house about ten minutes from here. Nicholas, Jo, and Decker are on their way there now. They'll take them back to the Enforcer house to be checked over, wiped, and sent back to their lives. This time for good."

Valerie let her breath out on a sigh, only realizing then that she'd been holding it. She'd been so worried that Ambrose may already have killed them.

"No. He only planned to kill you," Mortimer said, obviously reading her mind. "You were the difficult one who had seen the portrait. None of the others remembered anything that could have given him away."

"Then why did he take them at all?" Valerie asked with a frown. "From what I understand, he didn't need to take them to read them, he just had to get close. Why take the risk and kidnap them again when he knew they didn't know anything that could point a finger his way?"

Bricker grimaced. "He has a strange way of thinking. He kind of saw you ladies as his property."

"You mean his cattle," Valerie said grimly.

"Basically," Bricker acknowledged apologetically and then shrugged. "He wanted you all back where he felt you belonged."

"So that he could continue to bleed us dry of blood until we died?" Valerie suggested, eyes narrowed.

Bricker nodded. "I'm afraid so."

Valerie muttered under her breath with disgust.

"Did you find out how he got onto the women?" Anders asked. "How he knew they had no family and chose them?"

"Ah yes," Mortimer nodded. "Valerie, I gather you were going to work at the Teaching Hospital?"

"Teaching Hospital?" Anders asked, glancing to her.

"The college has a teaching hospital for animals, basically a veterinary clinic for students to hone their skills. The students perform the procedures, but they're overseen by the teaching staff who can step in if a situation arises. I was going to work there a couple days a week to keep my skills sharp and to practice a couple of new techniques I hoped to learn in my courses this year," she explained. "In fact, I was at the Teaching Hospital the afternoon I was kidnapped."

Mortimer nodded. "That's where he found his victims. He's on staff there. Cindy, Laura, and Kathy had taken their pets into the clinic hospital for one reason or another and he took the opportunity to ask questions and learn if they were likely victims for him or not. He met Billie in the bookstore coffee shop one afternoon when he was in the bookstore. He struck up a conversation with her, learned she was on her own with no one to care if she went missing and . . ." He shrugged.

Anders frowned and turned to Valerie to say, "But you saw Cindy in that other clinic we went to. Why would she go to both places?"

"She probably took her cat to the teaching hospital for an operation, spaying or neutering, or something," Valerie said grimly. "The biggest benefit of the clinic is that they don't charge as much for procedures like that. That's how they encourage people to bring their animals in. But for long-term care; yearly shots, flea pills, et cetera, she would need a regular vet." Valerie paused briefly, then glanced to Mortimer and shook her head. "I didn't see him at the teaching hospital. I was speaking to a woman, not Ambrose."

"He listened in. Caught part of it and got the rest of the info he was seeking from your interviewer. Apparently you told her that you have a clinic in Winnipeg and were just here temporarily?"

"Yes." She nodded and then grimaced. "I did tell her I have no family or friends here so I could work extra hours if they wanted."

"So . . . his name is Ambrose what?" Anders asked. "And just who the hell is he?"

"Just Ambrose," Mortimer said with a shrug. "He doesn't remember any more than that from his life as a mortal. And it may be his last name. He says it was on a name tag on his uniform."

"Uniform?" Anders asked with a frown.

"He was a soldier in World War I," Bricker explained. "He says his first memory is waking up in the middle of a battlefield; bombs going off everywhere, dead bodies all around him and some German fellow half blown up and lying across him, bleeding all over him."

"Ah hell," Anders muttered.

"What?" Valerie asked.

Rather than answer her, Anders arched an eyebrow at Mortimer. "An accidental turn?"

Mortimer nodded. "That's what we're thinking. He says he remembers pushing the German soldier off him and staggering to his feet. His head hurt, he felt it and it was soft and mushy, either half caved in or blown away. He felt dizzy and pain was gnawing at his head and gut. He passed out and when he woke up he was sucking on another soldier's open wound and feeling much better. The more blood he had, the better he felt and then the wound seemed to heal itself. He realized he was a vampire and has been living as one ever since, using whatever he could find on the subject as his guide."

"Which would be ridiculous fantasies like Dracula and such," Bricker pointed out with distaste.

Anders's mouth twisted, but he asked, "And he never got his memory back of his life before waking up on the battlefield?"

Mortimer shook his head. "He says not."

"Is that even possible?" Valerie asked. "I thought the nanos repaired things."

"They do, and they obviously repaired the physical damage done, but if the head wound was bad enough . . ." He pursed his lips. "The nanos may not have been able to recover the memories from the destroyed brain matter."

"I suppose that's possible," Anders said thoughtfully, and then sighed and shrugged the matter away.

"Wait . . ." Valerie said with a frown. "I get that the nanos repaired him, but I'm not sure I understand

how you think the nanos got there in the first place."
She glanced from one man to the other and asked
uncertainly, "Are you thinking that the soldier who
was bleeding on him was an immortal and that the
nanos were passed to him that way? That they got
into his wounds and just . . . took hold like a virus
or something?"

"Into his wounds, maybe his mouth. But yes, that's
probably what happened," Mortimer said.

"Does this happen a lot?" she asked with amazement.

"I've only heard of one other incident like it,"
Bricker said and raised his eyebrows as he glanced
to the others.

"Elvi's the only one I know of too," Mortimer said
at once.

"Same here," Anders agreed. "But it doesn't mean
there aren't more out there like him."

"Who's Elvi?" Valerie asked curiously.

"She's Victor's life mate," Anders said, and then
added, "Victor is Lucian's brother."

"And she was accidentally turned?" Valerie asked,
fascinated.

"It's a long story. I'll tell you later," Anders said
quietly.

When Valerie nodded, he glanced to the men and
said, "So he woke up in the middle of a war zone, a
vampire with no memory of his past, and managed
to survive unnoticed for almost a hundred years?"

"It would seem so," Mortimer agreed and shook
his head. "He's one lucky son of a bitch to have escaped our notice all this time."

"I'll say," Bricker muttered.

"And Igor?" Anders asked, glancing down at the

man still lying on the ground. Spotting the sun-flower sticking out of his chest, Anders scowled, but didn't pull it out.

"His name is Mickey Green," Mortimer said. "Ambrose met him in a bar six or seven months ago; liked him, decided he'd make a good flunky, and turned him." He eyed the sunflower stake sticking out of Igor—or Mickey Green's—chest and asked, "How long has he been staked?"

"He was staked earlier, but recovering. I put it back in just before you pulled into the driveway," Anders admitted, reaching for the sunflower stake now.

"We'll take it out once we have him chained up in the SUV," Mortimer said, stopping him. "He's a big guy. It's safer that way."

Anders nodded, but said, "I told Leigh I'd clean it for her. Most of the blood washes off, but the wood on the tip is a little stained and needs a bit of sanding."

"We'll take care of it back at the house," Mortimer assured him, and then added, "Speaking of which, I suppose we should get him in the SUV and take him there. We have a nice cell waiting for him next to Ambrose. The two can be neighbors until the council decides what to do with them."

Anders nodded. "I'll walk Valerie inside and tell Lucian you're here. He may want to talk to you."

He didn't wait for Mortimer's response to that, but caught Valerie's arm and urged her toward the front door. Roxy had lain down in a bit of shade nearby to watch them, but now got up and followed.

Valerie allowed Anders to lead her toward the house, but her mind was racing. He planned to walk her in, tell Lucian about the men being there and then leave her and head back to his own home . . . and she didn't want that. She wanted—actually, Valerie wasn't sure what she wanted. She knew what she didn't want though, and that was to be left here alone without him. But she didn't know what to do about it. He was determined to give her time to think and make her decision, and—the front door opening distracted her, and Valerie glanced toward it as Lucian stepped out.

"Mortimer and Bricker got some information out of Ambrose," Anders announced, slowing as the man pulled the door closed. "But I'll let them tell you about it. They'd be disappointed if I stole their thunder."

Lucian nodded as he approached, but his eyes slid from Anders to her as he neared. Slowing as he came abreast of them, he scowled at Valerie. "You still haven't asked?"

He didn't wait for a response, but simply shook his head and continued on toward the driveway.

"Asked me what?" Anders asked, glancing to her curiously.

Valerie hesitated and then simply spat it out. "Do you love me?"

Anders stilled, his breath leaving him in a long exhale. Then he just stood there staring at her until Valerie began to worry that the answer was no and he didn't want to admit it.

"If you don't, just say—" she began anxiously, but never finished because his mouth was suddenly on hers and he was kissing her.

Valerie quickly forgot about Igor, or whether Anders loved her and just about everything else. When he broke the kiss and lifted his head a moment later, she moaned in protest, and then blinked her eyes open when he said, "I love you."

"You do?" she asked with wonder, a smile curving her lips.

"Of course, I do. You're perfect. How could I not love you?"

"I'm not perfect," she said at once.

"You're perfect for me," he assured her. "You're beautiful, sexy, smart, brave . . ." He shook his head. "You're all I could have wanted and more, Valerie. I'm happy when I'm with you. I love you."

"Oh," she sighed and rested her head on his chest, admitting, "Lucian thinks I love you too."

"Great," Anders said dryly. "But what do *you* think?"

Pulling back, she met his gaze and said solemnly, "I think he's right. I love you too, Anders."

He closed his eyes briefly, as if savoring the words, then opened them again and asked cautiously, "So you'll agree to be my life mate?"

"Apparently I already am your life mate," she said wryly. "But if you mean will I agree to be turned, and marry you, and spend the rest of our very long lives together, than yes. I agree."

She caught a glimpse of the grin that claimed his face, but then gasped when he scooped her up and started to walk, saying, "Come on, Roxy."

"Wait! What are you doing?" Valerie cried, clutching at his shoulders.

"I'm taking you to my—*our* house," he corrected himself and then reminded her, "I promised that if you said yes, I'd rip your clothes off and make love to you until you couldn't stand and I intend to keep my promise. But not here."

"No, definitely not here," Valerie agreed, flushing. She wasn't exactly quiet when he made love to her. Besides, she liked the idea of having him all to herself.

When Anders paused beside his SUV, Valerie grabbed the door handle and opened it for him.

"See, you're perfect," Anders said with a grin as he set her on the passenger seat. "I didn't even have to ask. We're a good team."

Valerie just shook her head and laughed.

Smiling, Anders stepped back, and glanced down, saying, "In, Roxy."

The dog jumped up at once, settling on the floor between Valerie's legs as she had when they'd brought her back from Cambridge. She was smiling at the dog when Anders's face suddenly appeared before her as he leaned in. His lips brushed hers, then he whispered, "Seat belt," before closing the door.

Valerie did up her seat belt and watched him walk around to get in beside her to do up his own seat belt and start the SUV.

Anders reached for the gearshift, but paused when he saw that she was simply sitting there smiling at him. Tilting his head he asked, "What?"

"You know this is madness, right?" Valerie asked cheerfully. "We've only known each other a handful of days."

Anders pulled his door closed, and eyed her uncertainly. "Scared?"

"A little," she admitted.

"Second thoughts?"

"Oh, no, definitely not," she assured him with a laugh.

Relaxing, he leaned across the open space between them to give her a quick peck, but when he started to straighten again, she caught his face in her hands and whispered, "I do love you."

"And I love you," he assured her, and then kissed her again, this time a slow, soft, sweet kiss that left them both hungry for more. Raising an eyebrow, he asked, "Home?"

"Home," she agreed.

Anders shifted the SUV into gear and Valerie turned to peer out the front window and toward their future . . . together.

Lynsay Sands was born in Canada and is an award-winning author of over thirty books, which have made the Barnes & Noble and *New York Times* bestseller lists. She is best known for her Argeneau series, about a modern-day family of vampires.

Visit Lynsay's website at: www.lynsaysands.net

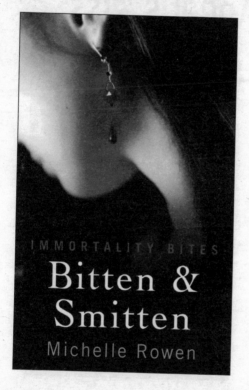